LIVING WITH MARKUS

FLORENCE OSMUND

ISBN-13: 978-0-9915185-5-5
ISBN-10: 0-9915185-5-1
LCCN: 2016905603

This is a work of fiction. Names, characters, places, and incidents are either the product of the author's imagination or are used fictitiously. Any resemblance to actual persons, living or dead, business establishments, events, or locales is entirely coincidental.

Acknowledgements

I wish to thank the following people for their assistance in creating this book.

To my editor, Carrie Cantor, thank you once again for keeping me on the straight and narrow and challenging me to become a better writer.

Thank you Deborah Bradseth of Tugboat Design for an eye-catching cover design and meticulous formatting.

To Barbara Mudd and Edward Kipp, thank you for your input related to CPFS and the Family Court systems in Illinois. Your feedback enabled me to create accurate scenes involving my fictional characters in need of a stable home environment.

Thank you John Konefes for your insight into the landscaping business and Illinois white deer population. Who would have thought that deer wouldn't eat hydrangeas?

To Jay a/k/a Ed Ochsner, thank you for sharing your knowledge of local craft beers. My characters enjoyed the variety throughout the story.

And finally, a special thanks to Marge Bousson for sharing her understanding of people afflicted with addictions, and for Beta reading and proofreading this book.

Chapter 1

Gabby let him know she was awake by stroking his back—her nimble fingers weaving their way down his body, dancing from one side of his spine to the other, the sensation of it sending a flood of warmth throughout his body. He responded by turning around and giving her a soft kiss.

"Are you seducing me, Miss Harding?" Marc asked. Aware of his own heartbeat, he edged closer to her with a hopeful expectation of what would soon follow.

She glanced at the bedside clock. "I started to, Mr. Nussbaum, but we need to get a move-on if we're going to make the opening in time."

It was Saturday, and they were going to the opening of what she considered to be a very important photography exhibit at the Milwaukee Art Museum. Somewhat less than enthralled by the exhibit itself, Marc still looked forward to spending the day with Gabby. He looked forward to spending every weekend with her.

She was up and out of bed before he could persuade her it wouldn't matter if they walked into the exhibit an hour later than planned. As she sauntered over to his closet where she kept a few outfits for her weekend visits, he eyed her well-toned body—a stark reminder of the gym membership she'd given him for Christmas the previous month.

Marc prepared to shave while Gabby showered. After raising the shaver up to his face, he hesitated, admiring the designer stubble look on himself. No match for Bradley Cooper, he thought, still not bad. He would have preferred to leave it, but Gabby liked clean-shaven men—men with manicured nails who knew the difference between a Shiraz and a Merlot and wore a sport coat to dinner, things that he took to heart only after he had started going out with her.

After filling their travel mugs with coffee, they donned their winter coats, grabbed their overnight bags, and descended the two flights of outside stairs running down the back of Marc's three-flat brownstone. The cold crisp January air—the kind that would leave your skin numb if you stayed out in it too long—stung their faces as they walked to the garage. After Marc warmed up his year-old

Range Rover for a few minutes, he pulled out onto Roscoe Street and began their northern journey to lower Wisconsin.

A sense of calm and ease fell upon him as he left his Chicago Lakeview neighborhood with his girlfriend by his side. He and Gabby had been dating for eighteen months, spending weekends together for the last six. At thirty, Marc was living the good life—single, successful landscaping business owner, completely unencumbered—and he didn't see himself settling down any time soon.

Spending weekends with Gabby meant giving up some things, like the Blackhawks home games Marc had faithfully attended since they'd won the 2010 Stanley Cup, something they hadn't achieved since the sixties. He still attended weekday games when he could, but weekends he kept open for her. Smart, fun, and pretty—even first thing in the morning with no makeup and mussed-up hair—Gabby's camaraderie easily beat out a bunch of rowdy hockey fans.

Relationships with women he'd dated in the past had never lasted very long. As soon as they mentioned "going to the next level," which they always did, Marc felt like going in the opposite direction, and he usually did. But Gabby had never done that. She had her own separate interests and a promising career at CEDA, a public service organization dedicated to helping low-income families. Only twenty-eight years old, she was already making a name for herself, both career-wise and in local politics after she worked tirelessly for the campaigns of two elected officials. And with family nearby and a wide circle of friends, she had her own life apart from him, which was how he preferred it.

"Thank you for coming with me today—I know it's not exactly your thing," she told him. "But wait until you see the exhibit. You'll be surprised at the talent of these teenagers." The exhibit they were attending included hundreds of photography entries in a local competition for which Gabby had been one of the judges. "Did you decide what you're going to do afterward while I'm at the judges luncheon?"

"I'll find something." He had thought about going on one of Milwaukee's many brewery tours but didn't want to tell her that until afterward. She probably expected him to do something more cultural—more cultural by her definition anyway.

"Did I tell you Glen called me yesterday?" she asked. Glen was her brother, an Air Force master sergeant.

"No. What did he have to say?"

"He wanted to let me know that he approved of you."

Marc has just met Glen for the first time, along with Gabby's parents, at Christmastime. They had all spent a few days at Mr. and Mrs. Harding's house on Lake Geneva. Marc had been nervous about meeting her family for the first time, but his fears had been quickly put to rest by her gracious parents and genial brother.

"Ha! That's a relief." Glen had impressed Marc as being near-perfect—

handsome, smart, well-traveled, and serving the country. "So he doesn't think of me as a lowly landscape worker like your mother?"

"She doesn't think that of you."

"She did in the beginning."

"Well, maybe. But she's come around."

"She used to call me 'lawn boy.'"

"One time."

"What does she call me now behind my back?"

"Marc."

"Mm-hm."

They talked about the presents they had exchanged with her family, the trip the guys had made to pick out a Christmas tree, and the old-fashioned fun they'd had decorating it. Marc's fear of being the only outsider had been allayed almost as soon as he'd walked in their door. Contrary to his dysfunctional family, Gabby's was idealistic. Of course, just about anyone's family outshined his: a father who brought new meaning to the word "pathetic" and a sister who couldn't support herself let alone her two fatherless children.

Easy to spot on the shore of Lake Michigan, the graceful sculpture of the art museum was artwork in itself with its huge movable steel louvers on either side that opened and closed twice daily simulating the wings of a bird. They pulled into the parking lot soon after the museum opened its doors. After Gabby checked in at the registration table for the judges, she led the way to the exhibit area.

Gabby was right—the photography was extraordinary. Hundreds of entries—action shots, still lifes, landscapes, portraits—as impressive as any Marc had ever seen. She proudly talked about the ones she had juried as though they had been created by her own children.

After they had seen the entire exhibit, they parted ways—she to her luncheon and he to the historic Lakefront Brewery where he hoped to enjoy an interesting tour followed by a beer or two. But as soon as Marc pulled into the crowded parking lot, his cell phone rang.

"I need a place to stay. Can you pick me up?"

He hadn't heard from Meinhard in months, and the piteous sound of his father's voice brought back painful memories of the past.

"I'm in Milwaukee. What's wrong?"

"I just said, I need a place to stay."

"I know what you said. What happened at wherever you were staying that you can't stay there anymore?" Meinhard had a history of flitting from one place to another—often running away from past-due rent or other debts.

"Doesn't matter, Markus, are you going to help me or not?"

Meinhard was the only one who still called him Markus. In an effort to distance himself from his father and his old world German mentality, he'd become *Marc* as soon as he'd turned eighteen. Meinhard had never accepted the change claiming *Marc,* spelled with a *c,* seemed too French—Meinhard hated the French.

"I can't do it, Dad. I'm not even coming home tonight."

"Let's not forget whose house you're living in."

Shortly after he'd arrived in the United States from East Germany in the late seventies, Meinhard had purchased a three-flat in a neighborhood that had once been a mecca for German-speaking immigrants. A few years later, his wife joined him, and they raised Marc and his sister Zenzi in the garden apartment, with tenants in the second- and third-floor apartments. Now Marc lived on the third floor by himself and had tenants on the other two.

"Let's not forget who's been paying the bills for the last twelve years," Marc said.

"I haven't asked you for a dime in—"

"Three months. Last October I gave you enough for the first and last month's rent for that flophouse you wanted to move into. What happened to that?"

"Never mind. That's what families do, you know. They help each other out when they need it."

"And the time before that I gave you six hundred dollars to pay off a debt you owed so the loan sharks wouldn't come after you."

"So I got into a little—"

"Let's see, and then the time before that—"

"Go to hell," Meinhard snapped and hung up.

Marc stared at the phone for several seconds. Even though he had told himself after the last bailout that he wasn't going to let Meinhard guilt him into another one, the thickness he felt in his throat caused him to question the way he had just treated his father. Poised to call him back, he looked at the last number in the call history. UNAVAILABLE. That meant something had happened to the cell phone he had given him.

Suddenly, going on the brewery tour didn't seem like such a good idea anymore. Instead, Marc drove back to the museum and wandered around the exhibits until it was time to meet Gabby. As much as he tried to concentrate on the artwork, his mind kept going back to Meinhard. Determined not to let this latest encounter with him ruin his day, he sat down on a bench in the museum's lobby and tried to calm down while waiting for her.

"Hey, handsome."

The sound of her voice pulled him into a happier place.

"Ready?"

"Let's go."

They headed for Milwaukee's arts and fashion district where they had planned to spend the afternoon in a variety of boutiques and galleries. Later, they would stay the night at the Pfister Hotel after attending the photography competition award dinner, at which time the three contest finalists in each category would find out which one would go on to compete nationally.

"Everything okay?" she asked him in the car.

"Sure. Why?"

"I don't know. You seem kind of quiet. What did you end up doing for the last two hours?"

"Nothing much. Went on one of those brewery tours and then came back here and looked at the other exhibits." He didn't like lying to her, but telling her about Meinhard's phone call seemed unnecessary and would only lead to a discussion about his father that he didn't want to have.

He parked near the Historic Third Ward where there were ample galleries and shops to keep them occupied until the banquet. In one of the galleries, he bought Gabby a silk scarf he'd found her admiring, and she in turn bought him a cashmere one that matched his good wool coat.

On the way to the hotel, his cell phone rang.

"Don't you want to get that?" she asked.

"I'll see who it is later," he said, thinking it was probably Meinhard.

After the short ride to the Pfister, Marc and Gabby walked arm-in-arm through its grand lobby admiring the hotel's vast collection of Victorian artwork. After checking into their room and changing into dinner clothes, they entered the Imperial Ballroom where they picked up a glass of wine at the bar and found their seats.

The program went on a little long for Marc's liking, but when two of the entries Gabby had designated as finalists made it to go on to the national competition, the pride and joy she exuded made it all worthwhile.

After the awards dinner, when Marc turned his cell phone back on, he saw that he had a message. He glanced at it and shoved the phone back into his pocket.

"Do you need to answer that?" she asked.

"It can wait."

"You sure? I can go on to the room myself." She smiled. "I'm a big girl."

He put his arm around her shoulders and gave her a squeeze. "Nope. I'm all yours."

"That kind of language can get you into trouble, you know."

"I certainly hope so," he said as they headed toward their room.

Chapter 2

Marc woke up to bright sunlight breaking through the tiny crack in the hotel room drapes. He lay there for a minute, savoring the soft texture of the lush bed linens against his skin before checking the other side of the bed.

Gabby's back was toward him—the gentle curves of her body hidden beneath the covers, her long near-black hair a stark contrast to the white pillowcase as it cascaded over it. She stirred. He stretched his neck in her direction to inhale her scent.

"Are you awake?" she whispered.

He didn't respond. Instead he walked his fingers down her back and around to the front of her naked body.

"You better get out of here fast. If my boyfriend catches you, we'll both be in big trouble."

"Screw him."

She rolled over to face him. "Okay."

* * *

After a quick shower, Marc headed to the hotel's indoor pool while Gabby took advantage of its spa services. Two hours later, they enjoyed a sumptuous breakfast in their room before checking out at noon.

"I had a wonderful time this weekend," she told him on the way home. "I hope you didn't hate it too much."

"I didn't hate it at all. I had a good time too. What do you want to do this afternoon? Just hang out?"

"Sounds good. I have tomorrow off. How about you?"

"What's tomorrow?"

"Martin Luther King Day."

"My guys are working, but I could probably take the rest of the day off after our usual Monday morning meetings. I could be home before noon."

With a landscaping business employing more than thirty part- and full-time workers, Marc's typical Monday morning routine called for visiting each of his three foreman's sites in Lake Forest, Evanston, and Glenview—all upscale suburban towns north of Chicago.

"Perfect. I have some after-Christmas shopping I can do while you're at work. And then maybe we could go see *Mr. Turner*?"

A movie based on an eccentric eighteenth-century British painter, *Mr. Turner* wouldn't have been Marc's first choice. *American Sniper* had just come out—now that was more his speed.

"Sounds good," he replied.

They made good time despite the icy roads. As they neared his house, Gabby leaned over toward him, slipped her arm into his, and whispered, "How about a fire in the fireplace, some Baileys hot chocolate, and a little ébats amoureux when we get inside?"

"How I love it when you talk dirty."

"You don't even know what I said."

"There's only one thing that can follow a fire in the fireplace and Baileys hot chocolate."

"What if I said it meant a trip to the gym?"

"I'd say you need a better translator."

He parked the car in the garage, and as they walked to the house, he hummed a nameless tune, a warmth radiating throughout his body despite the frigid temperature.

"You seem awfully cheery today," she said.

"I am."

"Anything in particular?"

"No. *Someone* in particular."

She squeezed his arm. "Me too," she said.

* * *

They were deciding between Mandarin Chinese or Thai takeout when the doorbell rang. Marc opened the door to find Zenzi and her two sons. He hadn't seen his sister in four years.

Marc barely recognized Riley, who had to have been no more than eleven by now but already looked like a teenager. He was big for his age, with dishwater-blond hair and blue eyes. Josh was a year younger. With brown eyes like his mother and lanky frame, he didn't look anything like his brother.

Marc fixed his gaze on Zenzi for several seconds before he could find the right words. Kreszentia—Zenzi for short—was one year and three days older than he and much thinner than when he'd last seen her. The dark circles under her eyes and uncombed hair made him wonder where she'd been. The last he had heard from her, she and the boys had been staying with a girlfriend.

He opened the door wider. "It's good to see you, Zen. It's been a long time," he said smiling but groaning inwardly at how this would all look to Gabby. "Come on in boys. Man, you sure are a lot bigger than the last time I saw you."

Neither boy smiled as they walked silently past Marc and into the kitchen.

Marc turned toward Zenzi. "So what's going on?" he asked as she stepped inside.

Gabby appeared in the kitchen, looking a little wary. He fumbled as he said, "Uh...this is my sister, Zenzi, and her two boys, Riley and Josh. Everyone, this is my girlfriend, Gabby."

"Well...it's nice to meet all of you," Gabby said.

An awkward silence filled the room.

Gabby turned to face Marc. "Do you need for me to—"

"We need to talk," Zenzi said to Marc. "And I don't care who hears it."

"Um...Gab, why don't you take the boys into the living room, see what's on TV, and give us a minute."

After the three of them had left, Marc turned to his sister. "What's going on?" he asked again as he pulled out a chair at the kitchen table for her. "Can I take your coat?"

"We need a place to stay," she said as she plopped herself down in the chair without removing her coat.

Over the years, Zenzi had approached him on a number of occasions to move into one of the apartments in the three-flat—usually between boyfriends—and each time Marc had agreed she could but only if she paid rent. He couldn't swing the mortgage payments and all the other costs associated with maintaining the property without it. Each time she had left in a huff. This time was different—she didn't look like she had any huff in her.

He took a seat across from her. "Where are you staying now?"

She looked down at her hands, which were tightly clasped and resting on the table. "We've been in a shelter for the last thirty days."

When she looked back up, her remorseful visage tugged at his emotions.

"A shelter?"

"I'm not proud of it, believe me," she said. "The boys deserve better."

Marc leaned back in his chair and stared past her, unable to continue looking directly into her eyes. He struggled to find the right words, and when he did, they caught in his throat.

"I have two renters here. I can't very well kick them out."

"What about here?"

"Zen, you know how much space I have."

"Does she live here too?"

"Just on weekends. She has her own place."

"Well, you need to think about freeing up one of the apartments for us."

It was unlike her to be this bold.

"I have leases, Zen. I can't just break them."

"Figure out a way, little brother."

Her pathetic circumstances aside, she was beginning to annoy him. "You know I need that income to keep things afloat, and it doesn't appear that you'd be able to pay any rent."

She leaned forward and looked him squarely in the eyes. "I know what you did."

"What are you talking about?"

"I know you assumed Dad's identity when you took over this place."

"I don't know what you're talking about," he said, stuttering.

"Don't lie to me. I had it checked out. What you did, are still doing, is a felony. You could go to prison, Marc." She gave him a quick, hard smile. "Like father, like son?"

"Don't compare me to him. And it's not like I stole anything from him. I earned the right to this place, and you know it. I've worked my ass off to keep this house, and I've put a ton of money into it. It's mine."

"Not legally."

He laughed out of nervousness. "So what are you doing? Blackmailing me?"

"Let's not call it that. Let's call it brotherly love. Or would that be sisterly love? You're the smart one. What shall we call it?"

Marc called it survival. When Marc was eighteen, Meinhard was thrown in jail for eighteen months on an aggravated assault charge. He had been working nights and sleeping during the day. One afternoon, after being awakened by the tinkling sound of the ice cream truck's bell for the third day in a row, he had stormed out of the house—baseball bat in hand—and threatened to beat the driver to a pulp if he ever drove down his street again. Luckily, he didn't actually make contact with the young man. Otherwise, it would have been a felony resulting in much longer jail time.

Shortly after that, Zenzi announced she was pregnant and moved in with a girlfriend, leaving Marc with sole responsibility for the house. Meinhard had left behind a number of overdue bills, including the mortgage, and Marc had found it more practical to pretend he was Meinhard instead of trying to transfer everything into his own name. He didn't think too much of it until he was forced to sign Meinhard's name to a bank document, and when that led to more signatures on other documents, he was in too deep to turn back without getting himself into trouble. He'd kept up the charade, and now Zenzi was going to use it against him.

Riley appeared in the doorway. "Where are we staying tonight?" he asked.

Zenzi looked at Marc with such smugness he wanted to slap it away.

"There are twin beds in the spare bedroom, and the sofa isn't half bad," he told her. "But it's temporary…until we figure something out."

"Go get our things," Zenzi told Riley.

"Hey, Josh!" Riley yelled from the kitchen. "We're moving in!"

Chapter 3

"You don't have to leave," Marc said to Gabby as she put on her coat. "That's okay. It's getting late."

As he followed her into the kitchen, Marc walked past Zenzi and the boys, who sat lined up on the sofa.

"We still on for tomorrow?" he asked Gabby.

"I'll call you," she said halfway out the door.

Marc grabbed his jacket and followed her. "Hey, can I explain what's going on?" he asked.

She turned to face him. "It doesn't matter, Marc. You've got your hands full right now. I'd just be in the way."

"Do I at least get a kiss good-bye?"

She gave him a quick kiss. "I'll call you tomorrow," she said before turning and descending the stairs. Within seconds, she was in her car and out of sight.

Unnerved by Gabby's brusqueness, Marc retreated to his apartment shaking his head and blaming his sister for ruining the rest of his weekend.

Riley greeted him in the kitchen. "We're hungry," he said.

"So am I," Marc said as he walked past him and into the living room.

"What was up *her* ass?" Zenzi asked. "Did you two have dinner already?"

"We were getting ready to order Chinese or something when you arrived."

"The boys have never had Chinese. They like pizza though."

"If you think—" Marc stopped short of telling her his immediate reaction to her impertinence, realizing he'd better reconcile what she had on him before pissing her off. He ordered enough pizza so they would have leftovers for lunch the next day.

"So what was her problem?" Zenzi asked again while they waited for the delivery. She got up and walked toward the kitchen. "You've got beer, I hope."

Marc's neck muscles tightened at the sound of the fridge door opening and closing. "She doesn't have a problem," he said when Zenzi reentered the living room.

"Sure looked like it to me."

"You and I need to talk later."

"Suit yourself."

The four of them watched the evening news in relative silence until the pizza arrived. After it came and Marc had gotten everyone settled in at the table, he excused himself to call Gabby. His call went directly to voice mail. He texted her.

Call me later.

By the time he returned to the kitchen, Zenzi and her boys had devoured an entire pizza and had started in on the second one. So much for leftovers.

He watched as Riley and Josh woofed down their slices of pizza. Even though Marc had no real tie to them, he felt sorry for Zenzi's sons. They were innocent victims in all this.

"So what grade are you boys in now?"

"I'm supposed to be in sixth," Riley said.

"He missed some school and had to stay back a grade," Zenzi explained.

"I'm in fifth too," Josh added. "Where are we going to go to school now?"

"We'll have to figure that out," Zenzi said. "Hey, maybe they'll go to our old school, huh, bro? What a hoot that would be. I wonder if the same rotten teachers are there. Probably not. They were old back then."

"Where were they going to school up until now?" Marc asked.

"There was a school not far from the shelter."

"That *sucked*," Riley added.

"Hurry up and finish eating, you guys. Your uncle and I have some talking to do."

Zenzi ate the last piece of pizza while Marc cleared the table.

"Go watch TV, boys," she ordered. "And don't touch anything." She turned toward Marc. "I see you still have OCD when it comes to housekeeping."

"I like neat and clean."

"I'll bet your tight-ass girlfriend does too."

"So, tell me, big sister of mine, what made you start snooping around into my private business?"

Zenzi leaned back in the chair and crossed her arms across her diminutive chest. "I got to thinking that this house is as much mine as it is yours, so—"

"Are you kidding me? What have you *ever* contributed to this household?"

"Doesn't matter. Nick says as long as—"

"Who's Nick?"

"Just someone I know, and he has a law degree, and he says I may have legal rights to this place."

"If you think for one minute I'm going to give up all the money and hard work I've put into this property for the last twelve years to you or anyone else, you'd better think again."

"You wouldn't be able to do much from jail."

"Look, Zen, I didn't willfully do anything wrong—I was just trying to keep from losing my home."

"Our home."

"I wouldn't have done it if I'd known it was illegal."

"Like Nick says, ignorance is no defense."

"So what do you want?" Marc asked, dreading the headache he felt coming on.

"You should have that eye looked into—it's twitching like crazy."

"What do you want?"

"I want one of the apartments. Doesn't matter which one."

"And you'll pay rent?"

"I couldn't pay it now even if I thought I should, which I don't."

"What happened to your blogging business?" At one time, Zenzi had been making money as a free-lance blog-writer. Small businesses, hobbyists, and others would throw a mess of vague ideas at her, and she'd turn it into something interesting, informative, entertaining, or whatever it was they were trying to accomplish. She'd been good at it. If she put her mind to it, Marc knew she could support herself and the boys on what she could make doing that.

"I haven't done that for a while."

"How come?"

"None of your business."

"You'd have to pay rent when you got back on your feet."

"Do you pay rent?"

"What do you mean 'Do I pay rent'? I pay the goddamn mortgage! And everything else that goes with it."

"I'd say you have a decision to make," she said on her way to the fridge for another beer. "Where do you keep your extra blankets?"

* * *

Marc awoke with a throbbing in his head he knew wouldn't be cured with any of the over-the-counter medications he had on hand. He pulled himself out of bed, threw on a robe, and rambled out of his bedroom to see if his sister and nephews were up.

Zenzi lay with her slight body draped over the sofa like a rag doll, one leg dangling over the side at such an angle Marc wasn't sure how she managed to avoid falling onto the floor. Empty beer bottles lay strewn on the coffee table—eight of them. He retreated down the hall, shaking his head.

When Marc opened the door to the spare bedroom he found Riley and Josh awake, dressed, and sitting on the edge of one of the twin beds.

"You're up! You can come out, you know. You don't have to stay in here with the door closed."

"Is Mom up?" Josh asked.

"Not yet."

"We'll stay in here until she's up and had her coffee," Riley said.

"I can make you some waffles for breakfast."

Josh's face lit up. "Really?" He rose to his feet only to have Riley tug on the back of his shirt, jerking him back down on the bed.

"We'll wait," Riley said.

"Okay, suit yourself."

Marc made coffee and stood at the kitchen window sipping it, feeling hollowed out and powerless but cautiously optimistic he could sort this mess out. It was out of character for Zenzi to use threats to get what she wanted, but then Marc didn't know her as well as he once did. Of course he felt sorry for her and what she and her boys must have gone through, especially living in a shelter, but she was disrupting his life.

It hadn't been easy for either one of them growing up. Losing their mother to cancer when he was seven and Zenzi eight had been difficult enough. Losing their father to alcohol afterward had in some ways been worse. While Meinhard worked sporadic manual labor jobs during the day and drank in neighborhood bars at night, Marc and Zenzi, mere teenagers, had maintained the household, with Marc supplementing the family income by cutting lawns in the summer and shoveling snow in the winter. He had managed to land on his feet. Zenzi hadn't.

Marc had mixed feelings about his sister—sympathetic toward her current state of affairs but irritated that she could be in a better place in life if she had put more effort into it. Other than take care of her, he didn't know what he could do for her, and that thought scared him.

"What's it take to get some coffee around here?" Zenzi bellowed, startling Marc and causing his coffee to slosh over the edge of the cup onto the floor.

"Oops... Cleanup in aisle three. Get out the mop and pail."

"You know, it would do you some good if you were to..."

"What? Be more like you?"

He reached over the counter and pulled off a sheet of paper toweling. "Coffee cups are in the cupboard next to the microwave," he told her as he sopped up the spill. "Still take it black?"

"I take it any way I can get it. Oh, you mean the coffee?"

"I was going to make waffles for the boys. Would you like some?" He struggled to come across as polite when what he really wanted was to be rid of her.

"And ruin this coffee? No, thanks. This is all I need until my first drink. You're out of beer, by the way."

"I noticed."

While Zenzi watched, Marc pulled out the griddle from the bottom cupboard and prepared to make a batch of blueberry waffles for the three of them.

"I checked the leases, by the way," he told her. "Neither one is up any time soon."

"Looks like you'll have to break one of them then."

Before he had gone to bed the night before, Marc had spent time Googling the ramifications of false impersonation. The enactments he found were called personation statutes, and while he didn't fully understand all the legalese, he understood enough to know he could be in serious trouble if caught—a minimum of a year in jail and $2,500 fine, and he could lose the house. What he didn't tell Zenzi was that the second-floor apartment lease had a "break clause" that might enable him to get the Bakers to move out within sixty days. It would kill him to break their lease—long-term tenants, nice people who paid their rent on time every month. It would also mean giving up the high-rent second-floor apartment.

"That's not something you can do overnight."

"Well, I guess we'll just have to stay here until you can make that happen."

She had him cornered, and she obviously knew it.

"Where did you stay before the shelter?"

"I had a boyfriend, but that didn't work out for us."

"Before then?"

"A girlfriend's, until her husband came back. What about Gabby's place?" she asked.

"What about it?"

"You could stay there and we could stay here until the other apartment is vacant."

"What?"

"Where does she live?"

"In Evanston, and that's out of the question." He wasn't about to vacate the premises and worry every minute of every day what his sister was up to.

"Just a suggestion."

"You want to tell the boys that breakfast is ready?"

"Boys! Breakfast is ready!" she shouted.

"I could have done that."

"Then why didn't you?"

* * *

When Gabby hadn't called by noon, Marc called her.

"I was just getting ready to call you," she said. "How's it going at your place?"

"Hectic…and crowded. It's a long story. Can we still get together today?"

"I'm sorry, but I thought you'd be busy with your sister and her kids there, so I made plans with my parents for today."

"Oh. Well, do you have time now? I'd like to explain what's going on."

"Only a minute. They're going to pick me up soon, and I still have some things I have to do before they get here."

"How about if I call you this evening? When will you be home?"

"I'm not sure. We're going out to dinner later. How about if I call you when I get home?"

"Okay."

Suddenly, Marc wasn't as happy with her busy "other life" as he had been before.

* * *

The following day, Marc asked Zenzi when she was going to enroll her children in school.

"It's a long walk. I thought maybe you'd drive us there," she said.

"We walked it all the time as kids."

"Well, I'm older now. And it snowed last night, and I don't have any boots."

"Have you talked to the school? Found out about tuition, what assistance is available?"

Zenzi shrugged.

"I have to make a few calls, and then I'll drive you."

First he called Nettlehorst Elementary School to ask about enrollment for the boys. Then he called his attorney, who confirmed his understanding of the clause in the Baker lease. He didn't know if he was relieved or disappointed—either way he dreaded having to tell them that they had to be out in sixty days.

After making two work-related calls, Marc dropped Zenzi and the boys off at the school while he went to the grocery store to pick up food for his burgeoning household. Into the top of the cart he threw a variety of items he thought they'd like, and in the bottom he put two cases of beer. Normally, two cases would last him a month, but with Zenzi in the house, he figured he'd be buying more the following week. False personation was going to prove to be a costly mistake any way he looked at it.

"How did it go?" he asked Zenzi after picking her and the boys up at the school.

"They can start next Monday if all the paperwork goes through," she said. "There's a few school supplies they'll need."

"Would you like to stop somewhere?"

"That would be nice."

Chapter 4

“To be honest, we’ve been dreading this moment,” Brian Baker told Marc. His wife, Maria, sat by his side with her hand on his knee. They had been Marc’s tenants for four years, ever since Brian had retired from his teaching job. “We figured something was up when your sister moved in with her two sons.”

“I hate doing this to you, believe me. You’re the best tenants anyone could ever ask for.”

“We knew that provision was in our lease, but quite frankly, we didn’t think you’d ever actually use it.”

“I hadn’t planned on it, but… How do you feel about the sixty days—will that be enough time?”

“No, but I guess it’s going to have to be,” Brian said. “That’s what’s in the lease.”

Marc had hoped this discussion would have gone smoother.

Maria appeared to be agitated. “I don’t know how we can possibly—”

Brian didn’t let his wife finish the sentence. “Never mind, Maria. We have no choice.”

“But what about—”

“We have no choice, dear.”

“I wish things were different,” Marc said.

Brian stood up. “So do we, Marc.”

Afterward, Marc told Zenzi of their conversation. “I just put a sweet retired couple out on the street. I hope you’re happy.”

“Happy? You think I’m happy?”

“Sorry. I probably shouldn’t have said that.”

“When will they be out?”

“Sixty days.”

“What until then?”

“We’ll just have to squeeze you in here until they’re out. Was everything you own in those few bags you came in with, or do you have some things stored somewhere?"

"A friend of mine is storing our beds in her basement and a few other things."

"Including your computer?"

"I don't have that anymore."

Great.

"If I'm not home in time for dinner, just eat without me," he told her. "There's food in the fridge."

* * *

After visiting his favorite nursery to put in an order for spring plantings, Marc drove to the posh Lake Forest neighborhood to check in with his top foreman Juan Baez. He relied on Juan to oversee the work done for the "Green Bay Six," his private term for the six lavish homes that faced each other on Green Bay Road, whose owners competed over who had the most impressive landscaping. Four of them were Marc's clients. The other two were maintained by another landscaping company, whose owner had a more caustic name for the group. Three crew foremen oversaw the aggregate of Marc's projects. Juan, who had been with him the longest, was the only one Marc trusted with his Green Bay Six clients.

Spotting his North Shore Landscaping pickup truck parked on the side of the road with its hood up, he pulled up behind it.

"Transmission again?"

Juan's head popped up from beneath the hood. "Yeah. I've tried the additive you gave me a few times now, but it's only a temporary fix. I think it's time to either rebuild or replace. What do you think?"

They talked about the problem and decided that while the transmission was being rebuilt, Juan would use his own vehicle for a few days, as Marc had no spare trucks in his small fleet. They spent another twenty minutes discussing a schedule for getting all the equipment ready for the spring busy season, and then Marc drove back to Chicago where he took care of some banking before going home for the day.

Exhausted, more mentally than physically, Marc climbed the stairs to his apartment looking forward to kicking back with an ice cold Revolution IPA he was anxious to try.

He didn't expect to find the kitchen in such chaos—dirty dishes on the table and in the sink, an open loaf of bread on the counter, crumbs everywhere, and a splat of mustard on the linoleum floor, a partial footprint in its center. He followed the trail of yellow splatters on the floor to the living room where he found the boys watching *Gilligan's Island* and Zenzi sleeping on the sofa surrounded by empty beer bottles.

"Who traipsed in mustard on their shoe from the kitchen?" he asked. Receiving no response, he raised his voice. "Ahem!"

Both boys turned around.

"What?" Riley asked.

"There's a trail of mustard going from the kitchen to in here."

"There is?"

"Check your shoes, and whoever did it, go in and clean it up."

"Not mine," Riley said after looking at the bottoms of his shoes.

"Mine either," Josh added.

"Then how about if both of you go in and clean it up!"

"What's all the shouting about?" Zenzi said, uncurling from a pretzel-like position on the sofa. She blinked her eyes a few times and ran her fingers through her tangled hair. "What time is it?"

"Boys, I told you to go clean up the kitchen floor—now!"

The boys looked at each other, shrugged their shoulders, and got up.

"Wasn't us," Riley mumbled on his way out of the room with Josh following close behind.

Fists firmly planted on his hips, Marc glared at Zenzi who was still in a half-horizontal position on the sofa.

"What's wrong with you?" she asked.

"What's wrong with *me*?"

"Yeah, that's what I said."

"I come home to a fucking disaster in my kitchen and you passed out on the sofa after guzzling half my beer, and you're asking what's wrong with *me*?" He walked away from her muttering, "This isn't going to happen every day, I can tell you that."

Checking the progress in the kitchen, he saw the boys had managed to smear the mustard stains into an even worse mess.

"Get out of here. Go to your room...anywhere but in here. I don't care."

"But we haven't finished—"

"You've done quite enough. Get out." He walked to the cupboard under the sink and pulled a household cleaner out from it. "Go! I'll finish in here."

Forty-five minutes later, Marc had the kitchen cleaned and three frozen pot pies in the oven.

"Your dinner's in the oven," he yelled at no one in particular. "Listen for the timer. I'm going out, and I expect this kitchen to be spotless when I return."

"Yes sir!" Zenzi yelled back.

* * *

After Marc returned from eating dinner out, he pulled his SUV into the garage next to his prize 2004 Mazda Miata. A client had sold it to him for a steal after Marc had constructed a complicated retaining wall on his property. A classic car that needed a lot of work, Marc had done most of it himself. He stared at it for a long moment—what he could get for it if he sold it could cover Zenzi's living expenses for a year…easily. That thought occupied his mind while he gathered up what he had purchased at the liquor store on his way home. After pulling out a few bottles of beer for himself, he stored the rest in his tool cabinet and then grabbed the other beverages, all non-alcoholic, to bring up to his apartment.

The kitchen, to Marc's astonishment, was in pristine condition—even the dishrag had been neatly folded and hung over the partition between the two sinks. A yellow sticky-note hung on the fridge. YOUR HOITY-TOITYNESS: WE HOPE THIS ROOM MEETS WITH YOUR APPROVAL. WE DARE YOU TO FIND A CRUMB ANYWHERE. NEATLY WRAPPED LEFTOVERS IN THE FRIDGE. LOVE, ZENZI AND THE BOYS.

He couldn't help but smile at the message and didn't care that she was making fun of him—he liked neat and clean. And quiet. Like it was now. No one was in the living room. He wondered where they all were.

Voices coming from behind the closed door of the spare bedroom door alerted Marc to their whereabouts. He knocked.

"Come in," one of the boys said.

The three of them were sprawled out on one of the twin beds watching a TV that hadn't been there when Marc had left. "Where did you get that?" he asked.

"The lady downstairs gave it to us. They're cleaning house for their move, and they didn't want to take this with them," Zenzi said. "I told her to just leave anything they don't want to take."

"That was nice of you."

"What? If it's stuff we could use, why throw it away?"

"Maybe they…never mind. The kitchen looks very nice by the way."

"Did you see our note?" Josh asked.

"Yes, I saw it. Very funny."

"Mom had to tell us what *hoity-toity* meant."

"I'll bet she did."

"I'll stay in here until the boys go to bed," Zenzi said.

"Thanks, but—"

"Don't argue. You're getting the living room to yourself for a few hours."

"Okay."

"You're out of beer."

"I know."

Marc settled himself in the living room and called Gabby.

"Hey!"

"Hey, yourself." Her tone of voice was not especially enthusiastic.

"I called to make plans for the weekend."

"This weekend?"

"Yes, this weekend." They hadn't missed a weekend together since they had started dating.

"Is your sister still there?"

"Yes, but I thought we could—"

"I'm sorry, Marc, but I made other plans."

"Oh?"

"A friend of mine from Charlotte is in town, and I invited her to stay here for the weekend. I figured you'd be busy."

"Is that all?"

"What do you mean?"

"Is that the only reason?"

"Reason?"

"For making other plans."

"Yes, why?"

"It just seems a little odd since we've spent every weekend for the past year and a half together that you'd make other plans without discussing it first, that's all."

"Like I said, I thought you'd be busy."

"I haven't had a chance to explain what's going on and—"

"Can I call you back? A friend of mine is over right now."

"Sure. Call me back."

A heaviness swept through his body as he hung up the phone—he hoped she wasn't slipping away.

Chapter 5

Seventy-five weekends. That was how many Marc had shared with Gabby—partial ones in the beginning, entire weekends for the past several months. He knew this number to be accurate because he had counted them himself the previous evening…while feeling sorry for himself and angry at Zenzi for messing up his life.

Marc plopped a dozen eggs into a pot of boiling water. Tired of hearing the boys constantly whine about being hungry, he figured they could snack on hard-boiled eggs between meals. When the eggs were almost done, Zenzi walked into the kitchen.

"So what are you going to do this weekend?" she asked him.

It had been twenty-two hours since Gabby had told him she had made other plans. He was aware of that number as well.

"Not sure."

"Nothing with what's-her-face?"

"Her name is Gabby."

"I thought she was your girlfriend."

"She is."

"So why aren't you doing something with her this weekend?"

Because you're here, stupid.

"A friend of hers is in town. What do you plan to do with the boys?" he asked, hoping they would leave for a period of time so he could have some time to be alone in his misery.

"Nothing. I have no money. No car."

"We have great public transportation, in case you've forgotten."

"I have no money, in case *you've* forgotten."

Now standing at the sink with his back toward her, Marc saw no reason to continue the conversation. He doused the fully boiled eggs in cold water.

"We're hungry," Riley said entering the kitchen. Josh wasn't far behind him.

Marc held out the pot of eggs. "Here, have a hard-boiled egg."

Both boys made faces.

"What?"

"Yuck," Josh said.

Zenzi laughed. "You mean you were boiling those eggs for *them*?"

"What's so funny?"

"They're not going to eat hard-boiled eggs."

"Why not? They're healthy, filling, and—"

"Sorry you wasted a dozen eggs on them, little brother. You should have asked me first."

"So what *can* we eat?" Josh asked.

Marc glared at him.

"Boys, I'd like to talk to your mother alone for a few minutes. Can you watch TV in your room for a while?"

"Can we take something to eat in there?" Josh asked.

"Yes. You can each have an egg."

The boys rolled their eyes and ambled out of the kitchen empty-handed. Marc waited until he heard the bedroom door close before he spoke.

"Look, Zenzi. I accept the fact that you have no other place to go, but let's get one thing straight—this isn't a cruise ship where you sit back and have everything done for you. You need to take responsibility for yourself and those kids, and that includes what they eat. Make a weekly grocery list, and I'll buy what's on it, but it's your responsibility to prepare their meals, get them to school, have clean clothes, and all the rest.

"And another thing—this is temporary. There is no reason you can't earn your own keep. And if you think for one minute you can get a free ride here because of something stupid I did that you can dangle over my head—"

"What the hell are—"

"Shut up. I'm not finished. If you need a computer to get back into your blogging business, you can have my old one. I'll set it up for you."

"I'm not going to—"

"You need to take hold of your life, Zenzi, and I don't see you doing that."

"Are you just about finished?"

"Yes."

"Good."

Marc retreated to the garage to work on the Miata, and for the next few hours, his emotions ran amok. He was glad he'd laid down the law with Zenzi but sorry he'd kicked her when she was already down. Further, he feared retaliation.

He thought about his own future—something he'd never done before, not in any serious way. Up until two years ago, he'd been too busy worrying about how he was going to make the mortgage payment, payroll, and all his other monthly expenses to think about long-range plans. And now with Gabby, he enjoyed the spontaneousness of their relationship too much to think about what could lie ahead for them.

Maybe he'd blown it with Gabby by keeping their relationship on middle ground. Maybe that's why she was finding it so easy to back away—she didn't have that much invested in it. Then why did he feel that he *did*?

Gabby had never talked to him about her expectations in the relationship, and he was only just beginning to wonder about his own. Having no expectations was easier of course. And safer. And now that he was thinking about it, rather aimless.

The sun had long since set, and the light wasn't that good in the garage, so Marc finished installing the new oil filter, put away his tools, and went into the tool cabinet to fetch a few bottles of beer for himself.

Only one of the two cases of beer he'd stashed there remained, and he hadn't been in that cabinet since placing them there four days earlier.

* * *

"Hey, babe."

"Hey, yourself."

It was Sunday evening, and Marc hoped Gabby's friend had left and that Gabby was alone...and missing him.

"How was your weekend?"

"Great. Heather and I had fun doing girl stuff."

"I'm almost afraid to ask, but what does that include?"

"You're a boy—can't tell you."

He was encouraged by her playful tone—up until then he had sensed ambiguity in her voice.

"Ah...should've known that. So are you free this coming weekend?"

"Of course."

Just those two words made his whole body relax.

"Good. I've missed you."

"I've missed you too."

"Let's plan on dinner for Friday then, and we can talk about the rest of the weekend later. Let me know if there's anything special you want to do."

"Do you want to stay here for the weekend?"

He had so hoped she would offer that.

"Sure."

After he hung up, Marc listened through his closed bedroom door for any noise coming from the living room across the hall. Hearing none, he cracked open the door and listened again. His attempts to avoid talking to Zenzi since telling her off had been successful, and he didn't want to spoil it for himself.

Thinking Zenzi had to be in the boys' bedroom down the hall, he slipped out of his room, past the spare bedroom, and into the kitchen where he retrieved a beer, the last one in the fridge, before going to bed.

"Got any more—"

"Jesus, Zen!" He swung around to face her. "You scared the crap out of me."

"How long did you think you could avoid me in this little shit hole?"

"This little shit hole is keeping a roof over your head, sister," he said as he opened his beer. "And will you keep your grubby little hands off my beer?"

Her posture changed, and the pained expression on her face caused Marc to think she was pretending to be upset by his remark—playing the part of a sad, broken-down soul who had just been unjustly attacked. Then the tears came, and he knew she wasn't pretending. She turned away and disappeared down the hallway.

"Wait, Zen. I'm sorry. I didn't—" He followed her to the spare bedroom only to have the door shut in his face. "Zen. Will you come out here, please?"

He let several seconds pass. "Zen?"

"Fine," he mumbled as he walked away. Grabbing the beer, he retreated to his bedroom to watch the ten o'clock news before going to bed.

I'll be so glad when she's out of here.

Chapter 6

On Friday morning, Marc hurried through things at work and went home earlier than usual to get ready for the weekend. He hadn't seen Gabby in twelve days. The timing for their reunion was perfect since the Bakers were moving out the following weekend, earlier than expected, and Marc would be too busy getting the apartment ready for Zenzi to spend much time with Gabby. He picked up a dozen roses for her on his way home. He'd made reservations at La Plume, her favorite Evanston restaurant, telling the person who answered the phone it was their anniversary so there would be a surprise dessert in it for them. Not a total lie—it would be the eighteen-month anniversary of their first date.

As soon as he opened his back door, a strange vibe in the room sent chills down his back.

"Zen?" he shouted.

"She left."

"What are *you* doing here?"

"That's a fine way to greet your father."

He hadn't seen Meinhard for three months, and then it had been only briefly to give him money.

"Where are Zenzi and the boys?"

Meinhard shrugged.

Marc dropped the roses on the counter. "What are you doing here?" he asked again.

"I need a place to—"

"How did you get in?"

"Zenzi."

"Why isn't she here? What happened?"

"She left."

"Look, old man, you better tell me what happened, and you better tell me right now. What gives?" he shouted.

"I'll just leave," Meinhard whimpered.

"Not until you tell me what happened to Zenzi."

"How do I know what happened? I came. She left. End of story."

"She had no place to go. Are you aware of that, Dad? Do you even care?"

"That's not my fault. Why are you yelling at me?"

Marc threw his keys down on the counter and marched into the spare bedroom. The closet was empty, and Zenzi's suitcases and bags were gone.

"How long ago did they leave?"

"Maybe an hour."

"You better hope that I find them," he said on his way out the back door. "And be the hell out of here when I get back!"

Marc was sick of Meinhard's irresponsible ways. If he wasn't asking him for money, he was asking him to pick him up somewhere or for a place to live. He had been a loser of a father when Marc was a kid and hadn't changed any over the years.

Before jumping into his SUV, Marc knocked on the Bakers' door hoping they had seen Zenzi and the boys leave. If they had, he would at least know in which direction to head. When he got no answer, he knocked on the door to the garden apartment. The tenant, Jessica, normally worked the second shift in a restaurant, so he wasn't surprised when she didn't answer.

Zenzi and their father had a history of bad blood, most of it emanating from her. It was odd how Zenzi seemed to despise the man even more than he did—Marc had ended up paying the bills and cleaning up his messes, not Zenzi.

He took a chance and drove down Halsted Street where there were restaurants, shops, and lots of activity, then drove north for a couple miles until he realized the pointlessness of his efforts. He pulled over and parked in a drug store parking lot where he Googled homeless shelters and soup kitchens within his ZIP code. An hour later, visits to them had turned up nothing.

Feeling helpless and guilty for having failed his sister, he headed for home, this time driving down Sheffield Avenue, still hoping to spot them.

He glanced at his watch. It was seven o'clock. *Gabby!*

He called her before thinking through what he was going to say.

"I was beginning to wonder about you," she said. "You're never late. Are you on your way?"

"No…ugh, well…there's a problem."

"What wrong?"

"Zenzi and the boys are missing, and I'm worried about them."

"Missing?"

"I got home and their things were gone. I'm out looking for them now."

"She's a big girl. Can't she take care of herself?"

"Not really. Not right now anyway."

"So what are you going to do?"

"I don't know, but—"

"Well, why don't you call me when you have it figured out?"

"You're upset."

"Maybe, but I understand. I really do. You need to go find her."

Marc wasn't sure if he believed she understood, and he wasn't sure if he did either. After all, Zenzi *was* an adult and *should* be able to take care of herself and her kids, and *he* should be with Gabby.

Instead of continuing his futile search for her, Marc headed home thinking that if he found Meinhard there, he would kill him, as he was sure he had had something to do with Zenzi leaving.

When he got home, both apartments, Jessica's and the Bakers', were dark so Marc didn't bother knocking on their doors again. His apartment appeared dark as well, but that didn't mean Meinhard wasn't lurking inside. He opened the door with caution.

After checking each room, Marc called the local police station and explained the situation. They told him that Zenzi leaving with her sons didn't appear to be a police matter but if they became aware of her whereabouts, they would call him.

Marc went to the fridge for a beer where he had put a six-pack the day before, but there was not a single beer in there now. It was eight-thirty, and it crossed his mind to forget about his sister and try to salvage the evening with Gabby, but in the end he couldn't leave without knowing what had happened to her. Now he wished Meinhard was still there so he could beat it out of him. A knock on his door interrupted his thoughts.

"Hi, Marc. May I come in?"

It was Maria Baker. She told him that she and her husband had heard yelling in his apartment during the afternoon.

"We heard a man's voice and knew you weren't home. We didn't know if we should get involved or not. Anyway, we didn't. I hope we did the right thing."

"That was probably my father, but he's gone now."

"I hope everything is all right."

"Yeah, me too."

So now he knew there had been some sort of argument between Zenzi and their father, which meant he had lied to him when he said he didn't know why she'd left.

❋ ❋ ❋

Blaring sirens jolted Marc awake after he'd fallen asleep on the sofa in front of the TV in the living room. *The Late Show* was just ending, so he knew it had to be past midnight. By the time he reached the front windows, the screaming vehicles had passed. Relieved they had nothing to do with him or his neighbors, he went to bed.

Unable to sleep, he pictured Zenzi and the boys somewhere in a park—cold, hungry, and scared. Meinhard had always managed to fend for himself, so he wasn't as worried about him. But Zenzi had invariably relied on others for a place to stay—boyfriends, girlfriends, the shelter, and now him.

By five a.m. he gave up on sleep, showered, and made a pot of coffee. He texted Gabby.

> R u up?

When he got no response, he retreated to the living room and turned on the news. During the weather report, his phone rang. Hoping it was Gabby, he grabbed his phone and looked at the caller ID. It wasn't a number he recognized.

"Hello."

"Is he still there?"

Thank God, it was Zenzi.

"Zen, where are you? I've been worried sick about you guys."

"Is he still there?"

"No. He's gone."

"Where?"

"I don't know. After I found him here yesterday, I went back out looking for you. When I got home, he was gone. Where are you?"

"And what if he comes back?"

"I'll tell him he can't stay."

"We're at Union Station."

"You stayed there all night?"

"Can you come get us?"

"Which entrance?" he asked. Union Station took up an entire city block and had multiple entrances on three sides.

"The one on Canal Street, near Madison."

"I'll be there as soon as I can."

Marc drove the five miles as fast as he could, stopping at the McDonalds drive-through along the way. When he arrived, the three of them were standing in front of the station. Zenzi climbed into the front seat while the boys jumped into the back.

"I smell food," Josh said.

Marc handed Zenzi the McDonald's bag. "Here's a snack for the ride home."

No one said a word on the way home. When they got in, Zenzi sent her sons to the spare bedroom.

"He's a bastard," she said.

"Tell me what happened."

"He came to the door, and like a fool I let him in. Honestly, I hardly recognized him."

"When's the last time you saw him?"

"God, it's been years. I've lost track of how many. Anyway, as soon as he realized you weren't here, he got all high and mighty on me. You know how he is. Said this was *his* house. He paid for it with *his* money. And he had a right to live here."

"I have a hell of a lot more invested in this place than him…just so you know," Marc told her.

"One thing led to another, and we had words, and he wasn't going to leave, and I wasn't going to stay in the same house with him, so we left."

"To Union Station?"

"No. First we walked over to Halsted Street, where this man handed me a twenty when he saw us standing on the corner looking like the lost souls that we were." She laughed. "I didn't ask him for it. He just shoved it in my hand. I would have tried to get more from other people, but Riley stopped me. Too embarrassed I guess."

"Thank—"

"Don't say it. Anyway, I didn't know where else to go, so we took a bus to Union Station where I knew it was warm and if we were asked to leave, I figured they'd know a place where we could spend the night. Then I got to thinking that I had just as much right to be here as he did, and that's when I called you."

"So you guys didn't sleep all night?"

"They slept some."

Marc shook his head. "The Bakers are moving out next weekend. So now you have a place to stay."

"Do you have any beer?"

He glared at her.

"Could you go get some? I have a few bucks left."

He knew it was the wrong thing to do, but he needed one too.

Chapter 7

"The Bakers are moving out on Saturday. I'm afraid I have a lot to do getting the apartment ready for Zenzi that weekend." Marc had been dreading having to tell Gabby he was unavailable all weekend.

"I understand," she said, but her tone indicated otherwise.

"Can we make plans for the following weekend?"

She hesitated before saying yes.

"I promise, no more family issues."

"Mm-hm."

"Can we make it a three-day weekend?" he asked her.

"You mean take Friday off?"

"Yeah."

"Maybe. I'd have to change some things at work."

"I'd like that."

"Okay."

"You'll come here then?" he asked.

"Okay."

"Thursday night?"

"You're trying to make up for things, aren't you?"

"Very much so."

"It's working."

"Damn, you don't know how glad I am to hear that."

* * *

On the morning the van arrived to move the Bakers, Marc took Zenzi and the boys out for breakfast at a local diner. Afterward, they all went to the supermarket to buy food to stock Zenzi's new kitchen. Marc bit his tongue when he saw Zenzi slip a case of beer into the cart amid the cereal boxes, frozen pizzas, and other items.

When they returned, the truck and the Bakers' car were gone, so the four of them went directly to the second-floor apartment to check it out. Given what Zenzi's friend had been storing in her basement for her and what the Bakers had left behind, Zenzi and her boys could exist comfortably without having to buy anything.

Marc spent the rest of the weekend with three of his crew cleaning the apartment, painting both bedrooms, and making sure everything worked properly when Zenzi moved in the following day—the same as he would do for any new tenant.

On move day, Marc sought Zenzi out for a private conversation.

"Look, Zen, I know you've had it rough for the past few months, and maybe even before that, I don't know, but I don't see you taking any initiative to get your life back on track, and that concerns me."

He told her he planned to set up his old computer in her bedroom and give her his WiFi password, so she had no excuse for not picking up her freelance blogger work.

"Loosen up, Marc. I'll get my shit together. Just give me a little time to get settled in."

"Promise?"

"Yeah."

Neither her words nor her tone were very convincing.

* * *

All week Marc looked forward to Gabby coming over on Thursday after work for a nice dinner out and a long three-day weekend. He wanted to make their time together special, and her playful texts during the week told him she was looking forward to it as much as he was.

Over the next couple of days, Marc checked on Zenzi periodically—not so often that she felt like she was under constant supervision but often enough to satisfy himself that she was behaving. Her friend had dropped off what she had been storing for her including Zenzi's collection of crazy cow stuff—salt-and-pepper shakers, coffee mugs, an umbrella, her keychain, a variety of refrigerator magnets. Even a pair of fuzzy slippers with giant cow heads on them that for some reason didn't embarrass her even when she wore them outside. How she had managed to hang on to these things given her nomadic lifestyle was beyond him. But maybe the larger question was why.

When Gabby arrived on Thursday, he greeted her with a box of Fannie May chocolates.

"If you think this will help you get back on my good side…well, you're right," she said before giving him a warm kiss. "I've missed you, you know that?"

"Not as much as I've missed you."

He had made a reservation with the upscale restaurant he had taken her to on the first anniversary of their dating. On the drive there, he filled her in on everything that had transpired since Zenzi had moved in, leaving out the real reason he was letting her have the second-floor apartment with no money and no job.

"I feel bad for Zenzi and especially her boys," she told him.

"I know. The whole situation with her is sad, and she has to get it together pretty quickly or it won't get any better."

"Do you think she will?"

"She has to. I'm not going to support her indefinitely."

After he parked the car, they walked hand-in-hand to the restaurant. Before entering, he took her aside and gave her a passionate kiss.

"What was that for?" she asked.

"For understanding what I'm going through."

"I'm trying."

"I can't ask for more than that."

During dinner, Gabby told Marc about how she had been asked by her boss to head up a needs assessment focus group that had to do with job skills training for people coming out of long-term incarceration. That her boss trusted her with taking full responsibility for the project excited her. As she was describing the types of people she wanted on her focus group, the waiter brought a miniature New York cheese cake dripping in raspberries to their table. She gave Marc a puzzled look.

"Happy anniversary, dear," he said.

"Anniversary?" she asked after the waiter had left.

"We met eighteen months ago. How could you not know that?"

"Okay, you get a point for that."

"Just one?"

Afterward in the car, Marc told Gabby that *Still Alice*, a Julianne Moore movie he thought she would want to see, was playing at the local movie theater, and they could catch the last show if they hurried.

"You know what I'd rather do?" she asked.

"What's that?"

"Watch a movie at your place. On the sofa. With a bottle of wine."

"Lights down low?"

"Now you're getting it."

After picking up some wine, they went back to Marc's apartment where they found *The Notebook* on Netflix. It was one of Gabby's favorite films.

"This is nice," she said halfway through the movie. Stretched out on the sofa, she lay on her back with her head resting on his lap. They had each consumed a glass of wine—their third one counting the two they had had at dinner.

"Good suggestion," he said. "Doing this in the theater would have surely drawn some attention."

His phone rang. He looked at the caller ID and turned the phone off.

"Not important?" she asked.

"Nope."

They watched another twenty minutes of the movie when someone knocked on Marc's door.

"Don't move. I'll be right back." He figured it was Zenzi, needing something.

But it wasn't her. It was Meinhard. Marc's stomach clenched at the sight of him.

"What are you doing here?"

"It's cold out here. Can I come in?"

Reluctantly, he opened the door and let him in. Disheveled and smelling like he hadn't showered in a while, Meinhard entered the kitchen.

"Look, I have company right now," he whispered. "Can this wait for another time?"

"I need some money. I have no place to go."

Marc pulled out his wallet and shoved two fifties into Meinhard's limp hand.

"Here. Now go."

He made brief eye contact with Marc before turning and heading toward the door.

"We can talk next week, okay?" Marc said to him.

Meinhard kept walking.

Taking a moment to free his mind of how he had just treated his father, Marc rejoined Gabby in the living room.

"Everything okay?" she asked.

"Mm-hm."

"Was that your father?"

"Yeah."

"You didn't ask him in?"

"I gave him what he needed."

"What was that?"

He stroked her hair. "Doesn't matter. He's gone now."

When the movie ended, they finished their wine and went to bed. After they made love and snuggled up against each other, Marc replayed in his head the scene with Meinhard, wondering what Gabby thought about it, and wishing the tightness in his chest would go away.

Chapter 8

The vibration of his cell phone woke Marc up. He grabbed it from beneath his pillow and slipped out of his bedroom to take the call. His heart sank when he heard Meinhard's voice.

"Can you come pick me up?" Meinhard asked.

"Where? Why?"

"The corner of Roosevelt and Clinton."

"And then what?"

"There's someone in Springfield who said I could stay with him. Could you drive me there?"

"Springfield? That's over three hours away. And it's one o'clock in the damn morning!"

"I'd really appreciate it. It's cold sitting here."

"You're sitting outside? Why do you need to leave town? And give me the real story."

"There was a truck...can I explain later? I'm borrowing this guy's phone and—"

"Dad?"

No response.

"Are you there?"

The glow of a full moon through the window was all Marc had to feel his way back into the bedroom. He eased his way into bed so as not to disturb her.

"That was him, wasn't it?" Gabby asked within seconds.

He lay there for a long moment before answering, allowing time for his muscles to relax, trying to guess what she was thinking by the tone in her voice. Five words wasn't much to go on.

"It was him."

He waited for her to say something, and when she didn't, he wished she had—it was better to know what she was thinking than to suppose the worst.

As he lay in bed, Marc considered whether to go rescue Meinhard or let him fend for himself. He had sounded so desperate on the phone, more so than usual. Soon the sinking feeling in his stomach guilted him into a decision.

He lay in bed for a few minutes longer until he thought Gabby had fallen back asleep. Then he got up, got dressed, grabbed a pen and paper, and wrote her a note telling her where he was going and that he would be home around midday at which time they could pick up where they'd left off and enjoy the rest of their weekend. He ended the note with a string of Xs and Os, hoping she would understand.

* * *

It was dark—sunrise was still a few hours away. Marc slowed the car as he approached the intersection where he expected to find Meinhard. At first, he didn't recognize him—the disheveled-looking old man at the bus stop slouched on the bench beside three black plastic bags.

He pulled up and rolled down the passenger-side window of his SUV. "Get in. You can throw your things in the—"

"Thought you'd never get here."

Marc didn't appreciate the comment, the tone, or much else about him at the moment.

"Do you know how to get there?" Meinhard asked.

"I know how to get to Springfield. Do you have an actual address?"

"Just drop me off at the edge of town. Then you can turn around and go back to Frenchie, if that's what you're concerned about."

In Meinhard's eyes, anyone named Gabrielle had to be French. Marc had told him more than once that Gabby's ancestors could be traced back to some of the first settlers of the Massachusetts Bay Commonwealth, but that didn't change anything.

"For someone who wants a favor, you're—"

"You're right. You're always right."

Marc stretched his neck in a failed attempt to keep the muscles from tightening any further. His father often had that effect on him.

"I suppose you want to put the address in that GPF thing of yours."

"It's GPS, and it's a handy thing to have when you don't know the area."

"Mm-hm."

Marc merged onto the I-90 ramp. "You said on the phone...something about a truck?"

"Doesn't matter. I made a mistake, that's all. It was a stupid truck, anyway."

"What kind of mistake this time?"

"Never mind. You've made your share of mistakes in life, and you're a hell of a lot younger than me."

"Than I."

"Don't get smart with me."

"So who's the woman?"

"What woman? I told you there's a *guy* in Springfield. He owes me some money. Said I could stay there a while."

"So tell me about the truck."

"It's nothing."

"Humor me."

"There's not too much to the story. I just kinda borrowed this guy's truck is all. To get to Springfield."

"And?"

"And...I had a little accident with it, but it wasn't working right and..."

"Translation: You stole a truck, and the police are looking for you...right?"

"He won't go to the police. There are... But I did hear... He's not someone to mess with, Markus."

"Who's the woman, Dad?"

"You think you're so smart."

Marc waited for the explanation he knew would eventually come.

"Someone who wrote me letters in prison. She wants to save my soul."

"And you're going to let her."

"For a while."

They got onto I-55.

"Are those bags all you have?" Marc asked him. "What happened to your furniture?"

"That junk? Anything I ever had of any value you now have."

If he hadn't been driving, if he had been face-to-face with him, he would have had a hard time keeping from punching him in the nose.

"What of yours do I have that doesn't rightfully belong to me, Dad?"

"Nothing, Markus. Nothing at all."

A heavy silence fell between them for several miles until Meinhard asked if they could stop for a bathroom break.

Marc pulled off on an exit where there were fast-food restaurants and a gas station.

"Are you hungry? When's the last time you ate?" Marc asked him.

"I could eat something."

Marc stopped at a McDonald's.

"Order whatever you want. My treat."

"You did that on purpose," Meinhard said when they were sitting down with their food.

"Did what?"

"Stopped here."

"What? You said you needed a bathroom break."

"You didn't have to pull off *here*."

Marc knew where he was going with this. They were in Pontiac, home of Pontiac Correctional Center, Meinhard's previous home away from home.

"I pulled off at the next exit after you said you needed to piss. Do you want to leave? Ask these nice folks for a doggie bag and drive somewhere else...drive somewhere else while the food gets cold?"

"You don't have to be such a wise-ass, Markus."

Marc shoved his food to the side and stood up.

"I've lost my appetite. You finish your food while I gas up."

Ten minutes later, for a fleeting moment as Marc gave the gas-tank cap a final turn, he contemplated taking off without Meinhard, the little boy in him wanting his father to know what it felt like to be abandoned.

When he drove back to McDonald's, Meinhard was outside waiting for him, a white paper bag in hand.

"I bagged up your food in case you get hungry later."

"If you give me that address, I'll put it in the GPS before we take off again. We'll be in Springfield in less than two hours."

He removed a scrap of paper from his jacket pocket and handed it to Marc.

"I do appreciate your driving me there, you know."

"I know."

"Sometimes I don't think you know how much I appreciate the things you do for me."

"I know, Dad."

"I wish your mother was still here. She'd have been proud of you."

The mention of his mother signaled that Meinhard was about to ask for something.

"I wish she were here too."

"She was a good woman." His German accent thickened—another telltale sign.

"I know."

"Didn't deserve to die so young."

"Mm-hm."

"I could use a little cash to get me by, if you can spare it."

"What happened to the hundred I just gave you?"

"Doesn't matter."

"It matters to me. What did you do with it?"

"I owed it to someone."

"I thought you were going to use it to get a room somewhere."

"Yeah, well, so did I."

"Have you ever met this woman, Dad?"

"What woman?"

"The woman I'm taking you to. Who else would I be talking about?"

"Did you hear what I said about the money?"

"Yes, I heard you. Have you ever met this woman?"

They were now at the outskirts of Springfield.

"We corresponded some. Talked to her on the phone once."

Marc was more concerned about the woman than he was about his father, but he asked the question anyway. "What do you know about her?"

"Enough."

"What happened to your cell phone, by the way?"

"It's in one of my bags, I think."

They approached a nicely maintained one-story cottage-style home, white picket fence and all. Standing tall in the center of the front yard was a religious statue surrounded by low evergreens.

"Want me to come in with you?"

"Not really."

"I'll at least wait until she opens the door, just to make sure she's home."

"Thanks."

"You have my cell phone number if you need me."

"Mm-hm."

Marc handed him a wad of small bills.

"Here you go. Spend it wisely, okay? And let me know how you're doing?"

"I will."

Marc watched him schlep himself and the three plastic bags to the front porch and ring the doorbell. The door opened. Marc thought the woman looked normal enough—middle-aged, hair up in a bun, wearing tan slacks and a brown sweater. Marc lingered until Meinhard disappeared into the house.

I hope she knows what she's getting herself into.

Before taking off for his journey home, Marc retrieved a text message that had come in during the drive. It was from Zenzi. In one of his weaker moments, he had bought her a prepaid phone until she could get back on her feet.

Hot stuff left here @ 6:30. Where r u?

From the second-floor apartment, Zenzi had a full view of the backyard and walkway leading to the garage and alleyway.

He glanced at the time on Zenzi's message. Six fifty-one. He pictured Gabby reading his note, crumpling it up, and leaving in a huff. He called her cell phone and got the voice-mail greeting. Not a good sign. He texted Zenzi back.

On way home.

Marc drove home, hoping Gabby was just out getting some breakfast and would be there when he returned.

Chapter 9

Relieved to see her Lexus Sport parked in its usual spot, Marc rushed up his back stairs and into the kitchen.

"Gab? I'm home!"

Gabby emerged from the hallway wearing a skimpy white nightie—her presence filling the entire room. He let his eyes rest on her long, shapely legs, seduced by the thought of her wrapping them around his back.

"I thought you'd never get back."

He sauntered toward her. "So what do you have on underneath there?"

Before he reached her, she turned around and sashayed toward the bedroom.

"Come find out," she said.

Once in bed, her touch alone drove him crazy. Afterward, as they lay cuddled together, three high-pitched beeps sounded from his cell phone. He felt her body tense up in his arms.

"Aren't you going to get that?" she asked.

"No. It can go to voice mail."

When the phone finally stopped beeping, he felt her relax.

Still lying close to each other, they talked about the rest of the weekend, and when his phone went off again, Marc got up, retrieved it from his pants pocket, and turned it off. When he turned around to face Gabby, she was sitting up in bed.

"You should listen to it. It could be important," she said without emotion.

"I'll listen later."

He crawled back into bed.

"So we were talking about—"

"I don't think we should plan anything for today."

"Why not?"

"You know he's going to call you back. He probably already has."

"I won't answer it. I'd rather be with you." He inched his way closer to her and draped his arm in her lap.

"Promise?"

"Scout's honor."

"You were never a Boy Scout."

"Yes, I was. Well, not a Boy Scout, but a Cub Scout."

"Mm-hm."

"Wanna see my badges?"

"I've never heard *that* line before," she said while giggling.

He loved it when she laughed like that—so melodic, soft, and restrained.

"So what do you want to do?" he asked her.

"Let's go ahead with the Egyptian exhibit at the Art Institute."

"Sounds like a plan. Lunch at Terzo's?"

"Perfect."

"I'm going to shower," she said as she rose out of bed. "Want to join me?"

Stupid question.

* * *

While Gabby blow-dried her hair, Marc retrieved his cell phone messages—all three from Meinhard, each one sounding more desperate than the last.

Call me right away, Markus. It's important.

Where are you, son? Pick up the goddamn phone.

If you don't call me soon, I may...

He paused after listening to the last one, which ended abruptly, and then called the number showing on his phone.

"It's about time. You gotta come get me."

"Where are you?"

"Hold on."

Marc fought to maintain self-control while he waited for Meinhard to get back on the phone.

"The corner of Pope and Laurel."

"In what town?"

"Springfield. Where else would I be?"

"What are you doing there?"

"Waiting for you to pick me up."

"What happened at—"

"I'll explain later. Just come get me."

"I just got home!"

"Took you long enough."

He wasn't about to explain the exhilarating hour he'd just spent with Gabby.

"Now you expect me to turn around and come get you? It's a three-and-a-half-hour drive."

"I have nowhere to go."

"Can't you stay there until tomorrow?"

"Where? I have no money."

"What happened to the money I gave you?"

"Can we discuss this later? I'm using this guy's phone."

"What happened to your phone?"

"Just come get me."

"I'm sure they have shelters there."

"I'm not near any shelters. I'm in the middle of nowhere."

"Are you near public transportation?"

"I just told you I'm in the middle of nowhere. Are you deaf?"

Marc counted to three before responding.

"I'll be there as soon as I can."

"I'll try my best to stay alive until then."

"Dad, are you serious or just being dramatic? Will you be okay until I get there?"

"I'll be fine."

Marc jumped at the sound of the back door slamming.

"Hold on!" He threw the phone down on the sofa and ran toward the kitchen. As he neared the back door, the lingering scent of Gabby's perfume confirmed his suspicion.

"Gabby!" he shouted from the doorway.

She picked up her pace as she walked toward her car.

"Wait!" he bellowed.

If he had had on more than just his boxer shorts, he would have run after her. Within seconds, she was in her car and gone.

"Damn him anyhow!"

Back in the living room, he glared at the phone—one flick of a finger could end the call. It was tempting.

"I need an address, Dad. For the GPS."

"Hold on."

Marc seethed while he waited—angry at Meinhard for his constant intrusions into his life, but angrier at himself for allowing it.

"Eighteen-oh-five South Pope."

"Fine. I'm on my way."

"Well, you don't have to sound so happy about it," Meinhard said. "You'll see a clump of bushes on the corner. I may be behind there."

Marc threw on the clothes he had ripped off earlier in the heat of passion and headed out.

Once on I-90, he set the cruise control speed to five miles over the limit and for the rest of the trip did his best to avoid reaching his snapping point after having to rescue his father for the second time in twelve hours.

* * *

When Marc finally arrived at the address, he found Meinhard standing on the sidewalk talking to a man with a dog. When he spotted Marc, he inconspicuously waved him on. Marc drove on, mumbling obscenities to himself, and then waited around the corner for the dog-walker to move on. When he went back a few minutes later, Meinhard was dragging his bags of worldly possessions out from underneath a forsythia bush.

"What happened?" he asked once Meinhard was situated in the car.

"Nothing. Just passing the time of day."

"I mean with the woman."

"How about 'Are you okay, Father?'"

Marc flashed him a bitter smile. "Are you okay, Father?"

"Do you care?"

After a couple of miles of driving, he got the story.

"That crazy bitch wanted to cast the evil out of me with a spell and then maybe something worse, who knows."

"Should have stayed. It might have done you some good."

"The last thing I need is your sarcasm."

"Sorry. Go on."

"Her house was filled with religious stuff, candles, crystals, and who knows what else. And it reeked...herbs or something, I don't know. She offered me a cup of some vile-smelling tea that could have been piss for all I know, and then she started to chant—just horrible—something about fire and water and circling the moon or some shit. A real nutcase."

Marc remained silent.

"Aren't you going to say anything?"

"Where do you want to go now?"

He let out a soft whimper. "I've been thinking about that, son. After all I've been through these past few months, maybe it's time I come home."

Marc recalled painful memories of all *he'd* been through, thanks to his father. Like having to evict the third-floor tenant after Meinhard had gone to prison and then moving into it with two roommates, both of whom had been complete slobs. He had kept the second-floor tenant and rented out the garden apartment to a young couple with a new baby. In order to make the mortgage payments and take care of unpaid bills Meinhard had left behind, Marc worked for two landscapers, often putting in sixty-hour weeks of back-breaking work.

Then when Meinhard was released, he'd waltzed home thinking he would move back in. When Marc told him there was no room, Meinhard had argued that it was *his* house. Marc had told him that if he wanted to pay him the same $100 a month he got from each roommate, he could move back in. After that, Marc didn't hear from him until he showed up on his doorstep again months later. Marc helped him find a cheap room elsewhere, paid the first two month's rent, and advised him to get a job. Ever since then, Marc had been bailing him out of one predicament after another.

"And just where do you think you're going to stay in the house?" Marc asked him.

"Who's in the garden apartment?"

"A paying tenant."

"How about with Zenzi then?"

"That would never work. And anyway, where would you sleep? Her apartment is full."

"That leaves only one place."

"No."

"You have two bedrooms."

"No."

"You'd deny your own father—"

"Would you like me to list the reasons why you can't move in with me?"

"No."

"When's the last time you had a job?"

"I have a job…at Lenny's…or *had* one until the unfortunate truck incident."

"Doing what?"

"Washing dishes. Sweeping up. Cleaning tables. Whatever Lenny needed me to do."

"Where were you living?"

"Over the restaurant with Lenny's deadbeat brother-in-law."

"Were you current on rent?"

"It wasn't a bad setup."

"Were you current on rent?"

He took his time answering. "Not always, but he'd deduct it from my pay when I wasn't. He didn't seem to have a problem with it."

"I'll bet."

"Look, Mister Hot Shot, not everyone is as—"

"You have two hours to figure out where you want me to drop you off. Then I have a relationship to mend, thanks to you."

"With Ms. Frenchie?"

Marc didn't respond.

"At least they take care of you in Germany when you're down and out," he mumbled under his breath. "You get respect there."

"If you're talking about their Socialist Party, that went defunct years ago. But I'll gladly buy you a plane ticket if you want, so you can see for yourself. Just say the word."

"Don't be a smart-ass."

"I'll try."

"I haven't eaten since that measly breakfast you bought me."

"Mine is still in a bag in the back seat. Help yourself."

They drove the rest of the way in silence, with Meinhard dozing off every now and again, the sound of his rattly breathing grating on Marc's nerves more and more with each mile. He didn't know what to do—he couldn't bring him home if there was any chance of reconnecting with Gabby. A half hour outside of Chicago, Marc woke him up.

"I'm going to take you to a shelter."

"You'd dump your own father at a shelter when you have room yourself."

Marc pulled in a slow breath and then released it before he spoke. "You can stay the weekend while you figure this out. But no longer."

Chapter 10

M arc pulled up in front of his garage. The space where Gabby normally parked was empty.

"Damnit!"

"What's the problem?" Meinhard asked.

"Nothing."

After he exited the car, Marc headed to the outside stairway that led up to his apartment. Meinhard followed, dragging with him his three bags of belongings.

"Not good enough to go in the front door?" Meinhard asked when he had caught up to him halfway up the stairs.

Marc swung around to face him. "Is that really where you want to go?" he snapped at him.

"Calm down, son. The back stairs are fine."

Marc unlocked his back door, and without turning around to see how Meinhard was managing the stairs with his baggage, entered his apartment. Leaving it up to his father to figure out where to put himself and his bags, Marc disappeared into the bathroom.

Sitting on the toilet-seat lid to avoid having to deal with his new houseguest for the moment, Marc scanned the bathroom walls. Eyeing Gabby's bath items in the shower stall gave him hope that she hadn't left for good. He made a mental note to look for a replacement tile for the one he had cracked when he'd installed the caddie for her toiletry items.

He turned his attention to the Art Deco ceiling fixture that he never liked and added that to his mental notes. The bath towel Gabby had left draped on the towel bar compelled him to get up and straighten it. It bugged her when he did that, probably as much as it bugged him to find it that way.

After spending an unreasonable amount of time scrutinizing every inch of the bathroom, Marc figured Meinhard had had sufficient time to get settled in his room. He proceeded to his own bedroom to check the closet for Gabby's clothes.

Still there. More hope.

Relieved to see the door to the spare bedroom closed, he headed for the living room. "I hope you stay in there the whole weekend," he muttered to himself.

Marc plopped down in his favorite chair, turned on the TV, and prepared to read his text messages. While he was reading the first one, a new one came in from Zenzi.

> Why is that sob here?

He searched for the right answer.

> Just 4 w/e. No place 2 go.

She responded within seconds.

> So?

He moved on to the next message. It was from Juan.

> Mrs. W wants workers on Sunday AM, party in PM.

Mrs. W was Mrs. Wilder, one of the Green Bay Six.

> Can u get a crew together?

> Yes

> Go ahead then.

The Green Bay Six weren't his only feuding clients. A far more serious battle was being fought among some other well-to-do Lake Forest families in another part of town, near the Middlefork Savannah Forest Preserve, and it revolved around whitetail deer. As a result, Marc learned that there were three distinct camps when it came to an overabundance of deer living near residential areas: those who had a strong affection for animals, those whose main concern was for the environment, and those who cared only about protecting their precious landscaping. Each of his three clients—none of whom understood or cared about the other's concerns—belonged to a different camp, making his job interesting and challenging. He referred to them as the Deer Campers.

No messages from Gabby, so he sent her one.

Can we talk?

Not receiving the usual "message sent" indicator caused a sinking feeling in his stomach. Had she blocked him?

"Got anything to eat?" Meinhard's voice startled him.

"I do, but why don't you come in here and sit for a minute first?"

"Why do I feel like there's a lecture about to come on?"

"No lecture. I just want to talk about a plan. A plan for where you're going to live...how you're going to live...how you plan to support your—"

"Maybe we should start by talking about this house. It's still in my name, or have you forgotten that?"

"Let me remind you that when you were carted off to prison, you were three months behind in your mortgage payments, and I was all of eighteen years old mowing yards ten and twelve hours a day trying to make ends meet, working weekends at Home Depot, and begging the bank to give you more time. I did whatever I could to keep a roof over our heads." The longer he talked, the angrier he became. "*I* was the one who had to deal with the deadbeat tenant you had in here. *I* was the one who—"

"Never mind. I can see where this is going, and I don't think we could live under the same roof anyway. I'll let you buy me out then."

Marc marched to his bedroom across the hall, his teeth clenched tight. He returned a minute later gripping a file folder in one hand.

"Would you like to know what you have invested in this place compared to what *I* have?" He didn't wait for an answer. "The day you left here, you had $40,000 equity in this property."

"You're crazy. I paid on that mortgage for twenty years."

"And you borrowed against it six times during those twenty years."

"That many?"

"Yes, that many. Since you've been gone, I've become current with the mortgage, put on a new roof, had every flat painted, upgraded the garden apartment kitchen and bathroom so I could charge a decent rent, landscaped the yard, upgraded the old circuit-breaker panel, and replaced half the windows. This in addition to normal maintenance, paying insurance premiums, taxes, and all the other shit that goes with it.

"So let's do a little rough math here. Let's say we split the cost of the home improvements since I lived here and you didn't. And split the real estate taxes, the insurance, and the normal maintenance. And let's talk about what it's cost me to bail you out of one stupid jam after another." He held up the file folder and waved it in the air. "You may be surprised to see that I've kept track of all this."

Marc tallied the numbers on his cell phone's calculator. "Now would you look at that," he said smugly. "It appears that you owe me roughly six grand."

Meinhard's eyes sent him a wordless but well-perceived message.

"What's the matter, Dad? Nothing to say?"

"I don't like your math," he finally said.

"There are a lot of things I don't like."

"Go on. Say it. Maybe it'll make you feel better, hothead."

I can hear u guys.

"What was that chirping sound?" Meinhard asked.

"My phone."

"Don't they ring anymore?"

"That was a text message."

"What's that?"

"Someone sent me a written message from their phone to mine."

"Who would do that?"

"Someone who had something to say to me."

"Why not call?"

"Texting is faster and usually more to the point. Quit changing the subject."

"Can I do that on my phone?"

"I thought you lost it. You had to borrow someone's to call me."

"I found it."

"Let me ask you this again. Where are you going to go, and how are you going to support yourself?"

"I don't know. I'll be seventy next month. What can I do?"

"You never did apply for Social Security, did you?"

"I don't want their money."

"It's not *their* money. You paid into it all those years you worked. It's *your* money. You need to go down to the Social Security office and apply for it, but first you need an address, and it would be helpful if you had a checking account."

"I don't trust banks."

"Just a suggestion."

"I bet they don't do it this way back home. There you're taken care of," Meinhard said.

"Right."

"This country is going to hell. This neighborhood is going to hell. Damn queers."

He was referring to the predominantly gay neighborhood two blocks east of their house known as Boys Town. When he had purchased the house in the early eighties, Boys Town had been much smaller and less conspicuous.

"I told you before that I can arrange for you to go back there."

"Don't be such a wise guy. I came here looking for the American dream. Why would I want to go back there? I could use a drink."

"Of what?"

"Anything. Beer, whiskey. I don't care."

"How about a soda?"

"So now you're going to deny me an occasional drink?"

"It's not occasional and you know it."

"Maybe you should have one too. Lighten up a little."

Marc's head hurt. "Dad, you need a place to live, and then I'll take you to the Social Security office to apply. Do you think you could get your job back from Lenny and live above the restaurant again?"

Meinhard shrugged without saying anything, appearing too tired or too uninterested to continue the conversation—a known strategy of his to get people off subjects he didn't want to discuss.

"Would you like me to make you a sandwich?" Marc asked.

"I thought you'd never ask."

As he prepared the meal, Marc was struck by the realization that he had no bond with Meinhard beyond the blood tie to him and questioned why he felt obligated to continue tolerating him at all.

Chapter 11

Marc knocked on Zenzi's door with the intent of explaining his plans for their father. Riley answered.

"You can't come in," he said. The earthy stench of cigarette smoke drifted out from behind him, causing Marc to wince.

"Why not?"

"Mom's not feeling very well."

"Oh? What's wrong?"

"Uh, probably the flu or something."

"Well, just tell her I'm here. I want to talk to her about something. It'll only take a minute."

"Sure. I'll tell her, and then she can call you...when she wakes up," he said as he closed the door.

Riley's words implied that everything was under control, but his facial expression told Marc something different. Marc stuck his foot in the door before it closed all the way.

"I'd like to come in."

"She wouldn't want you to see her like this."

"Like what?"

"Not feeling well."

"Does she need help?"

Riley shot him a look that Marc couldn't decipher.

"Riley?"

When he didn't respond, Marc pushed his way past him.

He found his sister in the living room sprawled out on the sofa, eyes shut and drool hanging out of her mouth. He checked her pulse. It felt weak to him but he didn't know anything about pulses. He called her name, and when he got no response, he lightly slapped her cheek.

"How long has she been like this?" he asked Riley.

"Not long."

She had just texted him a half hour earlier. Apparently, she had been okay then.

"Has this ever happened before?"

"Yeah. She'll wake up...in time."

Marc glanced around the cluttered room, picked up an empty bottle of vodka lying on the floor, and placed it on the coffee table.

"She needs medical attention. I'm calling 9-1-1."

"She told us never to do that."

"I don't give a rat's— She needs help. Where's Josh?"

"In Mom's bedroom...hiding under the covers, the last time I looked. He doesn't like it when she gets like this."

"Go tell him I'm here."

"Why?"

"So he knows someone is here."

"Fine."

Marc called 9-1-1 and stayed on the phone with the dispatcher until the EMTs arrived, trying to keep calm on the outside while his heart raced on the inside. He stared at the empty Absolut bottle and wondered if it was the one he'd kept in his freezer. If it was, she must have taken it before she moved out five days earlier. What a stupid blunder for him to have left it accessible.

When the two EMTs arrived, Riley and Josh came out into the living room, Josh hugging a stuffed penguin that Marc recognized from a zoo trip he'd taken with the boys when they were much younger.

"She's gonna be mad when she wakes up," Josh said to the EMTs.

"Are you a relative?" one of the EMTs asked Marc.

"I'm her brother, their uncle."

"So when we leave, they'll be in your care?"

"I'll look after them, if that's what you mean. Where will you be taking her?"

"Illinois Masonic. You know where that is?"

"Over on Wellington?"

"That's the one."

"What do you think caused her to pass out?" Marc asked, fearing he knew the answer but hoping he'd hear something different.

"There can be any number of causes for someone to pass out, but judging by her decreased vital signs, clammy skin, and that empty vodka bottle over there, I'd say there's a chance it's alcohol poisoning."

"She seemed okay an hour ago."

The EMT continued talking while he and his partner strapped Zenzi to the gurney. "If someone drinks a large volume of alcohol in a short period of time, it can cause them to black out. That may be what happened, but they'll know more at the hospital after they run tests."

"Should we follow you?" Marc asked.

"If you want, but my guess is that she's going to be out for a while." He looked at the boys. "The ER isn't the best place for children."

After the EMTs left, Riley said, "I wouldn't want to be around her when she wakes up."

"I'm sure they can handle her."

"So what happens now?" Riley asked.

"Well, I guess you can come up to my apartment until—"

"*No way.*"

"Why?"

"Because *he's* up there."

Marc could only imagine what Zenzi had told her sons about their grandfather—the amount of animosity she felt toward him was no secret.

"Well, you can't stay here alone."

"Sure we can. We're used to it."

"No. I'll stay down here with you until your mom comes home," he told them, hoping it wouldn't be more than one night.

"She won't like it," Josh said.

"Why not?"

"She just won't," he said with a quick shrug.

"Well, right now she has no say in the matter."

"Looks like we don't either," Riley said.

Marc didn't care for his tone.

"How long is she gonna be gone?" Josh asked.

"I don't know. Not too long I hope."

"This sucks," Riley said. "You never should have called for an ambulance." He picked up the empty vodka bottle and some of the other items that littered the living room and headed toward the kitchen. "C'mon, Josh, help me clean up this place."

With routineness and efficiency that suggested they had done it many times before, the boys carted off dirty dishes, glasses, food wrappers, various pieces of clothing, and garbage that were scattered about. When finished, they joined Marc in the living room.

"Do you have any Pepto-Bismol?" Riley asked.

"What for?"

"To drink. What else?"

"Why do you need Pepto-Bismol?"

"I get upset stomachs."

"Really."

He shrugged. "Whatever. So now what?"

"Now what what?"

"What do we do now?"

"What do you normally do?"

"Nothing much."

Well, I guess we'll do nothing much then.

"When she comes home, you're taking the shit for her being taken to the hospital," Riley told him.

The shit?

"Of course I will. I'm the one who called them."

"Be sure and tell her we had nothing to do with it," Josh added.

"I'll be sure to do that."

"So now what?" Riley asked again.

"If your mom was here, what would you guys be doing?"

They both shrugged.

"Do you have any homework?"

"Nope."

"Do you have any video games?"

They shook their heads.

"No Xbox or PlayStation?"

"Nope."

"I have an old PlayStation I never use, and—"

"You do?"

"Forget it, Josh. Mom wouldn't let us have it anyway."

Marc had no clue what to do with them. He glanced at his watch. "Are you hungry?"

"Sure."

"Where do you want to go?"

"Like out somewhere?"

"Yeah, like to a restaurant," Marc said.

"What if Mom calls?" Josh asked.

"She has my cell number."

"I'd rather stay here. Wouldn't you, Riley?"

"Yeah."

"Okay, so let's see what's in the fridge."

"There's nothing much left from when you took us to the store," Riley said.

Marc checked the freezer and found it bare. "How about if we drive over to

KFC and pick up some chicken? We can bring it back here," Marc said.

"Really?" Josh asked.

"Fine," Riley said with no enthusiasm.

"Uncle Marc?"

"Yes, Josh."

"Can we stop at the pet store first?"

"For what?"

"Crickets."

"Crickets?"

"Yeah. For Bart."

"Bart?"

"His new pet snake," Riley said rolling his eyes.

They had been in the apartment less than a week and already he had a pet?

"Where did you get a pet snake?"

"I brought him home from school today. Our teacher didn't want him there anymore."

"So you volunteered to take it?"

"No one else wanted him."

"And your mom said okay?"

"She said the first time she saw it out of its tank, she was going to flush it down the toilet."

"What did she say about the crickets?"

"We never got to that part."

"Well, we can't let the thing starve, I guess. The pet store it is then."

As Marc made his way through the kitchen, a crudely made heart cut from construction paper lying on the counter caught his attention. "What's this?" he asked.

"I made a Valentine's card for Mom," Josh said. "But she never got a chance to read it."

"When is Valentine's Day?" Marc asked, the image of Gabby's face flashing through his mind.

"Today."

Shit.

* * *

Later that day, after the boys had gone to bed, Marc called the hospital to see how Zenzi was doing. He was told she had acute alcohol poisoning, her blood alcohol content was .30, and the doctor had given her a strong cocktail of drugs to stabilize her.

They suggested he not come to see her for at least twenty-four hours and preferably forty-eight. Apparently, when she came to and they told her who had called 9-1-1, she'd spat out a string of derogatory remarks about her good-for-nothing brother that could be heard throughout the entire hospital wing.

Next, he called Gabby's cell phone. It rang ten times and never went to voice mail. He tried texting her again, but like before, it didn't go through. He pictured her out with friends, having a good time. Or maybe she was sitting home alone, stewing over being snubbed on Valentine's Day by her thoughtless boyfriend. Either way was distressful.

Stupid holiday. Pain-in-the-ass sister.

He called Meinhard, who'd been left unattended for several hours.

"Where the hell are you?"

"I'm down in Zenzi's apartment. She's in the hospital."

"What's the problem?"

"Are you okay while I take care of her boys down here? What are you doing?"

"What do you think I'm doing?"

"I hope you're putting together a plan for yourself. Have you called Lenny?"

He got no response.

"Dad, have you called Lenny for your job back?"

Still no response.

"Are you there?"

Marc closed his eyes. When he opened them, Riley was standing in front of him. He put down the phone.

"We can't sleep."

"What's the problem?"

Riley glared at him for an intense moment before saying, "What do you *think* is the problem, dumb-head?" He ran back into his bedroom, slamming the door behind him.

After contemplating what he should do, Marc knocked on the boys' bedroom door.

"Riley?"

"Go away!"

"Can I come in?"

"No!"

"Look, I know what you're going through and—"

"No, you don't!"

He opened the door. Both boys were sprawled out on the same twin bed.

"Okay, so maybe I don't. Look, I don't know what I said back there, but whatever it was, I'm sorry."

Josh ran to him and hugged his waist, the unmistakable sweaty-kid smell emanating from his body and the awkwardness of the hug causing Marc's muscles to tense up.

"She's never been in the hospital before," Josh blurted into his chest.

"Josh, stop being such a baby," Riley said.

Marc shot Riley a disparaging look.

"This is earth-quaking," Josh said through sobs, his face still buried in Marc's torso.

"That's earth-shattering, dummy."

"Can we stop with the name-calling?" Marc asked.

Riley rolled his eyes and then turned to stare out the window into the black night.

As Josh pulled away from Marc, with his small hands clenched into tight fists, he shouted, "You know what, I'm *glad* she's in the hospital. She needs help!"

Marc's phone rang from the living room. Thinking it could be Gabby, he left the boys' room to answer it. The sound of the door slamming behind him indicated that one of the boys didn't care much for his sudden departure, and now he regretted it too.

The caller ID said it was Meinhard.

"Dad?"

No response.

"Are you there?"

Torn between going upstairs to check on Meinhard and handling the situation at hand, Marc went back to the boys' bedroom to try to make amends.

Despite the forceful door slam—or maybe because of it—it hadn't shut all the way. Hearing Riley speaking calmly to his brother, Marc paused for a moment just outside the door to listen in on the conversation.

"Look, Josh, we need Mom back here or else they're going to take us away from her, and we don't want that, right? We could end up like Brady. Remember him from the after-school program? He was in a million foster homes after they took him away."

Marc knocked on the door. "Everything okay in there?"

After getting no response, Marc eased the door open but didn't go in.

"Everything okay?"

"I was just kidding about Mom needing help," Josh said. "She really doesn't. She's fine."

"Well, I'm not so sure about that. Look, I have to check on Grandpa. His phone went dead or something. Will you be okay for a little while? I'll be back in a few minutes."

"So are you gonna like sleep here?" Riley asked.

"On the sofa. So if—"

"Fine."

"But for now, I have to go upstairs for a few minutes. While I'm gone, you two get ready for bed."

"Fine."

After climbing the back stairs up to his own place, Marc found the door was locked. Luckily, he'd brought his key but when he used it to open the door, he found Meinhard had engaged the chain lock as well.

"Dad."

He waited for a response.

"Dad, unlock the door," he said louder.

Still no response.

"Dad!" he shouted.

"What are you shouting about? I'm right here."

Meinhard unlatched the chain.

"Why did you lock the door? I told you I'd be right back."

"To keep the queers out."

"First of all, stop calling them that."

"Why? That's what they are."

"Never mind. Just get it into your thick head that they don't want anything you've got. And they don't want anything I've got. They don't want anything. Don't worry about them."

"I don't trust 'em."

"Why on earth do you...? Forget it. What happened to your phone?"

"It stopped working."

"Does it need a charge?"

Meinhard sat slumped in a chair at the kitchen table. The overhead light shone on his face and hands, revealing a sprinkling of age spots that Marc hadn't noticed before.

"I'm going to have to spend the night downstairs with the boys. You'll be okay up here?"

"What do I look like, a five-year-old?"

Marc stared at Meinhard for a moment while he decided how to respond without saying something he would later regret.

"And I'll have to spend time with them until Zenzi gets home. That should give you time to get your shit together. Did you call Lenny?"

"How could I? That cheap phone you bought me is dead."

Marc wished he had stopped at the pharmacy before coming home—he was all out of Xanax, which had been prescribed for him two years earlier when he was having mild panic attacks. He hadn't taken it often but really needed it now.

"I'll check on you in the morning."

No response.

Chapter 12

"Hey, good lookin'!" she yelled up to him. "Haven't seen you in a while."
From the landing outside of Zenzi's back door, Marc peered down at Jessica, the tenant who lived in the garden apartment. The white waitress uniform peeking out from below the hem of her coat told him she had just come from work.

"Hey, yourself. You're getting home late."

"Double shift. Two waitresses didn't show up."

"Bummer. Hey, hold on a minute. I want to see what the special was tonight."

It was a standing joke between the two of them—most of the time Marc could tell what the daily special was by either the stains on her uniform or her smell.

Having known her for more than a year, Marc was amused by the attractive twenty-five-year-old blonde's frequent shameless flirtation. If not for her five-year-old son and an ex-husband who Marc suspected could still be in the picture, he would have made a play for her right after she had moved in.

"Let me see. It's hard to tell with you bundled up in that coat and everything, but I'm going to—"

She plucked one end of the collar of her uniform from beneath her coat and held it out for him to sniff.

"Roast beef."

"Uh-huh. And?"

"Garlic mashed potatoes."

"Glad to see you haven't lost your touch, ace."

"Where's Tyler?"

"With Al." She reached out to straighten his shirt collar. "Where's your coat?"

"I was just going from one apartment to another," he told her. "Didn't bother."

"Wanna come in for a cold one? I have a couple of Lincoln Park lagers in the fridge calling our names."

Jessica and Marc shared a taste for microbrews and had spent quite a few evenings sampling some of the local craft beers.

After explaining the current state of affairs with his family, he declined her offer.

"Hey, when is Al bringing Tyler back?"

"Tomorrow morning." She smiled and shot him a wink. "We'd be alone."

"You know you shouldn't tease me like that."

"I know. But it's fun to watch the blood slowly rise up your neck...like it's doing right now."

"You're too cute, Jess. Where I was going with that was I was thinking of taking the boys to Dimo's for pizza tomorrow night. Do you want to join us? It would sure help me out."

Even though Jessica's son was younger than Marc's nephews, he figured they would enjoy each other's company.

"Help you out?"

"I really don't know what to do with them. It's a little awkward."

"Sure. Will your dad be joining us too?"

"No. There's stuff in the fridge and freezer he can eat."

"What about Gabby?"

"Don't ask."

"What the hell? Something happen between you two?"

"Maybe. Not sure." He turned toward the stairs. "Six o'clock?"

"Works for me. See ya then, lover boy. Good luck 'til then."

Marc climbed the stairs to Zenzi's apartment where Josh and Riley sat at the kitchen table.

"Shouldn't you two be in bed?"

"Probably."

"Then why aren't you?" He glanced at his watch. "It's nine-thirty."

"We don't have any set bedtime, and besides we couldn't sleep," Riley said.

"Yeah, we thought maybe we could play Fact or Crap for a while," Josh added.

"What?"

"It's a game."

"Your mom lets you play this?"

"She plays it with us...sometimes. Wanna play?"

Playing a kid's game didn't thrill him. He pretended to be busy doing something in the kitchen sink.

"Uncle Marc?"

"How long does it take to play?"

Josh ran to their bedroom and emerged with a box.

"I didn't say I would, or even that—"

Josh had the game pieces out before he could finish his sentence.

"Fine, but it's late, so it'll have to be short."

The game involved one person reading a statement and the others determining whether it was factual or not. Riley explained the rules to Marc.

Riley read the first statement. "Cows dream if they lie down."

Josh was first to slap down the fact side of his paddle indicating he thought the statement was true.

"Uncle Marc, aren't you going to play?" Josh asked.

"How did you know that? How would *anyone* know that?"

"Just play, okay?" Riley said.

"Someone actually—"

"Uncle Marc."

Marc guessed crap.

"Josh is right. Take two tokens. Uncle Marc, you have to give up one. Next question. Flirty, foxy, and farty are all terms used to describe wine aroma."

Marc and Josh slapped down the crap sides of their paddles close to the same time.

"You're both right," Riley said. "But Josh was first so he gets two tokens." He looked at Marc. "You get one."

Josh's strategy appeared to be that if you don't know the answer, slap down any answer as quickly as you can—you have a 50/50 chance of being right and you get an extra point for being first if you are right. Marc picked up the next card off the pile and read the first statement. "Crickets have ears on their legs. What?"

Josh slapped down fact. Riley followed suit.

"You're both right. Take your tokens." He turned toward Josh. "Lucky guess again?"

"I know my bugs."

Marc looked at Riley, who rolled his eyes and nodded.

"Next question. *The Encyclopedia Britannica* was put together by a man named William Smellie."

The boys laughed. Josh slapped down fact. Riley guessed crap.

"Josh is right. Where do they get these questions?"

"We had that one before, Riley. Don't you remember? Mom thought I said Willie Nelson."

"Whatever."

"Okay, my last one. Rapper Vanilla Ice's real name is Robert van Winkle."

Josh guessed crap. Riley guessed fact. Riley was right.

They played for another half hour until Josh read the last question.

"All spiders have eyes. Okay, stop everything. This answer is wrong. All spiders *don't* have eyes."

"How do they see?" Marc asked.

Riley rolled his eyes. "Josh and his bugs."

"Spiders aren't bugs, stupid."

"What are they," Marc asked.

"Arthropods."

"How do you know this stuff?" Marc asked.

"I just do. Spiders can have two, four, six, or eight eyes. Or none."

"Is that right."

"And they have blue blood…just so you know."

"They do?"

"Yep."

"You're pretty smart."

"No, he's not," Riley said.

"I am too!"

"Not about most things."

"So how many tokens do you have, Riley?"

"Five."

"Well, I have nine! So now who's the smartest, bonehead?" Josh said to his brother.

"Shut up, Josh."

"I see you only have one, Uncle Marc."

"I know, but I didn't have a chance to answer the last one."

"So? Neither did I," said Riley.

Marc started to put the game back in the box. "Let's call it a night, huh?"

"I won, butt-munch!" Josh said to Riley.

"Josh!" Marc said. "How about being a good winner?"

"I *am* a good winner."

"I mean how about showing a little humility?"

"What?"

Marc searched for the right words.

"How about stop being such a dipshit about it," Riley said before getting up from his chair.

"Riley! Watch your mouth," Marc said as he and Josh gathered the game pieces and put them back in the box.

"He gets into trouble for using bad words all the time in school," Josh said. "And he's a sore loser."

"You both need to stop with the name-calling."

"Uncle Marc, can you explain the humanity thing?" Josh asked.

"The what?"

"About being a good winner."

"You mean humility?"

"Yeah."

"Having humility means you're not so sure of yourself, not so self-confident."

"My teacher says self-confidence helps you build up steam."

"Build up steam?"

"So I don't get it."

"What I meant was—"

"Don't be a dipshit about it," Riley said from another room.

"Okay," Josh said as he prepared to head to his bedroom. "Thanks for playing with us. Mom never lasted *that* long."

"Don't forget to brush your teeth, guys."

* * *

Marc awoke with a headache the next morning after having spent the night on his sister's sofa, which smelled of stale cigarettes. He checked his watch—six-forty-five. After finding an aspirin in the medicine cabinet, he listened for sounds coming from the boys' room. When he heard none, he tiptoed in and found them asleep in the same twin bed, Josh's feet within inches of Riley's face.

Knowing Gabby was an early riser, he took a chance and called her again. No luck, not even voice mail.

Finding the cupboards bare, Marc headed upstairs to his apartment to scrounge up something for breakfast. This time his door was unlocked though he was sure he had locked it the night before. Swearing under his breath at his father's carelessness, he walked to the spare bedroom and peered in. The bed had been crudely made, and there was no sign of Meinhard or his worldly possessions. He picked up a handwritten note from the nightstand.

Markus,

You have better things to do than watch over me, like take care of your family. I'll be fine.

Your father

P.S. I took what you had stashed in your sock drawer. You should be more careful with your money.

Pathetic old man.

No telling where he'd gone. Marc figured there'd been at least three hundred dollars stashed in the drawer—enough to tide Meinhard over for a while.

His father had a history of disappearing for long periods—he'd done that so frequently when Marc was young that his mother had just come to accept it. "He'll be back as soon as he sobers up," she'd say, and then they would spend time tidying up the place so it looked nice when he returned. One time, when he had been gone for five days, his mother started taking in other people's laundry to make ends meet. On the sixth day, he came home, like nothing happened. Marc remembered him sleeping on the couch for several nights afterward, the couch that had served as Marc's bed, leaving Marc to sleep in an upholstered chair.

* * *

"So what are we supposed to do today?" Josh asked Marc after the three of them had had breakfast. "Is Mom coming home?"

It was Saturday, and the more time Marc had spent with Riley and Josh, the more he resented having to babysit them because of his sister's reckless behavior. He felt little connection to his nephews and didn't see that changing any time soon.

"I doubt they'll release your mom this quick, but we'll see. I thought we'd go out for pizza tonight. I've invited Tyler and his mom to join us." They had met Jessica and Tyler just once since they'd moved in.

"Why?"

"Why what?"

"Why are we all going out?"

"Because I thought it might be a fun thing to do, and there's nothing to eat here."

"Whatever. So what do we do until then? Or do you have to take care of *him*?" Riley asked.

"First of all, *him* has a name. Grandpa Meinhard."

"Like we have more than one Grandpa?"

"I'm just trying to—"

The phone interrupted him. It was a doctor at the hospital.

"Mr. Nussbaum, I'm calling about Zenzi Nussbaum. She is your sister, correct?"

"Yes. How is she doing?"

"There was a problem here, but everything is under control now."

"Under control? What happened?"

"She broke out of her restraints and wreaked havoc in our detox ward."

"Restraints?"

"She became combative when she came to the ER. She had to be restrained so she wouldn't hurt herself or others."

"Is she okay?" He pictured her going completely berserk and hurting herself in the process.

"She'll be all right. May have gotten a bump on her head and a few bruises, but nothing serious."

"Anyone else hurt?" he asked, fearing the worst.

"She managed to knock down two staffers who required medical attention—one hit her head pretty hard when she was thrown against a food cart, and another injured his back trying to keep your sister from pulling out her IV. They'll be okay, but I can't say that for the things she destroyed along the way."

"Like what?"

"Like she threw a bedpan at one of the nurses. The nurse ducked, and the bedpan hit a light fixture. Glass everywhere. Then she ran into an orderly who was wheeling a cart. The cart went flying, spilling everything onto the floor. We're still recovering stuff. Would you like for me to go on?"

"No. I get the picture."

"I suggest you come here right away. Since there were injuries, we had to call the police, and you may want to talk to them."

"I'll be there as soon as I can."

"Where are you going?" Riley asked after he hung up.

"I'll call Jessica to see if you can go downstairs for a bit," he said, forcing a sense of calm into his voice.

"Where are you going?" Riley asked again, this time more insistent.

"That was the hospital. I need to check on your mother."

"Why? What's wrong?"

"I just need to check on her. That's all. You can stay downstairs. I won't be long."

"We don't need a babysitter. We stay home alone all the time. Even when she's here, we're usually alone. What difference does it make?" Riley demanded.

"Don't argue with me! Go to your room for now—both of you!"

The boys rushed off.

He clearly wasn't cut out for this. Couldn't the boys, Riley in particular, just cut him some slack?

After calling Jessica and arranging for the boys to go downstairs, he went to their room. Sitting in a hunched-over position on his bed, Josh looked as if he was about to cry. Riley looked like he was ready to punch someone. Marc scanned their faces for a long moment before speaking.

"Look, I'm sorry I yelled at you, but I've been under a lot of pressure lately and—"

"What's wrong with Mom?" Riley asked, crossing his arms over his chest.

"I'm not sure. I'm going to check on her."

"It's your fault she's in there."

"Shut up, Riley!" Josh said.

"Shut up yourself."

"Stop it!" Josh cried out and ran over to Marc where he pressed his face against Marc's chest. Through his sobs he managed to blurt out, "I don't want to end up like Brady."

* * *

Two policemen and a hospital security guard greeted Marc outside Zenzi's room.

"Marc Nussbaum?" one of the policemen asked.

"Yes, that's me."

The officers led him to a private area across the hall.

"Your sister is going to be arrested as soon as she's released from here."

"On what charges?"

The officer took a small pad of paper from his breast pocket.

"Assault, disorderly conduct, destruction of private property, and possession of marijuana."

"Possession of marijuana!"

"She was caught smoking a joint in the hospital bathroom."

"Good grief."

"We have a concern."

"Just one?"

"They'll keep her here until she's over the worst of her withdrawals, but if she goes from here directly to jail, she's going to have a rough time of it. Physically."

"What alternatives do we have?"

"They're telling us here she's in pretty bad shape, like she's been abusing alcohol and who knows what else for some time. She probably needs long-term rehab at this point. Not one of those thirty-day programs, something longer."

"Really?"

"Really. Unfortunately, they're not cheap, and they have long waiting lists."

"Like how much and how long?"

"Can't say, but you could ask if they have a social worker on staff here. They could tell you more."

Both policemen got up.

"We've seen people go through detox here, then straight to jail, and let's just say it doesn't usually end up very well. Good luck to you."

At the nursing station, Marc inquired about a social worker and was told they had two on staff. He waited while they summoned for one.

When the social worker arrived, she handed Marc a list of rehab centers in the state. "The ones listed on the first few pages are state funded, so they will be the most affordable," she explained. "Some are even free. You'll have to contact them to find out what they charge and how long of a wait list they have. I can't give you that information." Then she took the list back and crossed off two of the listings. "Unfortunately, Illinois has had some recent budget cuts, and I know these two have since closed."

Chapter 13

Marc picked up the boys from Jessica's apartment, and while they kept busy in their room, he went on the Internet checking out the rehab places on the list he'd received from the hospital social worker. He called twelve facilities within driving distance to find out what kind of waiting list they had, what they charged, and if they would even take Zenzi. What he found was not encouraging—waiting lists ranging from thirty days to six months, average monthly costs between $5,000 to $20,000 and as high as $50,000, and only half of them offering the dual diagnostic treatment that Zenzi needed.

Riley entered the living room.

"I'm hungry."

"Me too."

"There's nothing here to eat."

They walked into the kitchen to see if there wasn't something they could scrounge up for lunch and found Josh standing in the middle of the room, shoulders drooped, looking like he was about to cry.

"What's the matter?" Marc asked.

"Homer died."

"Who?"

"That stupid, smelly rodent," Riley said.

"He was my pet, fart-face!"

"Boys, please!"

"Get rid of it before it stinks up the whole house," Riley said.

Marc turned toward Josh. "First of all, what kind of animal was it?"

"A mouse."

"You had a pet mouse *and* a pet snake?"

"I kept them separated."

"Where did you get the mouse?"

"I found him by the garage. He was almost dead, but I got him better."

"Obviously, you didn't," Riley added.

"Riley. Where is he now?" Marc asked Josh.

Josh shrugged. "Heaven, I guess."

"I mean where's the physical body?"

"Still in his cage. I can't look at him."

"What do you want to do with him?"

"Bury him, I guess."

"Well, the ground is frozen, so we can't really bury it."

"I'll put him in the freezer so he stays fresh," Josh said.

"No! You can't put a dead mouse in the freezer. What's wrong with you?"

"But I want to bury him...and...and," he said through his sobs.

"Okay. Okay. Stop crying. Let's go see what we can use to wrap him up."

Marc found a roll of freezer paper in the cupboard and used most of it to package the rodent into what turned out to be quite an ominous-looking parcel. After clearly marking it HOMER - DEAD MOUSE, he offered to take the boys to Rock 'n' Roll McDonald's for lunch, thinking that getting out of the apartment might make dealing with the two of them somehow easier. Located near downtown, the fifties-style restaurant was a hit with kids, and they were excited to go.

At the restaurant, after they had their food and were seated, Riley dropped a bombshell.

"There's something we have to tell Mom."

"What's that?"

"Nick called."

"So?" Marc wondered if it was the same Nick who had prompted Zenzi to take advantage of Marc's mistake in judgement when he had assumed his father's identity.

"She needs to know."

"Do you know why he called?"

"Probably the same as before."

"And what's that?"

"For us to stay with him for a couple of days."

"Why would you do that?"

"Because the migration people are coming," Josh added.

"That's *im*migration, you—"

"What?" Marc asked.

"They always come when we go there," Riley said.

Nothing added up. Marc figured they didn't know what they were talking about.

"I'm not going to bother her with it."

"Okay, but you know she's married to him."

Marc choked on his bite of hamburger and had to take a swig of soda before he could respond.

"What are you talking about?"

"She had to."

"Marry him?"

"So he can stay in this country."

"I'll talk to her."

* * *

Jessica agreed to watch the boys while Marc drove to the hospital for the second time that day. There he found Zenzi in bed with restraints on her ankles and wrists. After he got over the initial shock of her appearance—pallid skin, expressionless eyes, and hair so thin you could see right through it—he asked her how she was doing.

"How do you think I'm doing?"

"Okay. Stupid question."

"How are my boys?"

"They're fine. They keep asking when you'll be home."

"Not soon enough."

When he confronted her about Nick, she confirmed he was her husband, at least in the legal sense of the word.

"You married this guy? A guy you don't even know? When did this happen?"

"Calm down, you lunatic. It's all good."

"So far, I see nothing good about it, Zen. Who *is* this guy?"

"Just someone I met who needed a green card. I did him a favor."

"A favor? You married him as a favor? Where'd you meet him?"

"Through Brenda."

"Who's Brenda?"

"A friend."

"So where was *he* when you were in the shelter?"

"He didn't know we were there."

"I don't get it. What do you get out of doing this?"

Zenzi didn't answer.

"What—did he pay you?" he asked half-jokingly.

"Maybe."

"What? How much?"

"What's it matter?"

"Maybe you're right. It's illegal regardless."

"It's not illegal when it's a favor."

"Don't be stupid. So now what?"

"Now what, what?"

"He called. What does he want?"

"How the hell do I know?"

"I think you do!"

She looked away.

"You better tell me."

"Stop trying to be my boss."

"'Fess up, Zen. Whether you want to admit it or not, you need me right now. What's he calling about?"

"Immigration comes by to check on us every so often."

"Check for what?"

"See if we're a family, I guess."

"The four of you."

"Five."

"You can't even count."

"We have a daughter."

"He has a daughter?"

"We."

"What do you mean, we?"

"I had a baby with him."

"What?"

"We had a baby."

"Had or have?"

"He has her."

"He has custody of her?"

She nodded.

"Legal custody?"

"No. But he wants to. Him and his girlfriend."

Marc sank into the chair beside her bed.

"So the boys know this?"

"Maybe. I don't know."

"What do you mean you don't know?"

She didn't respond.

"How did you explain the baby to them?"

"We didn't."

"You are something else." Marc paused to collect his thoughts. "Jesus, you are in so much trouble."

"I wouldn't be if it wasn't for you!"

"Me?"

"If you hadn't called for an ambulance, everything would be fine right now!"

"Exactly what are you calling 'fine'?"

A nurse came into the room and asked them to keep their voices down.

"Why don't you just leave!" Zenzi said to him.

"And what am I supposed to do with this Nick person?"

"I don't care. Dress up like a girl and pretend you're me."

"You're an idiot, you know that?"

"I thought you didn't like name-calling."

"Where's this guy from anyway?"

"Singapore...I think. Could be Nigeria though."

"There's a big difference between Sing—"

"Get out."

"Someday you'll thank me for what I did."

"Bastard."

"You need help. You know that."

"Not your kind of help."

"And we need to talk about plans for what you're going to do when you get out of jail."

"I already know what I'm going to do when I get out. Go straight to the liquor store and get me a nice big hug in a bottle."

"Your boys need you—and they need you sober."

"Well, let me tell you something, brother dear, alcohol is the only reliable friend I've *ever* had, and don't you *dare* try to tell me how to raise my kids. What the hell do you know?"

"I know how to recognize when two innocent boys are being   By the way, I need you to sign a permission card in case I have to pick them up from school while you're away." He took a card out of his wallet and handed it to her.

"I'll be home in no time. No need to."

"Zen...just in case?" He handed her a pen. She scribbled her name on it and tossed it back to him.

"Josh says Riley often gets into trouble at school."

"So?"

"So you're not concerned?"

"He's just going through a phase."

"Looks like more than just a phase to me."

"I don't think any of this is your business."

Marc threw his hands up in the air. "Fine."

"What do you know about raising kids?" She fought to escape from the restraints.

The orderly who had been stationed outside her door came in.

"Is everything okay in here?"

"Get him outta here!"

The guard glared at Marc. "Best you leave," he said.

He stopped by the nurse's station on his way out.

"Can you tell me who my sister's primary physician is while she's in here?"

"Dr. Dhir, but not for long."

"Why?"

"She's being transferred to County."

"County?"

"Cook County Hospital over on Ogden Avenue."

"Yes, I know where it is. But why the transfer?"

"I don't know the answer to that."

"Who would I ask?"

"You'd have to check with Admissions." She pointed him in the right direction.

When Marc found the Admissions department, he was invited to talk with one of their representatives.

"I understand your concern, Mr. Nussbaum, but we aren't equipped to care for your sister beyond the initial detox."

"I'm not sure that going to the county hospital would be best for her. I'd rather see her—"

"Mr. Nussbaum, she's not a minor."

"I know."

"And you're not her legal guardian."

"Your point?"

"None of us really have a say in the matter. She can go to County, and that's her choice, or she'll be discharged from here and then be arrested. Were you aware of that?"

"Yes."

"Is there anything else I can do for you today?"

Marc got up from his chair and left without responding.

On the way home, he reflected on the Zenzi he remembered from childhood—the one who saved food for him when he was busy cutting lawns and missed dinner, the one who helped him with his social studies homework, the one who played checkers with the grumpy old man who lived across the street. It appeared as though alcohol had destroyed that Zenzi...but he hoped not irreversibly.

* * *

As they drove to Dimo's Pizza Parlor, Marc wondered if Jessica was thinking the same thing he was—that to an outsider, they looked like the typical all-American family. While most of what came with being a family man did not appeal to him—namely less freedom and more commitments—there was something about being in the driver's seat with a pretty woman beside him and a backseat full of kids that he found curiously pleasing.

While waiting for their pizzas, they went to the game room where the boys played video games and Marc and Jessica challenged each other to a game of darts.

"Are you any good?" Marc asked her.

"I don't know. I've never played before."

"This ought to be a piece of cake then," he teased. "And since you're a girl, I'll spot you a hundred points."

She shot him a menacing look. "That's very gallant of you."

Not missing the sarcasm in her tone, he made a grandiose arm swing toward the dart board. "Ladies first," he said.

Jessica threw the first dart and missed the board altogether.

"Shut up," she said.

"I didn't say a thing!"

"You were thinking it."

"Step aside, mind-reader."

Marc threw a 20 inside the double ring. "Forty to nothing," he said.

She picked up the second dart. He could tell by the way she held it, she had never played before. He started to feel guilty spotting her only 100 points, but then she hit the red section of the bull's-eye.

"Fifty, smart-ass," she said.

"Beginner's luck." He paused. "How did you know it was fifty points?"

"Everybody knows that."

Marc hit near the center of the board with his next shot, but it bounced off and fell to the floor.

"You need to put a little more oomph behind it, Hercules," she said. "Watch and learn."

She tucked her hair behind her ears, rolled the dart between the palms of her hands a few turns to warm it up, and took aim. Marc couldn't help but stare at her backside where the top of her tramp stamp peeked out above her jeans. He had never seen below the top of it, but Jessica had told him what it said. ABANDONMENT—THE WOUND THAT NEVER HEALS. She had spent the first sixteen years of her life in foster homes and didn't know who her biological parents were.

She threw another bull's-eye, this time in the green section.

Her stand was all wrong. She threw like a girl. And she didn't have good follow-through. But two of her darts were in the bull's-eye.

"You are *so* lucky," he told her.

She walked up to him and put her hand on his shoulder. "Oh, yeah? How many bull's-eyes do I have to get before you recognize skill when you see it?"

"More than two."

She backed away from him so he could take his turn.

"So tell me, lover boy, what happened with Gabby? I thought you two had a thing going on."

"I thought we did too."

"So what happened?"

"She ran out on me."

For good?"

"Don't know."

"What did you do to her?"

"Nothing. Who can explain the actions of—"

"Careful, buddy."

"She left without saying anything. It may have had something to do with my spending the majority of Saturday hauling my father's ass all over the damn state."

"Saturday. Valentine's Day."

"I didn't know it was Valentine's Day at the time."

"Good one."

They bantered until their pizza was ready. Score: Jessica 750, Marc 580.

"Who won?" Riley asked Marc when they were seated back at the table.

"I was having a bad night," he responded.

"She beat you?" Riley asked.

"Like I said—"

"Never go up against my mom in darts," Tyler warned. "Did she pull that 'I've never played this before' trick on you?"

Marc shot a look at Jessica.

"But I'm just a girl," she said fluttering her eyelashes.

They talked, laughed, and poked fun at one another while they ate dinner. As they were leaving the restaurant, Josh pulled Marc aside.

"This was fun, Uncle Marc. Thanks."

* * *

The boys were in bed and Marc had collapsed on the sofa when he heard a knock at the door. It was Jessica. He invited her in.

"Are you okay?" she asked.

"Yeah. Why?"

"You're not upset over darts, are you?"

"Hell, no."

"Something's the matter."

He went to the fridge and got two Belgian ales from the six-pack he'd brought down from his apartment. The two sat down at the kitchen table where Marc filled her in on Zenzi's situation.

"I thought you were going to tell me more about Gabby."

"Nothing more to tell." He told her about Nick and the baby.

"Your sister has a daughter that you didn't know about?"

"Yep."

"What are you going to do?"

"About Zenzi?"

"Zenzi, the guy, the whole thing."

"I could pay for her to stay at a long-term rehab place, which is what she really needs, but that would cost megabucks. I'd have to take out a loan."

"Let her see what County's like. That might straighten her up."

"Do you know what it's like?"

"County?"

"Yeah."

She didn't respond right away. "It's like the difference between Dimo's pizza and the kind you get out of a vending machine. They each serve the same purpose but one is a lot more appetizing."

"Hmm."

"How long has she had a drinking problem?"

"Apparently, a long time. I knew she was drinking when Dad went to..."

Marc had never told Jessica about his father's prison time.

"Went where?"

He told her all the sordid details.

"Holy shit! How long was he in for?"

"A year and a half."

"And afterwards?"

"He's been drifting in and out of my life for years—*in* when he wants something."

"So what about Gab?"

"What about her?"

"Are you going to try to get her back?"

"She won't take my calls. I can't even get a text message to go through to her. I think she blocked me. Damn my family."

"You really miss her."

"Yeah. I do."

"Did you try Facebook?"

"Didn't think of that. You're a girl. If you were her, would you want me to stay away or keep trying to contact you so you would know how much I cared?"

She twirled her hair around her finger a few times. "That depends."

"On?"

"On how much I cared for *you*."

Chapter 14

"I want to see my sons!" Zenzi shouted at Marc. There was fire in her voice but not in her vacant eyes.

He'd just arrived at County Hospital after having driven forty minutes on unplowed streets just after a foot of snow had fallen. Once inside, he was pleased to note that her room wasn't as bad as he'd envisioned. It was small, fairly clean, and—because she was under house arrest—private.

"You can't have minor visitors, Zen. And would you really want them to see you like this?"

"I'm gonna get you for this—putting me in this hell hole."

"I had nothing to do with it. You were discharged. You could have—"

"I'm under house arrest, thanks to you." She yanked at the bedsheet to reveal an ankle monitor.

"Hey, that's not my fault."

"You called 9-1-1, remember?"

"Would you rather I had let you die there?"

"Maybe I would. Everyone would be better off."

"Don't say that. Your boys miss you."

"You're damn right they do. You know what I don't understand? How you can do this to your own sister."

"I'm not doing any—"

"You could get me out of here if you wanted to. I could go somewhere nice. That's what I need. Somewhere nice where I can get some help. Not in this place."

"You need to—"

"Don't tell me what I need. I never had a parent, and I don't need one now!"

Her agitated state made him wish he hadn't come. "I'm just trying to—"

"I know what you're trying to do, and I don't need your help."

"What I was going to say was—"

"Get out."

"Hold on, Zen. I need to know more about this Nick guy...and your daughter."

"What difference does it make?"

"It makes a big difference. I'm staying in *your* apartment, taking care of *your* kids, and if something is going to come down around this guy there, I need to know what I'm up against."

"Her name is Baby Emma. She'll be one in May."

"Baby Emma?"

"Yeah."

"So Emma is her name?"

"She's called *Baby* Emma. Don't ask me. It's some kind of custom where he's from."

"She's *your* daughter."

"I know."

"Emma. Emma what?"

"Emma Lee. That's his name. Nicholas Lee. He's not a bad person, and he has money."

"He's not a bad person? He's committing fraud against the federal government." Marc guessed at that—he didn't know for sure if that's what he was doing.

"Not my problem."

"It *is* your problem. You married him so he could get a green card. That makes you—"

"Shut up, will you? Someone will hear you, you idiot."

"Zenzi, look—"

"Just get out! I can manage my own affairs."

Marc stared at his sister—disheveled hair that looked like it hadn't been combed in days, a hospital gown hanging off one shoulder that revealed how thin she had become, and restraints on her ankles that prevented her from leaving the bed.

"Okay, I'm going. If you need me, you have my number. And so do the hospital staff."

"Good riddance."

Marc made his way out of the building, past dozens of poor souls who had no other choice but to go to a county hospital—people who lived under the poverty level and had no insurance in spite of Obamacare—not exactly like his sister but in ways all too similar.

Driving in his car, despite the frosty air temperature, beads of sweat dripped down Marc's face and into his eyes, muddling his eyesight. The Xanax he had taken before his visit with Zenzi had just about worn off. He pulled into an alleyway and parked, the heaviness in his chest pulling him downward—physically and emotionally. All too familiar with the symptoms of a panic attack, he sat motionless while he tried to relax.

It would have helped to have had someone to talk to as he felt so helpless. Someone like Gabby. He picked up his phone, pulled up the Facebook app, and searched for her name among his Facebook friends so he could send her a private message. Something soft and conciliatory.

Her name wasn't there among his friends. She'd unfriended him.

The pressure building up in his neck made him want to scream. She could have at least had the decency to break up with him face-to-face, or even over the phone, something.

He felt foolish that the unfriending had such a devastating impact on him—a stupid social media site—but it did. A few clicks on her keyboard had wiped him out of her life. One, two, three, delete.

Marc agonized over it for a few minutes before he thought that maybe it was for the best. She didn't even know about Zenzi and the boys.

After giving himself a few minutes to stop wallowing in self-pity, he drove home where he found Riley, Josh, Jessica, and Tyler shoveling the sidewalk and driveway.

"I'm sorry. I should have done that," he told Jessica.

"No problem. We're having fun. How is she?"

The boys stopped what they were doing and joined them.

"Alive and kicking...literally."

"What does that mean?" Josh asked.

"Your mother is doing fine, but she's not happy about being in the hospital."

"Gabby was here," Riley told him.

"What? What did she say?"

Riley shrugged.

His gaze went to Jessica. "What did she say?"

"I was inside."

Marc took Riley by the shoulders. "She must have said something, Riley. Think back. What did she say?"

"Chill out, man."

"Riley, tell me what she said!"

"Stop yelling at him!" Josh shouted.

Riley shook himself free from Marc's grip.

"She asked if you were here. I said 'no.' And then she left."

Marc swallowed through the thickness of his throat. "I'm sorry I... It's just that...uh...I need to talk to her, that's all. I shouldn't have yelled at you."

Looking like he was about to cry, Riley ran upstairs to their apartment.

"Good one, Uncle Marc," Josh said before he followed his brother up the stairs.

"They're going through a lot," Jessica said.

"I know. So am I."

"You really miss her."

Marc fought to keep his bottom lip from quivering. "Yeah."

"Did you try Facebook?"

"She unfriended me."

"Well, she came here today, so it looks like she wants to talk to you. Why not go to her house?"

"I've got the boys to—"

"Look, I was thinking of taking Tyler over to Lincoln Park Zoo for a few hours this afternoon. How about if Josh and Riley join us while you go patch things up with Gabby."

"Really?" He took two twenties out of his wallet. "Here, this is for lunch."

"Go!"

"You're a doll, you know that?" he said as he ran toward his car.

"Yeah, yeah, yeah. That's what they all say," she yelled after him.

It took Marc twenty minutes to drive to Gabby's townhome in Evanston.

Standing in front of her door, he was cautiously optimistic but braced for the possibility that this could also be the end. He rang her buzzer, and while he waited for her to respond, he was reminded of the first girl he had ever approached in high school—Melinda Lieberman. They'd had two classes together—math and literature. The math teacher had had them sit in alphabetical order, which put him right behind her—good for being close to her, bad for paying attention to the teacher. One day he mustered up the courage to talk to her. She told him to flake off. The sinking feeling in the pit of his stomach right after that was just like the feeling he was having right now.

When Gabby opened the door and Marc looked into her eyes, he found himself struggling to catch his breath.

"Hi," he said, barely getting the word out.

"Hi."

"Can we talk?"

"Sure."

Gabby's spacious townhome, a gift from her parents, was modern and tastefully furnished. She kept it neat and clean, no clutter and nothing out of place, one more thing he liked about her. She led him to the living room and asked him if he wanted something to drink.

Yes, a large scotch on the rocks.

"No, I'm fine."

They sat diagonally across from each other on a sofa that filled one corner of the room.

"I'd like to start by—"

"Please, let me go first," she said.

His gaze remained fixed on her while she spoke.

"I'm sorry I bolted on you like that on Friday."

"That's okay."

Right—like hell it is.

"It was Valentine's Day. Did you know that?" she asked.

"I didn't then."

"I could have gone with my parents to Palm Springs for the weekend to visit my grandmother, but instead I thought I was going to spend it with you."

"I'm sorry. I guess I—"

"Then your dad called and... And then I woke up to find your note. I was pissed."

He had never heard her use that word before.

"I don't blame you."

"And I left in a huff...for good I thought. And then I remembered the stuff I'd left behind, and I didn't want you to have it, or see it. I just wanted out—everything out."

"So you came back for your stuff?"

She nodded. "But by then I had calmed down...so I stayed."

"Then I came back and we made—"

"And when he called again and I heard you say, 'I'll be there as soon as I can,'— after specifically telling me you'd rather be with me—that did it. Like all I was good for was a booty call and then—"

"But it wasn't like that at all. I—"

"I don't care how you *meant* for it to be. I'm telling you how it felt to me to be on the receiving end of it. Here I give you a second chance, give you the benefit of the doubt, and that's what I get in return." She glared at him for a long moment. "*That's* why I left."

"It sounds so much worse when you tell it."

"Well, maybe you need to put yourself in my place. What would you have done?"

He shrugged.

"Look, I know what you're going through. I never told you this, but when Glen was fifteen or so, he got into drugs—big time. My parents bailed him out of more situations than I can count. For two years, maybe it was longer, it was like I didn't even exist—all their attention went to him. And it had to. I know that." She paused long enough for Marc to let that sink in. "I'll never forget how isolated that made me feel, like I was unworthy of their attention. I started bingeing on food. Anything I could get my hands on to compensate for the loneliness I suppose. I gained almost twenty pounds, but that didn't bother me. What bothered me was that my parents hadn't noticed."

"Gabby, I don't—"

"You don't have time for yourself, let alone me. That's just the reality of it. I understand it, and I accept it. It is what it is. I just know I can't go through that again."

"But what if—"

"And then there are all our differences. At first, I thought they didn't matter, but now…"

"What differences?"

"Our likes and dislikes, our backgrounds."

"But I like what you like."

"I know. But only because I like them. There's a difference."

"But—"

"The situation isn't going to change no matter what you say." She got up and walked toward the front door without looking back at him. "I hope everything works out for you. I really do." She turned around to face him. "I wish it could have worked out between us. I really mean that."

He walked toward her. "It doesn't have to end like—"

"Yes, it does." She opened the door and then leaned in to kiss him on the cheek. "Goodbye, Marc."

He stepped outside and then turned around to face her.

"But—"

She closed the door.

He stared at the brass door knocker for a few seconds before walking away.

On the drive home, he tried not to think about what he would miss most about her —the smell of her perfume, the sound of her voice, or cuddling up against her in bed. He was pretty sure he loved her and cursed himself for not having told her that when they were still together. Maybe that would have made a difference. If Meinhard hadn't called on Friday, he and Gabby would be making plans for the weekend right about now. Maybe she'd have worn that yellow sweater he gave her for Christmas. Maybe he would have told her then that he loved her.

Zenzi ran a close second when it came to blame. If she could get hold of herself and her drinking problem, maybe… He couldn't finish the thought. He was becoming his father—blaming things on everyone else—and he hated himself for that. He'd spent a lifetime trying not to be like his father.

Chapter 15

After returning home from his desolating talk with Gabby, Marc averted his attention to something that he feared wouldn't have a much better ending—continuing his search to find a rehab place for Zenzi. Using the last page of the list he had received from the hospital social worker, he started calling the rest of the facilities. Several phone calls later made him realize that the more affordable the facility, the longer the waiting list, and the ones with short wait lists were beyond his budget.

"Alcohol has been my only reliable friend," Zenzi had said. What a sad thought. He was about to contact the last agency on the list when a text came in from Juan.

> Mrs. W not happy. Not enough color at driveway. Guests arrive in 3 hrs. Any ideas?

Not enough color? It was February in Illinois. What did she expect?

> Capture 5 cardinals and make them stay at driveway.

He hoped Juan would appreciate the humor.

> LOL. Now get serious.

There was no way to know if it was a sincere "lol" or not.

> Buy some winter jasmine @ Pasquesis + red dyed twigs. Temp fix. Let me know if that works.

Marc wondered what it would be like to have the most pressing thing on his mind be the lack of color by his driveway.

His phone chirped again. The text was from Gabby.

Please throw my things in a box and send.

The final insult had been flung. Before he could stop trying to read some other meaning into it, another text message came in.

We r home now just so u know.

It was from Jessica. He wished they had stayed a little longer at the zoo—he wanted to be alone long enough to get over Gabby's parting words. He stalled as long as he thought he could without seeming disrespectful of Jessica's generosity before retrieving his nephews.

Jessica greeted him at her door.

"So?"

Marc shrugged.

"That bad, huh?"

"C'mon boys. Let's go home," he shouted, not knowing exactly where they were. "Say goodbye to Tyler. And what do you say to Tyler's mom?"

The boys came in, thanked Jessica, and told Tyler they'd see him later.

Jessica gave Marc a sympathetic parting look.

"So how was the zoo?" he asked them on their way upstairs.

"Awesome," Josh told him.

"What was your favorite animal?" Marc asked.

Josh thought about it for a few seconds. "The cheetah," he said. "Do you know how fast a cheetah can run?"

"How fast?"

"Zero to sixty in three seconds."

"That seems hard to believe." There weren't many cars that could do that.

"It's true. Fastest animal on earth."

"You know a lot about animals. Maybe you want to be a veterinarian someday."

Josh thought about that for a moment. "No, I like hamburgers too much."

Marc forced a smile.

"So how's your girlfriend?" Riley asked as they entered their apartment. "How come she's never around? Some girlfriend. She coming over later?"

"No."

"Why not?"

Marc didn't respond.

"Why isn't she coming over later?"

"She just isn't! Okay? Jesus, get off my back."

"Hey, don't take it out on us because you got dumped. C'mon, Josh, let's go play sock ball."

Seething over Riley's impudence, Marc grabbed a craft beer from the fridge before sitting down in front of the TV. He tried to focus on the opening segment of *60 Minutes,* but his mind kept wandering to the last time he and Gabby had drifted off to sleep in each other's arms, the last time she had poked him for snoring, the last time they had made love.

He finished his beer and got up to get another but then hesitated as he looked down the hall toward the boys' bedroom.

He rapped on their door.

"May I come in?" he asked.

"No."

"Please?"

"We're busy."

"I'd like to apologize for yelling at you."

When neither boy said anything, he continued. "I'm sorry I yelled at you, Riley." He opened the door. "This is when you say, 'Okay, Uncle Marc. We understand.'"

Josh looked at Riley. Riley glared at Marc for a long moment, and before Marc knew what was happening, Riley hurled a firmly packed sock ball that he had been holding behind his back, hitting Marc on the side of his face.

"Heads up!" Riley shouted, after it was too late.

Marc glared at him.

Josh got off the bed and backed away from them. "Now you're in trouble!"

"Yep," Marc said wearing a stern face. He picked up the ball and pretended to put it in his pocket but instead threw it back at Riley, hitting him in the gut and prompting a sock-ball free-for-all among the three of them.

After the last sock ball had been thrown and the boys had settled down, Marc asked them what they wanted to do for dinner.

"How about if we make something here?" Riley asked.

"Like what?"

"Like a regular meal."

"Yeah, let's do that," Josh added.

* * *

"C'mon boys. It's time for breakfast. You have twenty minutes to eat before the bus!" Marc had just finished making pancakes. After he'd put them out on the table and heard no signs of life coming from the boys' room, he peeked in to find Riley sitting up in bed.

"There's no school today."

"Sure there is. It's Monday."

"No, there's not. It's Presidents Day."

Marc had planned to leave for his Monday morning rounds with his three crew foremen after dropping the boys off at school.

"Oh. Well, I made pancakes. Can you guys—"

The boys were out of bed and racing down the hallway before he could finish the sentence.

"You guys are going to have to come with me to work this morning," he told them when they'd finished stuffing themselves. He didn't want to wear out his welcome with Jessica even though she didn't typically leave for work until late morning.

"Nah, we'll stay here," Riley told him.

"Look, I know you said your mother allowed you to stay alone, but I don't think that's a good idea, and since I'm responsible for you—"

"Fine."

"When's she coming home anyway?" Josh asked.

"I don't know."

"Why can't we talk to her?" Riley asked.

"She's in recovery. In treatment."

"Does she ask about us?"

"Of course she does."

He pulled his vibrating phone out of his pocket.

Can u swing by Blacks this morning?

It was Juan.

I'll be there in 1 hour.

"When are we leaving?"

"Now. Get your coats on."

"I don't feel so good," Josh moaned.

"You're fine. Get your coat on."

Marc sat down at the kitchen table and closed his eyes. All he needed was a sick kid.

Can you come by Abramskys first?

It was Juan again.

Sure

Based on Juan's messages, Marc suspected a conflict between the two Green Bay Six neighbors and didn't look forward to meeting with Gordon Black in particular. Black was an obsessive engineer who wanted everything perfect. The Abramskys were generally the peace-keeping members of the group—nothing really mattered to them as long as there was no arguing.

A rap at the back door startled him. It was Jessica.

"I know this is last-minute, but two waitresses didn't show up this morning, and I've been called in to work. There's no school. What are you doing with the boys?" she asked, giving Marc a piteous look no man could resist.

"I was about to take them with me to work for a few hours. Taylor can come too if you want."

"You're a doll," she said halfway down the stairs.

Marc and the three boys piled into the SUV and headed off for Lake Forest.

"My stomach still hurts," Josh said from the back seat.

"You didn't poop this morning," Riley told him. "That's why."

"Do you have to go now, Josh?" Marc asked.

"Probably."

Marc circled the block, re-parked in his driveway, and handed Riley the door key. "Go with him, okay?"

Fifteen minutes later, the boys returned.

"Feeling better now?" Marc asked.

"Yep! How long until we're there?"

"We haven't even left yet."

"I know. How long?"

"About a half hour, if traffic is good."

"What's for lunch?" Josh asked.

"We just had breakfast."

"I like to think ahead."

"We'll see where we are when it's lunchtime and then make a decision."

"How long will we be at work?"

"Where *is* your work?"

"I get dibs on the front seat on the way back."

"Are there any girls there who're gonna pinch our cheeks and say how cute we are?"

"Barf. That's gross."

"He's a landscaper, you dummies," Riley chimed in. "There aren't any girls."

"Oh, really?" Marc asked.

"You're kidding, right?"

"I have about thirty people working for me, and four of them are girls...I mean young women."

"What can *they* do?"

"What do you mean 'What can they do'? They do the same work as the men."

"Right."

"Riley, women can do—"

"I know that's what everyone says, Uncle Marc, but let's get real."

When they arrived, Juan was standing in the Abramskys' driveway talking with Jeff Abramsky.

"You guys stay in the truck until I'm finished. I won't be long." Marc winked at them. "Keep an eye out for girls."

Marc approached the two men.

"I don't want any trouble. You know that," Abramsky was saying.

Marc shook hands with Abramsky and asked him if there was a problem.

"Gordon over there claims my willow hedge blocks his view of cars coming off of Penny Court and onto Green Bay Road when he's coming out of his driveway. Now, you know I try to get along with everybody, and I surely don't want a fight over this, but I'm not removing a hedge that has taken ten years to get to the height it is. I won't do it."

Long before they had become his clients, the Abramskys had planted roughly one hundred feet of willow hedge on two sides of their corner lot, a hedge that was now almost eight feet tall.

"Mr. Black said he's almost been hit many times by cars he doesn't see coming off of Penny Court," Juan explained. "And he's going to go to the City Manager if we can't resolve it between ourselves."

"That hedge gives me privacy. I'm entitled to my privacy."

"I agree with you, Mr. Abramsky, but I can tell you I know of other cases where the City made someone trim back plantings that obstructed a critical view for drivers. I'm not saying they would do that here, but I have seen it happen."

"Black wants it removed entirely, and I won't do it! Maybe the City should take a look at that stone wall he has surrounding his property. I wonder if that's even code!" Abramsky said.

"I can vouch it's within code," Marc told him. "I'm the one who installed it, and we had a permit. Why can't we trim the hedge to a height that allows people to see cars coming off of Penny Court?" Marc asked.

"I looked at that," Juan said. "We'd have to trim it to a point that—"

"I would lose all privacy," Abramsky added. "And that won't do. Can't you go talk some sense into that guy, Marc?"

"I'll talk to him, Mr. Abramsky, and get back to you."

"Today?"

"I'll go over there right now."

Marc and Juan walked away from Abramsky's driveway, and when they were out of earshot, Marc asked Juan, "What should I expect from Black?"

"He's got pictures, documentation, witness statements, you name it."

Marc rolled his eyes. "Great."

Juan went to Marc's truck to keep the boys amused while Marc walked over to the Black residence. He hated this part of the job. As he walked, he recalled his first taste of squabbling neighbors. He had been about eight, old enough to shovel sidewalks. These two old curmudgeons, who were next-door neighbors, each thought their walk should be the first to be shoveled. Marc learned very quickly that there was no reasoning with these two, so he came up with a plan—he paid Zenzi to shovel one walk while he shoveled the other so they were done at exactly the same time. When he proudly told his father what he had done, his father told him to make sure Zenzi forked over half of what she had earned, the same as Marc had to do. His father had a hard time giving Marc credit for anything back then... and still did.

His wife standing by his side, Gordon Black presented Marc with a series of photos showing the blind spot the Abramsky hedge created when they backed out of their driveway. Backing out onto Green Bay Road was difficult enough without obstructions.

He then presented a log he had maintained over the past six months that included twenty-seven instances of them or their guests nearly getting hit by traffic coming off of Penny Court because their view had been obstructed by the Abramsky hedge. Some of the entries were accompanied by photos and a handwritten signed statement by the driver.

"We have utmost concern for our safety and the safety of our guests and people coming off of Penny Court," Gordon told Marc. "Now, I don't know if they had a permit to plant that hedge in the first place—the Building Review Board wouldn't give me that information—but if they didn't—"

"Let's see if we can settle this without going there," Marc said.

"If they don't remove that menacing hedge, I *will* go there," Gordon said. "I'm prepared to take this to the next level."

"I've looked at it, Mr. Black. The entire hedge wouldn't have to be removed. If we cut back ten feet or so on each side by the corner of their lot, people could easily see the cars coming off of Penny Court, and that would solve the problem."

"Just at the corner?"

"I think that's all that would be required."

"I envisioned the whole hedge being removed."

"If what you want to accomplish is for people coming out of your driveway to be able to see cars coming off of Penny Court, all that would be necessary is removing the hedge at the corner. Is there some other objective I'm not aware of?"

"No, that's our only concern," Slavina said. "Right, Gordy?"

"Yes, dear."

"Then let me discuss this with the Abramskys and see if we can resolve this today."

Marc swung by his truck, pulled out a pad of paper and pencil from the glove box, and started sketching out a plan with Juan. Josh and Riley rolled down their windows so they could see and hear what was going on.

"Looks good to me, boss," Juan said. "But this empty space on the corner looks a little bare."

"We'll come up with something. Some low-growing evergreens and annuals to brighten it up throughout the year."

Juan gave him a dubious look.

"Needs something more, doesn't it?"

"I think so."

"Uncle Marc?" Riley asked.

"Just a minute, Riley. We're in the middle of this."

"But I have an idea."

"Okay, what is it?"

"When we were at the zoo the other day, there was the same thing, by the flamingos."

Marc didn't welcome Riley wasting his time by sticking his nose in where it didn't belong but listened anyway.

"What same thing?"

"The same trees with the corner cut off."

"And?"

"In the empty space at the corner they put a water thingy."

"Riley, I appreciate your trying to help, but—"

"Wait, boss. I know what he's talking about. I've seen that water feature. That could work."

Juan took the pad and pencil from Marc and drew a sketch of what he and Riley had seen at the zoo.

"It's low. It fills the space. And it's interesting. Plant a few evergreens and annuals around it like you were talking about, and it would be the best looking corner in the neighborhood."

Marc looked at Riley and held up his hand for a high-five.

"You're all right, kid."

When Marc explained the plan to Abramsky, he liked it—no one else in the neighborhood had such a feature. They agreed on a start date in the following month when the weather was more conducive to the work that had to be done.

Marc climbed into his truck, thankful this neighbor spat had been resolved without too much angst, thanks in part to Riley.

"Where to now, Uncle Marc?" Josh asked.

"How about if we go to Margie's for turtle sundaes to celebrate Riley's genius idea?"

"Turtles on a sundae? I'm not going!" Josh yelped.

"Not real turtles, silly. It's ice cream with caramel and fudge sauce dripping all over it and nuts and whipped cream on top."

"How long 'til we get there?"

Chapter 16

"We don't have to go down there," Riley insisted. "We know how to get to the bus stop and back home on our own. You don't trust us. That's what it is."

Marc had just explained the new before-and-after-school routine he'd worked out with Jessica so he didn't have to drive them to school each day and lose so much work time. The plan called for his dropping the boys off at her apartment at 6:00 a.m. where they would have breakfast. She would then bring them and her own son to the school bus stop. Another boy's mother—a friend of Jessica's, whose son Zach was in Riley's class—would pick up all four of them at school and bring them back to her house, where either Jessica or Marc would pick them up, depending on their schedules.

"It's not that I don't trust you, it's that..."

"It's what then?"

"At your age, you can't always trust your own decisions. Your brain isn't fully developed yet." He had heard that on a Dr. Phil show.

"What decisions? There's only one way to get to school and home again."

Being challenged by an eleven-year-old was getting old.

"Look, I'm the one responsible for your well-being, so I'll make decisions based on—"

"In other words, 'because I said so.' We've heard *that* before."

"And you'll probably hear it again, so don't be surprised when you do. Now go to bed...because I said so."

Just when Marc thought the boys were asleep, Josh came out of their bedroom. "Riley doesn't want to go to Zach's house after school," he whispered to Marc.

"I know."

"Because they got into a fight once, and he's pretty sure once Zach's mom sees him, she'll remember it was him who clobbered Zach."

"Are you saying Riley never got caught for what he did?"

"Nope. And Zach didn't tell on him either. But Riley thinks his mom saw him running away that time, and if she sees him again, he thinks he's going to get into trouble."

"Okay. Go back to bed, and I'll deal with it."

After thinking about what Josh had said and not knowing how he should handle it, he called the hospital to discuss it with Zenzi.

"She's no longer a patient here," the hospital worker told her.

"What? As of when?"

"As of this morning."

"On her own?"

"What do you mean?"

"She was under house arrest."

"I don't know anything about that, sir. I just know she left this morning."

"Thank you."

"Who were you talking to?" The sound of Riley's voice surprised Marc. The boy must have wandered into the living room just as Marc was ending the call.

"No one. Just work."

"Problems at work?"

"Yeah, but someone else is taking care of it. Why aren't you in bed?"

"I heard you on the phone."

"Why are you still dressed?"

Riley looked down at his clothing. "This is what I'm wearing to school tomorrow."

"So you're sleeping in it?"

He shrugged. "Then I don't have to change in the morning."

Marc shook his head. "Go to bed. It's late."

"I'm not tired."

Marc glanced down at his phone and saw he had three voice-mail messages that must have come in when he had his phone turned off.

"Go to bed anyway."

"Why?"

"Because I said so!"

Marc waited until the echo of Riley's bedroom door slamming had subsided before listening to the messages in the order received.

Zenzi's voice.

Hey brat! I'm on the corner of Taylor and Racine. Come get me...now!

Zenzi again.

Thanks a lot, asshole.

A male voice.

Mr. Nussbaum, this is Officer Royke from Precinct 19 of the Chicago Police Department. We have your sister in custody here. She asked us to contact you to let you know her bail hearing is tomorrow. She may or may not be granted bail. Here's my phone number. Call if you have questions.

Apparently she hadn't been able to remove the ankle monitor, and that's how she was caught.

He closed his eyes wishing it would all go away.

* * *

Marc elected to not attend Zenzi's bail hearing. That afternoon he called Officer Royke, who told him Zenzi's bail had been set at $200,000—rather high since the court considered her a flight risk. Marc didn't figure she'd flee once out of jail, and he could have paid her bail by cashing in two of his CDs. Still, he hesitated doing it—Zenzi was too unpredictable. After considering a variety of potential scenarios, he decided not to post bail.

When Marc dropped Riley and Josh off at Jessica's the next day, he gave her money to cover their breakfasts for the week. While the arrangement for getting them to and from school technically worked, Marc was the first to admit it wasn't ideal in that it added an hour to the boys' daily routine and was dependent on Jessica and another mother. But for now, it would have to do. Making Marc feel even worse about the arrangement was Josh's departing comment.

"Thank you for paying her to feed us, Uncle Marc."

He had had the boys under his care for four days. On his way to work and feeling completely inadequate as their caregiver, Marc gave thought to talking to someone about their welfare in general—someone who knew more about children's needs than he did. But when he realized that could lead to one of two things—getting even more involved in their lives or being completely removed from them—he didn't do it.

After taking care of business at the nursery, Marc stopped by the Green Bay Six neighborhood and was surprised to find Juan de-icing the approach to the Montanas' driveway.

"What are you doing?" he asked him.

"Javier and Isaac didn't show up today. I'm filling in." Javier and Isaac were brothers Marc had hired as a favor to a supplier friend of his. They had been with him for less than three months.

"That's the third time this month," Marc said.

"Tell me about it."

"How's their work been lately, any improvement?"

"Not really."

"I've got at least a half-dozen names on my waiting list. Talk to them tomorrow and give them the 'shape-up-or-ship-out' spiel."

"With pleasure."

Good landscaping workers were hard to find, but when Marc did find them, they typically stayed with him for a long time. Seasoned workers took great pride in their work and put up with all sorts of crap—back-breaking tasks, safety hazards, inclement weather, and clients who thought they knew more about landscaping than the workers.

"By the way, Strom told me he got caught in the middle again between the MacCallums and Trinkos."

Rex Strom, one of the Deer Campers, lived next door to the MacCallums, who didn't like deer. They lived next door to the Trinkos, who were animal lovers. Rex Strom, who was primarily concerned with Mother Nature, often attempted to keep peace between the other two.

"Who did what this time?"

"Strom said the Trinkos put a salt block at the edge of their property to attract the deer, and of course that pissed off the MacCallums big time."

"Let me guess. They nibbled at one of the dogwood trees in the back."

"Actually, they did quite a number on two of them, including the trunks where it looks like they may have scraped off the bark with their antlers. We may have to replace them."

"Let's wait until spring and see if they come back. I kind of hope they don't make it though. Deer love dogwoods. I'd rather see a couple of gingkoes back there. How's that row of barberries doing?"

"Great. My guys hate them because of all the thorns, but then so do the deer."

"So is the salt block still there?"

"Rex convinced them it was better to let the deer find salt and other natural stuff they need on their own."

"Have to give Rex credit. Did he say how MacCallum reacted this time?" Arnie MacCallum was known for his mean-spiritedness and hot temper.

"Only that he was going to report them to the county because I guess the Trinkos put the salt block on forest-preserve property, not their own."

"The Trinkos shouldn't have done that."

"Nope."

After leaving Juan, Marc stopped for a beer. He rarely drank during the day, but today he felt like having a beer. Worse yet, he felt like he *needed* one, and that worried him.

When he reached his truck, his cell phone rang. It was Meinhard.

"Hello?"

There was no response.

"Hello...Dad...are you there?"

Still no response.

Marc was fairly certain Meinhard was trying to make it seem like he was in trouble by not responding. He'd done it before. Either that or he had forgotten how the phone worked.

"Dad, are you all right?"

He waited a few seconds before he hung up. He wasn't in the mood to deal with any of Meinhard's stupid shenanigans.

Within two blocks, his cell phone rang again.

Damn him.

This time it was the principal of the boys' school. Riley had gotten into a fight in the bathroom and was on his way to the Emergency Room with the school nurse.

Chapter 17

"How badly was he hurt?" Marc asked Riley's principal when he called to inform him of a fight in which Riley had been involved.

"The nurse thinks he may need a few stitches, but I would say it wasn't too serious."

"If anyone asks, I'm on my way. Can you get a message to his brother, Josh, that I'll pick him up on my way to the hospital?"

"Yes, of course."

This is why I don't have kids.

Josh and some man wearing a suit-and-tie were waiting in the school's circular driveway when Marc pulled up. They approached his truck. After Marc showed him his ID, he and Josh headed for the hospital.

"What did Riley do?" Josh asked him as soon as they pulled away.

"I'm not sure. We'll have to see when we get to the hospital."

"Same one as Mom?"

He hadn't told the boys of her escape. "No, a different one."

"Why not the same one?"

"They probably took him to the nearest one. Your mom's is way on the other side of town."

"Is he gonna get into trouble?"

"I guess that depends on what happened."

Marc felt enough stress over the situation without having to deal with questions from a ten-year-old.

"If Mom was here, it wouldn't matter what happened. He'd get away with it."

"He would?"

"He gets away with a lot."

Marc pulled into the hospital parking lot. "C'mon. Let's go see how he's doing."

"Uncle Marc?"

"What?"

"I'm glad it's you finding out how he's doing and not Mom."

* * *

"But he called her an alkie."

"I don't care what he called her. You shouldn't have hit him, Riley."

"What am I supposed to do? Let him call my mom names?"

"There are other ways to handle situations like that."

"Yeah, like what?"

It turned out Riley had hit the kid, and the kid had pushed him back. Riley had fallen and hit his head on the edge of the sink, which resulted in four stitches and a flyer on what to look out for in case of a concussion.

"Like walk away."

"I couldn't walk away. I was taking a pee."

Marc stifled a smile.

"Then maybe you should have just ignored his comment."

"Is that really what you'd do, Uncle Marc? If someone called your mom a bad name, you'd just ignore it?"

He hesitated. "Maybe we should talk about this after dinner."

"That means you wouldn't either."

They stopped at the grocery store to pick up the makings for BLTs, and when they got home, the three of them made sandwiches together. Marc had to admit it was kind of fun, especially since Riley behaved himself—no name calling, sour attitude, or anger. Marc didn't mind being around him when he was like that. Then the phone rang.

"I need a little cash," Meinhard said.

"Where are you?"

"I'm at Lenny's."

"Are you working there again?"

"Sort of."

"Are you living there too...sort of?"

"I can be, but I need a little cash...just until I put in enough hours for a paycheck."

"How much are we talking about?"

"A few hundred, that's all."

That's all?

"Dad, do I look like a—"

"Forget it then," he said and hung up.

He contemplated leaving his father to rely on his own defenses. To draw the line. Stop doing things for him that he should be capable of doing for himself.

After dinner and a short phone call to Jessica, Marc took the boys down to her apartment. Seeing that she was still wearing her waitress uniform, he moved in close to her and inhaled.

"Something Italian, right?"

"The orange splatters kinda give it away."

"Lasagna or spaghetti-and-meatballs?"

"Lasagna."

"Good. I've still got it." He turned to leave. "I'll make it up to you somehow."

"Promises, promises."

After a fifteen-minute drive into an ominous section of Chicago, Marc pulled his truck into the alley behind the restaurant. After letting himself in the back door, he peeked into the kitchen. One of the cooks asked him if he needed something.

"I'm looking for Meinhard Nussbaum."

"So's the boss. Good luck."

"Where can I find the boss?"

"In the front at the cash register."

Marc glanced at the customers as he walked through the restaurant—mostly men of varying ages and races, dressed like maybe they had just gotten off of work and hadn't yet changed out of their work clothes. The place reeked of the fried food that big-haired waitresses wearing too much blue eye shadow carried past him.

"I'm looking for Meinhard Nussbaum. Do you know where he is?"

The man at the cash register shook his head without looking up.

"Has he been here today?"

"Don't know him."

"Are you Lenny?"

The man grunted.

"Look, I'm his son. He called me saying...I'm just trying to—"

"Don't know him."

After leaving the restaurant, Marc looked up and down the street but saw no sign of Meinhard. Proceeding down the alley with the only light to guide him coming from a lone fixture mounted high on the side of the building, he walked back toward his truck. No one else was in the alley or what he could see of the parking lot—just him, along with two dumpsters and several garbage cans whose rancid smell caused him to wince.

Midway down the alley Marc sensed something behind him. As he jerked his head around to look over his shoulder, a rat the size of a small cat scampered across the pavement, disappearing into the shadows of the dumpsters. He quickened his step.

When he thought he heard footsteps behind him, he whirled around to find a dark-skinned man wearing a hoodie pointing a gun at his face.

"Your wallet," the young man said.

Frozen where he stood, Marc stared at the man's face without actually seeing it. He fished his wallet out of his back pocket and tossed it on the ground at the man's feet. As soon as the man ran off with it, Marc called 9-1-1, his hands trembling so badly he had to make repeated attempts at getting the numbers right.

Two policemen arrived within minutes. As Marc was describing the mugger to one of the officers, he caught a glimpse of Meinhard disappearing behind the restaurant.

Just as Marc finished his conversation with the first officer, the second one walked up to them and handed Marc his wallet.

"Found it down the block. Your ID is in there. Want to check it to see what's missing?"

"Just the cash," Marc told him after looking inside.

Still shaking, but feeling lucky that the thug hadn't shot him and had had the decency or ignorance to forgo taking his ID and credit cards, Marc drove home without continuing the search for Meinhard. Less than fifteen minutes after he arrived home, Meinhard called.

"Where the hell are you?" Marc asked him.

"Is that any way to—"

"Don't give me any crap. I just got mugged because of you. I'm still shaking from it."

"Me? What did I do?"

"I went to Lenny's looking for you, and some dirtbag mugged me. You saw it happen, didn't you?"

"That was you?"

Seething, Marc pulled the phone away from his ear and placed it face down on his lap.

"What do you want?" Marc yelled into the phone after a few seconds.

Meinhard hung up.

"What's going on?" Riley asked. Marc had assumed he was in his bedroom with Josh.

"Nothing! Have you and Josh finished your homework?"

"Looks like you're in a pretty shitty mood," Riley said.

"You got that right."

* * *

"Is this Markus Nussbaum?" a caller asked Marc the following morning.

No one except his father called him Markus anymore. "Yes, it is. Who's this?"

"My name is Rita Johansson. You don't know me. I live over on Newport."

"This is about my father, isn't it? Meinhard Nussbaum."

"Yes, I'm afraid it is. My son found him sleeping in our basement this morning. He begged us not to call the police. He said he lived nearby and that you'd come get him. Your number was in his wallet."

"What's your address? I'll be right there."

Rita Johansson and her teenage son lived one block away. When Marc arrived, Meinhard—dirty, smelly, and looking much older than his years—was sitting in a chair on their front stoop, a familiar black garbage bag alongside him. Marc apologized to Rita and thanked her for not calling the police.

"I couldn't remember the name of our street" was his explanation on their walk home.

"It's Roscoe."

"I know. It just slipped my mind for a minute."

"Where have you been?"

"Trying to get my old job and room back. Isn't that what you wanted?"

"What happened?"

"We had a little difference of opinion."

Once home, Meinhard sauntered off to the spare bedroom, his bag of personal belongings in tow. Marc followed him.

"Do you have clean clothes to put on?"

"No."

"Why don't you go take a shower, and I'll lay out something of mine for you on the bed. This weekend we'll buy you a few things."

"When's Zenzi coming home?"

"I'm not sure."

"Where is she?"

"She's being detained."

"She's in jail?"

"Yes."

"What's she in for?"

"Does it really matter?"

"She's my flesh and blood. I think I have a right to know."

"I don't think you have a—"

"Don't be disrespectful to your old man."

"Jesus, don't you ever quit? Look who's calling who disrespectful! I don't have a freakin' life because of you."

"Go to hell."

"You go to hell."

Meinhard left the bedroom and headed for the back door—without his coat. The temperature was just above freezing.

"Where are you going, you old fool? You'll freeze out there."

Meinhard turned around, ambled into the bathroom, and shut the door behind him.

"I'll be downstairs if you need me," Marc shouted at him through the door.

After laying out some of his clothes for Meinhard, Marc retreated to Zenzi's apartment. The first thing he did was split one of his Xanax pills in half and wash it down with a slug of beer.

Chapter 18

"So you're not going to bail me out of here?" Zenzi asked Marc over the phone. Marc lowered his voice to a whisper so the boys wouldn't hear. "You got yourself in there. You get yourself out."

"Asshole."

"Name-calling is a bad habit of yours—one I'm trying to break your kids of."

"Leave them out of this, jerk."

"Speaking of your kids, Riley got into a fight at school and had to have four stitches in his head."

"Did he win?"

"Are you kidding me?"

"He's a boy. Boys get into fights."

"It's not the first time."

"Stay out of it, Marc."

"It's a little hard when they're under my care."

He waited for a response.

"Zen?"

"Please come get me," she said softly. "I can't take it in here."

When Marc didn't respond right away, she hung up.

A few minutes later, Isabel Gunther from next door showed up with a plate of cookies. She and her husband, Johnny, had lived next door for as long as Marc could remember. He and Zenzi would drop in on them now and then when they were kids, mainly because there would always be something home-baked which would be freely offered. Now that he was older, she would occasionally bring the goodies to him.

"Hello, Markus…I mean Marc."

"Hello, Mrs. Gunther. Won't you come in?"

"I was hoping we could talk for a minute in private. Are you alone?"

"Zenzi's boys are in their room. Let me grab a coat. We can talk on the deck."

"I hope you don't think I'm being a nosy old busybody with nothing better to do," she said, "but we heard Zenzi had been arrested. Since then, we've watched you go back and forth between your apartment and hers…and, well, I just wanted to say we're here if you need us. If you need help, the boys are welcome here any time."

"That's very sweet of you to offer, and nice to know I can count on you for that. There have been times… It's been hard… May I ask you though, how did you know she'd been arrested? The boys don't even know that."

"Johnny has a police scanner."

"Oh. Well, she's going through a tough time right now."

"As long as those boys are all right…"

"They're fine."

She got up. "I don't want to keep you any longer. Remember, we're right next door. Whatever you need." She handed him the cookies. "Here. These are for the boys. Well, and for you too."

"Thank you, and if these are chocolate chip, well, the boys may not see many of them."

"Marc…"

"Just teasing."

No sooner had she left when Riley came out of his room and charged at Marc with his fists swinging, sending the cookies flying. "You didn't tell us Mom was in jail, you bastard!"

He held Riley at bay with one hand. "Calm down, son. I didn't—"

"Don't call me that!"

"Calm down, kid."

"And we don't have to…" Riley stopped mid-sentence, stopped his swinging, and backed away, his face looking like it was ready to explode.

"You don't have to what?"

Josh now joined them. "What's going on?"

"Nothing!" Riley yelled and stomped off to his room.

"What's wrong with him?" Josh asked.

"He's upset."

"So what else is new?"

"Does he get like this often?"

"Yes, and I'm getting a little tired of it." Josh rolled his eyes. "I gotta go," he said and headed toward his bedroom.

* * *

That night, Marc was lying awake on the sofa pondering what to do about Riley when a thunderous clunk from the floor above jerked him off the sofa.

"What the—"

He listened for more noises and, hearing none, threw on a shirt and headed toward his apartment. His back door was locked, so he used his key to open it, but Meinhard had engaged the chain lock again.

He rapped on the door.

There was no answer.

He rapped louder.

Still no answer.

He ran downstairs, grabbed his cell phone, ran back upstairs, and called Meinhard's phone. He heard it ring.

"Pick up the goddamn phone," he muttered. He pictured his pathetic father lying on the floor trapped beneath something heavy. "Damn him."

He pounded on the door and yelled, "Dad!" repeatedly.

When the window curtain moved, Meinhard peeked out from behind it and opened the door.

"What the hell is all that banging for?"

"Let me in."

"Is that any way to—"

"Listen to me, and listen to me good. You are *not* to chain this door...ever again. Is that clear?"

"Couldn't be any clearer. What's all the fuss about?"

"I heard a loud bang, a thud, up here, like something heavy fell on the floor."

"Oh, that. It was nothing."

"Don't tell me it was nothing! What was it?"

"Just something falling off the bed. You can go back downstairs now. Everything's fine here."

"What fell off the bed?" Marc walked past him toward the spare bedroom, turned on the light, and stared down at a leather briefcase lying on the floor. It was one he normally kept in the closet. "What's this?" He picked it up and laid it on the bed. "It weighs a ton. What's in here?"

The briefcase had been stuffed with his mother's silverware, the only thing she had ever owned of any value, the only material things Marc had of his mother's. It had been in Marc's closet ever since his father had gone to prison, right next to the briefcase.

He looked up at him. "Get out!"

Meinhard's dull glare grazed over Marc's face before he turned toward the back door and shuffled out into the cold February night, wearing nothing but boxer shorts and a t-shirt.

"Keep going, Dad. I hope you freeze to death," he yelled after him.

Marc waited a long agonizing moment before walking outside and finding Meinhard standing on the landing. Pushing his anger aside for the moment, Marc went to him, turned him around, and guided him back to his bedroom.

"Go back to sleep. I'll check on you in the morning."

Before he left, Marc removed the chain lock from the door. Then he gathered everything in the apartment that was small and of value, placed the items into a duffle bag, and brought the bag with him to Zenzi's apartment.

Riley and Josh were seated at the kitchen table.

"What are you guys doing up?"

"We couldn't sleep with all that racket going on upstairs," Riley said. "Where do you think *you're* going?" he asked Marc.

Marc glanced down at the duffle bag. "Oh, this? I'm not going anywhere. I brought down some things from upstairs that I needed. Do you know what time it is?"

"No, do you?"

Marc was in no mood for sarcasm, especially from a kid.

"It's a quarter to one. You guys need to go back to bed."

"We can't—"

"I don't care! Try!"

That was enough to make Josh cry. Riley put his arm around his shoulder and guided him toward their bedroom.

"C'mon Josh. *I'm* here for you," Riley said before slamming the bedroom door.

Marc felt the vibration of his phone.

Is everything ok up there?

It was Jessica.

No

Should I come up?

No

???

Just give me # for suicide hotline.

I'm coming up.

Chapter 19

"I'm worried about you," Jessica said. She wore no makeup, and her hair was in a sloppy knot on top of her head. The short ski jacket she had thrown on over her flannel nightgown and fuzzy pink slippers completed the look.

He smiled. "You look striking," he told her. He meant it—even her tousled hair looked good to him, but he was a sucker for blond hair.

"Very funny. Next time you mention suicide in the middle of the night, I'll just ignore it."

"I'm sorry. It's just that I've never seen you like..."

"Careful, buddy. It's almost that time of the month, and my sense of humor is somewhere down around my ankles."

Marc glanced at her feet.

"You have nice ankles by the way."

She flashed a weak smile.

"Beer?"

"Sure."

Marc retrieved two beers and gave her a quick recap on the latest episode with Meinhard. They kept their voices low so as not to alert the boys, especially Riley, that she was there.

"I guess technically it wouldn't be stealing the family silver if he's the head of the family...just sayin'," she said.

"When I add up all the money I've spent on this house, not to mention the time I've spent bailing him out of one screw-up after another, I think—"

"I hear ya. Can I change the subject?"

"Shoot."

"Riley said something to Tyler the other day that...well, maybe Tyler misunderstood him. You know how kids are."

"What did he say?"

"He told Tyler that he was lucky his father was gone."

"Lucky that Tyler's father was gone?"

"Yeah. I'm not sure what he meant by that."

Marc agreed. "Me neither."

"You told me once that neither boy knows his father, right?"

"Right."

"What about this Nick guy?"

"What about him?"

"I guess you could consider Nick to be Riley's stepdad. Could Riley have been thinking of *him* when he said it?" she asked.

Marc shrugged. "I don't know. I don't know what to think."

"It's a mess, isn't it?"

"Tell me about it."

"What are you going to do?"

"About what?"

Jessica smiled. "Any of it."

"I don't know."

"Overwhelmed?"

"Most of the time."

They talked for another hour over a few more beers. Tyler was spending the weekend with his father, so Jessica was free to stay without worrying about him being alone downstairs.

"You know there's a point when you have to just say 'No more.' You can only do so much. We're all human—we have limits."

"Believe me, if I could, I would. But I'm all they've got. If I didn't help them, who would?" He let out a sigh. "Do you want another beer?"

"Sure, why not."

Marc became more relaxed with each beer. "Look, Zenzi has a disease—you can't fault her for that. Until she gets sober and starts supporting herself, at least a little, I'll—"

"Allow her to keep right on drinking."

"Well, that's not fair."

"You give her a place to live. She doesn't have to work. You make excuses for her. She's not accountable to anyone."

"So what are you saying? That it's *my* fault she's the way she is?"

"I'm just saying don't forget to take care of yourself. That's all I'm saying, okay?" By the end of her sentence, her words were slurred.

"I won't."

"I better go." She got up to leave. At the door, she turned around to face Marc who was right behind her.

"I hope you're not mad at me, you big dope."

"No, I'm not mad at you. How could I ever be mad at you?"

She stepped toward him and put her arms around his neck. "I think I've had a bit too much to drink," she whispered.

Even through the ski jacket, he was enticed by the feel of her body up against his. He breathed in the scent of her hair and let out a soft moan.

She loosened her hold and leaned her head back to meet his gaze. After a few tempting seconds, their lips met, lightly at first, then progressively deeper until he was unzipping her jacket and reaching inside to explore her body.

They each backed away at precisely the same time and stared into each other's eyes for a long moment.

Marc grabbed her arm. "C'mon. Let's go in here," he said as he led her into Zenzi's bedroom. "And try not to make any noise," he whispered. "Riley's a really light sleeper."

* * *

When Marc opened his eyes, he had to think for a few seconds about where he was. He reached out for Jessica only to discover an empty side of the bed.

"Jess?" he whispered. "Where are you?" When he got no response, he turned on the bedside lamp. She wasn't in the room. The alarm clock said three a.m.

Sitting on the edge of the bed, Marc contemplated the events of the past few hours, which he vaguely remembered had included kissing Jessica. But he was fuzzy about what had happened after that—so fuzzy that he wasn't sure if they had gone any further than that. He did recall seeing her tramp stamp in its entirety, so he assumed they had.

* * *

The alarm clock flew off the coffee table when Marc attempted to hit the Off button. He had gotten very little sleep, waking up every half hour or so to a mélange of thoughts about Jessica.

Riley stood in the doorway of the living room.

"What's the matter?" Marc asked him.

"Are you freakin' kidding me?"

"Look, kid, you had better watch your language."

"Or what?"

That was a good question.

"Go back to your room and wake up Josh. School today."

Riley stomped off to his room, slamming the door behind him.

Will u be home later?

The text was from N Lee.

Who is this?

Zenzi u idiot.

I'll be out in the AM then home later. Why?

What time?

Why?

We want 2 talk 2 u.

Who's we?

Nick and me.

You're out of jail?

Yep

Marc hesitated a few seconds before responding.

Come at 12 b4 I pick up boys from school.

Ok

He slumped down on the sofa to think about their conversation. That she went from jail directly to Nick and not to him and the boys bothered him. Did she have plans other than coming home and relieving him of her parental responsibilities, and that's what she wanted to talk about?

Feeling like he was being sucked into her dysfunctional life even further, he allowed his thoughts to drift back to Jessica—he couldn't imagine how the next time he saw her would go. He mentally composed a series of potential opening sentences for the encounter.

Hi Jessica. Can you tell me if we had sex last night? I was too drunk to remember.
Hey gorgeous. When can I see you again?
Look, if you're still speaking to me...

The chances of Marc ever having a romantic relationship with Jessica was complicated by something she had shared with him about her past that caused him to believe it might not be over between her and her ex-husband. Apparently she had been attacked and raped when a senior in high school. Too embarrassed and ashamed to tell anyone except for Al, the nineteen-year-old she was dating, and seeing no purpose in reporting it when she couldn't identify her attacker, she had kept it a secret. When she discovered she was pregnant from the rape, Al asked her to marry him with the intention of raising the baby as their own. They married and a month later, Jessica miscarried the baby. Two years later, they had Tyler.

It wasn't until five years after Tyler was born that Al had admitted to her that he knew who her attacker had been—his younger brother, Jerry. Al had chosen to tell Jessica this only after his brother had died in a car accident. Jessica was furious that Al had waited so long to tell her, and she divorced him. That had been a little over a year and a half ago.

Jessica's story still on his mind, Marc went to the boys' room to make sure they were getting dressed. Only Josh was there.

"Where's Riley?"

"I don't know."

"You don't know or won't say?"

"I'm not lying!"

"Okay. I didn't mean anything by—"

"Wouldn't surprise me if he ran away."

"Why do you say that? Has he talked about it?"

"Yeah."

"Don't go anywhere," Marc said rushing out of the bedroom. "Start getting dressed for school," he yelled.

Marc threw on his coat and raced down the outside stairs to ground level. The sun had yet to rise, making it difficult to see much of anything. After scanning the area and not seeing any sign of Riley, he turned toward the house where Jessica was standing in her kitchen window staring at him.

He froze at the sight of her and couldn't think of what to do or say.

"Can't find Riley," he finally yelled.

She shrugged her shoulders and walked away, out of his sight.

Marc's insides pleaded for a Xanax as he climbed the stairs to his own apartment. As he got close, he could hear Meinhard's voice and then Riley's, which compelled him to bolt up the stairs two at a time. By the time he was ten feet from his apartment door, Riley's shouted words were clear.

"You caused this, you bastard!" It was painful to hear such a young voice use that kind of language and with so much rage.

"Calm down, son," Meinhard said. "I'll—"

"Don't call me that! I'm not your son!"

Marc barged through the door. "Hey, what's going on?" he asked.

"Nothing!" Riley snapped and headed toward the door.

Marc grabbed him by his jacket collar.

"Not so fast, young man."

"Let go of me! You're not my father!"

"We're going downstairs to have ourselves a little talk." Turning to Meinhard, he said, "I'll deal with you later."

"Me? What did I do?"

Still holding on to Riley's collar, Marc guided him out the door and down the stairs to their apartment with Riley fighting him the whole way.

"Let go of me!"

"I don't want you to run off."

"Yeah? Why not?"

Marc didn't respond as he ushered him into the kitchen of Zenzi's apartment.

"Sit down, Riley. We need to talk."

Still clearly agitated, Riley sat down. Marc attempted to calm him down, but it was no use—he was mad at the world.

Marc couldn't see sending Riley off to school in his current emotional state and called the school to inform them of his absence.. When Josh entered the kitchen, Marc said to him, "I want you to go down to Tyler's by yourself. Riley's not going to school today."

"That's not fair! Why does he get to skip school?"

"I'll explain later...when you're older. Now go."

"Maybe *I'll* run away then."

Marc grabbed Josh's arm. "Do I need to take you downstairs like a damn two-year-old?"

Josh broke free from Marc's grasp and spit on the kitchen floor.

"What did you do that for?"

"I hate you!"

"Riley, take Josh downstairs and make sure Tyler's mother knows you're not going to school today. And hurry. I have a meeting in Evanston in forty-five minutes, and you're coming with."

"No, I'm not."

"It's not up for discussion. Go!"

"I'd rather go to school."

"Too bad."

"Whatever."

Marc wished he had had what it took to man up and face Jessica and be done with it. Instead, he'd sent an eleven-year-old to cover for him.

Riley returned a few minutes later. "What's with you anyway?" he asked.

"Let's go. We'll stop at the McDonald's drive-thru, grab you some breakfast, and you can eat it on the way."

"Fine."

"Did you explain things to Tyler's mom?" Marc asked him on their way to McDonald's.

"I did what you ordered me to do."

"What did she say?"

"What was she supposed to say?"

"Nothing, I guess. I was just curious if she said anything."

After he got Riley situated with a breakfast, he drove north toward Evanston's Central Street neighborhood where one of his biggest clients lived—a client with a ten-thousand-square-foot home whose architectural design was inspired by Henry Wadsworth Longfellow's home in Cambridge, Massachusetts. The client wanted to talk about his plans to buy the property next door and move his pool and pool house there so he could expand his garage to accommodate more cars. He had asked Marc for an estimate on landscaping for the project.

The project was too big and too important to risk anything going wrong—Marc had to come up with a way to keep Riley on good behavior while he met with his client, and with Riley's current state of mind, he figured that wasn't going to be easy.

"Where are we going?" Riley asked.

"I have to meet with a client about a big landscaping project."

"Boooring."

"When you're old enough to work, you can pick a more exciting profession."

"I'll wait in the truck."

"No, you'll have to come with me."

"What am I supposed to do?"

"Listen. You might learn something."

"Right."

"There is one thing you could do."

117

"What?"

"I'm not sure if you can handle it."

"Try me."

"This client, he has a very odd habit."

"So?"

"In the middle of a sentence, he slips in the word *tick*."

"What?"

"He'll be talking, and all of a sudden he'll say the word *tick* and go right on with the sentence."

"That's crazy."

"I'm curious as to how many times he does this while we talk, so I want you to count them."

Riley laughed. "What?"

"Will you do that for me?"

"Sounds kinda dumb."

"Now, I don't want you to laugh at him—that would be rude. I want you to listen to our conversation and in your head count the times he says that word. Do you think you can do that?"

"Maybe."

"Good, because we're almost there." He glanced at Riley and pointed to his chin. "You have a little..."

Riley swiped his chin with his napkin.

"Gone?"

"Yep."

"Wouldn't want food on my chin in front of Mr. Tick."

Marc couldn't be sure, but he thought he caught Riley smiling. Good sign.

"No making fun of him now, you understand that?"

"Yep."

They spent the next hour walking the grounds with Marc's client and discussing landscaping schemes. Riley stayed close by but out of the way. Marc periodically tried to catch a glimpse of Riley's face to assess his frame of mind, but Riley kept dodging his looks.

When they finished, Marc and Riley climbed into Marc's truck, and before Marc had the key in the ignition, Riley blurted out, "Twenty-seven."

"Is that right? Twenty-seven times."

"Yep, and that doesn't count the time he said tick and meant it. When he said, 'My wife came in with a tick on her blouse,' I thought I was gonna bust a gut, really."

"Yeah, I knew I couldn't look at you when he said that."

"What now?"

"We're going to go home and talk, and then I have to meet with your Mom."

"You're going to go to the jail?"

"No, apparently she's out. She texted me this morning."

"So why didn't she come home?"

"I don't know. That will be one of the first things I ask her."

"So I'll get to see her?"

Marc's initial feeling was that allowing Riley to see his mom if she wasn't coming home to stay would just complicate matters. And not knowing what Zenzi and Nick wanted to talk about made him that much more uneasy about bringing Riley into it. Yet, denying Riley the chance to see his mother didn't seem right either.

"I'm going to ask you to trust me on something. Can you do that?"

"I don't know. Depends."

"Your mom and Nick have something specific on their minds that they want to talk to me about. Let me have that conversation first before you see her."

"Why?"

"This is where the trust part comes in. I want you to trust me that that's the better way to do this."

"So where am I supposed to go?"

"And this is where I'm going to trust you. I want you to go upstairs while they're here and be with your grandfather. Do you think you can do that?"

Riley didn't respond.

"And I think maybe an apology is in order."

"To who?"

"Your grandfather."

Riley sucked in his breath. "Fine."

"You think the two of you can get along while you're up there?"

Riley shrugged.

"I want you to be sure you can do this—sometimes with him you have to be more of the adult."

His face brightened. "I can do that. And Uncle Marc?"

"Yes."

"I guess I owe you an apology too."

"Oh?"

"For being such a jerk-wad lately. And one more thing."

"What's that?"

"Mr. Tick looks just like Homer Simpson—didn't you notice that?"

Stifling a smile was impossible—the boy was right.

Chapter 20

After Marc escorted Riley upstairs and was comfortable with the way he and Meinhard had greeted each other and started a conversation, Marc went back downstairs and let half a Xanax dissolve in his mouth while he waited for his sister. He had run a couple of scenarios through his head about what they could possibly want to discuss, but in the end, he didn't have a clue.

They arrived precisely at noon: Zenzi, Nick, Nick's girlfriend Sonya, and Baby Emma.

Zenzi was first to walk in the door—appearing pale and tired, even thinner than before and with a sadness in her expression that was painful to see. Marc went to hug her, but she backed away from him.

Nick followed—somewhere in his thirties, tall, good looking, and well-dressed. Nice enough smile. It was difficult to tell his ethnicity—light brown skin, thin facial features, wavy black hair. He and Marc shook hands.

Sonya was close behind—petite, younger than Nick and Zenzi. With dark hair and an olive complexion, she was notably attractive. It was Sonya who carried the baby, wrapped in a blanket that covered most of her face.

"She's sleeping," she told Marc after introducing herself.

Sonya and Nick made an interesting-looking couple—an intercontinental air about them. The way Nick attended to the baby while Sonya removed her coat and took a few things out of the diaper bag made them look like a solid family unit. Zenzi, who had gone on ahead to the living room on her own, appeared to be a fifth wheel.

They settled into the living room. Marc and Nick sat on opposite ends of the sofa, and Sonya settled herself and the sleeping baby into one of the chairs in the bay window on the other side of the room. As Zenzi positioned herself in the recliner across from the sofa, Marc noticed that her hands were shaking. The tension in the room was palpable.

Nick initiated the discussion. "First of all, we want to thank you for stepping in to watch over Zenzi's boys while she's been unavailable." His speech and mannerisms implied a good education. "Zenzi appreciates it. I appreciate it. We all appreciate it." A bare accent was perceptible.

"They're good boys," Marc said as he tried to gauge the man's character.

"We have a proposal. Zenzi and I are legally married, and I probably won't have my green card for another couple of months or so. It depends on whether they make me go through an audit or not. Our caseworker, who has visited us periodically for the past ten months, recently lost her job, and we now have a new one. I'm concerned about this."

His English was perfect—like maybe he had been schooled in English as opposed to his native language.

"Let's get one thing straight, Nicholas," Marc said. "You are in this country from...where are you from?"

"I am a citizen of Malaysia. My father was Malaysian. My mother was Nigerian."

"Okay. So you're a Malaysian who is fraudulently seeking U.S. citizenship. Do I have that right?"

"I am a Malaysian seeking U.S. citizenship. That is correct."

"And you've taken advantage of my sister in the process."

Nick turned toward Zenzi. "I trust that I have not done that." He turned back to face Marc. "I provide her with financial assistance, bailed her out of jail, and I am raising our daughter."

As if on cue, Emma woke up on Sonya's lap and started making noises. Sonya sat her upright allowing Marc to see her face. The baby smiled and flapped her arms a few times before settling down.

"She's adorable, Zen," Marc said. Getting no response from her, he turned back to Nick. "With all due respect, all you're doing for Zenzi is fueling her alcoholism with your money, and you probably didn't do her any favors by bailing her out of jail."

"Hey!" Zenzi blurted out. "You're talking about me like I'm not in the room."

"Look, Zenzi," Marc said, "one way or another, we need to get everything out on the table. You have an alcohol problem, and what you need is serious treatment. Look at you." He gestured toward her shaking hands. "You're probably in withdrawal right now."

Zenzi stared past Marc without responding.

"We understand what you're saying, Marc," Nick said through a feeble smile. "And that's why you may like our proposal."

Here it comes.

"I'm listening."

"We all agree that Zenzi needs treatment, and I can arrange for that. There's a place in Texas that will treat her for her addiction as well as address her physical, emotional, and any other needs she has. And they can admit her straight away."

Marc turned toward Zenzi. "And what do *you* think about that?" he asked her.

She shrugged. "Maybe that's what I need."

"How long does this treatment take?"

"As long as she needs it to take. Three months. Six months. A year."

"What's the rest of the proposal?"

"I'll live here, in this apartment, with the boys and Baby Emma until Zenzi gets better."

"Hold on one minute," Marc interjected. "The boys?"

"Of course, the boys. I am their stepfather."

"No. There's no 'of course' about it. You can call yourself anything you want, but from what I've seen, you've played no role in those boys' lives. You don't even know them."

"Of course I know them. I know them, and I care about them. Very much."

Marc didn't trust him or his words.

"I will not allow those two boys to live with you."

"Wait just a freakin' minute," Zenzi snapped. "I'm their mother. I think I get a say in this matter."

No one else spoke while Zenzi scanned each of their faces.

"For once, I'm with Marc," she said. "I don't want the boys living with you, Nick."

Nick arched an eyebrow at her but let her continue.

"They *don't* know you well enough, and you know that. Admit it—you want them with you for when the Department of Immigration sends over that social worker. So it looks like we're a family." She turned to Marc. "Can't they live with you upstairs? And whenever a social worker or whoever comes over, they can come down to my apartment and pretend they live there."

"Zen, now you're dragging children into an adult situation," Marc said. "Do you think that's fair?"

"Why not?" she asked.

"I am okay with that," Nick said. "Look, it will be two or three times at most, and I am certain that we can come up with reasonable explanations for them not being here some of the time."

Marc looked at Zenzi. "What about your daughter?"

She took her time answering.

"I'm okay with her staying with Nick. She seems to be doing fine," she said nodding her head but shrugging her shoulders at the same time.

"And then what?" Marc asked Nick. "How long does this go on?"

"As soon as I have my green card, we'll get a divorce."

Marc glanced at Sonya. "And how does she fit into this picture?"

"Sonya and I plan to marry as soon as I'm divorced."

"And what about the baby then?"

"Sonya and I will raise her."

Marc turned to face Zenzi, searching her face for a sign of emotion. "And you're okay with all this?" he asked her.

She seemed to be fighting to hold back tears. "Baby Emma's bonded with them. Both of them."

"You have rights, you know," Marc said gently.

"I know. And I also know what's best for my daughter."

"And then what happens to the boys?" Marc asked.

"That is for you and Zenzi to decide," Nick said.

Marc shook his head. "You're talking about this like it's all perfectly normal, like people do this all the time. Well, it's not—this whole scheme is preposterous. It's filled with holes, and it's fraudulent. I asked around, Nick. You're committing a federal crime that comes with jail time and fines."

"Think about it, Marc. There are no losers here. Zenzi gets the help she needs... immediately. I get my green card. The boys are taken care of. You're eventually relieved of your custodial responsibilities, which I'm sure have been a burden for you. Nobody gets hurt."

"Nobody gets hurt? Are you kidding? I can't go along with this!"

Marc rose from his chair. "I think we're done here," he said to Nick in a calm voice.

"Marc, please sit back down and—"

"Don't friggin' tell me what to do in my own house."

"It's *my* apartment," Zenzi said.

Marc shot her a look. "It's *my* house. It's *your* apartment only because I allow you to live in it."

"Calm down, brother."

"And don't you try to tell me what to do either." He headed toward the hallway.

"Where are you going?" Zenzi shouted.

He turned to face Nick.

"There will be no deal!"

"May I say something?" Sonya asked.

Marc hesitated at the doorway, then whirled around to face her.

"What is it?" he asked.

"Could you please come back here and sit with us again?"

He was curious as to what was on her mind.

"Go ahead," he said without sitting down.

"I realize this is none of my business, and no one asked for my opinion, but I can't just sit here and watch this whole thing fall apart. Marc, I've known Nicholas for over a year." She gave Nick a warm smile. "He's a good man and a very good father. While it may look like he's only in it to get legalized in this country, I can assure you he cares about Zenzi and appreciates what she's done for him. All he's trying to do is make a life for himself in this country, an honest life, and I'm hoping...no, I'm praying that you'll help him do that."

"Then why aren't *you* helping him get his green card?" Marc asked.

She didn't respond right away. "Unfortunately, I can't do that. I have something in my background that—"

"Oh, really? Like what?"

"Sonya is not at issue here," Nicholas interjected.

"No, Nick. I don't mind telling him." She turned her attention to Marc. "I was involved in a check-fraud scheme a couple of years ago. I'm a different person now, but it's on my record."

Oh, great! They'll both have criminal records.

He turned toward Nick. "So what difference would that make for you?"

"She was charged with a felony. If I'm seen as fraternizing with someone with a record, they might think twice about granting the green card," Nick said.

"No offense, but my concern is for Zenzi and the boys."

"Marc, let's face it," Nick said. "Zenzi cannot be a responsible parent without getting proper treatment. Are we in agreement on that?"

It bothered Marc that the three of them seemed to consider the ridiculous plan completely acceptable, like they were a group of friends planning a joint vacation or something, deciding whether to go to Wisconsin Dells or the Indiana Dunes. Why was he the only one who had any common sense about this? He sat back down on the sofa and considered Nick's question.

"Yes, I am in agreement with that."

"How long before you could get her into treatment?"

"Months."

"Think about the consequences of staying on the course you're on, Marc. How has that been working for you?"

"What do you do for a living, Nick?" Marc asked.

"I take small consulting jobs wherever I can get them. Without a green card, I can't do much."

"Tell him what you did in Singapore, Nick," Sonya said.

"I have a bachelor's degree from the Singapore Institute of Technology, a master's from Nanyang Technological University, and a law degree from Bricksfield. I worked in the executive branch of the Malaysian government developing computer systems and programs."

"Sounds like a good job. So why did you leave?"

"I discovered something going on that people in high places didn't want me to see, and I was asked to leave. It's not like here—I couldn't go to anyone with this information. After I left, I was blacklisted, so no one else would hire me."

"So what had you discovered?"

"I am not at liberty to say."

"Mm-hm. Well, I still don't like it. It's not right."

"Will you at least think about it? Would that be asking too much?"

"I'll do that." He turned toward his sister. "In the meantime, where will you stay, Zen?"

"We think it is best if she stays with me," Nick said. "If she were to move back here, she would get too involved with her sons again and wouldn't want to leave."

"This is your preference then, Zen?" Marc asked her.

Zenzi nodded.

"And you're okay with that?" Marc asked Sonya.

"Yes. Zenzi and I have become friends. I'm totally okay with that."

"And the boys?" Marc asked. "What do I tell them? Riley knows you're out of jail, Zen, and in fact he's upstairs waiting to see you."

"He is? Why isn't he in school?" she asked.

"There was an incident this morning, and I felt it was in his best interest to keep him home today. Zen, he wants to know why you didn't come home first after being released from jail."

Zenzi rose from her chair. "I want to see him."

"Can it wait until we're finished here?" Marc asked.

"C'mon. Let's get this over with."

Nick got up to leave. Sonya followed suit.

"Please consider our proposal, Marc," Nick said. "I think we all know it is in everyone's best interest." He turned to Zenzi. "We'll wait in the car while you spend a few minutes with Riley."

Before they left, Marc approached Zenzi's daughter who was wide awake and alert in Sonya's arms. "It was nice meeting you, Baby Emma," he said caressing the back of her hand. Maybe it was his imagination, but he thought she had Zenzi's eyes.

After Nick, Sonya and the baby left, Marc went upstairs to get Riley. After bringing him down and witnessing a rather awkward reunion between them— Zenzi wanting a big hug but Riley being hesitant—Marc excused himself so they could be alone.

As he turned to go, Zenzi whispered, "And that little secret about you assuming Dad's name and the house? Go along with this, and that could go away. Just remember that, little brother."

Chapter 21

"So how did it go with your Mom?" Marc asked Riley after she and the others left.

"Good."

"Did you have a nice talk?"

"Yeah."

"And what about with Grampa Meinhard?"

"Okay."

"What did you two talk about?"

He shrugged. "Not much."

"Were you in the same room?"

"Yeah."

"So who spoke first?"

"He did."

"Well, what did he say?"

"He asked how I was."

"Okay...and you said..."

"Fine."

Was I this difficult to talk to when I was eleven?

"Riley?"

Riley smiled. "I was just playin' with you. We actually had a nice talk. He asked me about school, and I told him what I was doing there. He asked about Josh too. And then he told me what it was like going to school in Germany."

He never talked to me about that.

"It was kind of interesting. He talked about how he crossed over from East Germany to West Germany, or maybe it was the other way around. I don't remember. Anyway, he hid in a truck with a bunch of dead pigs."

"What?"

"He said he hid under the pigs, and it was cold in there."

Marc had never heard that story.

"And he talked about the differences between East and West Germany."

"He did?"

"Yeah. How he was on the communist side."

"East Germany."

"He said communism means you take care of each other, not like here."

Well, there's a little more to it than that.

"Communism or socialism?" Marc asked.

"He used both words. I'm not sure what the difference is. But he said he was a teenager when the Berlin Wall went up and he watched it being built. Took pictures of it."

"Really."

"And he was sad when it came down."

"You know what the Berlin Wall was?"

"Yeah. Had it in history class."

"Did he say why he was sad when it came down?"

"He said he was afraid the people on each side wouldn't get along."

"Did you talk about anything else?"

"Not really. But he did ask me how Mom was."

"What did you tell him?"

"First I said fine, but then I told him she was sick."

"What did he say?"

"He said he knew that. That was pretty much it. What did you and Mom talk about?"

Marc had given careful thought to how much he would initially reveal to the boys about his discussion with Zenzi and Nick. They were smart kids but too young to understand all the nuances of alcoholism and details of Nick's immigration status. They deserved to know something—just how much would be a delicate balancing act for Marc, especially since he wasn't sure himself what he was going to do about Nick's proposal.

"We talked about the best treatment for your mother. She really needs help."

"Why is she staying with Nick? Why not here?"

"She'd like to stay here. She'd rather be back with you guys, but until she gets better..."

"I don't get it."

"She has to learn how to stay away from alcohol first, and that's not easy for some people."

"You just do it. What's the problem?"

"I wish that's how it worked, but it doesn't. You see, people like your mom are dependent on alcohol, their bodies crave it. It's like when you and I get hungry. Our bodies crave food, and we don't feel good without it. So we eat. For your mom, alcohol is like her food. Her body craves it, so she drinks. She knows it's wrong, but it's not something she can control."

"So how do they fix that?"

"I don't know what they do exactly, but it takes counseling and different therapies in a place where there are no distractions or opportunities to slip up."

"How long will that take?"

"That depends on your mom. Some people need longer than others."

Marc could tell that Riley was struggling to hold back tears as he said, "How much should we tell Josh? He's only ten, you know. He won't understand any of this, and he's very sensitive."

"We can tell him your mom is sick and we're figuring out the best way to get her well so she can come home. Then if he asks questions, we'll just be honest with him."

"I guess that'll work." Riley shrugged. "Uncle Marc?"

"Yes?"

"Are you going to stay with us until she gets straightened out?"

"For the time being...yes."

"Okay, what's really going on?"

"I told you what I know."

"Liar!"

"I don't know what—"

"You said you'd never lie to us."

"And I haven't."

"Then why did you say 'for the time being?'"

"Because we don't know the whole plan yet, Riley. I can't tell you what I don't know."

"Whose decision is it?"

"I suppose, in the end, it's your mother's decision about her treatment. She's an adult. No one can force her to do something she doesn't want to do. But..."

"But what?"

"It's complicated, Riley, and it's an adult subject. I can't tell you all the details, but nothing I've said to you has been a lie. I promise you that."

"Yeah, right."

* * *

Nick's proposal gave Marc much to consider in the days that followed, which provided him with a convenient excuse for not thinking about what had happened between him and Jessica. He thought about doing the right thing—talking it out and everything—but thinking about it was as far as he got. She hadn't made any effort to contact him either, and he wanted to believe it was because nothing had actually happened, though that seemed unlikely.

In the meantime, Marc debated whether to allow a complete stranger to live in his house under the pretense of being a loving husband to his sister and father-of-the-year to his nephews. If Marc didn't go along with it, Nick would likely get caught and be deported. Nick getting caught didn't bother him. What bothered him was what would then happen to Zenzi and the boys. And Emma. Now that he'd met her, he was thinking about her too.

Without Nick's influence and money, Zenzi would probably not stay in rehab and would want to come back and assume her former role—a semi-functional alcoholic raising two young boys. And then Marc wondered how long that would last, given there would be at least one government entity with knowledge of Nick's fraudulent behavior in which Zenzi was an involved party. Would she be culpable too? What if they investigated the situation and in the process determined she was an unfit mother? Would they take the boys away?

And if Marc *did* go along with their plan and Nick was caught, maybe he would be considered an accomplice and subsequently charged with something too.

Despite Sonya's heartfelt words, the primary reason Nick wanted to move in while Zenzi was getting help was to make the authorities think they were a family so he could get his green card. It didn't take a genius to figure out whose best interest was at the top of Nick's list.

While their proposal was definitely slanted in Nick's favor, Zenzi *would* get the treatment she really needed—she would be in one of the best treatment centers in the country.

Marc had to admit that it was in his best interest too in that he would be alleviated of the burden of Zenzi and the boys, at least for a while. And of course the matter of his assuming his father's name was at stake too.

But what about the boys—would it be in their best interest?

Chapter 22

"He has to leave!" Zenzi shouted into the phone at Marc the next morning, referring to their father. Apparently, Riley had told her that Grandpa Meinhard was living in Marc's apartment. Marc had had a fitful night's sleep, and the last thing he wanted to hear was one of Zenzi's rants.

"Zen, I'm trying to juggle a million different things right now. Will you give me a freakin' break? I'm looking for a place for Dad to go. These things take time. And don't forget I'm watching over your two kids and trying to maintain a business, which is about to—"

"Nick's plan is called off if that man is in the same house. I won't have it."

"What difference does it make? It's not like he's—"

"I don't want him anywhere around my kids! You never should have left Riley with him yesterday."

"I'm trying hard to find a place for him, but what's the difference if he's still here for a while after Nick moves into your apartment and the boys stay with me upstairs? The boys can have my bed, and I'll sleep on the sofa."

"Won't work."

"Why not?"

"He's evil."

"He's not evil. He's—"

"I don't care. He didn't give a shit about me."

"Why are you going back to… This is today. What are you—"

"That sonofabitch knew what Harley was doing to me for years, you dumb shit," she said through sobs. "And I won't have him in the same house as my daughter when I'm not there to protect her!"

"What the hell are you talking—"

She hung up.

It took Marc a moment to digest what she'd said, and when he did, he was certain he hadn't heard her right. The only Harley he knew was the kid who had lived two doors down from them when they were kids—Harley Cooper. He was a few years older than Marc, a bully who was always getting into trouble. Marc didn't know what he could have done to Zenzi that she was still so upset about or what that had to do with Baby Emma or anything else.

He replayed her words in his head. Unless she was talking about molestation or something, but that seemed far-fetched—she would have said something before now. Wouldn't she have?

He picked up his phone to call Zenzi back when the thought of Harley Cooper doing anything like that to his sister made him hurl it against the wall, pieces flying in multiple directions.

"What did you do that for?"

He hadn't heard Josh enter the room.

"Nothing you'd understand."

* * *

Marc discovered cell phones had gotten a lot more expensive in the last two years. The new one set him back three hundred dollars.

The first call he made was to Zenzi.

"Can we talk? Privately?"

"Why?"

"What you said yesterday."

"Doesn't matter."

"It matters to me."

She let out an audible sigh. "Nick's at work if you want to come over." Her voice was soft and calm. He couldn't tell if she'd been drinking. She gave him Nick's address, which was in an up-and-coming neighborhood in the South Loop, twenty minutes from his house.

After making sure Jessica's car wasn't in its usual parking space, he rushed down the stairs past her kitchen window and hopped into his SUV. He had managed to avoid her for thirty-six hours—not something he was proud of, just grateful.

When he arrived at Nick's apartment, Marc conducted a quick visual inventory of its contents—expensive furnishings, immaculately clean, view of Lake Michigan—not what he expected for someone who didn't have a steady job.

In a crumpled Cubs jersey and her usual baggy sweat pants, Zenzi sat on one end of the white leather sectional in the living room, her legs and feet tucked up under her. Marc sat on the other end where he spoke the opening sentence he had rehearsed on the way over.

"I know this is a sensitive area, but can you explain to me what you were talking about yesterday…about Harley Cooper?"

"It's in the past."

"Apparently not—it sparked quite a nerve yesterday."

"What do you want to hear, all the gory details?"

"No, of course not. I don't think so. I really don't know because I don't know what he did to you."

She lit a cigarette. "You can't figure it out?"

"He molested you?"

She nodded, blowing out a long breath of smoke up toward the ceiling. "When?"

"Started when I was pretty young."

"Like when Mom was alive?"

She took another long puff of her cigarette.

"When are you going to stop that disgusting—"

"When are you going to get off my ass about everything?" she snapped back.

"Sorry. So was Mom alive?"

"I don't think so. I don't remember how old I was. I don't want to remember."

"How long did it go on?"

Her eyes grew wide. "Until I figured out that I didn't have to put up with it."

"And you think Dad knew?"

"Harley *told* me he knew."

"Well, that doesn't mean he actually—"

"Stop trying to protect that bastard. He had to have known—it was happening right under his nose."

"I'm not trying to protect him, Zen. I'm just trying to understand so—"

"You don't need to understand. It happened. End of story."

"But it's not the end of story. You're still angry over it, and you—"

"Still? I'll *always* be angry over what he did to me."

"Maybe some therapy would—"

"Is that why you came over here, to tell me I need a shrink?"

"Well, no, but—"

"Then don't."

"I wish you had told me earlier. Why didn't you?"

"You don't get it, do you?" She put out her cigarette and lit another. "Do you know how humiliating this is? How I let him do that to me for all those years? How afterward I felt like it was *my* fault for letting him do it? How ashamed I was." She rocked the upper half of her body to-and-fro against the sofa back as she talked, her jaw tightening more with each sentence. "Do you know what it's like to have a father you can't trust? Do you have any idea how alone I've felt over the years?"

"I'm sorry you had to go through that, Zen. I can't even imagine what it's done to you."

"I lose another little piece of myself every day because of that pathetic bastard. And there's not that much left to lose, believe me."

"Are you talking about Dad now?"

"Yes, Dad! He let it happen!"

"You don't know that for sure."

"Oh, I'm sure he knew. And even if he didn't, he *should* have!"

"Does anyone else know about this?"

"Just Nick."

Emma's cry interrupted their conversation. Marc had forgotten all about the baby. Zenzi got up and walked toward the hallway.

"She's probably wet and hungry," she said with her back to Marc. "You can stay if you want. Or you can leave. I'm done talking."

A few minutes later Zenzi emerged with Emma in her arms and sat down. The pink-cheeked child looked at Marc with wide inquisitive eyes, cautiously checking him out before flashing him a toothless smile.

"She's so pretty," he said.

"Like I used to be. Is that what you're thinking?"

"No, of course not."

"So I wasn't pretty?"

"You know what I meant."

"I was, you know."

"You still are."

"Liar."

"I can't win with you."

"So don't try."

"Why are you so angry?"

"Wouldn't you be if you were in my situation?"

He didn't know how to answer that.

"Nick's plan," he said.

"What about it?"

"What do *you* want to do?"

"I don't have much choice, do I? If I don't get into some kind of rehab, I'll probably go to jail, and then they'll take my kids away from me."

"But what Nick is doing is illegal."

"Well, hot shot, what do you advise me to do?"

"You don't even know this guy."

"I know him well enough to trust him. That's more than I can say about anyone else in my life."

"Including me?"

"Tell me you'll go along with it, and then I'll let you know."

"That doesn't make any sense."

"Yeah, well, I don't tend to make much sense until I've had my third drink for the day, and I've only had two."

"Zen, it's only—"

"Don't lecture me, okay?"

He studied the face of innocence on her lap wondering what would be best for her.

"Have Nick and Sonya raised her from the beginning?" he asked her.

"Yep."

"And they've been good parents?"

"They're excellent parents."

"There is an upside to this crazy plan. I see that, but—"

"Then say you'll go along with it," she said. "If anything goes wrong, you can just say you didn't know."

"Didn't know what?"

"Don't make me say it, okay?"

"Know that the only reason the two of you married was so he could get his green card?"

"Bingo."

When Emma started fussing, Marc got up to leave. "I'll let you know by Friday," he said before walking out the door.

Marc had two days to decide what to do about Zenzi's situation—agree to let Nick and Emma move into Zenzi's flat while she got the treatment she needed or say no and live with the consequences, which could involve Zenzi's health, her going to jail, and her losing custody of the boys. Furthermore, if he opted to go along with it, he had less than a week to find other living accommodations for Meinhard.

Later that day after he fed them dinner, he arranged for the boys to stay next door with the Gunthers for a couple of hours. Then he called Meinhard to tell him he was going to stop by in a bit with some Chinese takeout.

"Don't bother with that crap. I don't know how those Chinks can eat that stuff every day."

"What would you like for dinner then, Dad? I'll pick up whatever you want."

"Doesn't matter. I'm not fussy."

Marc picked up a bucket of Kentucky Fried Chicken and decided if his father didn't like it, he would throw it at him.

"Fried chicken?" Meinhard said when Marc arrived with dinner.

"I asked you what you wanted."

"Whatever. It's your money."

"Ya know..."

Marc didn't finish his thought. Instead, he remained silent while he set the table for the two of them.

"You're eating here?"

"Is that okay?"

"What about those kids?"

"They're next door."

"Why?"

"Because."

"So what's up? You send the kids next door, come up here with food. What's going on?"

"Nothing. Can't we just enjoy a meal together?"

"You're up to something," he mumbled.

"Fine. I am up to something. Forget the food." He pushed his plate away hard enough for a biscuit to fly off and roll toward Meinhard.

"Look, Zenzi needs to come home, but she won't unless you're gone. So we need to find a place for you to go."

He figured it wasn't a big lie—eventually, Zenzi *would* be coming back. And the more he contemplated Meinhard's sour expression, the more he didn't care if he had lied.

"Maybe that's not her call. Is her name on the deed?"

"You know it isn't."

"End of discussion."

Marc felt his muscles tense up as the blood slowly rose up his neck. He kept his fists, clenched and ready, under the table.

"I know about Harley," Marc said, the words spewing from his mouth like vomit.

"What are you talking about?"

"I know what Harley did to Zenzi while she was growing up. She told me everything."

"Harley—the kid from down the street? What did he do?"

"Do you want me to spell it out for you?"

"Looks like you're going to have to because I'm at a loss here."

"She said he molested her and you knew about it."

"What? How many drinks did she have under her belt when she said this?"

"She wasn't drunk."

"She's full of shit."

"You knew nothing about Harley taking advantage of her? She said it went on for years."

"I don't believe it."

Marc knew there would be no point in further discussion.

"Here's the deal, Dad. I'm moving back into this apartment, and you need to find somewhere else to live."

"Just like that? My own house. Because she's making up some shit."

"That's not the reason, and goddamnit, it's not your house anymore! You haven't been around for years."

He stared at Marc with a blank expression for a long moment. "You have a spare bedroom."

"You need to be independent."

"Like Zenzi?"

Marc heaved a sigh. "What's it going to take for you to find another place to live?"

"I'd need money to do that."

Here it comes.

"How much?"

"Deposit on an apartment, first month's rent. You're the smart one. You figure it out."

"And then what? Who's going to pay the second month's rent?"

"Exactly."

"Let's see…how about you?"

"I'm old and my health isn't good."

"You look okay to me."

"I have spells."

"What kind of spells?"

"Sometimes I forget things."

"Like what sort of things?"

"Just things."

"Well, I have news for you. We all do that."

"Like where I am."

"Mm-hm."

"And I think I'm depressed."

"Yeah? Well, me too."

"You're not taking me seriously."

"I'm going to look into financial assistance for you."

"Don't bother."

"Why not?"

"No handouts."

"But you'd take a handout from me!"

"That's different."

"Well, you may not have a say in this."

"Oh, yeah?"

"You just said sometimes you don't even know where you are. I'll have you declared incompetent." He had no idea if that was even possible.

"I'm not budging."

Marc got up and turned toward the door.

"You better think about it, old man," he said before closing the door behind him.

Chapter 23

"You boys are going to have to bear with me for the next few days while I take care of a number of things for your grandfather. The Gunthers were nice enough to say you can go there after school while I do this. Mr. Gunther will pick you up from school."

"Why can't we stay at Tyler's like before?" Josh asked.

"Just for a few days."

"Why?" asked Riley.

"Just because. It's complicated."

"I don't see why we can't stay here by ourselves," Riley argued.

"We've been over this before, Riley. Like a million times."

"So stupid. I'm almost twelve. Kids in my class babysit all the time."

"I don't care what other kids do, I—"

"Now you sound like Mom," Josh said, rolling his eyes.

"And what's going to happen to Mom, anyway?" Riley asked.

"She's going to get the treatment she needs."

"Where?"

"There's a place in Texas that—"

"Texas!"

"Yes, Texas."

"Why so far away?" Riley asked.

"Can I see her before she goes? Riley got to," Josh said.

"We'll see." Marc wasn't sure how soon Nick could get her into the facility.

"Can we visit her there?" Riley asked.

"Well, it's in Texas, and that's pretty far from here. And besides, sometimes there are no visitors at these places anyway."

"That's not fair!" Riley shouted. "When is she leaving?"

"I don't know that for sure. Those details haven't been worked out yet. Look, you want her to get better, don't you?"

Both boys nodded.

"Well, if that means no visitors, wouldn't you be for that?"

A blank stare from both boys.

Riley turned away from Marc. Josh followed.

"This shit stinks!" Riley said before disappearing into his room.

"Yeah," Josh said.

Marc headed for their room. When he was within a few feet of it, the door flew shut. He changed his direction and retrieved a beer from the fridge.

* * *

The following morning Zenzi called to tell him she would be able to go to rehab the following Monday—four days away.

"So are you going to go along with this, or what?" she asked him.

"I'm in."

"Good choice."

Marc agreed to drop the boys off at Nick's apartment on Friday after school so they could spend the weekend with her there.

Later that day—in between discussions with Arnie MacCallum about installing motion-sensitive floodlights in his backyard to scare away the deer at night and listening to him rant about how the best thing that could happen to the baby deer in the forest preserve behind his house was a band of hungry coyotes—Marc met with the Social Security Administration and Department of Human Services to make sure he understood all the benefits to which Meinhard was entitled. Before they could get the processes started, they needed a copy of his birth certificate, Social Security card, and a few other documents. He asked Meinhard for these things.

"I don't have one."

"One what?"

"A Social Security card."

"What do you mean you don't have one? You lost it?"

"No. I never had one."

"Dad, you had to have had one. Otherwise you wouldn't have been able to work."

"Apparently not, because I never had one."

Marc knew he had to be mistaken.

"How about your birth certificate?"

"Nope."

"What do you mean 'nope?'"

"Don't have one of those either."

"You *were* born, weren't you?"

"Don't be a smart-ass."

"We'll have to write to the German government and have them send us a duplicate then."

"Good luck."

"Okay, why do you say that?"

"Because I never had one."

"Of course you did. What's wrong with you?"

"I was adopted in Germany."

"What? You never told us that. Because that's not true, is it? But even if it is, it shouldn't make any difference. They'll have a record of it."

"It wasn't done exactly legally."

"What?"

"Are you deaf or something?"

"You're telling me that you've gone your whole life without a birth certificate and Social Security card?"

"Looks that way."

"How did you become a citizen without—"

Oh shit.

"You're not a citizen."

Meinhard raised one eyebrow and then looked down.

"Was Mom legal?"

"No."

"Are you kidding me? How did you buy a house if you weren't a citizen?"

"I had the down payment and a job. The bank didn't care."

Neither of them said anything for several seconds.

"And you know what else?" Meinhard asked.

"What, there's more?"

"If I had known Harley Cooper was doing anything to Zenzi, I would have killed him. I would have fucking killed him. Will you please tell her that for me?"

* * *

"I'm told I can't get him any public assistance if he's not a citizen," Marc told Zenzi and Nick over the phone. "Not unless it's an emergency." Marc had asked them to put him on speakerphone so he could explain things to both of them at the same time.

"I'm afraid you're right, Marc," Nick confirmed. "I know that part of the law."

"Quite honestly, I don't know what to do with him."

"Kick him out and let the sonofabitch fend for himself," Zenzi said. "He seemed to do okay before."

"He's seventy, Zen. He can't do that anymore."

"So you're supporting him, even after what I told you."

"When we're done here, can I talk to you privately about something?"

When she didn't respond, Marc continued. "He's not well, you know."

"That's bullshit. He'll outlive all of us!" Zenzi said.

"I'm not so sure of that."

"Well, this plan won't work if he's living there. I won't allow it."

"Are you sure he's not a citizen, Marc?" Nick asked.

"He says he's not. You've got the law degree. How can I prove or disprove it?"

"Do you think you could get power-of-attorney over him?"

"I don't know."

"Well, if you could, then it would be easy to check. But it would still take time, and time we don't have. We expect a visit from the social worker next week."

"After Zenzi is gone?" Marc asked.

"Yes, toward the end of the week. They know she's going into rehab. If I can find a place for your father to stay, are you still with us on this plan?"

"I still don't like it, but yes, I'm in."

"What if he stays here, in my apartment, until we can figure something else out?" Nick offered.

"Here?" Zenzi said. "No way."

"Why not?" Nick asked. "You'll be in Texas. Baby Emma and I will be in your apartment. Marc will be upstairs with your sons. What's wrong with him staying here?"

"And treat that louse like a king?"

"Do you have a better idea?"

"C'mon Zen. Let's do it," Marc said after a long awkward silence. "Just make sure you lock up your valuables and nail down anything you want to find there when you return. Nick, I need a minute with Zenzi alone, if you don't mind."

"He's gone, and you're off speaker," she told Marc. "What's up?"

"Dad told me he was never aware of Harley Cooper doing anything to you, and I believe him. He said if he had, he would have killed him."

"Well, you go right ahead and believe him. I don't."

"Zen..."

"That son of a bitch lied to us the whole time we were growing up—where he was half the time, who he was with, what happened to his paycheck. Let me tell you something. I don't know if you know this or not, but after Mom died, I started wetting the bed. Well, Dad didn't want to have to deal with that, so you know what he told me? He said kids who wet the bed are taken away from their homes by the police. You know how many nights I slept in the bathtub after that? So tell me why should I believe him now."

Marc hung up the phone wishing he could go back in time and be a better protector for his sister. He had never considered the effect losing their mother must have had on her—the effect it would have had on any five-year-old girl.

A text message came in from Jessica.

Asshole

Chapter 24

Without having told anyone where he was going, Marc drove north on I-294. It was Saturday morning. He had dropped the boys off at Nick's apartment the previous night for their weekend with Zenzi. He felt rested, uninhibited, and strangely calm.

He had stayed only a short time at Nick's—long enough to witness a heartwarming reunion between Zenzi and her boys. Nick and Sonya had been warm and welcoming to them as well, and Marc felt at ease leaving them there. Sonya had invited him to stay for dinner, but he'd declined.

The duffle bag on the passenger seat contained a change of clothes, toiletries, and his laptop. He planned to get as far away as he could—away from all the drama that was consuming his life.

53 MILES TO MILWAUKEE, the highway sign said.

He concentrated on his driving and nothing else. The farther he drove, the farther away he wanted to be.

His cell phone chirped five times during the first hour of his journey. He ignored it each time.

At the Milwaukee city limits, he contemplated one exit ramp after another—then after passing the last one, kept on driving. A short time later, he found himself in Sheboygan, and needing gas and a restroom, pulled off the expressway and into the first gas station. Deciding on a snack for the road—a can of cream soda and a package of beef jerky—was easy. Deciding on a destination wasn't.

"How far is it to Green Bay?" he asked the man behind the counter.

"Fifty miles or so. Want to buy a map?"

"No, thanks, but I'll take a pack of Newports."

Marc hadn't smoked a cigarette since high school when he thought it was the cool thing to do, so buying a pack now was inexplicable, but he did it anyway.

After paying the man, Marc headed north.

Halfway to Green Bay, he took the Manitowoc exit and drove on county roads the rest of the way. Nothing but farms and rolling hills. Peace and quiet. He turned down the radio, slowed to five miles below the posted speed limit, and engaged the cruise control. The calm emptiness—void of all people, their problems, expectations, and demands—allowed him to concentrate solely on the road ahead of him. No other thoughts were required.

Six hours after leaving home, Marc pulled into a Motel 6 parking lot. He checked in, turned off his phone, and without regard for any of the messages, collapsed on the bed and fell asleep.

* * *

The irritating sound of a backup beeper coming from outside Marc's motel room was enough to waken him, the musty smell of his surroundings reminding him where he had spent the night. The clock on the nightstand said seven-fifteen—he had slept almost ten hours.

From the window he mindlessly watched a big rig going in reverse in the parking lot not twenty feet from his room. When the lengthy truck had finally passed, the bright light from the new-day sun momentarily blinded him, forcing him to close his eyes for a minute and allow the warm rays to calm his face. When the sun disappeared behind a mass of low, hazy clouds that had rolled in, his thoughts reverted to his current state of affairs. Within seconds, rain pellets smacked hard against the window.

Marc's phone had logged two voice-mail and eleven text messages. Both voice-mail messages were from Jessica as were five of the text messages. Zenzi had sent him three texts, Juan two, and there was one from Nick.

Afraid of what Jessica had to say, he skipped to Juan's texts.

Lite crew 2day. Will be working myself.

Big blower busted again. Needs repair.

Then Zenzi's.

Going 2 rehab Monday.

Nick wants 2 move in Thursday at latest.

Why don't u answer?

And from Nick.

Can u call or text asap?

After a long lukewarm shower, Marc emerged from the bathroom and for several seconds stared at the faded image of a lone sunflower that hung slightly crooked on the dingy grey wall behind the bed, wondering why anyone would have purchased something so depressing for a motel room. After straightening it, he retrieved a towel from the bathroom and laid it across the soiled upholstered seat of the only chair in the room.

He glanced at his open duffle bag, which revealed a photo of himself and Gabby that he had taped to the cover of his laptop. It was the only photo he had of her—a selfie he had taken when they were in Millennium Park one day, the mirror-like Cloud Gate sculpture in the background reflecting their backs and the Chicago skyline down Michigan Avenue. He removed it from the laptop and smiled at the quirky upward tilt of her mouth that she got whenever she had to hold a smile too long. He crumpled it up and lobbed it toward the wastebasket in the corner of the room and missed.

After a while, he couldn't stand seeing the defaced photo lying on the floor any longer and finally picked it up and dropped it in the wastebasket. He stared at it for several more seconds before returning to the chair.

Why he had chosen this cheap, run-down motel room to clear his head and soothe his wounded state of mind eluded him.

His thoughts drifted to his screwed-up family and how that affected his purpose in life. He pictured himself fifty years in the future, slouched in a shabby recliner in some god-forsaken old folks' home, being asked what his greatest accomplishment in life had been. His biggest fear was that his answer would be surviving the care and handling of his dysfunctional family members.

Tired of the energy he was having to spend on others, he thought about ways out from underneath it all—the sacrifices, the aggravation, and the frustration of dealing with things he couldn't control. "Family is everything" Marc had heard people say a million times. He wanted to accept that as a fundamental truth, but hard as he tried, he couldn't. *Freedom is everything*, he thought.

Why should he have to take care of everybody? Nick had money. Let him take care of Zenzi and the boys. And if not him, the state. And his father? Screw him— he'd never been there for Marc.

He closed his eyes and tried to relax the muscles in his face and then down the rest of his body as he reminded himself of the purpose for this trip.

After several minutes, Marc checked his phone—no new messages. He considered opening the ones Jessica had sent earlier but then decided against it. After responding to the messages from Juan, Zenzi, and Nick, he called Meinhard's cell phone. His call went directly to voice mail, an indication that Meinhard had been fiddling with the settings again.

For the next hour, Marc contemplated what his life had become, what he'd rather it be, and what he could do about it. Five minutes before checkout time, having more questions than answers, he packed up his things and took one last look at the dismal room, relinquished photo, and unopened pack of Newports.

He emerged from the motel and stood in the doorway under the shelter of the building's eaves while the rain came down in ragged diagonal sheets, the echo of the massive raindrops hammering against his vehicle making it seem like he was in the middle of a battlefield rather than a Motel 6 parking lot. Wincing as the rain pelted his face, he ran to his car, dove into the driver's seat, and slammed the door shut. With nothing but the previous day's dirty laundry to his avail, he wiped his face, blotted his hair, and sopped up the water puddles on the seat.

Dark thick clouds and heavy rain meant turning on the car's headlights in order to see anything in front of him. As he drove through the lot, water trickled down his neck and torso, the dampness on his skin causing him to shiver as he pulled out onto the glassy street that led to the highway. He slowed down as he approached Main Street. A right turn would lead him home. Left meant distancing himself further from it. An impatient driver behind him blew his horn. Marc turned right.

As he drove, one question kept coming back to nag him: What was he most grateful for? Jessica had asked him this during one of their late-night talks after they'd had a few beers, and for some reason it had never left his mind. He was pretty sure the answer to that question would lead him down the right path, but he didn't know the answer when Jessica had asked and didn't know it now.

By the time he was halfway home, a throbbing headache had such a tight grip on him that he felt compelled to pull off the expressway and into a strip-mall parking lot. He parked in the most remote spot, rested his head against the headrest, and closed his eyes. When he opened them, he felt no better and pounded his fist on the dashboard, causing his GPS device to detach from the windshield and fall to the floor. Not bothering to see where it had landed, he reached across the passenger seat for his duffle bag where he kept his Xanax and aspirin—the crunching sound of plastic from his stepping on the GPS device only adding to his despair.

To ensure the weekend was a complete disaster, he finally decided to see what Jessica had on her mind. He read her five text messages in the order they had been received.

Can we talk?

Where r u?

R the boys with u?

Not asking 2 much 2 talk. U owe me that much.

I hate you.

Then her two voice-mail messages.

All I can say Marc Nussbaum is that you better be lying in a ditch somewhere unable to return my calls because if you're not, so help me...

I hope you're okay.

Instead of driving out of the parking lot and heading south toward home, Marc pointed the car east, in the direction of Lake Michigan. Twenty minutes later, when he neared the lake, he pulled into a lot adjacent to the local yacht club and parked in the first row, close to the water.

Looking out over the vast milky grey surface of the water under the dingy post-storm sky, he became mesmerized by a series of ill-defined clouds drifting in from the north. A silvery veil of mist floated close to the surface of the water, indicating the air was cooler than the water beneath it. He watched the mist move from side to side, then front to back as though hiding something within its billowy orb. He studied its seductive movements and wanted to be in it, wanted to be the something it was hiding.

A breeze brought the moisture to his face, filling his nostrils with sweet dampness. He closed his eyes, welcoming the graveyard quiet of the surroundings that encircled him.

The intensity of the moment held him captive for he didn't know how long. He perceived himself floating around in the mist, inside the suspended water particles, in space somewhere between fantasy and reality. It felt good being there—isolated, carefree, as though under water—out of touch with whatever was going on above the surface.

He pictured Gabby inside of it with him, blissfully floating around in the thick, silent air where everything moved slower than in the world outside. He fantasized hearing her laugh again, the feel of her touch, and the sound of his cell phone's ring tone when she called. "I Hope You Dance" was her favorite song. They had often listened to it, sometimes while they made love.

Promise me that you'll give faith a fighting chance,
And when you get the choice to sit it out or dance,
I hope you dance.

He allowed his mind to wander while he gave thought to the meaning of the lyrics when suddenly Jessica's question about what he was grateful for started to have meaning. He turned the question around and asked himself what would he be most grateful for in life if he could turn back time and have anything he wanted. The answer to that question was clear.

While he let that thought simmer, it also became clear to him that the faith he needed to give a fighting chance was the faith he had in himself—faith to make the right choices in life.

A soft breeze swept in and pushed out the mist, leaving the flat surface of the water a still blank canvas. He closed his eyes while the song played in his head until he reached a line that jolted him into a disturbing realization about what he had almost done.

When you come close to sellin' out reconsider

Marc took in one last dose of the quietude before getting in the car and pointing it south—toward home.

It was time to dance.

Chapter 25

On the rest of the drive home, Marc couldn't stop himself from recalling his worst memories from childhood—feelings he had suppressed over the years because they were so painful—scared he wouldn't earn enough money cutting lawns and shoveling snow to help put food on the table, feeling unwanted when his father chose to be in a bar rather than home, ashamed of what they didn't have and jealous of what other kids did. And then it occurred to him that what he currently wanted for himself and those around him was the antithesis of these feelings. Thinking about his childhood from that perspective was insightful—a welcome change.

A few blocks from home, needing a few minutes to mentally prepare for whatever he was going to find there, he turned into a drugstore parking lot and drove to the farthest corner. Unlike the past, the churning in his stomach wasn't telling him he should be avoiding a certain situation—it was motivating him to delve in and do something about it.

After collecting his thoughts, Marc headed for home, but not before running into the drugstore to buy the biggest box of chocolates they had. The meeting with Jessica wasn't going to be easy.

* * *

Once inside Zenzi's apartment, Marc settled in on the living room sofa and texted her to let her know he was home. She responded.

>Will drop boys off tomorrow 7 AM. Will u be home?

>Yes

>Then for the harder one.

IOU apology, explanation, more. I'm such a jerk. Can we please talk?

Jessica didn't respond right away. Her car was parked out back, so he knew she was home. Ten agonizing minutes later, she replied.

Esp the jerk part. Tyler is with Al. Where r the boys?

With Zenzi n Nick until tomorrow AM.

U can come down if u want.

Be right there.

He grabbed the chocolates and a six-pack from the fridge before proceeding down to her apartment. She greeted him at the door.

"Please don't hate me," he told her.

"I'll let you know how I feel after I hear what you have to say for yourself."

He handed her the chocolates.

"And don't think for a minute that this will make everything okay," she said waving the box in the air.

"I know. It was just a little something I thought couldn't hurt."

She snatched the beer from him and put it in her fridge. "I want to talk without involving any of this."

"Okay. That's fair."

He followed her into the living room where he heard a song he recognized from *The Magic Flute,* an opera Gabby had dragged him to after they'd first met.

"I didn't know you liked classical music."

"There's a lot you don't know about me."

He sat on one end of the sofa, and she sat on the other with her legs tucked up underneath her, looking directly at him with an expressionless face and not saying a word.

"You're not going to make this easy for me, are you?"

She still didn't say anything.

"Okay. First of all, I'm sorry I've been avoiding you these past few days."

"It's been a week."

"A week. I know it's been a week."

"Eight days to be exact."

"Eight days. Eight days is too long. I know. Can I ask you a question before I

151

do the explaining part?"

"Depends on the question."

"Why did you leave that night?"

Her piercing stare made him more uncomfortable than he already was if that was possible. After a long moment, she responded. "I left because...you dozed off, leaving me there to try to figure out on my own what had just happened. I got mad and left."

"What *had* just happened?" he asked.

"I don't know. Thanks to you, I still don't know what to think."

"Well, I don't know either. In fact..."

"In fact what?"

"This is going to sound really stupid, but I don't even know *what* we did."

"Isn't that what we were just talking about?"

"No, I mean the act. I don't know what we physically did."

"You're kidding."

"I was drunk. I don't remember much past taking our clothes off."

"Thanks a lot, Romeo. I impressed you that much?"

"No, that's not...so we *did* do it?"

"You really don't know, do you?"

"I'm afraid not."

"The heart-shaped birthmark on your ass was a pleasant surprise. Does that clear things up for you?"

"Shit! I'm sorry I missed the event," he said through a grimace.

"Yeah, well, you should be."

"Were we careful?"

"It's a good thing one of us was thinking clearly. Yes, we were careful."

"How careful?"

"You had a condom in your wallet."

"Whew!"

"You're too much."

"We were talking about what happened...in the significance sense," he continued. "And that's probably why I kept avoiding you—because I didn't know how to interpret what had happened. That, and I didn't know what you were thinking, so—"

"We don't seem to be getting anywhere."

"You're right. So let's...as I recall, I don't think either one of us made the first move. We kind of made it together. Agree?"

She nodded. "And there was alcohol involved."

"Excessive alcohol," he said.

"Yep."

"So we're in agreement, I think, that maybe we both wanted something to happen, but alcohol turned that 'maybe' into 'let's do it.' How am I doing?"

"The question is how much of a role did the alcohol play," she said.

"Yeah."

They locked gazes for a long moment. She was the first to look away.

"Is this as uncomfortable for you as it is for me?" he asked.

"Look, we need to get it out in the open whether we have feelings for each other...without any alcohol involved. There—I said it."

"Yep. You said it."

"So?"

"I have to go first?"

Her look answered his question.

"I'll be honest, Jessica, when you first moved in, I thought to myself, now there's one hot chick. Sorry, 'attractive woman' is what I meant to say."

"Whatever...thanks for the compliment."

"You're welcome. Anyway, that's what I thought. But then after you told me what happened between you and Al and your divorce was so fresh and I could see your feelings were raw, well, I..."

"You what?"

"I thought maybe it wasn't over between the two of you, and that meant hands off for me."

She rolled her eyes. "Hmph."

"What does that mean?"

"Means...you may have been right."

"May have been or am?"

"I honestly don't know."

They sat and stared at each other while the silence swelled between them.

"Want to know what I think?" he asked.

She nodded.

"If there's any chance of you and Al getting back together, it would be a bad idea for us to explore anything further between us."

She stayed silent for a while and then smiled. "And an even worse idea would be to have too much to drink together...ever again."

He stood up and reached out his hand. "Can we shake on this and officially make up?"

She laughed and followed his lead. "Go back to just friends again?" she asked.

"Like before. Now...how about a beer? I know I could sure use one."

She walked toward the kitchen. "Only one. I'm keeping the rest though."

"There's something else I want to say."

"What's that?" she asked as she handed him a beer.

"Whatever feelings I have...you've been...I mean, I can like be having the worst day, and then we talk, and well, you..."

"I what?"

"Somehow, you make me—"

"Make you what?"

"I'm really bungling this, aren't I?"

"What are you trying to say?"

"I'm not sure, but I want it to be a compliment."

"Hmmm."

"Can I start over?"

"Sure you want to?"

"No."

"I'd say quit while you're ahead, but you're not."

"Can I change the subject then?"

"Go for it."

"Do you find that all men are jerks?"

She smiled. "Your words, not mine." She took a sip of beer. "And you didn't change the subject, by the way."

They sat without talking until it became uncomfortable.

"What about that Malaysian airplane that disappeared into thin air?" he asked.

"Have they found it yet?"

"Last I heard on the news, no."

"Over two hundred people on board."

"Weird."

"Yeah. Pretty weird."

When Marc left her apartment, he climbed the stairs to Zenzi's knowing one thing for sure—he didn't feel the same way about Jessica as he did about Gabby. Of course, they were such different people, how could he? But then he was a different person when he was around Jessica than he had been around Gabby. He wasn't sure what to make of that.

Later, as he showered, he realized he didn't even know exactly what he expected from a relationship—any relationship. He needed to figure that out. But it would have to wait. It had been a long day.

* * *

The next morning, Zenzi, Nick, and the boys arrived promptly at seven. Nick stayed just long enough to say goodbye to the boys before he went to his car to wait for Zenzi who wanted some alone time with Marc.

After the boys went to their bedroom, Marc asked her how the weekend went.

"It was hard. Nick and I talked about it beforehand. We wanted it to be a nice weekend because I won't be seeing them for a while, but like Nick said, if we made it too good, they'd wonder why I had to go away."

"So did it go okay?"

"Yeah. Nick made sure it did." She paused. "He's not such a bad person, you know."

"You're in agreement this is the best thing…for you *and* the boys. Right?"

She shrugged.

"Zenzi."

"I suppose."

The distant look in her eyes said something else.

"You sure?"

"Yeah."

"You don't sound it."

"Look, in a few hours I'll be on a plane to a place a thousand miles away where I can't drink or see my boys, with people I don't know making me do things I'm sure I won't want to do. Don't expect me to be excited about this."

"I don't. Is that all that's bothering you, or is there something else?"

"That's not enough?"

"That's not what I meant. I only—"

"I'll get through it…somehow."

"And it'll be worth it in the end, right?"

She nodded. "Nick's going with me to Texas to make sure I get settled in okay."

"That's good. So was Sonya there this weekend too?"

"No. Just the five of us. She came by a couple of times but didn't stay. Baby Emma missed her, I could tell. So did Nick, I suppose."

Zenzi said her last goodbyes to the boys and raced out of the apartment without saying anything more to Marc. When Marc went to the boys' room to tell them to get ready for school, Riley gave him a look that Marc didn't know how to interpret.

"What's wrong?"

"Nothing."

"Do you want to talk about your visit at Nick's?"

No response.

"Did you have a good time?"

"Yeah," Riley said.

"What all did you do?"

155

"Nothing…just family stuff."

Family stuff?

"What are we having for dinner?" Josh asked.

"We can talk about it in the car on the way to school," he told him. "Let's go. So what all did you do there?"

"Can we cook something here for dinner?" Josh asked.

"Like what?"

"Nick cooked hamburgers on the grill. I liked that."

"He has a grill?"

"Yeah. On the balcony."

"They were awesome," Riley added.

"Well, we don't have a grill," Marc said.

"Maybe we could buy one."

"Maybe."

"Nick had barbecue potato chips too."

"Thanks. That's good to know." He paused while he took in their somber expressions. "If you don't want to talk about the weekend, that's okay."

"We're just sad she's gone," Josh said.

"Me too."

Chapter 26

The next day, Marc helped Jessica move her refrigerator in order for her to retrieve something important Tyler had shoved under it. When he was halfway up the stairs going back to Zenzi's apartment, he heard screaming.

"What's going on in here?" he shouted as soon as he entered the kitchen.

"We're in here," Riley shouted back.

Marc rushed to the boys' bedroom where Riley was hovering over Josh who was lying on the floor next to an overturned vacuum cleaner, his body twisted around it like a pretzel. The smell of burnt rubber permeated the room.

"What on earth?"

"Josh's shirt got sucked into the vacuum," Riley explained.

"What?" Marc kneeled down to assess the situation and then turned around to make sure the vacuum cleaner had been unplugged. "How in God's name did you manage to do this?"

"Can you just get me outta this thing?" he wailed.

Marc tried to turn the brush-rollers in reverse in order to release Josh's t-shirt, but it was wrapped around it so tightly, it wouldn't budge.

"I don't understand how—"

"The wheel or something is poking me in the ribs, can you *please* get me—"

"I'm going to have to cut you out of this. Riley, go get a pair of scissors."

"Scissors?"

"Yes. Scissors."

"I don't think we have any."

"You don't have scissors?"

"My ribs hurt!"

"Riley, go down to Jessica's and ask her if she has a pair of scissors we can borrow."

"So *everybody* has to know?" Josh asked.

"Do you want out of this or not? Riley, go!"

A few minutes later, Riley came back with a small pair of blunt-tip scissors designed for young children.

"What's this?" Marc asked.

"It's what she gave me."

"Can't you just rip it off of me? I think I'm getting rogame."

"Rogame?"

Marc looked at Riley for a translation.

"Beats me," he said.

"Rogame. Your skin gets red when you've rubbed it on the carpet or something."

"That's rug burn, you moron," Riley said.

"Stop calling me names!"

"Will you both shut up for a minute?" Marc stood up. "Don't anyone move. I'll get a better pair of scissors from upstairs."

"You know *I* won't be going anywhere," Josh mumbled.

"Would a razor blade work?" Riley asked.

"You've got one?"

"In the medicine cabinet."

Marc took one blade from the box and then put the box in his pocket for safekeeping.

"Josh, your shirt is wound so tight against your body, I'm afraid I'll cut you if I try to do it with this blade. Riley, hand that little scissors back to me. It might work after all."

Marc went to work on his shirt.

"Ow!"

"Stop wriggling, okay?"

Josh stopped moving but let out a plaintive moan.

"Josh, you're going to have to let me poke this scissors between your shirt and skin. It's blunt—so it won't hurt you."

"That's easy for you to say!"

"Well, hold your breath or something."

When Marc finally did get the scissors in position, it took him a long time to cut the fabric just an inch due to the dullness of the blades. When he had a few inches cut, he was able to tear it the rest of the way, freeing Josh from his predicament.

"Turn around," Marc told him. "Let me look at you."

Josh lifted up what was left of his t-shirt and turned around.

"I don't see any cuts or anything, just some redness."

"It felt like my skin was being ripped off, and now I'm kinda stiff."

Marc pressed lightly on his chest, stomach, and back. "Does anything hurt?"

"Not too much. I really thought I was going to ventilate down there."

"Ventilate?"

"Hyperventilate?" Riley asked, rolling his eyes.

Josh nodded.

"So tell me, how did this happen?" Marc asked.

"Well, it all started when Mrs. Gunther brought over some oatmeal raisin cookies, you know, the kind with the smashed red thing in the middle?" Josh explained.

"The Maraschino cherry?"

"Whatever. Anyway, I brought one in here and got crumbs on the floor, and I thought I better get rid of them before you got back, so I got the vacuum and tried to use it but the crumbs were too close to the wall so I laid the vacuum cleaner down and got down on my hands and knees to brush them away from the wall so the vacuum cleaner could get to them and that's when my shirt got caught and it sucked me in."

"Why did you lay it down?" Marc asked. The vacuum cleaner was an upright.

Josh shrugged.

"Well, I'd say you're lucky you didn't hurt yourself even more doing that. From now on, don't touch anything that has an on-off switch unless I'm around."

"What about the lights?" Josh asked.

"Okay, except the lights. You can touch those."

"The toaster?"

"Okay, the toaster too."

"What about a flashlight? Sometimes I need one to find things under my bed."

"What's for dinner?" Riley asked.

"My Fart Blaster gun takes batteries, and it's got an on-off switch. Does that count?"

"What do you want for dinner?" Marc asked.

"Wanna see it?"

"See what?" Marc asked.

"My Fart Blaster gun."

"No, that's okay."

"Can we have pizza?"

"Can I have a cookie first?"

"Yes to pizza. No to the cookie until after dinner. Let's have the pizza delivered, and while we wait, I need to talk to you about something."

"About the vacuum cleaner?"

"No, about something—"

Marc's phone interrupted him. It was Meinhard.

"There's nothing here for dinner," he said.

"Did you look in the freezer?"

"I told you there's nothing here."

"Hold on a minute." Marc put his hand over the phone. "Are you guys okay with Grandpa joining us for pizza? He needs to be part of this discussion anyway."

The boys each shrugged.

"Can you come down here, Dad? I need to talk to you, and then you can join the boys and me for pizza if you want."

"What are we talking about?"

"Can you just come down to find out, please?"

"Fine."

Marc called in the pizza order.

"How long?" Josh asked.

"An hour."

"Is he coming down?"

"Yes."

The back door opened and Meinhard walked into the kitchen.

"Where are we sitting? In here?"

"I thought we would, unless, of course, you'd be more comfortable in the living room."

Meinhard sat in the only remaining seat at the table. "Speak," he said.

"There's going to be a change in the living arrangements," Marc said.

"And we don't get any say in it, right?" Riley asked.

"Smart kid," Meinhard mumbled.

Marc reconsidered what he was about to say to Meinhard's remark. "Dad, you will be moving into an apartment in the South Loop," he said instead.

"What the—"

"It's a nice apartment right on Michigan Ave—"

"What the hell am I supposed to—"

"Dad. Your language."

"So what the heck am I supposed to do there?"

"It's temporary until you find a permanent place to live."

"Why can't I stay upstairs...in my own house?"

"First of all...never mind that. Because the boys and I are going to stay there."

"What?" Riley asked.

"What the..." Josh added.

"So who's going to live here?" Riley asked.

"Nick and Baby Emma."

"Who?" Meinhard asked.

Marc was about to respond when there was a knock at the back door. He paid the pizza delivery guy, asked the boys to set the table, and made sure everyone had drinks and pizza before continuing the conversation.

"Dad, you don't know this but last year Zenzi married a man named Nicholas Lee, and they had a baby girl. They call her Baby Emma."

"You've got to be kidding. Like she—"

"Dad, this may be a good time to keep your opinions to yourself."

"So why don't they live together? Or is that none of my business too?"

"Their relationship is complicated. That's about all I can say about it."

"So why all this shuffling around?" Meinhard asked. "Or is that—"

"Like I said, it's all a little complicated."

"But why would—"

"Dad, I'm telling you all I know at this time. Can you just accept it for now?"

"I'm not one of your kids."

Josh faced his grandfather with wide eyes. "Neither are we."

Chapter 27

"What the hell am I supposed to do there?" Meinhard asked Marc the day he was to move to Nick's apartment.

"What do you do here?" he asked him.

"Nothing. You stick me upstairs all by myself with a TV that you need a college degree to use and expect me to be grateful...in my own house. Prisoners are treated better."

"You can always find another place to stay if you don't like these arrangements."

"You'd like that, wouldn't you?"

"Don't push me, Dad. I'm in a frame of mind these days that...never mind."

"What am I supposed to eat there? Or do I get to eat?"

"Really? Is that your biggest concern? You want to know what *my* biggest concern is?"

"Not really."

"I didn't think so."

Marc grabbed Meinhard's bag of possessions.

"Do I need to check this for anything of mine that just happened to make its way in there?"

"I found my old camera in your closet. I took it. You got a problem with that?"

Marc had completely forgotten about his father's passion for photography, initially in Germany and then to a lesser degree when he came to the U.S. One of the few things Marc admired about his father was his ability to shoot extraordinary photographs of buildings, landscapes, animals, strangers—unfortunately, never the family.

"What ever happened to all the photos you had?"

"Found those too." He took the bag from Marc and headed toward the back door. Marc followed.

They drove to Nick's apartment, and immediately after entering, Meinhard selected a bedroom and shut the door. Marc checked the fridge, freezer, and cupboards where he found at least a week's worth of food readily available. Nick—who was staying with Sonya until Zenzi's apartment was ready for him to move into—had at least thought of that.

"Call me if you need anything, Dad," he shouted. "And plug your phone in every once in a while, will you?"

No response.

Marc took a quick mental inventory of Nick's belongings and left.

It was a warm day, warmer than usual for the middle of March, and when Marc returned home, Riley and Josh were sitting on Zenzi's small deck.

"We're not moving," Riley said.

"You're not moving from those chairs, or you're not moving upstairs?"

"Upstairs."

"Why?"

"This is our home."

"Well, you have no choice. You're moving upstairs. It's temporary. Get over it."

As soon as he said it, he realized he shouldn't have.

Josh burst into tears.

"Now look what you've done," Riley said. He got up to console his brother, mumbling under his breath, "Idiot," loud enough for Marc to hear.

Marc followed the boys into their apartment and sat down at the kitchen table. His chirping phone showed an incoming text message.

I'd like to move in tomorrow AM. Is everything ready?

It was from Nick.

What time?

Around 9.

Ok. We'll be out by then.

Marc went into the boys' room.

"Josh?"

"Yeah."

"Are you okay?"

"No."

"I'm sorry I was so..."

"Mean?"

"I'm sorry. Look, boys, I don't like all this moving around any more than you do. But sometimes we have to do things we don't really want to do. That's life. It's not always fair. The move is temporary, just until Nick can get established."

"Where?" Riley asked.

"I don't know where."

"What about the baby?"

"What about her?"

"Will she stay with Nick?" Riley asked.

"Yes, I think so."

"Hmph," Riley said with a scowl.

"What's the matter?" Marc asked.

"Nothing."

"Why the face?"

"Nothing!" Riley spat out and left the room.

Marc looked at Josh.

"We were thinking..."

"What were you thinking?"

"That maybe when Mom gets home, we'd be a family or something," Josh said.

"Who all would be a family?"

"Mom, Nick, and us."

"Oh."

Marc let that sink in for a moment.

"Not Baby Emma?" Marc asked.

"Nope."

"You have a big mouth, turd-face," Riley said as he reentered the room.

"Quit calling me names, jerk-bucket."

"Both of you stop it," Marc said. He turned to Riley. "So what's wrong with Emma?"

"We just don't like her."

"But she's your sister."

"She doesn't feel like a sister. She never even lived with us."

"Pets are better," Josh added.

"I know some of this doesn't make sense to you. To be honest, it doesn't all make sense to me either, but for now I'm asking you real nice to go along with the plan. Can you do that for me?"

"Fine."

"Fine."

"Okay, let's grab your things and get you settled in."

Their closet didn't contain much—a couple of shirts hanging lopsided on hangers and one bathrobe. He checked their dresser drawers and found only a couple of pairs of pants, shorts, and t-shirts for each of them. No underwear or socks. He checked the laundry basket in their closet. It was half full.

"Are these all your clothes?"

"Yeah."

"C'mon boys. Let's go."

"Where?"

"Shopping."

"For what?"

"Clothes."

"And a grill?" Josh asked.

"And a grill."

They drove to the nearby Sears store, and by the time they had finished, Marc had a small outdoor grill and each boy had a week's worth of clothing for school and a few more outfits for play. When they arrived home, he helped them cart their things upstairs and get settled in the spare bedroom, the one Meinhard had vacated.

"It kinda smells in here," Josh said.

Marc agreed—hadn't Meinhard been showering? He retrieved the air freshener from the bathroom and sprayed the room.

"What about you guys? Have you been taking showers?"

"Sometimes," Josh said.

"How often is sometimes?"

"When I think of it and it's not too late."

"Like every other day?" Marc asked.

Josh shook his head.

"Every three days?"

He shrugged.

"Okay, here's the deal. I'll always shower in the morning before you guys get up. Josh, you shower Monday, Wednesday, and Friday. Riley, you've got Tuesday, Thursday, and Saturday. How does that sound?"

"Clean. It sounds really clean," Josh said.

"And wash your hair too," Marc added.

"With shampoo?"

"Yes, with shampoo."

"What about Sunday?"

"You'll have a reprieve on Sunday."

Josh's face lit up. "We're getting a dog?"

"Not a retriever, you dope," said Riley. "A repriever."

Marc smiled. "You're both wrong, but that's okay. No one has to shower on Sunday. How's that?"

"Why didn't you just say that in the first place? Here I thought we were getting a dog."

* * *

A week later, Marc got a call from Nick, who had moved into Zenzi's apartment with Emma a few days earlier. He had not seen him since the move.

"Can the boys come home now? Mrs. Schmidt from the Department of Immigration is here and wants to talk with them for a minute." Marc could tell he was on a speakerphone. It was a call Marc had been expecting—he just hadn't known when it would come.

"Yes, of course. They'll be right down."

"Boys," he called to them. Riley and Josh had also been expecting the call.

"The lady from the Department of Immigration is downstairs. You know the drill."

Riley saluted. Josh followed suit.

"I'm serious, guys. This is important."

"We know," Riley said with attitude.

"I'll see you in a bit."

All he could hope for was that the boys went along with the story—that they lived with Nick and Emma and everything was normal except for their mother being in a hospital in Texas. Nick was their stepdad, Emma was their stepsister, and Uncle Marc lived upstairs. One big happy family, he thought as he popped a Xanax.

A half hour later they returned.

"So how'd it go?" he asked.

They shrugged.

"What did you talk about?"

"Nothing," Riley said.

"She asked to see our room," Josh added.

"And what did she say when she saw it?"

"She said it was pretty neat for a boys' room."

"And then what did you say?"

"Nothing."

"Anything else?"

"It's a lot neater down there, not like we left it."

"Sounds good to me."

"Not as neat as it is here though. Nobody's *that* neat."

Marc wanted to take that as a compliment but was sure Riley was being critical, not patting him on the back.

As soon as Riley went back to his room, Marc called Nick.

"So how did it go?"

"I think it went fine. Hard to tell."

"Were the boys okay?"

"Yes. Maybe a little rehearsed, but they were fine. We should probably mess up their room a little for next time though."

"When will that be?"

"I can't get advance notice with this one, so I don't know."

"What did she say about Zenzi being away?"

"She knew the story before she got here. She asked for a contact name there. That's about all."

"Probably to verify she's there."

"Probably."

"Is everything okay down there? Do you need anything?"

"Don't worry about me," Nick said. "If I need anything, I'll get it on my own."

Marc had a difficult time dealing with Nick's enigmatic personality. He was charming—there was no disputing that. And at times he appeared to be giving and considerate. But an underlying aura of slyness and dishonesty tainted any positive characteristics Nick had and kept Marc from trusting him.

"Okay. Talk to you later."

"So why did you have to call Nick when we already told you how it went?" Riley asked.

"Yeah. Why did you have to do that?" Josh added.

"Sometimes a child's perspective isn't the same as an adult's. I just wanted to—"

"Just say it. You still don't trust us!" Riley snapped. "C'mon, Josh."

The angry thump of their footsteps echoing down the hall was followed by the deafening slamming of their bedroom door.

Marc marched after them and swung their door open so hard it shook the wall.

"That does it! If you slam this door, or any other door, one more time, I'm going to beat your behinds with a—"

Josh immediately started crying.

"You can't touch us," Riley said. "We'll call DCFS."

"Oh, yeah? And then where will you end up? Leave this door open...always!"

Marc retreated to the living room and collapsed in his easy chair. Just the other evening he had Googled a few articles on raising preadolescent boys that included tips on how to keep from losing your temper. He made a mental note to reread them.

Chapter 28

"How much longer until you get your green card, and then what happens after that?" Marc asked Nick.

A week had passed since Nick had moved into the second-floor apartment, and Marc didn't know any more about Nick's situation than he had at their initial meeting.

"At this point, it will take as long as they want. I have no way of knowing. My guess is that they will grant it when they're satisfied with how I'm living, my future plans, etc. As far as what's next, a green card is good for ten years. It will allow me to get a job, a Social Security card, a driver's license. I can be a regular citizen...at least for ten years."

"So you get this green card and what happens to you and Zenzi?"

"As we've said before, we will get a divorce."

"And that won't raise a few eyebrows with the Immigration Department?"

"I know others who have done it, and they are still here."

"Are you going to move back to your apartment right after you get it?"

"That is my intent. How is your father doing there?"

"Okay, I guess. I haven't checked up on him yet."

"Sonya is going to spend weekends here, if that is okay with you."

Marc gave that a moment's thought.

"I don't see a problem with that."

"Are we okay then?" Nick asked.

"I guess so."

It didn't feel right. After he hung up, Marc went on the Internet, found the local number for the Department of Immigration, and put it in his wallet along with the number he had found earlier for the Department of Children and Family Services. Then he contemplated contacting Jessica...to talk some things through like they had done so many times before. They had run into each other a few times since "the fling" talk but had not really spent much time together.

Can we talk?

She didn't respond right away, causing Marc to think maybe he should have put more into his text about what it was he wanted to talk about. Five minutes passed. Then five more, increasing Marc's angst.

Come down if u want.

Be right there.

He poured himself a cup of coffee and took it down to her apartment.

"What's up, Markus?" she asked.

"No one but my father ever calls me that."

"I know," she said without smiling.

She was in her work uniform.

"When do you have to leave for work?"

"Half hour."

"That may not be enough time."

"For what?"

"For all that's going on, and I need a second opinion, someone to tell me I'm not going crazy."

"Maybe you are."

"You'd tell me if I was?"

"Not my area of expertise."

They sat down at her kitchen table.

"So what's making you feel crazy?"

"Being away those two days allowed me to do a lot of thinking—about the important things in life. And things were pretty clear in my head on the drive home, but now..."

"Not so clear?"

"I have so many thoughts running through there, I can't seem to keep them all straight—if I could just put some order to them and take one at a time, it would help."

"You want orderly thoughts."

"Saying it that way makes it sound really stupid."

She laughed.

"What's so funny?"

"You."

"Why?"

"Because everything about you has to be orderly. In its proper place. Easy to find. Perfect."

"What are you talking about?"

"That's how you are."

"Give me an example."

She paused for a few seconds. "Like your sock drawer."

"My sock drawer? How do you know what's in my sock drawer?"

"So I'm nosy. I peeked one day."

"What's wrong with my sock drawer?"

"Please." She used her hands to further illustrate her point. "On the left side of the drawer are all your socks—each pair neatly rolled into the same-size little bundle, lined up by color. The first row is all black, then brown, and they go on to the last row which are white."

"So I'm neat."

"Then there's a divider, actually there are two dividers."

"What did you do—take pictures?"

"In the middle section are your handkerchiefs. All neatly folded. Two piles—one for the whites, and the other for the coloreds."

"All I—"

"Then in the last compartment are your ties, again all perfectly folded and displayed."

"Okay, so how did Al keep his socks?"

"After I washed them, I threw them in a drawer, and when he needed a pair, he fished around until he found two that matched."

"My system is much more efficient."

"Everything in its proper place. Easy to find. Perfect."

"How did we get on this subject anyway?"

"Your disorderly thoughts."

"Oh, yeah. Now you've distracted me. Lost my train of thought." A warm flush crept across his cheeks. "I think what I was going to say is that I keep changing my mind about how I feel about things, and then I go back to my original thoughts, and then I don't know what to do. I don't want to make wrong decisions and regret them later. That's what I meant by disorderly thoughts."

"Too bad they're not all perfectly folded and lined up in neat rows."

"You're making a really important point, aren't you?"

"I'm trying."

He stared at her until he had to look away.

"Does all this have to do with the boys, or something else?" she asked.

"They're part of it. Sometimes I feel like I'm doing more harm than good by watching over them. Like what do I know about raising kids? I never even babysat, for crissake, and here I am responsible for two boys. I don't know what I'm doing, yet I have decisions to make all the time with them."

"Wanna know what Riley and Josh think?"

"I don't know. Will it make me feel better or worse?"

"Do you want me to tell you or not?"

"Lay it on me."

"They think you run hot and cold. At times, you're the best uncle they could ever ask for, and then there are other times they think about running away."

"I know about the running-away thing. When I thought Riley had actually done that a while back, it scared the crap out of me."

"Just so you know, I made them promise me that if they do decide to run away that they run away to here."

"Thank you for that. I guess I do run hot and cold. Yesterday, I almost ripped their bedroom door off the hinges so they would never be able to slam it again. Totally lost it."

"I know."

"You heard it all the way down here?"

"Certain noises travel through the heating system."

"I'll have to look into that."

"When Al and I separated, Tyler showed me every chance he got that he was *not* happy with that decision, and he blamed me for it. He had just turned three, and his speech was pretty good—we could understand most of what he said. Well, he stopped talking, but only when he was with me. With Al he was fine. And even though he had been potty-trained for over a year, he started having accidents...only with me and always when we were in the car on our way to somewhere or out in public."

"How awful."

"Tell me about it. And, of course, I was also dealing with the reason I left Al in the first place. And not very well, I have to admit. Then my boss told me if I was late for work one more time, he was going to fire me. There were days I didn't think I could take any more."

"So what did you do?"

"I Googled it."

"Been there too."

"I found out that it helps to understand emotions."

"Yours or the kid's?"

"Everybody's. Now, I know that's hard for most of you guys, but with kids especially, you have to go there. Deal with the emotion, and you're dealing with the problem."

"And that worked with Tyler?"

"Yep. And Al too."

"There should be classes in this stuff."

"I know. And now I have to go, or I'll be late for work."

He got up to leave. "Is being thankful an emotion?"

She smiled. "They say if you can feel it, it's an emotion. You're not going to get all sappy on me now, are you?"

"Come here, you." Marc got up from his chair and reached out to her for a hug. "Thanks for listening."

As Marc climbed the two flights of stairs to his apartment, he took his wallet out of his pocket, retrieved the piece of paper with the number for DCFS, and crumpled it up. Then he went straight to his sock drawer and ransacked it.

* * *

The next day, Marc drove to Lake Forest, and after meeting with Juan about a problem with an irrigation system, they drove to the Trinkos' property where Juan wanted to show him something he had discovered—thanks to their adversarial neighbor Arnie MacCallum—that was growing near the back of the Trinko property line.

After Juan pointed out the bed of plants in question, Marc broke off the stem of one of them and examined it.

"I think this is Farkelberry," he told Juan.

"Never heard of it."

"You don't see it much this far north." He looked at the breadth of the entire patch. "This didn't grow here wild. It was planted. You never noticed it before?"

"I can tell you it wasn't here last spring. I would've remembered it."

Marc stooped down and snipped off a piece of another nearby plant that appeared to be out of place, this one with a hairy stem and irregular-shaped two-tone green leaflets. He sniffed it.

"Might be red clover, but it's hard to tell because it's not blooming yet."

"That's what MacCallum thought too."

"This had to have been planted too—the rows are too even. Why did MacCallum bring this to your attention?"

"He saw deer eating it."

"Ah."

Looking more closely at the bed, Marc noted some of the leaves had been twisted off their stems. Deer alright. Unlike most other mammals, deer didn't have upper central incisors and therefore couldn't clip off vegetation. They had to yank it off.

Juan looked past Marc. "Here he comes," he said.

"What the hell do I have to do to get these morons to stop feeding the goddamn deer?" MacCallum bellowed.

Marc held out his hand. "Hello, Mr. MacCallum. Juan was just showing me these plants."

Arnie's handshake was firm, a little too firm for a friendly conversation.

"Last summer, they put in all those stupid geraniums—or whatever they were that the deer loved—and then in the fall there were all those blasted apples they left to rot on the ground for the deer. Each season it's something new." He turned toward his own yard. "Look at my dogwoods. They'll never be the same. Do you know how much those varmints have cost me ever since the Dinkos moved in here? Well, I'll tell you. It's in the thousands, not to mention the time that Marcia and I put into our garden the first two years, before we fenced it in on all sides including the top of it so the deer couldn't jump in. That was another five hundred. Damn Kinkos."

"It's Trinkos."

"What kind of stupid name is that anyway?"

"I'll talk to them when they get back from vacation, if you like."

"Somebody better, or I'm going to take matters into my own hands!" MacCallum stomped away mumbling obscenities, leaving Marc and Juan looking at each other in silence.

"When do the Trinkos get back?" Juan asked.

"Sunday."

"You're going to call them then?"

"I'm going to call on Rex first. Maybe he'll mediate again."

Marc dropped Juan off at his truck and drove to the boys' school to pick them up.

"So how was school today, boys?" he asked when they were settled in the back seat.

"Okay," Riley said. Josh didn't respond.

"What did you learn, Riley?"

"Not much."

"Well, you must have learned something. Didn't you tell me you were doing fractions?"

"Yeah."

"Well, did you do any of that today?"

"Yeah."

"So how did that go?"

"Okay."

"How about you, Josh? You've been awfully quiet back there. What subjects did you study today?"

"Maryanne Tobin tried to kiss me in the locker room," he blurted out.

"She did? What did you do?"

"I socked her in the arm."

"Josh, you can't hit a girl!"

"She tried to kiss me! Of course I'm gonna hit her."

"You should never hit a girl. And why would you hit someone who was trying to let you know she liked you anyway?"

"I don't like *her.*"

"Why not?"

"She's a girl."

"He'll change," Riley said. "I used to be the same way."

"And now?"

"Girls are okay. They get better later on, Josh. Trust me."

"Yeah, right."

"Can we agree that you'll never hit a girl again?" Marc asked as he pulled into his driveway.

"Not if one tries to kiss me."

Josh was out the door and halfway to the house before Marc could think of a response.

* * *

Lying in bed that night, thinking about Jessica's advice on understanding emotions, Marc analyzed his conversation with Josh about the kissing incident.

When the girl had tried to kiss him, he must have been surprised. Then he got angry. Or maybe embarrassed. Or maybe just annoyed. Repulsed? Uneasy? Confused? Even if Marc guessed right, then what was he supposed to do with that information? He couldn't remember what Jessica had said.

He thought back to his own first kiss. He was sixteen—much older than Josh—and had just gotten his driver's license. He and Martha Kingsley had been an item in school for several months but had never kissed. After relentless hounding, his father had finally given in to Marc borrowing the car to take her to the movies. Marc had given kissing her a lot of thought and had even watched a number of kissing scenes on TV to get pointers. After the movie, they stopped for an ice cream, a decision he'd regretted all the way back to her house when his queasy stomach threatened to throw it back up. When he pulled into her driveway, he knew it was then or never.

He went for it, but afterward he wished he had watched those kissing scenes more closely, because he'd missed her mouth and had ended up kissing her right below her nose, which meant she had kissed his chin. The next day at school Marc heard that she was telling her friends he wasn't a very good kisser. And that was the end of Martha Kingsley.

Chapter 29

"I see Nick has moved out," Jessica said to Marc when they ran into each other coming home at the same time. It had been a month since Nick had moved in.

"Nice try, Jessica. April Fools to you, too."

"I'm not fooling. I saw him load up a van this morning."

"What!"

"Maybe I'm wrong, but it looked to me like he was moving out. All the baby's things, luggage, boxes."

Marc ran up to the second-floor apartment and knocked. When he got no response, he used his key and entered the apartment.

"Anybody home? Nick?"

He walked in. The baby furniture and toys were gone. He texted Nick.

Where r u?

He continued scanning the apartment while he waited for a response. A small white envelope on the kitchen table caught his eye. Inside were a note and key.

April 1, 2015

Dear Marc,

I apologize for leaving in such a hurry, but circumstances were such that it behooved me to move out today. I was granted a green card last week and have made new arrangements for myself and Baby Emma.

I will be in touch with Zenzi regarding the divorce.

Your father may stay in my apartment until the end of the month.
Then he will have to leave as my lease ends at that time.

Thank you for all your help.

Regards,
Nick

So he'd left as soon as he'd gotten what he wanted, without saying a word. Thinking about it, Marc decided that having Nick out of their lives was a good thing, regardless of how unceremoniously he'd left. After he locked up the apartment and went to his own, he called the rehab facility in Texas to leave a message for Zenzi as to what was going on.

"She's no longer here, Mr. Nussbaum."

"What do you mean she's no longer there?"

"She left on Thursday of last week."

"And no one called me?"

"She is of age, sir."

"Do you know where she went?"

"No, I don't."

"She just walked out? What happened?"

Riley entered the living room. "Who walked out?" he asked.

"Just a minute. No, not you. I'm sorry. How could she do that?"

"Our residents are not held captive here. They can leave if they want. We strongly discourage it, of course, but unless they're here under court order, we can't legally detain them."

"Did she have any visitors while she was there?"

"I'm really not at liberty to—"

"Look, I'm very concerned about her. I'm taking care of her two small sons, and I need to know where she is. This is important."

"Hold on a minute."

"What happened to Mom?" Riley asked.

"I'm not sure."

"Where is she?"

"I don't know."

"She had a visitor on Thursday of last week, the day she left. A Mr. Alfonso Ray."

"Did she leave with him then?"

He could hear the woman on the phone talking to another person in the background.

"She left by taxi, alone."

"Where's Mom?" Riley sounded more agitated now.

"Okay. Thank you."

So she had money, at least enough for a taxi. Marc figured Nick must have had this Alfonso guy give her some money so she could leave. No use paying for her rehab once he'd gotten what he wanted from her.

He glanced at Riley, who was now joined by Josh.

"Well, your mom has left the treatment center, but I don't know where she is."

"Just call her on her cell," Riley said.

"She wasn't allowed to bring it with her."

"Well, that sucks!"

"I know. I wish she hadn't left without getting in touch with me. I wish she hadn't left at all." She had been there just a little over a month—not long enough to make much of a difference.

"So now what?" Riley asked.

"Yeah, now what?" Josh added.

"We just have to wait. I have no way of reaching her."

"What about Nick? Maybe she's with him."

He texted Nick.

Do u know where Zenzi is?

"He didn't answer my last text."

"Call him."

Marc called Nick's cell phone. It went to voice mail.

"Nick, please call me. I don't know where Zenzi is, and I'm worried about her. Call me back ASAP."

"He was too nice," Riley said.

"Who?"

"Nick."

"Why do you say that?"

"No one is that nice unless they're up to something."

* * *

Over the course of the next two days, Marc called Nick twice more and texted him once again before Nick finally called him back.

"I don't know where she is, Marc."

"How much money did you give her?"

"Excuse me?"

"You had someone give her money on Thursday of last week, right?"

"Yes."

"How much?"

"Enough to get her home if that's what she wanted to do."

"How much?"

"Five hundred."

"You gave an alcoholic who could walk out of rehab any time she wanted five hundred dollars?"

"She was going to leave one way or another. Would you rather she be out on the street with no money?"

"Thanks a lot, asshole."

Marc hung up on him.

He pictured Zenzi in some fleabag motel room drowning herself in booze. Or worse, lying somewhere passed out with no one around to help her. It had been a week since she had left rehab. He did some quick math and figured five hundred dollars wouldn't last much more than a week given a cheap motel room, a fifth of vodka a day, and some occasional fast food. And of course that wouldn't leave anything for a plane ticket home, not even a bus ticket.

He felt like punching Nick in the face. What was he thinking?

R u coming out today?

The text was from Juan. Marc hadn't been out to any of his sites in two days.

In crisis here. What's wrong?

Can't take more of Mrs. Montana crap. Her grass isn't as green as Hunters. Told her I'd spray paint it. That pissed her off. U deal with her. I'm thru.

I'm on my way.

Marc hoped Juan meant he was through dealing with the clients and not that he was through with his job in general. He shouldn't have made the remark about spray-painting the grass, but it *was* kind of funny.

From his truck, Marc called Tom Wilds, the landscaper who maintained the Hunters' lawn, found out what product he was using, and picked up some of the stuff on his way to meet with Mrs. Montana. It wasn't what he would have recommended to use on their lawn, which was mostly fescue grass, but if it would appease her, so be it.

Damn rich people.

* * *

"Come get me."

It was Zenzi, and she was slurring her words.

"Where are you?"

"Houston...I think."

"How can I come get you if you don't even know where you are?"

She laughed. "Maybe I'm confused, but this too shall piss. I mean pass. I have to piss. That's why I said that."

"It's not funny, Zen."

"Yes, it is."

"Well, you're the only one laughing."

"Well, I'm the only one drunk!"

"I can't help you from a thousand miles away. You need to get help where you are. Find a shelter or something. Get sober, and then call me back. Do you have any money?"

"Do you think I'd be calling you if I had money?"

Marc heard her talking to someone else.

"Who's with you?"

"Somebody I borrowed their phone from someone. Did that make any sense?"

His stomach immediately hardened.

"Can that person help you sober up?"

"He wants to know if you can sober up me?"

"She says 'no.' I gotta go," she said and then hung up.

"Shit."

At least he knew she was alive. His mind went berserk trying to decide what he should or could do. He glanced at his watch. Soccer practice was over and he was late to pick up the boys. Remembering how he felt as a kid who wasn't involved in any extracurricular activities, he'd given in to them when they'd asked to join the soccer team, even though Zenzi hadn't allowed it in the past. He didn't regret having made that decision, but this was totally messing up the routine he had for getting them to and from school.

When he arrived at the soccer field twenty minutes late, Riley and Josh were sitting on the grass, alone.

"It's about time you got here!"

"I'm really sorry, guys. I got here as fast as I could."

"Right."

"I said I was sorry."

Riley mumbled something that sounded a lot like "bullshit."

"What did you say?"

"Nothing."

"What did you say, Riley?"

"I said nothing!"

Feelings. Emotions. He couldn't remember how he was supposed to handle them—he was too angry.

"What's for dinner?" Riley asked.

Marc didn't respond.

"I *said* what's for dinner?"

"Cold cereal, and if you complain about it, you won't even get *that*!"

He wanted to take it back.

"Your mom called."

"She did?" Josh asked.

"Yes."

"Is she coming home?"

"Not right away."

"When then?"

"I'm not sure."

"What did she say?" Riley asked. "Or is that none of our business like everything else?"

"You know, Riley, if you..." He paused, composed himself, and continued. "She wants to come home, but she doesn't have any money."

"So she's going to stay in rehab?"

Marc had never referred to the place where Zenzi was staying as *rehab* in front of the boys. Riley must have figured that out on his own.

"No, she left there."

"Where's she staying then?"

"She had to hang up before she could tell me. She had borrowed someone's phone, and I guess they wanted it back."

"So what's going to happen to her?"

"I told her to find a place to stay until we could figure this all out."

Josh let out a loud whimper.

"Now you made him cry again," Riley said.

"Riley, if I hadn't told you your mom called, you'd have given me shit for that. I can't seem to win here."

"Nice mouth."

"Riley... Josh, what's upsetting you? What are you feeling right now?"

"I'm sad."

"Tell me why, buddy."

"I'm sad that Mom is lost."

"I don't think she's lost." But that's an interesting interpretation, Marc thought.

"And I'm scared."

"What are you scared of?"

"I'm scared that something bad will happen to her. Like a cat trophy."

"A cat trophy?"

"He means catastrophe."

Marc rolled to a stop at the red light and turned around to face the boys. "You know what, Josh?"

"What?"

"I'm scared too."

Chapter 30

"Look, Nick, you had no business sending her money when you knew she could walk out of that rehab at any time. And I'm holding you responsible for her well-being." It was now twenty-four hours since Marc had heard from Zenzi. Out of frustration he had called Nick.

"What do you expect me to do?" Nick asked, his tone indicating annoyance.

"I expect you to find her and either convince her to go back to rehab, and I mean give her good reason to go back, or bring her home. One or the other."

"How am I supposed to find her?"

"You should have thought about that before."

"I don't have the resources to traipse all over Houston looking for her. She's *your* sister."

"And she's *your* wife."

"I can't control what she does."

"Well, maybe you need to rethink that, my friend. Oh, excuse me for a moment while I take this other call. Oh look, it's from the Department of Immigration."

Marc waited several seconds for him to respond.

"I have a contact in Houston. I'll see what I can do to find her."

"You need to do better than that, bro."

"I will find her."

"Just so we understand each other."

"I got your message, Marc."

* * *

"When are you going to go to Texas and bring Mom home?" Riley demanded. "And don't give us any bull."

"How old are you?"

"You know I'm eleven."

"Just making sure. Look, I want her to either go back to treatment or come home just as much as you do, but there's only so much I can do. Nick has someone in Houston looking for her. He's going to try to convince her to go back into treatment, and if she won't do that, then she'll come home, but that doesn't mean she doesn't need more treatment. Your mom is still very sick. I want her to get better. Believe me, more than anything in this world, I want her to get better."

"How come you never say she's in rehab? That's where she is," Riley said.

"Where she's at, or where she was, is more than rehab. It's a treatment center where there are doctors who look at everything. Treating her alcoholism is only part of it. Do you understand that?"

"We're not stupid," Riley responded.

"I know that. And I didn't mean to—"

Marc's phone chirped.

Taking Larry to the ER. Lawnmower accident.

What hospital?

Lake Forest.

On my way. How serious?

Not sure. Could be very.

"What's going on?" Riley asked.

"One of my employees got hurt. You guys can go over to the Gunthers' while I—"

"They aren't home."

"How do you know that?"

"I saw Mrs. Gunther after school yesterday, and she said they were going to visit their daughter for a week. She asked me if I could take in their papers."

"Then you'll have to come with me."

"We have homework."

"You can do it in the truck."

"No, we can't."

"Just get your coats on and let's go."

"Riley, will you help me find my homework? I don't know where—"

"Will you forget about your damn—" Marc stopped himself from finishing the sentence.

"If we get bad grades, it'll be your fault."

"Fine."

"Fine."

"Fine."

It was a thirty-mile drive to Lake Forest Hospital. On the way, Riley asked Marc a question he had asked himself earlier.

"What if Mom comes home and starts drinking again?"

"I'm going to try to make sure that doesn't happen."

"How are you going to do that?"

"I can't. She needs professional help."

"Don't they have it around here?"

"They do, but there are long waiting lists."

"Is she on a waiting list?"

"Actually, I took her off when she entered the treatment center in Texas."

"Shouldn't have done that," Riley mumbled under his breath.

"When is your next soccer game, Riley?"

"Saturday. Why?"

"Just curious."

"You changed the subject."

"Yes, I did."

"Why?"

"Because I have that right."

Larry was in surgery when Marc and the boys arrived. According to Juan, Larry had been cutting someone's lawn on the riding lawnmower when he ran over a child's metal toy. A piece of the toy had shot out from underneath the mower, ricocheted off of something nearby, and embedded itself in his face, missing his eye by a few millimeters. Juan told Marc that the ER doctor who initially treated him said he thought he would make a full recovery, but they wouldn't be certain until he was out of surgery.

"Do you have anyone on the waiting list?" Juan asked. "He's going to be out for a while, and I can't be that short-handed."

"I'm afraid not."

Juan gave him a look that required little interpretation.

"I haven't had time to—"

"That's okay, man, but when one of the Green Bay Six-ers gets upset because someone's lawn across the street looks better than theirs, I'm the one who has to deal with it. I can't take care of twelve lawns, three crews, listen to these rich nutcases complain about the stupidest things, *and* be short-handed. I just can't do it."

"I hear ya. It hasn't been fair to you with me being gone so much. I know. I'm trying to take care of family business, and—"

"I have family business, too. I have a ten-year-old with ADHD, but I don't take off any work because of it." Juan got up to leave. "I have to go back to the job site. See ya later."

"He's mad at you," Riley said.

Marc didn't respond.

They stayed at the hospital until Larry's wife arrived and Larry was out of danger. On the way home, Marc stopped at a drive-through restaurant to pick up dinner. A block from his house, he thought he heard Josh crying in the back seat.

"What's the matter, Josh?"

Josh didn't respond, and when Marc pulled into the driveway Josh bolted out the door.

"Do you know what's wrong, Riley?"

"Nope."

They followed Josh up the stairs.

"What's the matter, buddy?"

"It's our fault!"

"What's your fault?" Marc asked as he unlocked the door.

Josh ran inside. Marc followed him into his bedroom.

"What's your fault, Josh?"

"It's our fault Juan is mad at you."

"What are you talking about? You had nothing to do with it."

"If you didn't have to spend so much time with us, you'd be at work more, and he wouldn't have to do your job."

"That's not true, Josh. Juan—"

"Yes, it is," Riley said when he entered the room. "Admit it."

"Look, everyone has to juggle things around at times, and sometimes..."

"Sometimes what?"

"Sometimes things don't work out perfectly. We all just do the best we can. And Juan will get through this. We'll *all* get through this. Maybe we'll make mistakes along the way. Maybe things won't go as planned, but we'll get through it. I promise. And, Josh, it's *so* not your fault. Do you understand that?"

"I guess so."

"Riley?"

"Sure."

"I want Mom to come home," Josh added.

"I know, buddy. I know." After a brief pause, he said, "So, are you guys hungry?"

"You have to ask?"

After the boys had gone to bed that evening, Marc popped open a can of beer and turned on the news—another unarmed kid killed by a policeman, ISIS threats closer to home, a second earthquake in Nepal. He turned it off.

After taking a long pull on his beer, he rested his head on the back of the chair and closed his eyes.

Sometimes things don't work out perfectly—isn't that the truth.

Chapter 31

"Come pick me up. I'm at the Greyhound bus station."

The sound of Zenzi's voice gave Marc some relief—she was alive.

"Where are you? I'm in Glenview right now. Where's the Greyhound bus station?"

"The one in Chicago."

"Zenzi, that's not a place I…what's the address? Or at least the cross-streets? Give me something."

"Hell if I know."

"Could you maybe ask someone?"

"Hold on."

He heard her talking to someone.

"Harrison and Jefferson. How soon can you get here?"

Marc glanced at his watch. "I have to pick up the boys at three-thirty. I don't—"

"Good, then I can go with you to pick them up."

"What I was going to say is—"

She hung up.

"…that I don't think I can pick you up first and still make it to the school on time," he said into the dead phone.

She had sounded sober. If he didn't pick her up right away, he wasn't sure if she would stay that way.

As he drove toward Chicago, he called his client and asked her if he could check out her magnolia tree the next day instead. She agreed. Then he called the Chalet Nursery and asked them if they would hold the mulch he had told them he was going to pick up.

It took him forty minutes to get to the Greyhound station and another ten to spot her sitting on a bench outside. She looked a mess—tangled hair, no coat, sweater with a ripped sleeve and buttoned incorrectly.

"C'mon, get in," he told her.

"Took you long enough." As she climbed in, he noticed she was wearing only one sock.

"I got here as soon as I could. Where's your other sock?"

"I have it in my bag. It got wet."

"You can't see your boys looking like that. I'm going to drop you off at your apartment so you can get cleaned up and changed. Where are your things?"

"What things?"

"Personal items? Clothes?"

"Don't take me home. I want to see my boys."

"Zenzi, you look like hell."

"Gee, thanks a lot. That's what you say to me after all I've been through?"

"I just think it would be better if they saw you a little more put together."

"Where's Daddy dearest?"

"As far as I know, he's still in Nick's old apartment."

"What do you mean, as far as you know? You're not keeping an eye on that good-for-nothing—"

"My plate's been a little full lately."

"I suppose you're going to rub that in my face for the rest of my life."

"I'm not rubbing anything in."

"How long?"

"How long for what?"

"Him being at Nick's."

"He has to be out at the end of the month."

"Then what?"

"How about let's talk about what's next for you."

"I'm home now. Everything's good."

"Everything's *not* good, Zen. You've got a serious problem and two children who need you sober...at all times."

"I *am* sober."

"For how long?"

She didn't respond.

"When did you last have a drink, Zenzi?"

"A while ago."

"How long ago?"

Several seconds passed before Marc broke the silence.

"I can drop you off at a shelter, you know."

"You'd do that, wouldn't you?"

"How'd you get money for a bus ticket?"

"I didn't get any money. Some friend of Nick's hunted me down and handed the ticket to me."

"You need help. You need help to get all the way sober and stay that way. If you go back home and try to pick up where you left off, you're going to go right back to drinking."

"I did okay for myself."

"I found you passed out in front of your kids. Or don't you remember that?"

"All I remember is I was doing okay until you got involved."

"Doing okay is being sober and working to support you and your kids."

"Get off your high horse. You think you know it all, don't you?"

"No, I don't. But I think I know a hell of a lot more than you do about what's real."

They were within a block of the boys' school. Marc pulled into the first empty parking spot he saw and faced Zenzi.

"Look, I want to help you. I want to help you get sober and independent. That's my goal."

"I don't need your help."

"You obviously do! You're living under my roof."

"That's just as much my roof as it is yours."

"Oh, really? And exactly how much have you contributed to it all these years?"

"So kick me out."

The boys came bounding toward the truck.

"Smooth out your hair or something, will you?"

"Mom!" Josh shouted.

Zenzi got out of the car and held her arms out to catch Josh.

"You're home!"

"Yes, sweetie. I'm home."

She embraced Riley. "Hey, I think you've grown an inch taller since the last time I saw you, you little bastard."

The boys jumped into the back seat. Zenzi climbed back in next to Marc.

"Just like old times, huh, Uncle Marc?" she said.

"Yep—just like old times."

* * *

During the next several days, Marc checked in on Zenzi often, praying that she would stay sober while he focused on what to do with Meinhard. He made sure she had plenty of food in the house and everything else she needed or wanted—except booze and money to buy booze. Thinking the best thing for her was to get back into a long-term treatment center, he had called the same facilities he had contacted in February and put her on two waiting lists.

Late one evening, four days after Zenzi had come home, Marc was having a rare moment of downtime in front of the TV—happily watching his favorite actress, Reese Witherspoon, on *David Letterman*—when a loud rap at his door startled him.

He opened the door to find Meinhard standing there, clothes askew, the little hair he had left on his head a mess, and his signature black plastic bag by his side.

"What are you doing here?" He had another week left in Nick's old apartment.

"Can I come in?"

Marc nodded.

"So, what's up?" Marc asked him as they stood awkwardly in the kitchen.

"Do you have anything to eat?"

"I could make you a sandwich."

"Good. I haven't eaten in days."

"Why not?"

"Could you make it now and ask questions later?"

"Put your things over there for now. I'll make you something."

"I can't pay you for it."

"You don't have to pay me for it, Dad."

"Thank you. You're very kind."

After making him a sandwich, Marc joined him at the kitchen table. He waited for him to take a couple of bites before he asked him again.

"So what happened at Nick's apartment?"

"Do you have another one of those?" he asked, gesturing toward Marc's beer.

Marc fetched a beer and placed it in front of him.

"What happened?"

"Nothing."

"Why did you leave Nick's apartment?"

"No reason."

"Spill it, Dad."

"Too highfalutin for me. Didn't like it there."

"What happened?"

Meinhard stared past him.

Marc couldn't be too hard on him—he appeared to be disoriented.

"You may as well tell me. Sooner or later I'll find out anyway."

"I sort of got caught going through one of the washing machines in their laundry room."

"What?"

"I was looking for my clothes."

"Because you had put them in one of the washing machines?"

"I couldn't remember if I did or not, so I was looking for them."

"And someone thought you were trying to steal their clothes?"

He nodded.

"You left here with clothes. What happened?"

"I can't find them."

"And you couldn't have called me for help?"

"No phone."

"Where's your phone?"

"I lost it somewhere."

"When did this happen?"

"A few days ago."

"Dad, whoever found it has probably run up a million dollars in charges by now."

"Someone could do that?"

Marc got up from his chair. "Don't go away." He ran to his bedroom, grabbed an old cell phone bill from his desk, and called the number to report the lost phone.

"You mean every time you make a call, it costs?" Meinhard asked when Marc returned.

"Not for local calls. But overseas, yes. And you can rack up data charges and maybe roaming charges. I don't know what all there is. I reported it lost, so if you do happen to find it, be sure to let me know."

"Well, you should have told me."

"So this is my fault?"

"Looks that way."

Marc finished his sandwich, took the last swig of beer, and retrieved another one from the fridge.

"You know where the spare bedroom is. I'll be in the living room lusting over Reese."

"Busting over grease?"

There was no point in responding.

* * *

The next day, Marc received a phone call from Tom Wilds, a competitor of Marc's in the landscaping business but also a friend.

"Juan called me today," he told Marc. "He kind of felt me out for whether I knew of any foreman positions open in the area. I thought you'd want to know."

"Hey, thanks, man, for telling me. What did you tell him?"

"That I myself didn't have anything open. But between you and me, even if I did, I wouldn't do that to you, not without talking to you first."

"I appreciate that, man."

"Any time. You'd do the same for me."

Marc couldn't afford to lose Juan. Things had to change.

He texted Juan.

On my way with beefs from Portillos.

Great!

Marc figured that buying Juan one of the best Italian beef sandwiches in town for lunch wouldn't necessarily keep him from looking for another job, but it couldn't hurt.

On his way down the stairs, as Marc passed over Zenzi's landing, he thought he heard arguing. He paused, and after listening for several seconds and hearing no more, proceeded to his truck. Zenzi had been home for five days without incident, and Marc had a lead on a local rehab facility that he wanted to talk to her about.

He met up with Juan at one of his smaller job sites. They ate their sandwiches in Marc's truck.

The first thing Juan told him was that his wife was pregnant.

Marc fist-bumped him. "Congrats, old man. That's number four, isn't it?"

"And that's it. No more kids."

"Isn't that what you said after the last one?"

"You're right, but then we wanted to try for a girl this time."

"So do you know what this one is?"

"It's a girl."

"How old is your oldest now? Ten, twelve?"

"Just turned thirteen, and he's already talking about a driver's license. Iyiyi! Do you know that when he turns eighteen, I'll have three teenagers in the house?"

"It'll keep you young, man."

"Or put me in a grave."

They talked about the schedule for the upcoming weeks.

"We'll have to do this more often," Marc told him before leaving. "I know I've been off track for a while, but I'm back now."

"I hope so, man."

After Marc visited the foremen at his other two sites, he stopped at the hardware store to pick up a few things he needed for work and a can of paint for the spare bedroom, which the boys had managed to scuff up pretty badly during their short stay. Then he stopped at the grocery store so that Meinhard couldn't complain there was nothing in the house to eat.

When he arrived home at six-thirty, he put away the groceries, popped a frozen pizza in the oven, and settled down in front of the television. Half-listening to the news, he went through his mail and browsed through the current issue of *Landscape Management*. When the oven timer went off, he knocked on Meinhard's door.

"You want any pizza?" he asked through the door.

"No."

"Are you hungry? Do you want something else?"

"No."

Too tired to probe into the reason for Meinhard's odd behavior of turning down food, Marc left him alone. After dinner he showered and then read through his text messages while he listened to a Bruno Mars CD that Gabby had once given him.

At ten-fifteen his phone chirped.

> Everything ok?

It was Jessica.

> Sure. Why?

> What happened today.

Marc laughed out loud.

> Is that a question or statement?

> U don't know.

> Know what?

> Have u talked 2 Zenzi 2day?

> No. Why?

> Can I come up?

> Sure

Marc threw on a t-shirt and went to the back door to meet Jessica.

"C'mon in. What's this all about?"

She held his gaze for several seconds, her expression solemn.

"What?"

"The police were here today," she told him.

Chapter 32

"Come in, Jess. Sit down. What do you know about the police being here?"

"Isabel Gunther from next door told me."

"Told you what?"

"That the police had been here earlier. And they took Zenzi away."

"What? Why? What did she do? Where are the boys?"

"We think DCFS took them."

"What?"

"Isabel said they had heard a commotion over here earlier, but it stopped, so they didn't worry about it too much afterward. Then the police came, and they stayed in her apartment for a long time, she said. Then two women came, and the boys left with them. She said Zenzi was screaming on her way out, followed by the boys screaming for their mom. Said it was just awful. Isabel went outside to talk with the two women to tell them she could take the boys until you got home, but they wouldn't have any of it."

Marc held his head in his hands, his fingers rubbing both temples. "Who do I call? I don't know who to call!" he hollered.

"Calm down. Can you come down to my place? Tyler's alone. We'll figure this out."

Marc followed her down the stairs. Once inside, she pulled out her laptop and started searching.

"Write this down." She gave him the number to the local DCFS office. "I don't know if that's the right number but if not, I'm sure they can give it to you. While you call them, I'll see if I can find out where they took Zenzi."

Marc remembered writing down and then discarding the DCFS number a month earlier. Maybe if he had called them then, he wouldn't be calling them now.

To his relief, a human being answered the phone but, then he was transferred around to several people before he was able to talk to someone who knew about the boys.

"I understand," he said. "When can I pick them up?"

"I'm afraid it doesn't work like that."

"But I'm their uncle. They're family!"

"We do prefer that children removed from the custody of their parents are placed with a relative, but once they're in foster care, there are steps that have to be taken before they are released to a relative, usually a judge deciding what is best for the child at a petition for guardianship hearing. I suggest you consult with a family-law attorney."

"But that takes time! What about those two boys in the meantime?"

"I can assure you they are being well cared for, Mr. Nussbaum."

"Can I visit them?"

"Only biological and stepparents have visitation rights, and a judge has to approve that as well."

"They're in foster care," he told Jessica after he hung up.

"I heard."

"They advised me to get a family-law attorney and petition for guardianship."

"Can you visit them?"

"Only a parent. What did you find?"

"She's in Cook County Jail."

"Twenty-ninth and California?"

"Yep."

"Holy shit. That's where they send hardened criminals. What are the charges, do you know?"

Jessica glanced down at her notes. "Illegal possession of a firearm, disorderly conduct, child endangerment, and child neglect."

"Holy shit."

"You already said that. There's a bail hearing tomorrow."

"Why are you looking at me that way?" he asked.

"Are you going to pay her bail?"

Marc stared at her, a heaviness throughout his body making it difficult to speak.

"You're scaring me, Marc. Say something."

"I don't know what I'm going to do."

* * *

Marc found a lawyer who handled family law matters, specifically DCFS cases. He immediately wired her the $2,500 retainer fee so she could get started on the case. Then he met with her—at a cost of $225 an hour—on the boys' third day in foster care.

"The first thing we'll do is determine whether your sister will agree to appoint you as their legal guardian. If she does, that will make this a lot easier."

"Why wouldn't she?" he asked.

"I've had cases where a parent thought it would be easier to get their children back if they were in foster care than if they were safe with another family member, or if there's bad blood between the parent and relatives, sometimes the parent will try to fight guardianship by them."

"And if she's not agreeable?"

"Then we'll file a petition with the court for short-term guardianship. I'm assuming your intention is to provide for them until which time your sister can do that for herself. Is that correct?"

"Yes. Of course."

"Short-term guardianship can be for up to a year."

"Well, let's hope it doesn't take that long."

"Where's the father?" she asked.

"I don't know."

"Do you think your sister knows where he is?"

"Honestly, she has told me she's not even sure *who* their fathers are. But there is a husband involved."

"Oh?"

"They're estranged."

"Did he legally adopt the boys?"

"No. He didn't really have much of a relationship with them...or with her for that matter."

"Okay."

"Can we find out how DCFS got involved in the first place? Why the police were called?" he asked.

"I can get a copy of the police report, but not the DCFS case file. That information is kept confidential except for legal proceedings."

"Let me ask you this—what if Zenzi still isn't able to care for them after she gets out of jail?"

"The court will make that determination. DCFS will prepare a detailed plan for her—attending parenting classes, going to rehab, becoming employed, whatever they deem necessary for her to become a responsible parent—and the court works closely with DCFS. She won't qualify for custody until she completes the plan."

"Do the kids have any say in who is granted guardianship?"

"If they're under twelve, they generally don't."

"Will Zenzi know of the petition if we go that route?"

"Yes, she'll be notified."

"Even if she's in jail?"

"Yes."

"Will she be able to attend the hearing if she's in jail?"

"Oh, yes. And she can dispute the petition if she wants to, but she'll have to prove her case, just like we do."

"Will she need a lawyer to do that?"

"No, she can present her case without one, or she can be represented by a public defender. Are you anticipating she'll fight this?"

"I'm just trying to cover all bases."

Marc left the meeting with a dull ache deep inside his belly. He thought he was doing right by the boys by trying to get guardianship, but he suspected Zenzi might not take that very well, just as he suspected she hadn't taken well to his not posting bail for her.

When Marc arrived home, Meinhard was sitting at the kitchen table eating a bowl of cereal. Ever since Zenzi and the boys had been removed from the premises, Meinhard had been suspiciously unavailable—always napping or in the bathroom whenever Marc came home. He sat down across the table from him.

"So you've been unusually quiet these past few days. What's on your mind?" Marc asked him.

"Nothing's on my mind."

"Let me ask you something. Where were you when the police came to Zenzi's apartment the other day?"

"Here, I guess."

"Are you aware of what happened?"

Meinhard got up to leave.

"Where are you going?"

"I'm tired. Think I'll take a nap."

"You've been taking a lot of naps lately."

"I'm old. Wait until you're this age," he said right before he closed the bedroom door.

Marc followed him and knocked on the door. When he received no response, he opened it.

"What! Can't a man have a little privacy in this place?"

"I want to talk to you."

Marc sat down on the opposite end of the bed from him.

"So what all did you see the other day when the police came?"

"Nothing."

"Well, you must have seen something. I heard there were three police cars here at one point."

"No, didn't see anything. Must have been taking a nap. Kind of like what I want to do right now."

"You know that Riley and Josh are in foster care, right?"

"Who?"

"Riley and Josh. Zenzi's kids?"

"No, I didn't know that." He looked genuinely surprised.

"Where did you think they were?"

He shrugged. "With Zenzi, I guess. Like always."

"Don't you want to know why they're there?"

"Where?"

"In foster care."

"I suppose because Zenzi's in jail."

"How do you know she's in jail?"

"You said so."

"No, I didn't."

"I guess I assumed it then."

"I thought you said you didn't see anything."

"I didn't."

"How did you find out the police were here?"

"I don't remember. I just knew."

"You called them, didn't you?" Marc asked, trying hard to maintain his cool.

"Of course not!"

"Yes, you did. I can tell by the way you're acting."

"You're wrong."

"No, I'm not. Why did you call them?"

"What is this, an interrogation?"

"Call it what you want. Now answer my question."

"You need to calm down."

Trying hard to suppress his anger, Marc continued in a calm voice. "Tell me why you called the police."

Wide-eyed and visibly trembling, Meinhard finally blurted out, "I couldn't sleep with all that racket going on down there."

"What racket?"

"Her yelling. The kids yelling. Sounded like things were being thrown."

"So you called the police because of the noise?"

"It was terrible."

"Why didn't you call me? I would have handled things. I always do."

"I didn't have your number."

Marc marched into the kitchen, grabbled the sticky note from the fridge door, and shoved it at Meinhard.

"What's this, you fool?"

"Your number?"

"You beat everything, you know that? Do you have any idea what those boys are going through and what I have to go through to get them back? Do you? Do you?"

"I called because of the noise. How did I know they'd take away the kids?"

"What did you think would happen to them?"

"Don't blame me. I—"

"Oh, I *am* blaming you, Dad. Big time."

Marc left the bedroom and went into his own room, slamming the door hard behind him. When the items on top of his dresser stopped rattling, he kicked at nothing in particular, and when his big toe connected with the wrought-iron leg of his bed, he unshackled a silent scream in his head that caused an immediate headache.

Chapter 33

Marc met his attorney at the Daley Center in Chicago's Loop district fifteen minutes before the guardianship hearing was to begin. The boys had now been in foster care for ten days—ten agonizing days—and Marc had not been allowed to even talk to them on the phone.

"Are you okay?" she asked him.

"I'm nervous as hell. I have a headache that won't quit, and I keep thinking I have to throw up. I wish I would. Maybe I'd feel better."

A week earlier, the lawyer had called Marc to tell him Zenzi had not signed the appointment form for Marc to have temporary guardianship and that they would have to petition for it on their own. That was followed by a visit from DCFS to interview Marc and check out his living conditions.

"I can't tell you how this will turn out, but I know the judge, and he's extremely fair, if that makes you feel any better."

"Some. How long do you think we'll be in there?"

"My guess is not long. Fortunately, and unfortunately, they have heavy caseloads, and they have to get through them quickly." She handed him a piece of paper. "Here's a copy of the police report."

DEPUTIES ALTON AND CASSIDY ARRIVED AT THE HOME OF KRESZENTIA NUSSBAUM AT 833 ROSCOE AT APPROXIMATELY 10:00 A.M. ON APRIL 11, 2015 RESPONDING TO AN ANONYMOUS COMPLAINT OF A DISTURBANCE INVOLVING CHILDREN. RILEY NUSSBAUM, A JUVENILE, ANSWERED THE DOOR. THE DEPUTIES OBSERVED AN ADULT FEMALE LYING ON THE LIVING ROOM FLOOR AND ENTERED THE APARTMENT.

AFTER CALLING FOR EMT ASSISTANCE, DEPUTY CASSIDY ATTENDED TO THE UNCONSCIOUS FEMALE WHILE DEPUTY ALTON SEARCHED THE APARTMENT AND FOUND A SECOND CHILD, JOSHUA NUSSBAUM, AND THE FOLLOWING CONDITIONS:

1. DIRTY DISHES PILED HIGH IN THE KITCHEN SINK AND ON THE COUNTERS.
2. AN EMPTY BOTTLE OF VODKA ON THE COFFEE TABLE.

3.   A 6-INCH SERRATED KNIFE ON THE KITCHEN COUNTER.

4.   A LOADED S&W 9MM HANDGUN ON THE NIGHTSTAND IN THE MASTER BEDROOM.

5.   A STRONG STENCH OF URINE ON THE UNCONSCIOUS FEMALE.

DEPUTY ALTON SPOKE WITH THE TWO MINOR CHILDREN AND AFTERWARD CALLED DCFS FOR AN EVALUATION.

THE EMTS ARRIVED AT APPROXIMATELY 10:20 A.M. AND WHILE THEY WERE WORKING ON THE PATIENT, SHE BECAME CONSCIOUS AND COMBATIVE, CAUSING THE EMTS TO PUT HER IN RESTRAINTS.

TWO DCFS CASEWORKERS ARRIVED AT APPROXIMATELY 10:45 A.M., EVALUATED THE SITUATION, AND REMOVED THE CHILDREN FROM THE HOME.

CHARGES: ILLEGAL POSSESSION OF A FIREARM, DISORDERLY CONDUCT, CHILD ENDANGERMENT, AND CHILD NEGLECT."

"Those poor kids," Marc said.

"It's time to go in. Do you have any questions?"

"No."

"If you're asked to say anything, just be honest. Be yourself. Like I explained, you may not have to say a word. That's *my* job."

They entered the small quiet courtroom and sat down. The only other people in the room were the clerk who had motioned for them to come in and the woman from DCFS who had interviewed Marc. The nameplate on the bench read William T. Morehouse.

Five minutes later, the judge entered the room and, after going through the papers before him, addressed Marc and his attorney.

"Ms. Nussbaum has relinquished her right to be here, so we can get started."

Marc wondered if ten days of jail time with no alcohol had caused Zenzi to come to her senses. He held on to that hope throughout the hearing.

The judge asked the DCFS caseworker and Marc's attorney a series of questions that appeared to be confirmation of what the judge already knew. Then he asked Marc several questions about his past relationship with the boys—how involved he had been in their lives, what kind of relationship they had, how much responsibility he had assumed and for how long.

When he had finished asking questions, the judge spent a few long minutes flipping through the papers in front of him.

Finally, he looked up and addressed his words to Marc. "I am granting de facto guardianship to you, Mr. Nussbaum, on a temporary basis not to exceed one year. DCFS will be in touch with you as to their expectations. Do you have any questions?"

"No, Your Honor."

"Court adjourned. Please see the bailiff to sign the documents."

* * *

The next morning at promptly nine a.m., Marc opened the kitchen door to have Josh jump right into his arms. Riley remained still, standing close to the DCFS caseworker who had escorted them home.

"Hey, buddy. It's so good to have you back home."

"Is Mom here?"

"No. It's just me."

Riley walked past Marc and Josh toward his bedroom.

"Riley?"

"Don't mind him. He's mad at the world these days," Josh explained.

Marc managed a polite smile at the social worker. "Is there anything we need to talk about?"

"Not right now. We'll be in touch a little later."

When the caseworker left, Josh broke into tears.

"It was awful, Uncle Marc. I don't never want to go back there again."

"I'm sorry, buddy," Marc said as he hugged him. "But you're here now and..."

"And what?"

"Let's go get Riley. I want to talk to you boys."

"I'll get him!"

Riley slinked his way out of his bedroom and into the living room.

"Welcome home, buddy."

"Can you not call me that?"

"I'm sorry. I didn't know—"

"I have a name."

"Sorry. Are you okay?"

"No, we're *not* okay. Do you have any idea what we went through?"

"Well, no, I don't, but—"

"Do you even *want* to know what we went through?"

"Of course I do. I care about you guys. I—"

"You didn't care enough about us to keep us out of foster care."

"Riley, I got you out as soon as I could. What are you talking about?"

"We were there ten days."

"With Mr. and Mrs. Dumbfart and their stupid dogs," Josh added.

"Tell me that wasn't really their last name."

"Oh, yes, it was."

Marc stared at Riley. "Really?"

"It was Dumfar. And they were really bad."

"Tell me about it."

"First of all, Mrs. Dumbfart had these statues all over the house, like in church. And their eyes followed you when you went by them. And if we didn't look at them every once in a while and say how nice they were, she'd get upset. And they had three dogs, and they weren't friendly."

"Yeah, and sometimes the little one pooped in the house."

"And then there was Mr. Dumbfart," Riley said.

"You probably shouldn't call them that."

"I don't care. He made us do all this work, like we were his slaves. Do this. Do that. Don't do this. Don't do that."

"And he had huge dandruff," Josh added.

"And her cooking was crappy, but we had to eat it anyhow. We didn't even know what it was half the time."

"Well, you're home now."

"Where's Mom?" Riley asked.

"I'm afraid your mother is in jail."

"Why? She's an alcoholic, not a criminal."

"The police have charged her with a few things, and now she's waiting for her day in court."

"Can't you bail her out?"

"I thought it was more important to bail you guys out."

"What do you mean?"

"I had to go to court and get a judge to agree to you living with me. It's called being your legal guardian. So until your mother gets things straightened out for herself, you'll be living with me...legally."

"Here?"

"Mm-hm. Your grandfather is back upstairs."

"So when does Mom go to court?"

"I don't know the date."

"Is she in big trouble?"

"You might say that."

"We didn't call the police," Josh said.

"I know that." Marc had no intention of ever telling them who had. "Hey, boys, I came down here yesterday and cleaned up a bit, did some laundry, and didn't find the clothes we bought together. Did you bring them to the foster home?"

"No. What we brought are in those bags over there."

"Then where are the new clothes?"

Both boys looked away.

"Boys..."

"We think Mom gave them away…to charity or something," Riley said.

"Why would she do that?"

"She said there was nothing wrong with the ones we had."

"I liked our new clothes," Josh said with a shrug.

"Did you tell her that?"

"Are you kidding? We *never* question what Mom does."

Chapter 34

The next day, when Marc drove up in front of their school, the boys were waiting for him on the curb as instructed.

"How'd it go?" he asked them.

"Fine," Josh responded.

"One kid in my class found out we were in a foster home somehow and asked me how it was," Riley said.

"What did you tell him?"

"I told him it sucked."

"Riley said you're going to buy us clothes again," Josh said.

The boys looked like a couple of street kids in their well-worn clothes. Marc figured legal guardianship came with some inalienable rights—like providing them with proper clothing, whether Zenzi liked it or not.

"That's right."

"Can we shop at Old Navy for clothes this time?" Riley asked.

Though Sears was more in line with his budget, he heard himself say, "Old Navy it is."

When they got home after shopping, Marc allowed the boys to enter the apartment first and then waited in the kitchen for their reaction to what he had bought for them earlier in the day.

"No way!" Riley screeched.

"Look, Riley, it's Zoo Tycoon. Awesome!"

"I got Call of Duty. Sweet!"

They ran into the kitchen, their wide grins making Marc feel slightly better about the ten days they had to spend in foster care.

"Thanks, Uncle Marc," Riley said. "But how'd you know which games to buy?"

"I heard you guys talking about them."

"There's only one problem."

"What's that?"

"Mom won't let us keep them. The new TV maybe, but not the Xbox stuff."

"We'll deal with that when the time comes."

* * *

The next day Marc received a scrawled letter from Zenzi.

> *If you think for one minute you're going to take my kids away from me, think again. I'm a good mother and you know it. Those boys love me and want to be with ME. Nick will take care of us. You'll see!*

> *Z*

> *PS And keep that SOB father of ours that you keep helping away from my boys!*

It was the idea of Nick "taking care of us" that troubled Marc the most. As far as Marc knew, Nick hadn't started divorce proceedings yet and they were still legally married. He wondered if there was now some other plan.

Marc called the lawyer who had handled his guardianship hearing and read the letter to her.

"Could Zenzi's estranged husband ever get custody of her boys?" Marc asked her.

"He could try, but from what you've told me, I doubt if he'd have much of a chance. Now, if he had legally adopted them, that would be another story. Then his chances go way up."

"Since I'm the legal guardian, would I be informed if he were to start any proceeding to get custody of them or adopt them or anything?"

"Yes, we would be notified. Nothing would take place without your involvement. Send a copy of the letter to me."

"What are you going to do with it?"

"Nothing for now. Let me know if anything more transpires."

After he hung up the phone, he re-read the letter. Her postscript confirmed his suspicion that she resented him in part because he continued to help their father—a regrettable circumstance for everyone involved.

His chirping phone disrupted his thoughts.

Do u know where your father is?

It was Jessica.

Upstairs I think.

U may want 2 check.

Why?

I think I just saw him on the street.

At your work?

Yes

Marc ran upstairs to his apartment to find it empty, but Meinhard's belongings were still piled in the corner of the spare bedroom.

Jessica worked at a diner in the Bucktown neighborhood, on the opposite side of town from where he needed to be for his first appointment of the day. Unable to imagine what Meinhard would be doing there, he got in his truck and drove in that direction. After cruising up and down a few streets without spotting him, Marc went into the diner to talk further with Jessica about what she'd seen.

"I could have been mistaken, but it looked like him," she said as she poured his coffee.

"I tooled around the area but I didn't see him. Did he look okay?"

"When he walked by, he was slumped over, looking down."

"That would be normal for him."

"Like I said..."

"What was he wearing?"

"A green-and-black plaid shirt."

"I'm sure that was him. He rarely takes that shirt off. He sleeps in it, for all I know. If you see him again, do you think you could grab him and then call me?"

"I'll try." She lowered her voice to a whisper. "I can't talk really, but I thought you would want to know that the girl who I saw with Zenzi's boyfriend or husband, whatever he is, walked by the house this morning. She didn't look my way or anything. She just kept on walking down Roscoe."

"Sonya."

"Is that her name? I never knew. Anyway, I just thought it was a little weird she was in our neighborhood. I gotta go. Call me later if you want."

Marc finished his coffee and then combed the streets once more before heading to his appointment.

* * *

"Why can't we visit her?" Riley asked. "She probably misses us."

"I'm sure she does, but they don't allow visitors in jail."

"That stinks."

They had just come home from scouring the neighborhood where Jessica thought she had seen his father. The effort had turned up nothing as did phone calls to nearby hospitals and a visit to his local police precinct where Marc had filed a missing person report.

"When's she coming home?" Josh asked. "I made her a present." He showed Marc a card fashioned from yellow construction paper. On the front was a drawing of a bird with its wings outstretched. Underneath he had written:

Welcum home from jale MOM

Inside he wrote:

We reely missed you.

Love, Josh

"And no one helped me with it either," he said.

"It's a great card, Josh. I really like the bird," Marc told him. "To answer your question, I don't know when she's coming home. Not before her court date is all I know. And then it depends on what the judge says."

"I want to talk to that judge," Riley said.

"I'm afraid you can't do that."

"What does he know about our mom? Nothing."

"He'll know enough about her."

"He could be a real jerk. How do we know?"

"Well, Riley, I guess we don't. But people don't get to be judges if they're jerks."

Marc wasn't sure if he believed that, but what else could he say to an eleven-year-old?

"What about Judge Judy?" Josh asked.

"What about her?"

"She never even gives the people a chance to talk."

"Well, that's TV. Your Mom will have a real judge."

"Judge Judy is a real judge," Riley added. "It says so right before the show."

"Look, boys, I don't know anything about Judge Judy. All I know is she won't be your mother's judge."

"Can you find out who it will be?"

"Why all this concern over the judge?"

"She's our mom."

* * *

Your father is here.

The text was from Jessica.

Where r u?

Home

Be right down.

"Where were you?" he asked Meinhard after retrieving him from Jessica's apartment and settling him in at the kitchen table. It was eight o'clock in the evening—almost seven hours since Jessica had seen him in front of her restaurant.

"I'm not sure. I was on a bus though."

"You're not sure where you were?"

His gaze was blank.

"What day is it?" Meinhard asked.

"Friday."

"I'd like to go to bed now."

"Will you promise me you won't leave the apartment again...unless I'm with you?"

"I'm tired. I'm going to bed."

Marc went straight down to the garage and rummaged through his workbench until he found an old cowbell he'd inherited from a previous tenant. He rigged it so it chimed whenever his apartment door opened. This way, he would know if Meinhard left the apartment—provided Marc was at home. When he wasn't home, he'd ask the Gunthers next door if they could keep an ear out for it.

Chapter 35

"Nicholas Lee is seeking legal adoption of Riley and Josh," Marc's attorney told him over the phone.

"Are you freakin' kidding me?"

"I have a copy of the paperwork in front of me."

"So he and my sister must still be married, right?"

"Yes."

"Now what?"

"Do you want to fight it?"

"My first reaction to that question is yes, I want to fight it, but I need to think about this."

"There's a hearing in two weeks, on the fifteenth."

"And I can be there?"

"As the boys' legal guardian, you have the right to be there."

"Can I get back to you on this?"

"Within forty-eight hours would be best."

Marc hung up the phone shaking his head. The only perceivable reason for Nick wanting to adopt the boys was that Zenzi and Nick were planning to stay together after she was released—a definite change in the plan that they had presented to him. But he wanted to hear it from Zenzi that that was the case before he made any decisions. After spending an hour on the Cook County Jail website and then talking to an administrator, he learned that the best way to connect with her would be by completing an application for visitation. The only other way was if she were to call him. It would take three to five days to process the visitation application, and if it was approved, he would have to wait for the day of the week that visitation was scheduled for the division in which she was housed. He didn't have that kind of time.

He struggled over the pros and cons of doing nothing versus fighting the adoption. Afterward, feeling no more confident in what to do than he did before, he texted Jessica.

Can we talk 2nite?

At 9 after Tyler goes 2 bed.

Meet u on deck. I'll bring beer.

Just 1 each.

☺

After Marc and the boys grilled burgers for dinner that night and the dishes had been washed, he called for a family meeting.

"Are we in trouble?" Josh asked.

"No, you're not in trouble."

"Whew! So the school didn't call you to—"

"Shut up, dummy," Riley interjected.

"Why would the school call me?"

"I don't know."

"Josh."

"Sometimes they just call to see how you're doing."

"Josh."

Josh looked to Riley for help.

"Too late now, blabbermouth."

"What happened?" Marc asked.

Riley took the lead. "They let us outside at lunchtime today. It was kinda warm, I guess. Anyway, I saw Josh at the other end of the playground, and it looked like him and this other kid were arguing or something, so I went over there to see what was going on. That kid was a lot bigger than Josh, I mean a lot, and it looked like he was getting ready to punch him, so I pushed him out of the way." Riley threw up his hands. "That's all I did."

"How hard did you push him?"

"Not hard."

"So he wasn't hurt or anything?"

"Nope."

"So why would the school call me for that?"

Josh jumped in. "Maybe because I waited until he had his back turned and then I slugged him from behind."

"Why did you do that after Riley took care of things for you?!"

Josh shrugged.

"Where did you hit him? Was he hurt?"

Riley answered for him. "He barely touched him and besides, Josh couldn't hurt this guy if he tried—he's half his size. Tell him Josh. Tell him why you slugged him."

"Because he called me a jailbird baby."

"Do you know the saying 'Sticks and stones will break my bones, but words will never hurt me'?" Marc asked.

"That's a stupid saying, Uncle Marc," Riley said.

It *was* a stupid saying, Marc had to agree.

"I don't even know what it means," Josh added.

"Look, you can't let what others say get to you. If what they're saying isn't true, then that makes them ignorant, and that's their problem, not yours."

"What if it *is* true?" Riley asked.

"Then you either ignore it or own up to it."

"What if he calls me that again, or calls me something way badder? What am I supposed to do?"

"Way worse. Just ignore him."

"But that makes me look like a wuss."

"It makes you look smart."

"I want to say something really good back at him. Something to shut him up."

Marc thought about it for a few seconds.

"What's his name?"

"Kurt."

"What if you said, 'Why don't you get a life, Kurt, and leave mine alone?'"

"Well...I don't know."

It didn't sound that good to Marc either. He'd Google something later.

"So why did you think the school would have called me?"

"Because we all got pulled into the principal's office."

"What did he say?"

"To stop arguing and try to get along."

"Well, that was good advice."

"So what did you want to talk about?" Riley asked.

"Are we done with the Kurt incident? Is there any more to it I should know about?"

"Nope."

"Okay...if you...if something were to...um, if your mom..."

The boys remained silent as he struggled to find the right words.

"You know, it's not that important. Why don't you guys go do your homework now."

After the boys had gone to bed, Marc met Jessica out on the deck as planned.

It was warm for April, and the cloudless sky and full moon provided enough light for them to see each other while they talked. Jessica had changed out of her work uniform and into jeans and a lightweight hoodie. He handed her a Goose Island lager before they sat down.

"So what's going on?" she asked.

She wore her hair down—unlike most days when it was either in a lopsided ponytail or piled up on top of her head.

"Your hair looks nice that way."

"Al likes it this way too."

Her facial expression always changed when she mentioned his name—not much, but enough to be noticeable.

Marc explained how Nick was pursuing legal adoption of the boys.

"Why wouldn't Zenzi want you to have custody of them at least while she's in jail? That doesn't make sense to me."

"I'm not sure, but she seems to view me as the enemy."

"Why?"

"One, I'm not helping her to return to life as she knew it before, which is pretty much drinking it away. Two, I'm providing food and shelter for our father, whom she despises. And three, maybe she's of the mindset that she and Nick will have a life together. I don't know. That's all I can come up with."

"Did I tell you I bumped into him once?"

"When was that?"

"I was coming out of my back door on my way to work one day, had to have been right after Zenzi came here to live, when this couple got out of their car in the alley and walked toward me. They were strangers to me, so I asked if I could help them find someone. They said they were here to see Zenzi and that was pretty much it. But I have to tell you, he kind of gave me the creeps."

"How's that?"

"I don't know. Just the way he looked at me, I think, and maybe that's not fair. But I got the feeling if his girlfriend hadn't been there, maybe he would have hit on me. I don't know, maybe it was my imagination."

"Were you flirting with him?"

"Of course not!"

"Just asking."

"I'm not like that."

"Are you kidding me? You are such a flirt."

"Just with you."

"Oh, really?"

"Yeah, really."

"Well, let's not go there, okay?"

They clinked bottles in agreement.

"So why would *he* fight for custody of them?" she asked. "You said he was never close to them."

"Either he and Zenzi are planning to be a couple when she gets out, which the more I think about seems so unlikely, or he thinks there's something in it for him. I don't know."

"What about his girlfriend?"

"Exactly. The plan was for them to get married and raise Emma."

"There's more to it, isn't there?"

"More to what?"

"More to what's bothering you."

"Yeah. To be honest…I'm not sure I want to get into this fight."

"Not exactly what you signed up for?"

"It's that, but even if it was, I'm not sure I'm the right person for the job."

"You appear to be doing okay from where I sit."

"Shit. I'm clueless what to do half the time with those two. Am I being too harsh or not harsh enough? When I have something I want to talk to them about, will I find the right words? Sometimes they have problems with other kids at school. Should I get involved, or should I let them work it out? When they do something wrong, do I punish them or try to understand what they're going through? It's never-ending."

"Half the time isn't bad you know."

Marc laughed. "Look, maybe living with Nick and Sonya or whoever and their half-sister would be a better deal for them—two parent figures, probably more money, living in a better neighborhood, in a better school district. I can't offer them that much and…"

"And what?"

"And I don't know how to handle them—just when I think things are going pretty well, they pull something new."

"So? They're kids. They're always going to pull new things. Look, the questions you keep asking yourself? I'm here to tell you that all parents second-guess themselves when it comes to their kids. It comes with the job."

"I'm not sure that makes me feel any better."

"And your comment about being better off with two parents and more money— I've got news for you. That's no guaranty for a happy childhood."

"Yeah, but it helps."

"You know what's wrong with you?"

"Oh, boy, here it comes."

"Okay, then, I won't tell you."

"No, please tell me. I want to hear this."

Jessica got up to leave. Marc grabbed her arm.

"I'm sorry. I *do* want to hear what you think."

"Make that *two* things wrong with you."

"I'm listening."

"We've talked about this before. You want everything neat and clean, no jagged edges, and then tied up with a pretty bow, just like your apartment, your cars... your life."

"Before you said it was just my sock drawer."

"That was just one example."

"I'm not like that."

"And I'm not a flirt."

"Well, you *are* a flirt."

"Think about it."

"So what's wrong with being neat and clean?"

"Nothing, unless you let it run your life."

"That's ridiculous. I don't do that."

"Do I have to remind you how you avoided me like the plague after we had that...whatever it was we had that night? Why? Because it had jagged edges. Wasn't very neat and clean, was it?"

"That's a bad example."

"Really? Okay, why don't you ever take your fancy little sports car out for a drive—the one that's been sitting in your garage for how long?"

"Not that long. I've been working on it."

"Is it drivable?"

"Well, yes, but— "

"But it's not perfect yet, is it?"

"It needs work."

"What needs to be done on it?"

"It's technical—you wouldn't understand."

"Mm-hm."

"That's another bad example. We're talking—"

"All I'm saying is you're going to miss out if you keep waiting for perfect." She got up to leave. "And one more thing. You wouldn't have brought this up if you had no intention of fighting for them."

Later that evening, after two more beers, Marc fell asleep watching TV, thinking of what Jessica had said. And how he couldn't take the Miata out with only one smoked headlight housing.

* * *

Early the next morning, Marc received a text from Juan.

Montana wants lawn cut 1.5 inches. Mower won't do that. Buy new mower just for him? LOL

Do I need 2 call him?

I can't deal with him.

I'll take care of it.

Carlos walked off job.

Why?

Fight with wife in AM. Fight with Louis in PM. Who knows?

Do u know Ryan in Mike's group?

Skinny dude with red hair?

Yep. His cousin ready 2 work, 5 yrs exp.

Can he start tomorrow?

I'll see.

Marc called his attorney to ask a couple of questions about Zenzi's upcoming court date. Apparently, Riley had overheard his conversation because as soon as he finished the call, Riley asked if he could take off school to attend it.

"I'm afraid not, Riley. This is adult court, talking about adult matters."

"That sucks."

"It may seem like it sucks now, but—"

"Well I'm tired of being treated like a kid."

"Sometimes we just have to accept things the way they are. I've had to do that before."

"Right."

"What I mean is you *are* a kid. A smart kid—I'll give you that. But you're still only eleven."

"Doesn't matter what you say, it still sucks."

"Why does it suck?"

"*Someone* has to look out for her."

"Is that what you think your role is—to look out for your mom?"

"*Someone* has to."

"That's not your responsibility."

"Then who?"

"Well, she has an attorney for the legal stuff. We have to find someone for medical stuff. And when that's all done, she'll be able to take care of herself...and you guys."

"I can tell you right now that's not going to happen."

"Which part?"

"Her taking care of us."

"She has to. That's her job."

"I'm just sayin'."

"Whether she does or not is yet to be seen, but one thing is for sure, you shouldn't be worrying about taking care of *her*. You need to concentrate on being a kid."

"That sounds all good and everything, but it's not going to happen. I know my mom."

Marc's phone chirped another incoming text message. It was from Jessica.

Playing PI tonight. Will call u tomorrow.

Chapter 36

"Okay, here's the scoop," Jessica said to Marc over the phone the next morning. She explained that she'd learned from Isabel next door that Sonya's mother lived in an apartment building at the end of their block, and that was probably why Jessica kept seeing Sonya pass by their house—she was getting off the bus on Halsted and walking to her mom's. Isabel also told Jessica that she played Bingo with Sonya's mother every Thursday night.

"Do I really need to know her Bingo schedule?" he asked.

"Hold on. So I planted a few questions related to Sonya and Nicholas in Isabel's head yesterday morning and then made sure I was outside when she came home last night after Bingo."

"Bingo gossip? C'mon, Jess."

"Do you want to hear this or not?"

"Proceed."

"I don't have to—"

"No, go ahead. I'm all ears."

She told him that the way Sonya had met Nick was in a bar, and at first her mother wasn't very keen on the relationship, but as she got to know Nick, she came to like him well enough. Apparently, he treats Sonya well, buys her things, takes her places. And she said her daughter adores Emma."

"Well, that's good to hear—the Emma part."

According to her mother, Sonya pictured her and Nick getting married and raising a family as soon as he had his green card, something her mother initially approved of.

"Did her mother mention that Nick was already married?"

"No, not that Isabel said, but she *was* aware of Zenzi and the boys because she said Sonya was having second thoughts about marrying him when he told her he was going to try to adopt Riley and Josh."

"Now that's interesting." So it didn't appear that Nick and Zenzi had plans to get together—otherwise, Sonya would be having more than just second thoughts. There had to be something else in it for Nick, Marc thought, or he wouldn't be doing it.

"I thought so too."

"Here's something else that's interesting. Nick apparently once served jail time for some kind of obstruction of justice charge."

"In this country?"

"She didn't say."

It had to have been before he had his green card, so Marc wondered why he wasn't deported, unless it happened in his native country.

"What are you thinking?" she asked him.

Marc didn't respond.

"Marc?"

"What?"

"What are you thinking?"

"I'm going to fight for those boys."

"Marc?"

"Yeah?"

"I knew you would."

* * *

The next morning, Marc searched for a website that archived English-language Malaysian newspapers. After more than an hour of tiresome hunting, he unearthed an article from 2013 announcing the mysterious death of one of the deputy ministers of finance in the Malaysian government. According to the article, the former deputy minister had been previously charged with financial fraud and was serving prison time when he died. It went on to give details of the scandal including what had prompted the investigation—the department's senior software engineer, a Nicholas R. Lee, had brought the deputy minister's transgressions to the attention of the prime minister and then left his position with the department soon afterward. During the preliminary stages of the deputy minister's court case, Mr. Lee had been charged with witness tampering and served nine months in federal prison.

He immediately called Nick.

"Look, my friend, I'm sure you mean well, but I'm here to tell you as the boys' legal guardian, I believe it's not in their best interest to live with you, and I am going to do everything in my power to stop you from adopting them."

"I'll see you in court then," Nick said and then hung up.

Marc called his attorney and told her of his conversation with Nick. She immediately advised him against any further communication with him.

"So you want to proceed with fighting him on his adoption petition?" she asked.

"Yes."

"Okay. I'll notify the court that we will be present at the hearing."

* * *

The resounding ring of the cowbell awakened Marc with such a start that he fell off the sofa and crashed his head into the coffee table, sending an empty beer bottle and loose change flying. Riley came running out of his bedroom.

"What's going on?" Riley shouted.

"Nothing," Marc said as he picked himself up off the floor rubbing his forehead. "Go back to bed."

"I heard an alarm or something."

"I'm going to take care of it," Marc said on his way out.

Marc opened the back door and calmly went after Meinhard, who was by then halfway down the staircase.

"Where do you think you're going, Dad?"

Meinhard turned to him. "Just out for a walk."

"In your underwear?"

He looked down. "Must have forgotten my pants."

"C'mon. Let's go back upstairs. It's the middle of the night."

"It is?"

"Yes, it is."

A movement by his garage caught his attention. Who would be hanging around there at two in the morning? Stepping backward into the shadow of his house, he observed a man and a woman standing within a few feet of each other. After a few seconds, they gave each other a quick kiss, and the man walked away.

Jessica's silhouette was unmistakable. Marc stayed pinned to the side of the house out of her line of sight while she walked toward her apartment.

Meinhard, now at the second-floor landing, stared at Riley, who was standing in the second-floor doorway. "What's he doing up? Shouldn't he be in bed?" he asked Marc.

"Yes, he should. I'll deal with him next."

Marc escorted Meinhard up the last flight of stairs to his apartment door.

"Tomorrow's Saturday, Dad. I'm taking the boys to Six Flags. Would you like to come with? You could keep me company while the boys go on the rides."

"What flags?"

"An amusement park. Like Kiddieland. Remember Kiddieland?"

"I remember taking my children there."

"Well, it's like Kiddieland but a lot bigger. You're welcome to come with us."

"I'd like that."

Marc settled back into his makeshift bed in the living room. His last thought before drifting off to sleep was whether the man Jessica had been kissing was her ex-husband Al or someone else.

* * *

Marc had invited Jessica and Tyler to join them at Six Flags, but Jessica had to work, so just Tyler came. The five of them piled in Marc's SUV and headed for the town of Gurnee, a forty-mile drive from Chicago. Marc and the three boys played a variety of car games along the way, some of which Marc had played as a child himself, like the alphabet game. Meinhard, sitting in the passenger's seat, remained silent the whole way.

None of the boys had ever been to Six Flags. Marc started them out by taking them to the little kids' rides. Marc and Meinhard sat on the bench watching the boys whiz past them as they went from one attraction to another.

It wasn't long before the boys said they wanted to go on the faster rides, like the roller coasters. After Marc was assured they met the height requirement, he allowed them to go on the tamest one. Seeing Riley and Josh so thoroughly delighted—smiling big and laughing hard—tugged at Marc's heart. He hadn't witnessed anything remotely close to it since they had moved in.

"I can't remember their names."

"Whose names, Dad?"

"Your kids."

"The taller one is Riley. The shorter—and younger—one is Josh."

"Nice names. What about the other one?"

"That's their friend, Tyler." He turned toward Meinhard. "Riley and Josh are Zenzi's kids."

His face lit up. "Zenzi?"

"Mm-hm."

"How is she?"

"She's fine."

"Why didn't she come today?"

"She had other things she had to do. She couldn't make it."

"I see. Too bad. She'd have fun here. Do you remember us going to Kiddieland?"

"I do remember that. It was fun."

"Zenzi liked the train. She would have gone on it all day long if we'd let her."

"I remember that too."

"I don't remember stuff much anymore."

The wistful tone in his voice pulled on Marc's emotions.

"I know, Dad. I know."

Chapter 37

Zenzi entered the courtroom looking years beyond her actual age of thirty-two—dark circles under expressionless eyes, ill-fitting clothes, and a shuffle to her walk that reminded Marc of their father. She caught Marc's eye before sitting down—her glare was brief. He didn't have to be within earshot to know that she asked her attorney why he was there.

The charges against her were painful to hear as they were being presented in rapid-fire succession by the prosecuting attorney: disorderly conduct, child endangerment, child neglect, and illegal possession of a firearm. Zenzi had pleaded guilty to all charges except child neglect.

Marc understood the charges, even agreed with them, but didn't know how and why she had come into possession of a gun. But his gut told him Nick had to have had something to do with it.

The prosecuting attorney made his case by calling to the witness stand one of the policemen who had responded to Meinhard's complaint, who detailed what they had found when they entered her apartment. That was followed by testimony from the DCFS caseworker who talked about what she had found.

Zenzi's public defender pleaded her case by talking about her addiction to alcohol and her desire to get the help she needed to become a clean and sober functioning member of society and devoted mother. She talked about the love Zenzi had for her children and admitted how her addiction negatively affected her ability to make good decisions, especially when it came to parenting. She emphasized the fact that dependence on alcohol was a disease—characterized by altered brain structure and function—that required specific treatment not unlike any other medical disorder. She informed the court Zenzi was twenty-three days sober and committed to staying that way.

The sentencing hearing lasted an hour, with the judge asking many questions—pertinent questions in Marc's opinion—about the mitigating and aggravating factors in the case. Marc felt a painful twist in his stomach when the judge asked about Nicholas Lee.

Zenzi's attorney explained Zenzi and Nick's relationship, making the household sound like a scene right out of *The Brady Bunch*. When the judge asked if Nick was present in the courtroom, she was told that he was not. When the judge asked if he had custody of the boys, Zenzi's public defender stated Marc's name and his relationship to Zenzi.

Based on the judge's tone and facial expressions throughout the hearing, Marc sensed the outcome wasn't going to go in Zenzi's favor. And he was right. The judge ordered two hundred hours of community service for the disorderly conduct charge, six months in county jail for each of three remaining charges, twelve months of probation, and a thousand-dollar fine. Afterward, Zenzi was handcuffed and escorted out of the courtroom.

Eighteen months in county jail. Marc couldn't imagine her spending that long confined to a six-by-eight cell in a facility that housed thousands of criminals, many of them serious offenders.

* * *

"That's not fair!" Riley yelped.

"Calm down, Riley," Marc warned him.

"She's not a bad person. She's a freakin' alcoholic!"

"She broke the law, son."

"Don't call me that!"

Riley stomped out of the living room and into his bedroom, slamming the door behind him.

Marc held his breath in a futile attempt to calm his nerves. He struggled to remember some of the advice Jessica had given him about what to do in these emotional situations.

He knocked on Riley's door.

"Go away!"

"I want to talk to you, Riley."

"Well, I don't want to talk to you."

"You have no choice. I'm the one in charge here."

"Yeah? Well, maybe that's the problem."

Marc's stomach lurched, causing him to pause for a moment before opening the door.

"What are you feeling right now, Riley?"

"Are you kidding me? Our mom is going to be in jail for eighteen months, and you're asking me how I feel about that?"

"Yes, that's what I'm asking," he said trying to convince himself that it wasn't a stupid question. "Are you angry? Sad? Confused? Tell me so we can talk it through."

"All of it."

"You know what? Me too."

Josh, who'd been downstairs playing with Tyler, returned.

"What's going on?" he asked.

"Mom got eighteen months, that's what's going on."

"What does that mean?" Josh asked.

"She's going to be in some shitty jail cell for a year and a half, that's what it means."

"I know you're upset, Riley, but you're going to have to watch your language. It's inappropriate."

"Inappropriate? Mom's in jail right now. *That's* what's inappropriate."

"Actually, it's not. She broke the law."

"She's sick."

"That doesn't excuse her from breaking the law."

"What did she do?" Josh asked.

He hesitated, not sure how much to tell them. "Some people thought that she wasn't providing a safe environment for you guys."

"They don't even know us," Riley added.

"They did an investigation, and that's what they came up with."

"So what? Now that's over and so she should come home."

"She has to pay for it, Riley. That's how it works."

"Yeah? Well, I think it stinks."

"I don't," Josh said.

Riley and Marc turned to look at Josh.

"C'mon, Riley, you know she didn't take care of us. Half the time we don't have food in the house, and when there is we have to make our own meals. Other kids don't have to do that."

"You're something else, butt-face."

"Riley! You apologize to your brother, and if you keep using that kind of language…"

"What? You're gonna throw me in jail too?"

"First of all, I wasn't the one who put your mother in jail—she did that herself. And secondly, young man, I'm the one who got you out of foster care, and I'm the one who…"

"Can do what?"

"Look, I'm on *your* side. I'm the one who's going to be there for you when you need it. Do I know what I'm doing all the time? No. Do I have all the answers? Of course not. I'm new at this. But I think we can get through this together. But only if you work with me, not against me."

Josh nodded.

Riley stared out the window.

"Riley?"

"Whatever."

"Why are you upset?"

"I'm not upset—okay?"

Marc got up. "Okay. I invited Jessica and Tyler up for a cookout tonight. Let's go to the store and buy what we need for it."

"Whatever."

* * *

The cowbell jolted Marc from a deep sleep—it was happening more and more lately. Meinhard didn't have a problem staying inside the apartment during daylight hours, but something was triggering him to wander out at night.

Marc threw on his pants and stumbled out the back door, catching Meinhard halfway down the steps.

"Dad, come on back. It's two-thirty."

Meinhard kept on walking until he reached ground level.

"Dad! Stop walking, will you?" When he caught up with him, he grabbed him gently by the arm. "Dad...stop."

Meinhard turned to face him and said, "Who are you?"

"I'm Marc...Markus, your son."

"Oh."

"You need to come back to the apartment. It's the middle of the night."

"Yes, I know. I work nights."

Marc held on to his arm and guided him back up the stairs. "C'mon. Let's get you back to bed."

"But I'll be late for work."

"I'll explain it to your boss. It'll be okay."

* * *

Marc spent the afternoon searching the Internet for assisted living places for Meinhard. He found several decent-looking ones averaging $3,000 a month, much more than he could afford. He called a few agencies about live-in help and learned the cost of that would be about the same.

"I may know someone," Jessica told Marc over a couple of pale ales in his living room that evening after the boys had gone to bed.

Jessica proceeded to tell Marc about a waitress at work who had a brother with Down Syndrome. He functioned well—was mostly affected physically and in his speech. According to his sister, Ruby, his IQ was in the low-normal range. Jessica said she'd met him a few times, and he'd seemed fine to her, a very nice young man.

"He's turning twenty-three next month, and wherever he's staying won't let them stay past that age," she told Marc. "Why I even bring this up is because he babysits, and apparently he's good at it. He sits for the kids of two aldermen and several families at their church. He's been doing it for years. It's his life."

"I'm not sure that's what Meinhard needs."

"From what Ruby has told me, parents love Denver—"

"Denver?"

"Yeah. That's his name."

"Okay."

"Anyway, the parents and the kids love him."

"But Dad isn't a child."

"But sometimes he behaves like one, right?"

"Yeah, he does."

"And he needs supervision...like a child."

"He does, but if this Denver person needs supervision himself, how can he be trusted to supervise my dad."

"I don't know. I guess you'd have to talk to his sister about that. I explained the situation here, and she seemed to think it could work out. You never know."

Marc gave it a moment's thought.

"I'll call her," he said.

* * *

"It's nice to meet you, Mr. Nussbaum." Denver had a big smile on his face as he held out his hand to Marc. He was barely five feet tall, neatly dressed. His voice was soft and his speech slow and deliberate, like he had to think about each word before saying it.

"And it's nice to meet you, too, Denver. That's an unusual name you have."

"No, it's not. In the twenties, over eight million babies were named Denver." His pronunciation of certain words was poor, and he omitted the endings of some of the longer words, but not so much that Marc didn't understand what he was saying.

"Is that right?"

"Yes, it is. You can check it out if you want. It's on Wikipedia."

"You go on the Internet?"

"Yes, sir."

"You must be pretty smart."

"I am smart. Would you like to know why I am so smart?"

"Why?"

"Because I remember things. If you don't remember things, people will think you're not smart, even if you are. So I make sure I remember things."

"That's very insightful."

"I know."

"Tell me about your babysitting experience, Denver."

"I've watched over babies and other children for five years and four months, and I have never had a...anything I couldn't handle. Would you like to hear about the worst thing I ever had to handle?"

"Yes, I would."

"I was watching Binny. He's two. That's not his real name. His real name is Bernard, but his parents call him Binny. So I call him Binny too. Binny does everything fast. Everything. He stuck his head in between two of the wooden... things by the stairs and couldn't get out. I tried, but I couldn't get him out either. So I called 9-1-1 and told them what happened. I waited for them to get there, and then I called Binny's parents, who were at a restaurant so they could hear what was going on. The police said they would have to cut the post. I asked Binny's dad if that was okay, and he said yes. He told me where the police could find a saw. They didn't have to come home. They finished dinner there. I handled everything by myself."

"That was very smart of you. I don't know if I could have handled that any better."

"Probably not."

"It sounds like Binny's parents trusted you too."

"They all do."

"So what would you think about taking care of an adult?"

"Why would an adult need to be taken care of?"

"The adult is my father. He lives upstairs. He doesn't always remember what to do or where he can and can't go. He needs supervision."

"I could do that."

"What if he started to wander off and wouldn't listen to you when you told him to come back? What would you do?"

"I'd bring him back by the hand. And I'd tell him why."

"What if he wouldn't listen?"

"If they know I'm the one in charge, they usually listen."

He was believable.

"Would you like to meet him?"

"Sure."

Marc led Denver up the stairs to his apartment where they found Meinhard standing in front of the hall mirror with a dazed expression.

"Are you all right, Dad?"

Meinhard turned around. "Huh?"

"Are you okay?"

"The same, I suppose."

Marc took his arm. "Let's go sit at the table."

The three of them sat down at the kitchen table, where Meinhard's cell phone lay in several pieces.

"What happened?" Marc asked.

"It broke."

He introduced Meinhard to Denver, and the two shook hands.

"Denver here is looking for a place to live, maybe with a roommate."

"That's nice."

"This apartment has two bedrooms."

"Mm-hm."

"I'm going to be living in Zenzi's apartment downstairs for quite some time."

"I think you told me that before."

"So my bedroom will be empty for a while."

"Oh."

"May I ask him something, Mr. Nussbaum?" Denver asked Marc.

"Yes, of course."

"Meinhard, do you play checkers?"

"I used to. Loved that game. Don't have anyone to play with anymore."

"I play checkers, and I'm good. I could probably beat you."

"I doubt it."

Denver picked up the main piece of Meinhard's phone and inspected it.

"Do you want me to fix this for you?"

Meinhard gave him a questioning look. "Sure."

Denver continued talking while he fiddled with the phone.

"So can I challenge you to a game of checkers?"

"I'll get the board."

Meinhard got up and headed toward his bedroom.

"How did you know my father liked checkers?"

"There's one in his shirt pocket. I can tell by the shape."

Marc stared at him.

"Here. It's fixed," he said as he handed the phone to Marc. "Do I have the job?"

"We haven't talked about pay."

"I know you'll be fair."

"You've got the job."

Chapter 38

The call came two weeks after Zenzi's sentencing.

"This is the assistant executive director of the Cook County Department of Corrections. May I please speak with Mr. Marc Nussbaum?"

"This is he."

"I'm very sorry to have to tell you this over the phone, Mr. Nussbaum, but early this morning your sister Kreszentia was found unresponsive in her jail cell. The executive director has asked me to convey his deepest sympathy to you and your family."

"Deepest sympathy? What! Why? She...died?"

"Yes. I'm afraid so."

A wave of dizziness overtook him—he sat down on the bed to keep from falling. "What? I don't understand. How could that happen?"

"A guard went to bring her breakfast this morning and couldn't wake her. CHS was called right away, but she had already passed."

"CHS?"

"They're our on-site health service."

"I can't believe this! How did she die?"

"I really can't tell you anything more at this time, but I can give you the number of the Cook County Medical Examiner, who handles all our deaths. He—"

"All your deaths! How many do you have?"

"We house over nine thousand inmates on any given day, sir."

"Wow."

"I'm very sorry for your loss."

Marc called the Medical Examiner's office and was told he'd have to come in with proper next-of-kin documentation so they could discuss their preliminary findings and next steps.

Marc hung up the phone, and grateful that the boys were in school, buried his head in his hands and sobbed.

How could they let her die in jail? Weren't there signs she was in trouble? Had she asked for help and not received any? What kind of jail was that?

He moaned at the thought of how he would find the right words to tell the boys, if in fact there were any: "Passed away," "departed," and "in heaven" all meant the same thing—she was dead.

As he mulled over what the consequences of her death would mean, he stared at the cow-head cookie jar on the counter, which didn't seem stupid or silly at all now. Her eccentric collection of cow things was part of her personality...part of her.

He searched his brain for the last conversation he'd had with her. It bothered him that he couldn't remember when that was. It had to have been when she was still at home because he hadn't talked to her since she'd gone to jail.

I should have bailed her out.

Closing his eyes, he pictured her as she'd looked when she walked into the courtroom— so pathetic in the ill-fitting outfit she had obviously not picked out herself. His last glimpse of her had been when they'd handcuffed her and escorted her out of the courtroom. She hadn't looked back at him.

Marc's throat thickened with the thought of how she might have died. Did she suffer? No one should have to die alone.

I should have been there.

She wasn't a bad person, just messed up. And sick. Alcoholism was a sickness, he reminded himself. A sickness she couldn't manage on her own. More tears came when he thought about her last moments on earth—alone in a jail cell.

The boys would miss her, and Baby Emma would never get to know her.

I wish I hadn't been so hard on her.

Thinking back to some of their last conversations, it tore at his heart that she died without receiving any reconciliation for being molested by Harley Cooper. Whether it was the truth or her alcoholic brain conjuring up a story that she believed was true didn't matter—she had died believing her father had known about it and had done nothing.

The boys would be out of school at 3:45 and were expecting him to pick them up to drive them to soccer practice. Marc thought of ways he could get someone else to pick them up and bring them home. But in the end, he knew he had to be the one to do it, even though he didn't know where he would find the strength to make the half-mile drive there and back without losing it.

There would be arrangements to make, affairs to settle, the boys' future to think about. Until now, he had handled things day by day. Contemplating the boys' future brought overseeing their welfare to a whole different level, and it terrified him.

When he arrived at their school, Riley and Josh were talking to a small group of boys their age. Riley ran over to his truck.

"We're going to go to practice with Will. His mom's driving. Sorry you made the trip for nothing."

"No. Come with me. Go get Josh."

"C'mon. We want to go with them. What's the problem?"

"Get Josh and come home with me."

"What the—"

"Just go! I mean come. Just get your brother, damn it!"

The boys climbed into the back seat, buckled up, and said nothing on the ride home. Once there, Marc told them to go into the living room.

"Sit down, boys. There's something I have to tell you."

"Are we in trouble?" Josh asked. "I don't remember doing anything wrong today."

"No, you're not in trouble. This has to do with your mom." He choked on the last two words, something he had hoped he wouldn't do. He sat down in front of them and looked into their eyes a long moment before speaking.

"Sometime during the night, your mom passed away." He swallowed hard in a failed attempt to hold back his emotions. His gaze went from one boy to the other as the tightness in his chest rose up into his neck. "I'm so sorry, guys," he blurted out. He fell to his knees in front of them and wrapped his arms around them. "I'm so sorry," he said into Josh's chest.

Josh sobbed. Riley broke away.

"She died? How'd she do that?" Riley snapped.

"How?"

"How'd she die? Don't they take care of people in jail? They just let them die there?"

"No, they don't just let people die there. What—"

"Then what happened?" Riley insisted.

Marc rose to his feet, wiped away his tears, and faced Riley. "They found her in her jail cell this morning."

"Was she sick?" Josh asked.

"It doesn't matter, Josh," Riley said. "She's dead!"

"What about us?" he cried out. "What's going to happen to us?"

Before Marc could respond, Josh broke into long, hard sobs. Marc took him in his arms and rocked him back and forth until his cries diminished into whimpers.

"Well, I hate her!" Riley shouted and ran into his bedroom, slamming the door behind him.

Josh pulled away from Marc and followed his brother.

"Josh, wait."

Josh turned around, wiping his face in the sleeve of his shirt.

"Let's let him be alone for a little while, okay?"

Josh froze, apparently torn between listening to Marc and being with his brother. He chose his brother.

* * *

The next day, Marc told Jessica about Zenzi's death and left the boys with her while he went to the Medical Examiner's office. There he was told by the ME's assistant that Zenzi had likely had a seizure, as she had bitten through her tongue.

Marc's stomach instantly knotted up. "Bit through her tongue?"

"I'm afraid it's common with seizures. She also had a rather significant contusion on her head, and I mention that because head trauma can cause seizures."

"Or maybe she had a seizure and fell and hit her head?"

"Possibly."

"Could you tell how recent the injury to her head was?"

"Perhaps during the autopsy they can, especially if it's relatively recent."

"What else causes seizures?" Marc asked.

"A whole laundry list of things—brain tumors, kidney disease, encephalitis, heart disease, epilepsy, just to name a few. It will probably come out in the toxicology report."

"How long does that take?"

"Figure four to six weeks. By then the autopsy will have been completed as well."

"It takes that long for an autopsy?"

"We perform over five thousand autopsies a year, and right now we only have twelve doctors. If there's a big backlog, it takes longer. Hard to tell."

Marc drove home thinking that if Zenzi had been mistreated in jail in any way and if that had caused her death, or if it came out that she had been neglected when in need of medical attention, someone would pay.

* * *

Zenzi had died on a Monday and was scheduled to be buried the following Thursday, the day after the initial autopsy. Marc kept the boys home from school for the week. One of the first calls he made was to Nick.

"I'm very sorry for your loss, Marc," Nick said after Marc told him of Zenzi's death. "Sonya and I will, of course, tell Baby Emma about her mother when she's old enough to understand. Is there anything we can do in the meantime?" He detected no emotion in Nick's voice. He expected him to say more.

"No, I can't think of anything. I'll let you know the arrangements when they've been finalized."

"Thank you."

In the meantime, Riley's sometimes withdrawn, sometimes angry behavior worried Marc more than Josh's sudden and frequent crying outbursts—at least Josh was releasing some of what he was feeling. Marc didn't know *what* Riley was feeling. He was convinced that in between Riley's outbursts, when he exhibited an unwavering coolness, it was his way to show Marc and maybe even himself that he was in control of his emotions. Marc had personal knowledge of this tactic—he had done the same thing as a kid.

On the day before the funeral, Marc was in the backyard talking to Jessica when an ear-piercing sound of glass breaking caused them both to jump. When Marc saw a stool come flying out of the second-story window along with shards of glass, he pushed Jessica out of the way to keep her from getting hit.

The stool shattered when it hit the ground, with pieces of it flying in every direction. When he looked up to see from where it had come, Marc saw Riley glaring down at them from behind the broken window—with his hands on his hips and an obstinate look on his face.

Marc stared at the remnants of the stool on the ground—like broken pieces of a child's life. "Excuse me while I try to handle this," he told Jessica.

"Marc?"

"Yes."

"Feelings."

"I know."

"Send Josh down here if you want," she told him.

"Okay."

Marc found Riley sitting on his bed, his head hung down so low that Marc couldn't see his face.

"Do you want to talk about this?" Marc asked him.

"Not really," Riley said almost inaudibly.

"Well, we're going to. That stool almost hit Tyler's mom," Marc said in a remarkably calm tone.

Riley looked up. "I wasn't aiming it at her. Can you tell her that?"

"No, because you're going to tell her that when you go down there and apologize to her."

"I'll pay for the window."

"Yes, you will. You can work it off until it's completely paid for." He tried to read Riley's facial expression. "What made you do it?"

Riley looked past Marc and shrugged his shoulders.

"Mad at something?"

"I guess."

"At who?"

"Mom."

"Why your mom?"

"'Cause all this is her fault."

"We've talked about this before, Riley. Your mom was sick—she had a disease."

"Then she should have gotten help sooner."

"I wish she *had* gotten help sooner."

"You should have *made* her get help sooner!"

"Me? But she—"

"At least Nick tried."

So now Nick is the hero?

"Look, Riley..." Marc stopped short of saying something he knew he'd later regret.

"What?"

"I understand you're angry. I do." Marc moved closer to him, but Riley backed away. "And I wish none of this had ever happened, but it did. And now we have to deal with it."

Riley jumped up and moved toward the door.

"*You* deal with it," he said before exiting the room.

"Riley," he called after him.

"What."

"We're not finished."

Riley returned with a scowl on his face and leaned up against the doorframe. Marc didn't know whether to shake him or hug him.

"Look, I'm having the same problems you're having with—"

"Right."

"No, I am. I don't know how I'm going to get through this either."

Marc could tell by the annoyed look on Riley's face that he didn't want to talk any longer, and even though ending the conversation would have alleviated his own angst, he went on.

"For as far back as I can remember, whenever I was sick, it didn't matter what it was, your mother would throw a can of chicken noodle soup on the stove and make me eat the whole thing. I could have twisted my ankle, and that was her remedy. Like chicken soup would cure anything."

Riley smirked. "She did that to us too, and I hate chicken noodle soup."

"And what about the way she couldn't tell a joke without messing up the punchline, but she would laugh that goofy laugh in the end anyway."

Riley laughed. "You got that right. Mom could screw up a knock-knock joke."

"And what about her singing?"

"Oh, my god! We used to close the windows when she sang so the neighbors didn't hear." He threw his hands in the air. "She'd crank up the stereo with that old Bon Jovi CD of hers and sing 'Livin' on a Prayer' over and over again. It was the only one she knew the words to."

"And she couldn't carry a tune to save her life."

"She was bad." Riley said with a trembling chin. He laughed. "And don't even get me started on the cows."

"I'm going to miss her."

"Me too," Riley said through overdue tears.

Marc got up and let him bury his face in his shirt.

"It's okay to cry, buddy. Let it all out."

After a moment, still holding on to Marc, Riley asked, "Do you think she wanted to die?"

He hesitated before answering. "I don't think so—she wanted to be with you guys more than anything. That I know for sure."

Riley backed out of Marc's hold. "That's what I still don't get—she wanted alcohol more than us."

"That's so not true. One thing I've learned about alcoholism is that it controls you, you don't control it. She loved you guys. I know that for a fact."

Riley's demeanor shifted. "So do you think she's happy now?"

"In heaven, you mean?"

"Yeah."

"I think whenever she looks down at the two of you, she is."

"I hope so."

"Feeling better now?"

"I guess so."

Chapter 39

Marc was grateful to Jessica when she offered to handle Zenzi's funeral arrangements—he had more than he could handle dealing with the boys' reaction to her death in addition to his own grief. They agreed on a small private service with just Marc, the boys, and Jessica—and Nick if he came. Marc suspected Zenzi had kept to herself, probably to hide her drinking, even though the boys said she knew lots of people. His suspicions were confirmed when he couldn't find evidence of any names, phone numbers, or e-mail addresses among her things. They put a death notice in the *Chicago Tribune* just in case.

Marc went back and forth when it came to deciding whether to tell Meinhard. In the end, he decided not to since the last time he had mentioned her name, Meinhard had asked who she was.

The days prior to the funeral were draining, as Marc dealt with the boys' bouts of anger, sadness, and confusion. One minute they would appear to be fine—in acceptance of what had happened to their mother—and then something would trigger a burst of emotion that required Marc's attention. His time alone after the boys went to bed offered little solace—he had his own emotions to manage.

Marc woke up on the day of the funeral and looked out the window at a beautiful blue sky. The middle of May seemed like a cruel time to have to bury someone—just when birds were building their nests, rabbits were hopping around in the yard, and plants were coming back to life after a long cold winter—a time for birth and rebirth, not death.

When he woke the boys that morning, he found them sleeping in the same twin bed—Riley's body cupped around his younger brother's in a protective posture. He gently shook Riley's shoulder until he awoke.

"Time to get up, bud."

Riley rubbed his eyes, pointed to Josh, and said, "He had a bad night."

"You're a good big brother, you know that?"

"Yeah, I guess."

Riley shook Josh until he awoke.

"C'mon, Josh. Time to get up." He looked at Marc. "What time do we have to go?"

"In a couple of hours. I thought I'd make pancakes for breakfast."

"With sliced banana on top?" Josh asked with a sad face.

"Is that how your mom used to make them?"

Josh struggled to keep back the tears. "A long time ago she did that. Chocolate milk too?"

Marc nodded. "I think I saw cocoa in the cupboard."

While they ate, Marc explained what they could expect at the service. When he got to the part about their mother's presence, in the casket, Josh's eyes grew big.

"No way," Josh said.

"Remember when Robin Williams died and they showed it on TV?" Riley asked Josh.

"Robin who?"

"Mork."

"Oh. Yeah, but he wasn't there."

"Yes, he was. He was in that long box."

"No way. Mom's going to be in a box like that?"

"Yes, but keep in mind all that's in there is her body," Marc explained. "Her soul went to heaven right after she died."

"So she won't have a body in heaven?" Josh asked.

"I'm pretty sure we must get new bodies in heaven. Maybe what happens is we get the body we had way before we died, when everything was working right."

"Do animals go to heaven?" Josh asked.

"Um…I would think so."

"So Mom will be with all the animals I've buried?"

"How many have you buried?" Marc asked.

"Lots. Mostly bugs."

"Well, I suppose so."

"She isn't going to like that part."

"I don't think bugs in heaven bother people. Things are pretty peaceful up there."

"I hope so."

"Do you guys have any other questions about today?" Marc asked them.

"Can we say goodbye to Mom even though her body is empty?" Josh asked.

"Of course. And she'll hear you from heaven."

"Really?"

"You can count on it."

The service took place in a small outdoor Interment Chapel in a Protestant cemetery where years earlier Marc's father had purchased four plots, one of which contained Marc's mother. Arriving a few minutes early, they entered the open-air pavilion that served as a chapel. The first thing they saw was Zenzi's casket at the front, draped in a crème-colored pall with deep red borders and crosses.

"Are you ready to say goodbye, boys?"

They walked past several rows of empty church-like pews toward the casket, which Marc had decided to keep closed during the service. Riley, who hadn't said anything on the ride over, kept off to one side while Marc and Josh stood near the casket.

Josh looked up at him. "Are you sure she's in there?" he whispered.

"Yes, I'm sure."

Out of his jacket pocket he retrieved a small cow figurine.

"This was her favorite cow. I thought she might want it with her."

Marc swiped a tear from his cheek. "We'll give it to the pastor afterward, and he'll make sure she gets it."

Josh told his mother about the cow and that he was going to miss her. "And Mom, good luck with God," he said.

"Riley? Did you want to say anything to your mom?"

He shook his head.

Marc said a silent goodbye to his sister, and when he turned around to face the rows of pews, he couldn't believe what he saw—they were half full of people.

Marc and the boys joined Jessica who was sitting alone in the front row. "Who are all these people?" he whispered to her.

Jessica shrugged.

Thinking the people in the pews must be at the wrong funeral service, he figured they'd realize it as soon as Zenzi's name was mentioned.

Marc had asked Pastor Whitlow from the Methodist church where he and Zenzi had gone to Sunday school to preside over the service. He entered the chapel from behind a screen near the small alter, acknowledged Marc with a nod, and began the service by leading the group in the Lord's Prayer.

Not a very religious man, Marc still found the pastor's words spiritually soothing. He glanced down at the boys every so often during the service to see how they were taking it all in. They listened intently, and when the pastor said he had a poem for God from Zenzi's sons, they looked at Marc and smiled.

If flowers grow in heaven God,
Please pick a bunch for me.
Place them in my mother's arms,
And tell her they're from me.

Josh became emotional as the poem was being read, as did Jessica and many of the mourners still seated behind them. Marc placed an arm around Josh's shoulder. To his surprise, Riley, the tough guy, buried his head in Marc's side.

Next the pastor said a few words about Zenzi that Jessica had provided for him, talking about the love she'd had for her family, especially her two sons, her beloved Cubs team, and anything patterned like a cow. The cow humor provided some relief.

The pastor then recited a verse from John 14.

In my Father's house are many rooms; if it were not so, I would have told you. I am going there to prepare a place for you.

The pastor talked about Zenzi's journey home to God and ended the service with a reading from Ecclesiastes 3:1-2.

To every thing there is a season, and a time to every purpose under the heaven:
A time to be born, and a time to die;
A time to plant, and a time to pluck up that which is planted.

Marc was shocked to learn that the lyrics to a Byrds song—one of Zenzi's favorites—had biblical roots.

When the pastor had finished, Marc turned around to look at the other mourners, catching a glimpse of Nick as he walked away from the group.

A woman in the row behind him stood up. About Marc's age, wearing what appeared to be a man's coat and worn jeans, she reached out for Marc's hand.

"You don't know me, but your sister used to come to the corner of Cottage Grove and 112th Street where I used to sit looking for handouts. She'd always put change in my cup. Even in the winter. Or when it was raining cats and dogs. And I know she didn't have any other business on that corner. And another thing, I know she didn't have much herself. I'll bet she did that for two years. I'll never forget her for that."

"Thank you for coming and sharing that story. May I ask you, how did you hear of her death?" he asked.

"Oh, word gets around in my neighborhood, like wildfire."

The woman seated next to her relayed a similar story to Marc—she had been a victim of domestic violence with a then two-year-old daughter. "I met her at the shelter. She gave me a pair of socks when she saw I didn't have any, and it was winter. On the first day, she gave them to me. She didn't even know me. She was like that. Half the people here are from the shelter. We all feel real bad she died."

One by one, the people in attendance, mostly women, relayed to Marc how they knew Zenzi and how her kindness and generosity to them when they had been down and out would never be forgotten. He listened intently, and with each one he became more disappointed in himself for not being aware of this side of his sister.

After everyone had left, Marc thanked the pastor, gave him the cow figurine, and led the way out of the chapel with Riley, Josh, and Jessica in tow. As he neared the rear of the chapel, he felt a tug on the back of his jacket.

"Uncle Marc, I have something to say to Mom," Riley said. "Alone."

"We'll wait for you by the car."

Marc watched Riley walk toward the casket, so proud of him.

Jessica had suggested that Marc and the boys go somewhere together afterward, just the three of them, somewhere other than their apartment, somewhere quiet where they could talk if needed. So he drove the boys to Belmont Harbor—a tranquil setting where they could reflect on times with their mom if that's what they felt like doing.

They each sat on a boulder near the water's edge. Under the overcast sky, a silvery mist floated right above the water's surface—eerily similar to the one Marc had encountered when he had visited another section of the Lake Michigan shoreline two months earlier, when life seemed so uncertain for *him*.

Josh interrupted his thoughts. "You know what I was thinking when that preacher was talking?"

Until now, Marc hadn't noticed how much Josh took after his mother—same eyes, same square jaw line.

"What?"

"That maybe I should die too."

"Why would you say that, bud?"

"So I could be with Mom."

"What about us?" Marc asked.

"We could all die. Together. Then we'd be a family again."

"And someday we will...not all at the same time though...and not until we're old and gray and walking with canes."

Josh smiled. "I don't really want to die."

"I'm glad to hear that, because I'd really miss you."

"You would?"

"Of course I would."

"No, you wouldn't," Riley added.

"Why do you think that?" Marc asked.

"You're not our dad or anything."

"I don't have to be your dad to love you...and miss you."

"You *love* us?" Josh asked.

I haven't made that clear? After all I've done?

"Of course I do. If I didn't—"

"He has to, Josh," Riley said. "He's our legal guardian."

This wasn't how Marc had envisioned the discussion going.

"That's not why," Marc told them.

"Why then?" Riley asked, clearly irritated with the conversation.

"You want to know something?"

There was no response.

"Remember that day I knocked on your door and you answered it, Riley. Your mom was in trouble that day. I think that was the first time I realized exactly how much trouble she was in. Anyway—I'm going to be completely honest with you here—the last thing on my mind was to take care of you guys. I didn't know you very well. Hell, I didn't really know you guys at all."

"Hey—watch your language," Riley said with a smile.

"All right. I had that coming. Anyway, I didn't know what to do with you. I just hoped your mom would hurry up and get better so I could get on with my life." He paused to find the right words. "But then the more I got to know you, the more I cared about you, and it may have taken me a while, but it got to a point where I knew I'd do anything for the two of you. And that's where I am now."

"Where?" Josh asked. "I don't get it."

"Sitting at Belmont Harbor, you goofball," Riley quipped.

"You know what we should do?" Marc asked.

"What?"

"Let's go to the nursery and buy some things to make a garden in the backyard in memory of your mom. We'll get some small bushes, some perennials, some annuals, some—"

"Some what?" Josh asked.

"C'mon, let's go. I'll explain it in the car. And some stones or 'lawn art,' as they call it in Lake Forest. What do you say? Good idea?"

"Great idea," Riley said.

"I guess so," Josh added. "What's for lunch?"

Later that day, after the boys had gone to bed, Marc went through Zenzi's dresser drawers, taking stock of what items he could donate to the women's shelter where she had made so many friends. In the top drawer, he found a note card. Written on it in her handwriting was, "Be grateful to those who were there for you, and when it's their time, return the favor." He found the sentiment ironic given that he had never received one word of gratitude from her.

Also in the drawer was an envelope containing several pamphlets—Addiction

Treatment Services in Illinois, Finding Treatment for Alcohol and Drug Addiction, and Alcoholics Anonymous for the Woman that included a list of local AA meeting places. On the front of this pamphlet, she had written in big block letters, When the alcohol wears off, the problems are still there. He assumed she had never gotten past reading the pamphlets.

After rummaging through what appeared to be every picture and card her boys had ever drawn for her, Marc found a photograph of his mother that must have been taken well before she had died. He'd never seen it before. Beneath it were twenty or so photocopies of the same photo, causing Marc to wonder if Zenzi had been afraid of losing it.

Tucked into the far corner of another drawer, he found a bunch of letters bundled together with a rubber band. The return address for the one on top read PFC Gerard Hill, Baghdad, Iraq. He opened it and read the first page—it thanked Zenzi for a crossword puzzle book, gum, Q-tips, and her sons' artwork. He flipped though the other envelopes—each from a different serviceman.

The bottom drawer was filled with Skittles, a few dozen small boxes of them, in every flavor imaginable. Marc smiled as he remembered Zenzi as a small child loving Skittles but not being able to have them—they barely had enough money for food. When she was old enough to get a little job helping out a neighbor, the first thing she had done with her pay was go to the corner store and buy a box of Skittles. When Dad found out, he'd made her return it and give him the money to teach her a lesson not to waste money on candy. At some point, she must have decided she'd never go without Skittles again.

Feeling somewhat consoled by going through his sister's things, Marc put everything back and wished for the umpteenth time that her life hadn't ended the way it had and that he had played a better role in it.

Chapter 40

"He can't do that!" Marc told his attorney over the phone. Just when things had started to settle down into a reasonable routine for the family that Marc was working so hard to regenerate, he'd received a summons to appear in court—Nicholas Lee was seeking ownership and occupancy of Marc's house.

"Let me do some further digging, and I'll get back to you," his attorney told him.

She called him back the next day.

"Who is Meinhard Nussbaum?" she asked him.

"My father."

"Apparently your father signed over the deed to your house to Nicholas Lee."

"What?!"

"Did your father own the house you're living in at one time?"

"Technically, he still does, but I've been the one maintaining it, paying taxes and everything, for years. When did he do this?"

"The transfer documents are dated May 23 of this year."

Four days after Zenzi's death.

"Are you freakin' kidding me? What can we do?"

"Do you know why your father would do such a thing?"

"My father is not in his right mind. Anyone could probably talk him into doing anything."

"Do you have power of attorney over him?"

"No."

"Do you have any medical diagnosis that would support your claim of his mental incapacity?"

"No."

"For now, gather any documents you have proving you have maintained the property for as far back as it goes, and we'll take him to court."

After he hung up, Marc marched upstairs where he found Meinhard taking a nap in the living room. Denver was sitting in a chair in the same room wearing headphones.

"Dad! Wake up!"

Denver pulled off the headphones. "Is everything all right, Mr. Nussbaum? You look upset."

"I'm upset all right." He turned to face Meinhard and yelled, "Dad!"

"His hearing is getting worse. I meant to tell you that the other day when you were here."

Marc shook Meinhard's arm.

"What's going on?" Meinhard asked.

"I need to talk to you."

"Okay."

"Would you like me to leave, Mr. Nussbaum?"

"No, Denver. You can stay."

Marc waved the summons in front of Meinhard's face. "Did you sign a document that gave ownership of this house to Nicholas Lee?"

"I don't know what you're talking about."

"Do you know who Nicholas Lee is?"

"No."

"Did you sign anything within the last thirty days?"

Meinhard sat up. "I don't think so. I don't know."

"Denver, has anyone come to the door since you've been here?"

"Just you. And my sister once."

"Has he been out of your sight at all since you've been here?"

"No, sir." He hesitated. "Well, there was this one day when we were in the backyard. This man came over. He said he wanted to talk to Meinhard in private, so I went by the garage, but I watched him the whole time."

"What did he look like?"

"He had on a suit."

"Could he have given my father a paper to sign?"

"Maybe. His back was to me, so—"

"What's the matter with you, boy? You're supposed to be watching him!"

"I'm sorry, Mr.—"

"I pay you to watch him... Do you know what this means? Forget it! Of course you don't."

Denver's face went pale. "I don't want you to be mad at me."

"Tell me that when we don't have a house to live in anymore."

"I'm really—"

"Go to your room."

"What's all the yellin' about?" Meinhard asked.

Marc swatted him on the head with the summons. "Sometimes I wish you were…"

* * *

Later that day, after most of the rage had left his body, Marc went back to his apartment to apologize to Denver.

"I can be a jerk when I'm upset," he told him.

Denver stared at Marc for several seconds without blinking.

"You're not going to disagree with me, are you?" Marc asked.

"No, sir."

Marc couldn't hold back a smile.

"I went off on you, and you didn't deserve it. I didn't mean to. And I'm sorry."

Denver's expression indicated to Marc that he needed to hear more.

"Whatever my father signed wasn't your fault. I was yelling at the wrong person. And I'm really sorry."

Still no reaction.

"Um, I was a jerk. I think I already said that. Oh, and I haven't told you lately what a good job you're doing. And I really mean that. I completely rely on you to watch over him, and you do a great job. Better than I've ever done."

Denver smiled.

"Is that what you were waiting for?"

"Yes, sir."

"So you forgive me?"

"Yes, sir."

"Friends?" Marc raised his arm for a high-five.

Denver did the same.

"Whew! Because I don't know what I'd do without you, Denver."

"You don't?"

"No, I don't."

"Can we agree on something?" Denver asked.

"Sure. What is it?"

"If you act like a jerk again, can I tell you you're acting like a jerk?"

Marc paused to reflect on previous occasions when situations had gotten the better of him.

"Yes. In fact, I insist on it."

* * *

Marc's attorney had asked that Meinhard accompany them to court for the hearing of their complaint against Nick's attempt to take possession of the house. Marc asked Denver to come as well, not only to watch over his father but also to demonstrate that his father needed watching over.

Nick's attorney explained to the judge that Meinhard had signed over his house to his client after his client's wife had died, that the house should have been in her name all along but signing it over to her was something Meinhard had neglected to do for years. Someone who wasn't privy to the real set of circumstances would have heard a heartfelt and convincing argument.

Marc's attorney took her time painting the real picture—Zenzi's addiction to alcohol, the real reason she and Nick had married, Marc's sole responsibility for the house for the past twelve years, his guardianship over Riley and Josh, and his father's failing health. Marc had asked his attorney not to mention why Zenzi had married Nick unless it was absolutely necessary. Apparently, his attorney thought it was.

The judge asked numerous questions and, after thirty minutes of discussion, asked Meinhard to stand.

Meinhard didn't stand.

The judge asked him again to stand.

Meinhard stared in another direction as if he hadn't heard the judge.

Denver stood up.

Oh, dear God.

"Your Honor, may I speak?"

The judge stared at Denver a long moment before asking him to identify himself.

"My name is Denver A. Pollack. P-O-L-L-A-C-K. The 'A' stands for Alvin, but I don't tell many people that. And in case it matters, I have Down Syndrome, but I'm still pretty smart."

"I can see that. And what is it you want to tell me, Mr. Pollack?"

"I am Mr. Nussbaum's caregiver." He pointed at Meinhard. "*This* Mr. Nussbaum. I call him Meinhard. He didn't stand up because his hearing is bad, and he doesn't always understand what's going on. Sometimes he does. But not always." He pointed toward Nick. "*That* man, that man sitting over there, he came to our house one day. He wanted to talk to Meinhard…in private, so I let him. I shouldn't have done that, but I didn't know that then." He pointed toward Marc. "I told Mr. Nussbaum I was sorry." He turned toward Marc. "Didn't I?"

Marc smiled. "Yes, you did."

The judge asked Denver a few questions before instructing him to sit down. After shuffling the papers in front of her for a long minute, she spoke.

"I am denying your petition for now, Mr. Lee, while I investigate this matter further. Court is adjourned."

No one spoke. Marc glanced over at Nick's expressionless face, wondering what was going through his head at the moment.

Marc, his attorney, Meinhard, and Denver walked out of the courtroom together. Once in the hallway, Marc reached out to shake Denver's hand.

"Thank you, Mr. Denver A. Pollack."

"For what?"

"I think you may have saved my house, but I do have to tell you that you may have been mistaken about one thing."

"What was that?"

"The 'A' in your name doesn't stand for Alvin."

"Yes, it does."

"Nope. It stands for Awesome."

Later that day, Marc called Denver's sister and, after a short discussion, drove into town to order an appropriate thank-you gift for Denver.

* * *

"Where's Josh?" Marc asked Riley later that evening. "In his room?"

"I guess."

"He's been spending a lot of time in there by himself lately."

"Really? I hadn't noticed."

Riley didn't look at Marc when he spoke. Marc suspected he was withholding something.

"Is he okay?"

"Mom just died. What do you think?"

"What was that?" Marc asked.

"What was what?"

"That noise. That scratching noise."

"I didn't hear anything."

"There it goes again. Is that coming from your room?" Marc got up and walked to the boys' room.

"Uncle Marc?" Riley called from the living room.

"What?"

"Can you come back here for a minute?"

They're up to something.

Marc opened the bedroom door where Josh was lying on the floor, face down, the upper half of his body under his bed.

"What are you doing down there?" Marc asked.

"Nothing."

"Josh?"

"Yes?"

"Come out from under there, will you?"

"Do I have to?"

"Yes, you have to!"

Josh came slithering out from underneath the bed and then sat crossed-legged on the floor. "What do you want?"

"What are you doing—"

The same scratching noise interrupted him.

"What was that?"

"I didn't hear anything."

"Josh, what's under your bed?"

"Dust?"

"What else is under there?"

Josh shrugged.

"You know it's been a long time since we cleaned under there. I'll go get the dust mop and shove it under there a few times so—"

"No!"

"Why?"

Just then a black cat ran out from underneath the bed and out the door.

"What was that?"

"A cat."

"I know it's a cat. Where did it come from?"

"Under the bed."

"Josh, where did you get it?"

"Hey, Josh," Riley yelled. "You better come out here!"

Josh darted toward the door.

"Not so fast, young man." Marc grabbed the back of his shirt. "You have some explaining to do."

"Can Riley be present?"

Marc couldn't stifle a smile.

"Let's go."

Riley was in the kitchen trying to corner the cat but wasn't having any luck.

"Okay, everyone sit down." He motioned toward the kitchen table. "Forget about the cat for now. Where did it come from?"

Josh looked at Riley.

"Don't look at me. This is all yours."

"I found it in our bushes. He was crying and everything."

"When?"

"Two days ago."

"You've had that thing here for two days without telling me?"

"I guess so."

"What do you mean you 'guess so'? Either you did or you didn't."

"What was the question?"

"First of all, I don't like cats. And second of—"

"Why not?"

"I just don't. And second of—"

"But why? You must have a reason."

"Because they're not dogs. How's that?"

"I don't think that's a good reason, Uncle Marc."

"Quit trying to get me off track. The cat's got to go."

"But—"

"It's got to go. What have you been feeding it?"

"Milk."

"That's it?"

"And Mrs. Gunther gave me some cat food."

"She did?"

"I sorta told her we had a new cat and you didn't have time to go to the store for food yet."

He didn't have the heart to yell at him for lying. "Riley, go see if you can find it."

"Josh, you know you did wrong by trying to hide it here. You had to know I'd find out sooner or later. And where has it been going to the bathroom?"

Josh shrugged.

"You don't know?"

"It kinda smells in our closet."

Riley came in carrying the cat.

"He seems kind of scrawny to me. When's the last time you fed him?"

"I ran out of food this morning."

"Riley, go next door to the Gunthers and ask them if we can borrow some more cat food. Tell them I'll pay them back."

"So we can keep him?" Josh asked.

"I didn't say that. I'll call the Anti-Cruelty Society and see if we can bring it in."

"But I named him and everything."

Marc stared at the frantic look on Josh's face.

"What did you name him?"

"Ralph."

"Ralph?"

"Yeah. He looks like a Ralph, don't you think?"

"You can't keep him, buddy."

"But look at his face."

Refusing to look at the cat's face, Marc turned his back on Josh and left the room.

"A cat could make me a little happy. You want me to be happy, don't you, Uncle Marc?"

That was so unfair.

Chapter 41

During the weeks following Zenzi's death, Riley and Josh continued to be moody—laughing one minute and crying the next. Riley would sometimes become withdrawn, not talking for an entire day at a time. Josh was more willing to express in words how he was feeling—talking about how sad or angry he was about his mother's death, or that he missed her, or he wished he could see her just one more time.

Both boys expressed feelings of guilt from time to time, bringing up instances when they had misbehaved when she was still alive, saying if only they hadn't done that maybe she wouldn't have gotten mad and drunk more because of it. Marc would explain again and again that they had nothing to do with her death, that alcoholism was a disease, a concept neither boy completely bought into.

Josh took to going into his mother's bedroom in the middle of the night and sleeping in her bed, usually accompanied by Ralph—who had escaped a trip to the animal shelter. Josh said he liked the way his Mom's bed smelled, that it reminded him of her, and that he was afraid of forgetting what she was like.

One day, about a month after Zenzi's death, Denver called Marc at work to tell him that Meinhard was acting strange—more than usual—and he was worried about him. He said Meinhard had stopped in the middle of a checkers game to ask what game they were playing. And he'd forgotten that he'd just taken a shower and took another one. That evening Marc paid Meinhard a visit.

"How are you doing today, old man?" he asked him.

Meinhard gave him a blank stare.

"Feeling okay?"

"Eh. And you?"

"I'm feeling great."

Meinhard gazed at him through clouded eyes without much expression. "You remind me of my son."

"Really?"

"I don't know what happened to him."

"You don't?" Marc asked.

"No, and it's a shame. He was such a good boy."

For a brief moment, Marc forgot about Meinhard's apparent dementia—that was the first kind word about him he had ever heard him utter.

"How old is your son?" Marc asked him.

"He's a man now. A good man. I miss him."

"You don't know where he is?"

"Maybe I do, but I don't remember. I don't remember very good anymore."

"Sometimes that happens as we get older. Sometimes I forget why I entered a room," Marc admitted.

"Sometimes I forget where I am."

"Do you know where you are now?"

"I'm home."

"Do you have any other children, Meinhard?"

"No, just the son."

The two men sat in silence for a moment.

"I like talking to you. Will you come visit again?" Meinhard asked.

"Sure. I'll come more often."

"That would be nice. Denver here is a good cook. Maybe you could come for dinner sometime."

"Okay. And maybe we could have a game of checkers too."

"I'd like that," Meinhard said.

The next day, Marc's attorney informed him that the court had officially denied Nick's petition to gain ownership of his house, and Nick was under investigation. Jessica called shortly afterward to let him know that, according to Mrs. Gunther's conversation at the latest Bingo game, Sonya had left Nick. Sonya's mother was pleased.

Marc wasn't. What did this mean for Emma?

* * *

It's a girl!

The text was from Juan.

Congrats old man! What's her name?

Sophia Nicole

Nice name.

Can I have tomorrow off?

No

???

But u can have rest of week off – paid.

You're alright no matter what they say about u. ☺

LOL

Now 4 bad news. Trinkos dog died. Vet thinks it was poisoned. Waiting 4 lab results. Not good.

What could have happened?

Shouldn't say this but MacCallum hated that dog.

Marc called Jessica to see if she could take the boys earlier than usual before school for the next three days so he could cover for Juan. She agreed as long as Marc picked up a bag of Garrett's popcorn for her the next time he was downtown, to which he agreed.

His next call was to the Trinkos.

"I'm so sorry to hear about Demetrius, Mrs. Trinko." Demetrius, a three-year-old Cockapoo, had unquestionably been Lynda Trinko's dog—Marc had never seen one without the other.

Her voice quivered as she spoke. "He was our child," she said. "Our only child. Here's Fred."

"He's not going to get away with this, I'll tell you that," Fred said with more assertiveness than Marc had ever heard before. Both Trinkos were very mild-mannered people.

"Do you know for sure what—"

"We just found out he died from carbamate poisoning."

Marc knew that carbamate was an insecticide but not much else. He had never used it. He wasn't licensed to use it.

"Really?"

"Yes, really."

"I'm so sorry."

"I know MacCallum did it. He's been after us for one thing after another ever since we moved here. He's threatened us. He's harassed us. And now he's gone too far. I know he's a client of yours too, so I shouldn't say anything more, except he's going to pay."

"But why would he poison your dog?"

"Oh, he's complained about him many times. Either barking or peeing through the fence onto his property. It's always something with him."

"Well, I don't know quite what to say except I'm sorry."

"I know you are."

* * *

Two months after the court hearing about the house, Marc's attorney called to say that Nick was being deported to Malaysia. Marc's first concern was for Emma. He asked about her.

"That's the other reason I called you, Marc. The child is in foster care."

"What?"

"Once Nick is back in his native country, he can appeal that decision, of course. I know of cases where the child was allowed to be reunited with the parent once they were reestablished in their native country, another one where the parent relinquished his parental rights in favor of the child being raised in the U. S., and one where the parent was allowed to reapply to stay in the U.S. because of the child."

"Why wouldn't they have contacted me? I'm her uncle!"

"There are no living relatives listed on the documentation I saw."

"Where is he now?"

"He's been incarcerated, waiting for deportation."

"Emma is family. I want her with us." The words were out before Marc had given it any thought.

"I can start those proceedings right away. You're talking legal guardianship, right?"

"Yes, and the sooner the better."

Marc hung up the phone, sat back in his easy chair, and contemplated what he had just done. He texted Jessica.

Help!

Now what?

Remember when I said I was in over my head?

Many times.

Well now I'm drowning.

Wanna talk?

You're wonderful.

Be right up.

Jessica arrived five minutes later carrying a sleeping Tyler. "Can I put him on Zenzi's bed? He has bronchitis, and I didn't want to leave him alone."

"Sure, go ahead."

Marc opened two beers.

Jessica hadn't changed out of her waitress uniform yet. He stood up when she reentered the living room and approached her.

"That's new," he said after sniffing her sleeve. "He's never made that before. New cook?"

"You're good. Harry quit the other day. New cook changed the menu."

Marc took another sniff.

"There's garlic in it. That's about all I can tell."

"Veal cutlets in red sauce."

"Sounds like a step up."

Ralph walked into the room. Jessica bent down to pet him.

"Hey, fella," she said.

Marc rolled his eyes. "I'm afraid 'he' turned out to be a 'she.'"

"Ha! You need a female in this household."

"Funny you should say that." Marc explained the situation with Emma.

She laughed.

"What exactly do you find so funny about this?"

"Oh, you're going to be such a pushover with that little girl. I can see it all now. She'll bat those big eyes at you, and you'll cave in big time, give her anything she asks for. I can't wait to see this."

"Jessica, I came to you telling you I'm drowning. What part of that don't you get?"

"You're not drowning, Marc."

"Yeah? Well, it feels like it."

"You're not drowning. You're flourishing."

"That's just a trick word for drowning."

"Those boys are lucky to have you, you know that?"

"I'm not so sure they would agree with you...at least not all the time."

"No parent gets that lucky."

"What on earth am I going to do with a one-year-old little girl?"

"The same thing you're doing with those two little boys—giving them lots of love and keeping them safe."

"And fed."

"That's a big one."

"But she's a girl. What do I know about little girls?"

"What did you know about little boys?"

"Nothing."

"Everyone seems to be surviving—you just do it."

Tyler came stumbling out of Zenzi's bedroom.

"I better go. He needs another dose of antibiotics." She scooped up her son, who was way too big for her to be carrying. Glancing over her shoulder, she said, "You'll do fine, my friend. Trust me."

* * *

For the next three days, Marc slept little, barely ate, and maxed out on Xanax. Mindlessly, he went to work and dealt with clients, staff, and plant life, but was mostly just going through the motions. When the week finally ended, he brought home the usual Friday-night pizza and sat the boys down in the living room.

"Boys—"

Riley interrupted him. "You know when he starts out like that, it can't be good."

Marc laughed. "Now, I don't know why you'd say that."

"Really, Uncle Marc?"

"Do I do that often?"

"Duh."

"Looks like I'll have to change up my routine. Anyway, what I wanted to share with you is that Nick has gone back to his native country, Malaysia, and was unable to take Baby Emma with him."

"Why not?"

"Because she was born in the U. S., and that makes her a U.S. citizen, so there were complications bringing her to his country."

"So why didn't he stay here then?" Josh asked.

"I'm afraid he's been deported."

"He's dead too?" Josh asked.

"Not de*part*ed, you ninny. De*port*ed!" Riley interjected.

"Oh."

"Deported means you have to go back to the country where you were born."

"What country was I born in?" Josh asked.

"Here. In the U. S."

"Good."

"Anyway, Baby Emma is in foster care, and I'm trying to get the same legal guardianship for her as I have for you."

"But she's not gonna live here," Riley said.

"Well, yes, that would be the plan."

"What? We're cramped as it is."

"We're not cramped. There's plenty of room."

"Where would she sleep?"

Marc hadn't thought of that. Not wanting to disturb Zenzi's bedroom, he was still sleeping on the living room sofa.

"She's just a baby. She can sleep anywhere."

"Well, I vote no," Riley said.

"This isn't a democracy."

"Mom was a Republican, I think," Josh added.

"Not Democrat, you—"

"What if Ralph doesn't like her?" Josh asked, cutting Riley short.

"I thought you were going to rename her to a girl's name?"

"I did. Ralphina, so I can still call her Ralph for short."

"I see. Riley, why are you against Emma coming here to live?" Marc asked. "She's your sister."

"Half-sister," Riley corrected him. "Can she even walk yet?"

"I'm not sure. Anyway, there's very little difference between a sister and a half-sister. Your mom gave birth to her just like she did you two."

"Mom gave birth to us?" Josh asked.

"How else do you think we got here? By stork?" Riley asked.

"Something like that."

"Josh, think about it," Riley said.

"How does that work, Uncle Marc?" Josh asked.

"Can we get back on the subject please?" Marc pleaded.

"I still vote no."

"I don't," Josh said. "I don't want to see *anyone* go to a foster home. It sucks. Big time."

"I like the way you think, Josh," Marc told him.

"But a baby in the house? She's probably still in diapers. Eeww. And a girl." Riley argued.

"I thought you liked girls," Marc said.

"Not that kind."

"Does she like pizza?" Josh asked.

"Only if it comes in a jar," Riley responded.

"You'll get used to having her around, I promise."

Look at what I had to get used to.

"Can we give her back if it doesn't work out?"

Chapter 42

Shortly after Zenzi's death, while Riley and Josh were at Jessica's for Tyler's birthday party, Marc and Meinhard enjoyed one of Denver's specialties—homemade meatloaf.

"So what do you do for a living?" Meinhard asked Marc.

"I have a landscaping business."

"Really? So did my son, I think."

Meinhard appeared more tired than usual.

"Tell me about him," Marc said.

"He was a good kid. A good kid then, and a good man now. Better than I ever was. He inherited that from his mother."

"When was the last time you saw him?"

"Oh, I don't know anymore. It's been years." He turned toward the kitchen and shouted, "Denver, do you know when I last saw..." He turned back toward Marc, his eyes vacant. "I've forgotten his name. I don't remember a lot these days."

When Denver came into the living room, Marc asked him how things were going.

"Pretty good."

"How about you?" Marc asked his father. "Is Denver here taking care of things okay?"

"He's a good kid. I wish my son could meet him. He'd like him."

"Yes, I bet he would."

"How about your father? Does he live around here?" he asked Marc.

"Not too far."

"He must be very proud of you."

Marc groped for the right words to respond. Finding none, he let Meinhard's words echo in his head long after he left their apartment.

* * *

Marc read Jessica's text.

Can we talk later?

Sure. What time?

After the boys r in bed.

Ok

I'll come up.

Marc was expecting her to contact him—Riley had confessed to him the day before that he and Tyler had had a fight at school. Tyler, three years Riley's junior and six inches shorter, had taken a swing at him and missed. That had incensed Tyler and prompted him to call Riley every dirty name he knew. It had happened on school property, and a teacher had overheard the fight and reported it to the principal. Neither child had received any punishment, just a warning. Marc had asked Riley what the fight was about.

"His dad."

"What about his dad?"

"Tyler was telling other kids his dad was coming back to live with them, and all I said was maybe he should cool it until it actually happened."

That news caught Marc by surprise—Jessica hadn't mentioned anything.

"And he took a swipe at you for saying that?"

"Yep."

He advised Riley that when it came to personal matters, it was usually best to just listen to what someone had to say and not comment.

So now Jessica wanted to talk.

The boys went to bed, and an hour later, Jessica rapped on his door.

Marc led her to the kitchen table where the boys would be less apt to hear them. He pulled two local ales from the fridge and then placed a two-gallon tin of Garrett popcorn in front of her.

"I meant a small bag, you goofus."

"I figured I owed you more than that."

"You're too much, you know that?"

"I try."

"So here's the deal." She cleared her throat. "Al and I have been doing some serious talking. A lot. And we've decided…well, we've decided to give it another try."

Marc forced a smile. "Hey, I'm happy for you. I really am."

"You sure?" she asked.

"Of course, I'm sure."

"Thanks. I told him I was willing to give it another try, but it wasn't going to go back to how it was before, at least not for me. Tyler, yes. But with me, that's going to take time."

"That seems fair to me."

"I thought so. Anyway, I wanted to check with you first."

"Check with me?"

"How you feel about him moving in."

"I guess that means the end of us then," he said with a straight face.

Her mouth fell open, but no words came out.

They stared at each other for several seconds, and then Marc smiled.

"You're playing with me, aren't you?" she asked.

"Guilty."

"You are so bad. I meant how you—as my *landlord*—felt about him moving in. But you knew that."

"Of course I did."

"Smart-ass."

"You know I love it when you talk dirty."

"So you're good with it?"

"Of course."

She got up. "I better go. Tyler is downstairs alone." She reached for the popcorn tin and headed for the door, laughing. "And stop checking out my butt!"

"I'm a guy, Jess. That's what we do. Hell, I've been known to check out department store mannequins' butts."

"Gee, thanks."

"Yours is cuter. Jessica?"

She turned around. "Yeah."

"I hope it works out for you guys."

"Yeah, me too."

After finishing his beer, Marc went to bed and fell asleep thinking what it would be like married to Jessica. Sometime later, he was jolted awake.

"Wake up! Uncle Marc, wake up!" Riley was yelling at him.

"What? What's wrong?"

"It's Josh. He's not in our room."

"Are you sure?" he asked when he was halfway to the boys' bedroom.

"I looked everywhere."

"Under the bed?"

"Yeah."

"In the closet?"

"Yeah."

"What about the bathroom?" The boys' window was open—wide enough for a small kid to go through. "Why is this open?"

"We like to sleep with it open."

"But there's no screen on it."

"It falls out sometimes."

Marc stuck his head out the window and looked down. The screen was lying on the ground below, but there was no sign of Josh.

"You stay here!" Marc ran back to the living room and threw on a t-shirt and a pair of sweat pants. "I'll go look for him."

He flew down the stairs and into the garage where he quickly found a high-powered flashlight. Its beam lit up the alley halfway to Halsted Street to the west and Clark Street to the east.

There was no sign of Josh.

He ran to the front of the house and looked up and down the sidewalk in each direction.

"Josh!" he bellowed as loud as he could. He didn't know what time it was—only that everyone except third-shift factory workers and people with severe insomnia were likely asleep.

He yelled Josh's name two more times. Several lights went on in nearby homes. Cell phone in hand, he was about to call 9-1-1 when he heard Josh's voice.

"I'm over here, Uncle Marc."

He followed the sound of Josh's voice with his flashlight. There he stood, in his Spider-Man pajamas, holding Ralph the cat.

"What on earth are you doing out here?"

"Ralph jumped out of the window. I *had* to find her."

"You scared the hell out of me."

"I'm sorry," he whimpered.

"Come here, you." Marc comforted him until his sobbing stopped. "Promise me you'll come to me if anything like that happens again?"

Josh nodded.

"Uncle Marc," Josh said as they walked up the back stairs to their apartment.

"Yes."

"There's something I have to tell you."

"What's that?"

"I think Ralph is going to have kittens."

* * *

The next day at breakfast, Riley asked how the talk with Tyler's mom had gone.

"Fine. Turned out she wanted to talk about something else."

"What did she want to talk about?"

"Adult things."

"I'm almost twelve."

"That's not an adult. It's not even a teenager."

"I'm into puberty, you know."

"Oh, really? And what makes you think that?"

"Well, for one thing I'm getting very hairy."

Marc was reminded of when he had gotten his first chest hair—literally one hair. He had immediately put on a button-down shirt and left the top three buttons open so that the hair was visible. He dressed like that for a week, until one morning after his shower, he looked down and the hair was gone. It had been a devastating moment.

Marc took Riley's chin in his hand and inspected his face. "I don't see any here."

"Not on my chin! And I use deodorant."

"Oh? Whose?"

"Yours."

"Riley, let's get one thing straight. Men don't share deodorant. That's one of our man rules. Unless it's a spray, which mine isn't. I'll buy you your own. What else?"

"That's it I guess."

"Good, because that's about all I can handle right now."

"So you're not going to tell me what Tyler's mom talked to you about."

"I'll tell you as soon as you get your first chin hair."

After Riley left, Marc Googled "puberty" and stopped reading when he found this definition.

NOUN: THE PERIOD DURING WHICH ADOLESCENTS REACH SEXUAL MATURITY AND BECOME CAPABLE OF REPRODUCTION.

Shit!

Chapter 43

"If this falls through," Marc told Jessica, "I will never forgive myself." The court hearing for Marc's legal guardianship over Emma was a few days away. "I can't let that little girl grow up without her family. And we're her family."

"Marc, Marc, Marc. Let me take you back to—"

"I know what you're going to say. Don't even go there."

"Okay. I just wanted to—"

"People change. I changed."

"Ya think?"

"Stop looking at me like that."

"You're pretty special, you know that?"

"Shut up." He could feel the flush creeping up his neck. "You're making me blush. How are things with you and Al by the way?"

A soft smile came over her face. "We're good. Things are good."

"Think you'll remarry?"

She shrugged and nodded at the same time. "Hey, did you see the FOR SALE sign next door?"

"Which way?"

"The Gunthers."

"No way. They're moving?"

"Isabel said now that they're empty-nesters, that house is too big for them, so they're downsizing," Jessica told him.

"Bummer. I've known them my whole life. Best neighbors anyone could ask for. Neighborhood won't feel the same without them."

"I know. What are we going to do without her cookies?"

"Exactly. Baby Emma won't know what she's missing."

"Can I ask you something?" she asked. "If you get custody of her, are you going to keep calling her Baby Emma?"

"I guess so. Why?"

"I don't know. It sounds a little odd to me."

"Apparently, it's a custom in Malaysia to call babies Baby Whatever until they're of age. Or maybe it's in Nigeria they do that. Anyway, wherever Nick's family is from, that's what they do."

"He seems to be out of the picture though."

"I know, and there's not much about that man I respect, but he *is* her father, her only living parent, and somehow it doesn't seem right to go against his culture."

"Good point. Who all will be in court today?"

"My attorney, the DCFS caseworker, Denver, my father, the kids, and me."

"The whole family."

"The whole family." Marc pondered the words and feigned a smile. "Sometimes I look back and wonder how the hell I ever got to this point."

"Want to know what I think?"

"Sure."

"You made it to this point because this is where you were destined to be."

"Everything happens for a reason?"

"Yeah, something like that."

"Can I ask you something?"

"Sure."

"What changed your mind about Al? About giving him a second chance."

She didn't answer for several seconds. "You."

"Did you understand my question?"

"Perfectly."

"Explain."

"I watched you in action dish out second chances one after another. And then I saw what happened as a result."

"I'm not following you."

"You gave everyone in your life a second chance. You gave Zenzi a second chance—and a third and a fourth—even after she treated you like... Your father—same thing. And you could have left those two boys in foster care, but you didn't, so they got their second chance, thanks to you. Hell, even Ralph got a second chance from you."

He laughed. "But not the kittens. We are *not* keeping all those kittens."

I learned by watching you that it's not just the receiver who benefits from a second chance—so does the giver.

"We're not keeping those kittens."

* * *

269

The hearing for Emma's guardianship was to start in two hours, and things on the home front were not going as planned. The boys were playing on their Xbox even though Marc had asked them three times to get off it to get dressed. Denver had called and told Marc that Meinhard had refused to change out of his badly worn plaid flannel shirt and baggy army-green pants in favor of the nice outfit Denver had picked out for him. The instructions on the back of Marc's Pepto-Bismol bottle said he should take no more than eight doses every twenty-four hours, and he was already on number six.

Somehow it all came together, and with no time to spare, everyone climbed into Marc's SUV and rode to the courthouse.

"Tell me again why I have to go to court," Meinhard said to no one in particular.

"Because we said so," said Denver.

I like that kid.

It was the same family court he had attended for the boys' guardianship hearing, and when they entered the courtroom and Marc realized it was the same judge as well, he was pleased and relieved.

Marc's attorney answered the judge's initial questions with ease, affirming Marc's suitability for guardianship of Emma. The hearing appeared to be going in Marc's favor, until the judge picked up a piece of paper from her bench and waved it in the air.

"I'm going to ask that the children be escorted out of this courtroom," she said. The caseworker from DCFS accompanied them out, and when they were gone, the judge addressed Marc.

"Mr. Nussbaum, can you please stand?"

Marc did as he was instructed, as did Meinhard.

"The young Mr. Nussbaum."

"Why thank you, judge," Meinhard.

Marc turned to face Meinhard and gestured for him to sit down. After giving Marc a puzzled look, he sat down.

"Yes, Your Honor," Marc addressed the judge.

"What is Call of Duty?"

"I'm not sure I understand your question."

"I see in one of the social worker's notes that your nephews are playing a video game that is intended for seventeen-year-olds. Are you aware of that?"

"I guess I am, Your Honor."

"Your nephews are how old?"

"Ten and eleven, almost twelve." He wished he hadn't added the last part.

"I'm aware that twelve does generally follow eleven. Where did they get this game that is intended for much older players?"

"I'm afraid I bought it for the older one...Your Honor."

"Then the younger child has no access to this game, right?"

"Well, no. They kind of share a room."

"So now we have two young children with access to a video game that is clearly intended for a seventeen-year-old, and I say 'clearly' because it says so right on the package."

Unsure how to respond, Marc said nothing.

"Do you know why this game is tagged for a young adult and not a child, Mr. Nussbaum?"

"I've never actually seen it played, Your Honor."

"How would you describe that parenting style?"

"Irresponsible?"

"Are you asking me?"

"Irresponsible."

"And now you're asking this court to allow you to parent a third child."

"Your Honor, may I say something in my defense?" Marc asked.

"Go ahead."

"I'm new at this, and I know I'm going to make mistakes...hopefully none worse than this one. But one mistake I'll never make is to forget how important my sister's children are to me, to society, to this world. Whatever they need, they will get from me. Will I occasionally make a bad decision? Probably. I can't promise you I won't. But I'll learn from them. That I *can* promise you."

The judge stared past Marc for a long moment and then directed her gaze toward Denver. "Mr. Denver A. Pollack. Will you stand please?"

"It's nice to see you again, Your Honor."

"And it's nice to see you too. How are things going with Mr. Nussbaum?"

"Which one?"

"The man sitting next to you."

"Things are going fine, Your Honor," Denver said. "We have good and bad days, but I can handle them."

"Tell me, Mr. Pollack, do you ever make mistakes when looking out for Mr. Nussbaum?"

"Yes ma'am. I made a big one last month."

"Tell me about it."

"I let a stranger talk to him, and Mr. Nussbaum almost lost his house over it."

"And how did you feel afterward?"

"Bad. Real bad."

"Did you take any steps to make sure nothing like that ever happens again?"

"I wrote myself a sticky note and put it on my mirror so I see it every day."

The judge turned to Marc. "Mr. Pollack here is a very smart young man. You could learn from him."

"I will, Your Honor."

"I'm going to grant you temporary legal guardianship of Miss Emma for up to one year. A DCFS caseworker will drop in periodically to see how she's doing, how the entire household is doing. I want you to know that Mr. Lee's attorney has informed this court that as long as Emma is in your care, he has no intention of fighting for custody."

Marc's sigh of relief was audible.

"Thank you, Your Honor."

"I have one last question. I don't see the child's birthday on any of this paperwork."

"It's in May, but I'm afraid I don't know the exact date. I'd have to check her birth certificate," he said.

"Your Honor?" Denver rose to his feet.

"Yes."

"It's May 30. Emma's birthday is today."

"Thank you, Mr. Pollack," the judge said, peering at Marc over the top of her reading glasses. "Emma and her caseworker have been in a holding room during this hearing, so please wait for them in the hallway. They'll follow you home if you don't have room in your car. Court adjourned."

Marc and the others marched in single file out of the courtroom and into the wide hallway where they joined Riley, Josh, and the caseworker.

"Well?" Riley asked.

Before Marc could respond, a woman carrying Emma approached them. Marc held his arms out for his niece.

"C'mon, boys. Let's take your baby sister home."

He turned to Denver. "How did you know today was her birthday?"

"Riley told me."

"How did you know?" he asked Riley.

"Mom told us."

"So everyone knew that but me?"

"It looks that way, Mr. Nussbaum," said Denver. "But that's how it works."

"That's how what works?"

"You're there for us when we need you, and we're there for you when you need us." He looked at Riley and Josh. "Right, boys?"

The three of them gave each other high-fives. Marc knew if he tried to speak, nothing would come out, so he didn't.

They drove home, the caseworker following close behind. At the back door,

Marc picked up a package wrapped in brown paper. No name, no writing at all. He brought it inside and placed it on the fireplace mantle.

After everyone was inside, the caseworker handed Emma to Marc. He barely had her in his arms when she began to cry. Before the caseworker was out the door, her sobs had transitioned into screams.

"It will take time for her to get used to the change," the caseworker shouted. "She'll be fine. I promise you. It may take several weeks. Be patient."

"Welcome home, Baby Emma," Marc said, his words heard by no one but himself.

Chapter 44

An hour after they had returned home from court, Riley asked Marc, "So is this how it's going to be from now on?"

Emma hadn't stopped crying. After holding her for five minutes, Marc was quite sure she didn't want to be in his arms, so he had put her in the convertible car seat that she'd come in and placed it on the kitchen table. Meinhard couldn't take the crying and went into the living room where he waited for Denver to come out of the bathroom so they could go upstairs.

"You heard the caseworker," Marc said. "She has to get used to us. She's probably scared to death, the poor thing." He turned his back on Emma and the boys while he fished around in a kitchen drawer for a piece of paper and pencil to make a shopping list. Emma had come with quite a few things, but Marc knew from a Google search that he needed to buy more.

When the crying stopped, Marc wheeled around to see what had changed. Denver was holding Emma, and she was gazing up at him as quiet as she could be, inspecting every inch of his face.

"I have a way with babies," Denver said.

"I see that."

Denver agreed to continue watching Emma while Marc and the boys went out to pick up the needed items for her, most importantly a crib. Afterward, they stopped at the grocery store where Marc bought frozen pizzas for dinner, a variety of baby food, and everything required for a belated Memorial Day barbecue over the weekend. Marc's objective for the barbecue was threefold—to officially welcome Emma into their family, to honor Denver with the thank-you gift he had recently bought for him, and to start things off on the right foot as a new family.

When they arrived home, Marc found Denver, Meinhard, and Johnny Gunther from next door playing gin rummy—something they routinely did when Isabel was at Bingo—with Emma nearby asleep in her car seat.

Marc invited Johnny to stay for dinner. After they finished eating, Meinhard and Denver went upstairs to their apartment, Riley and Josh retreated to their room to play anything but Call of Duty, and Marc and Johnny retired to the living room to enjoy a cold beer before they tackled assembling Emma's new bed. Johnny told him of their intention to downsize, which led to a discussion about Marc needing to upsize.

Two hours later, after they had successfully assembled the bed and Johnny had left, Marc opened the package he'd found at the back door. Inside were three books, all from the *For Dummies* series: *Your Baby's First Year*, *Parenting*, and *Potty Training*. There was no card inside, but Marc knew who they were from. He smiled. Jessica must have assumed the court would rule in his favor.

* * *

Marc hadn't ever hosted a party before but figured it couldn't be that hard. It wasn't going to be a big affair—just his burgeoning family, Denver, Denver's sister Ruby, and the Gunthers. He had invited Jessica, Tyler, and Al but they had had other plans. Only two days had passed since Marc had brought Emma home, and despite having read the last eight chapters of *Your Baby's First Year* where they talked about what to expect from a one-year-old, he still felt like he was in a fog when it came to attending to her needs.

Josh was a big help with the attention he paid to his sister, but that came with a price when it came to his relationship with Riley. When Marc caught Riley calling Josh a "girlie little mermaid" for playing with Emma while Marc prepared for the party, Marc sat Riley down for a talk.

"Let me explain something to you," he said to Riley.

Riley plopped down on his bed and rolled his eyes.

"And don't roll your eyes. This is important."

"Right."

"Number one."

"Here we go," Riley said under his breath.

"Number one. What Josh is doing with his sister is one of the most important things a big brother can do, and that is form a bond that will last a lifetime. You do that and later on you'll have each other's back. You'll confide in each other. You'll trust each other. Like you and Josh do now."

"Number two?" Riley asked, sarcastically.

"Number two. I know she doesn't seem like much now—she sleeps a lot, eats, and cries—but there's a little person in there, and someday when she's five or ten or sixteen, she'll need you, or you'll need her, and well, that's what family is all about."

"What about you and Mom? How'd that work out for you?" Riley asked.

It was a loaded question.

"You wouldn't be sitting here with me right now if your mom and I didn't have that bond. Look, I'm not asking you to spend time with Emma if you don't want to. What I'm asking you to do is not lose what you have with Josh. You're a great big brother, and I'd like to be able to count on you to continue being that."

Riley shrugged.

"Think about it."

"Fine."

By one o'clock everyone was sitting around the picnic table eating hamburgers, hot dogs, potato salad, chips, watermelon, and a red, white, and blue Jell-O mold that Riley had made from a recipe he'd found on the Internet. Apparently, Riley had been hiding the fact all this time that he could do things in the kitchen.

After everyone had finished eating, Marc excused himself from the table to fetch the welcome cake for Emma and gift for Denver. Riley and Josh had asked for chocolate cake with white frosting. But when Marc had gone to the bakery, the only cake they'd had with those flavors was one with the words GOOD BYE AND GOOD LUCK written in blue icing on the top. He'd bought it, taken it home, and swiped a knife through the colorful letters, transforming them into a bunch of wayward swirls.

"Before we have cake in celebration of Baby Emma's homecoming, I have something for you, Denver."

Denver's face lit up. "I like the sound of that," he said.

Marc handed him an awkwardly wrapped present. Denver looked at his sister for support.

"Go ahead. Open it," she told him.

Denver carefully peeled off the wrapping paper. When he saw the gift, he stared down at it for a long moment. No one spoke. When he looked up, he had tears streaming down his cheeks. Still not saying anything, he got up, walked over to Marc, and hugged him.

The large gold trophy was engraved with Denver's name on a prominent star that sat atop of it. Across the bottom was written BEST CAREGIVER EVER. His sister had told Marc that more than anything in the world, Denver wanted to win a trophy.

"That's the nicest thing anyone ever did for me," he blurted into Marc's neck.

* * *

"I'll hire another foreman," Marc said to Juan as they stood together at one of their job sites contemplating how to divvy up the summertime work. June was the bus-

iest month of the year for landscaping. In previous years, Marc had spent seventy-
and eighty-hour weeks at work during that month. But not this year.

"Save your money. Another foreman isn't going to help any. It's *you* we need,
the person who can make the hard decisions, deal with the clients, make purchases."

"Well, I can't put in the hours like I used to." He stared past Juan for a moment
as an interesting thought ran through his mind.

"Tell me what it is about my job that would keep *you* from doing it."

Juan answered without hesitation. "You don't pay me enough to deal with the
clients."

"What if I did?"

"What are you saying?"

"I'm saying you know enough about this business to run it. What would you
say to a partnership? Split the work and split the profits. Then I could solicit more
business, add more crews, and there would be enough profit for the both of us." He
shared some rough projections with him.

"You're serious."

"Hell, yes, I'm serious. Look, man, I need someone with me at the top. I have a
family now, and I can't put in the hours like I used to. And your family is growing.
Wouldn't the extra money come in handy?"

"Are you kidding?"

"Think about it?"

"Yeah, I'll think about it."

During the week, Marc and Juan met on two more occasions to discuss Marc's
offer, and after some friendly negotiations, they reached a mutual agreement.

Two days later, Marc sat reading the local Lake Forest newspaper over his
morning coffee. The headline read:

SEVEN DEER FOUND DEAD

IN MIDDLEFORK SAVANNAH FOREST PRESERVE

The carcasses of four fawns, two does, and one buck had been discovered by
a forest preserve worker within shouting distance of property belonging to Marc's
Deer Camper clients. Preliminary lab results showed they died of massive doses
of the insecticide carbamate, the same substance that had killed the Trinkos' dog
earlier in the month. Fred Trinko had told Marc that, much to his dismay, the police
hadn't been able to find any evidence that Arnie MacCallum had had anything to
do with their dog's death, and so no charges had been filed.

The story nagged at Marc the rest of the day as he dealt with all of his family
challenges. Contributing to the chaos was Meinhard's deteriorating mental state,

prompting Marc to seek power of attorney over his finances and medical care.

That afternoon, Marc went upstairs to explain to Meinhard what it meant for him to have authority to make financial and medical decisions on his behalf. Then he talked to him about the house.

"Technically, you own this house, and what I want to do is sell it and buy the house next door so we can all live in the same space." This was the first time Marc had mentioned to anyone in his family what he and the Gunthers from next door had been discussing for weeks. It hadn't been an easy decision for Marc to make financially, but after discussing it with his bank, he was able to secure a small business loan that would hold him over until his new enlarged landscaping business took hold.

"Who's all of us?" Meinhard asked.

"You, Denver, Riley and Josh, Baby Emma, and me. You'd have your own bedroom, like you have now, and Denver would have one too. But instead of being in two separate apartments, we'd be in one big house."

"Is there a kitchen?"

"Yes, a big kitchen."

"A place to play checkers?"

"Plenty of space for checkers."

"It's fine with me."

"Do you know who I am?"

"Sometimes."

"Do you know right now?"

"No, but it will come to me. My memory isn't so good these days."

The next day, they drove to the attorney's office, and Meinhard signed the form without asking any questions. When Marc helped him back into the car afterward, he said, "Thanks, Markus."

Markus—he remembered my name.

Markus—I can live with that.

* * *

Armed with the letter for power of attorney over his father's affairs, Marc proceeded with the house-swap transaction with the Gunthers, who had decided to move into the garden apartment where there were fewer stairs to navigate. Marc discussed this with Jessica, hoping that she would be in favor of moving into one of the larger apartments.

"As soon as you told us about the house swap, Al and I talked about it," she said. "And we think it's best we find another place to live. One with a third bedroom."

Behind a wide smile, Marc suppressed an emotion he didn't quite understand. "You're pregnant, aren't you."

She nodded.

"I'm happy for you, Jess."

"Yeah?"

"Very happy."

* * *

"If you boys don't get off of that Xbox this minute, I'm going to throw it in the garbage!"

Marc and the Gunthers had closed on their house-swap deal the previous day, and Marc needed everyone's full cooperation in order to make the moves go smoothly.

"I want those moving boxes filled with all your things by eleven!"

The plan was for the Gunthers to have all their belongings moved into their backyard by noon. Then Marc would move his father's things into the Gunthers' house, leaving the third-floor apartment empty for Jessica and her family to live in temporarily until they closed on their new house in a nearby neighborhood. Then the Gunthers could move into the garden apartment, and Marc could move his things from the second and third floors into the Gunthers' house. It had looked good on paper.

After dealing with Zenzi's sofa getting stuck going through the back door, Emma throwing one of her finest tantrums, his father pulling another one of his disappearing acts, and Josh getting locked in the bathroom with no toilet paper, they were moved into their new house.

That evening, after Marc checked on everyone to make sure they were all in the right places before he collapsed in his own bed, the phone rang. It was Fred Trinko.

"I thought you'd want to know that Tom Wilds was arrested this morning."

Marc was shocked to hear these words. Tom was the landscaper friend of his who had called months earlier to let him know Juan had approached him for a job.

"For using restricted-use pesticides to poison deer."

"What? Tom poisoned the deer?"

"And indirectly our dog. The police think the deer probably carried some of the poison to our yard and Demetrius got into it. Apparently, it doesn't take much to kill a dog his size."

"So it wasn't MacCallum after all."

"No. And I called him right away and apologized for accusing him. Much to my surprise, he was pretty gracious about it."

"Did they say why Tom did it?"

"Apparently, his contract with the Pinkertons down the road includes a two-year replacement guaranty instead of the usual one-year, and he was taking a big hit replacing plants that had been damaged by deer."

Marc was aware of the contract—Tom had told Marc that he had agreed to it in a weak moment, just to get the contract. The Pinkertons owned a two-acre lot with lots of landscaping.

"So he killed the deer?"

"The police traced the sale of the poison to him and found more of it in his basement."

Marc was aware that Tom had a license to purchase Restricted Use pesticides.

"I know Tom. That's not like him to do something so irrational."

"Well, I thought you'd want to know."

"Yeah, thanks."

An hour after Trinko's phone call, not yet over the shock of what Tom Wilds had done, Marc received a call from Tom's lawyer.

"He wants to sell his business to you…that is, if you're interested."

They talked for twenty minutes about potential terms of a deal and agreed to meet the next day in the lawyer's office.

Still reeling from what was happening to Tom, Marc peeked in on Emma—she had managed to fall asleep with her knees tucked up to her chin and her tiny butt high in the air. It didn't appear to be comfortable, but the peaceful look on her face told him it worked for her. He stood there for a long time staring at her before snapping a photo of her with his phone—a pose too cute not to be captured.

The previous day, Josh had gotten her to say her first word, *no*. That was followed soon afterward by her second word, *bye*. And her third word, *doter*. No one had a clue what *doter* meant, but she kept repeating it, so they knew it had meaning for her.

Emma stirred, straightening out her little body in the process. The angelic look on her face while she slept was in such contrast to the facial expression she wore when having one of her many tantrums that it was hard to believe it was the same child. She opened her eyes.

"Hey, sweetheart, did you have a good nap?" He walked closer to the crib.

She gazed up at him with a smile full of innocence and promise. Then in a sweet, clear voice, she said, "Doter."

That's her name for me!

Marc knew then that it was all over—that child was his. He picked her up, and even the pungent smell that drifted up from her diaper wasn't enough to spoil the moment.

Just as he finished putting a new diaper on her, his phone beeped. It was someone from the Medical Examiner's office.

"The Medical Examiner has finished his report," he was told. "You may pick up a copy of it, if you like. Would you like to know the findings now or wait for the report?"

"Now, please."

"Your sister died from a grand mal seizure, Mr. Nussbaum."

"How does someone die from that?"

"In her case, it was severe enough and lasted long enough to stop her breathing."

"Do you know what caused it?"

"Your sister was diabetic. Did you know that?"

"No, I didn't."

"She should have been on medication."

"I didn't find any medication among her things."

"She also had kidney disease."

"I didn't know that either."

"She may not have known that herself. It was in the beginning stages. And she had a recent concussion. I think we talked about that before. Do you know anything about that?"

"No."

"Seizures can be caused by any number of conditions. Kidney disease, diabetes, and head injuries are all possibilities. Likely one of those caused it, or a combination of them. Did your sister have a problem with alcohol?"

"Yes."

"Alcohol withdrawal can also cause seizures."

Marc hung up the phone wondering at what point his sister's life had taken such a horrible turn. It had been two months since her death but seemed longer. The boys didn't talk about her too often, and Marc didn't know whether that was good, bad, or indifferent. Soon after the funeral, they had planted a garden in the backyard—one he planned to transplant into their new yard—that included many of Zenzi's favorite flowers. He had purchased a small stone engraved with the words IN MEMORY OF ZENZI NUSSBAUM. Marc had made a point to visit it every day, and often one or both boys would join him.

On one such visit, Josh asked Marc why he came to the garden every day.

"Because she was my sister, and I miss her," Marc said.

"I don't."

"You don't?"

"Nope. Because I still have her in my heart," he said.

Epilogue

It was a bitter cold day in December, just days before Christmas, when Marc walked into the Cook County Family Courtroom for what he hoped would be the last time. Accompanying him were his father, Riley, Josh, Emma, Denver, a DCFS caseworker, and Marc's attorney.

Denver had made sure everyone was dressed in their finest "court clothes," as he called them. Marc, his attorney, and the caseworker took seats at the table in front of the judge's bench. The rest of the clan sat in the front row of the spectator seats.

"Mr. Nussbaum," the judge began, "your family has grown since the first time you visited my courtroom."

"Yes, it has, Your Honor."

She glanced down at her bench and shuffled through some papers. "I see you have Mr. Denver A. Pollack listed as the children's caregiver when you're not home."

"That's correct."

"Mr. Pollack?"

Marc glanced over at Denver and motioned for him to stand.

"Mr. Pollack, how nice to see you again."

"It's nice to see you again too, Your Honor."

"Have you been working hard to keep everyone in the Nussbaum family in line?"

"Yes, very hard."

"And what's it like working in the Nussbaum household?"

"I like it there very much."

She gestured toward Marc. "How is he to work for? What kind of boss is he?"

"Mr. Nussbaum is the nicest man I know. Do you want to know what he did for me for my birthday?"

"What did he do?"

"He took me to the Indie 500. I'd never been there, but I've had a poster of it on my wall ever since I was five years old. I love fast cars."

"He did that, did he?"

"Yes, and it was just the two of us. It was special."

"I see. Thank you for sharing that. You may sit down now." The judge looked directly at Riley and Josh. "Boys, will you stand please?"

Marc had not expected the boys would be asked any questions.

"Do you boys know why we're here today?"

They nodded.

"Tell me why."

Riley spoke. "Uncle Marc wants to adopt us...legally."

"And how do you feel about that?"

"We're both for it."

"So we have your vote?"

Both boys nodded.

After asking Marc, his attorney, and the caseworker several more questions, she spoke directly to Marc.

"Mr. Nussbaum, I am going to sign the decree for your adoption of Riley Nussbaum, Joshua Nussbaum, and Emma Lee, and I am also going to sign the name change form for Miss Emma to Emma Lee Nussbaum. Good luck to you."

A feeling of calm swept through Marc's entire body. He looked to his left at the five people sitting in the front row of the courtroom and wept.

"Before you go, would you like for me to take the very first picture of all of you now that you're a legal family?" the judge asked.

Stunned by the question and still choked up by her decision, Marc accepted the judge's offer.

"Everyone come up here. Mr. Pollack, I want you to sit way up there in my chair. Everyone else line up in front of the bench."

With everyone situated, the judge took Marc's phone and snapped several pictures—with Denver holding the judge's gavel high in the air in each one of them.

Later that evening Riley, who had become Denver's sidekick in the kitchen, helped make a celebratory dinner of spaghetti and meatballs, everyone's favorite. After Emma had been put to bed, they all watched *Night at the Museum*. Even his father enjoyed watching it, although he didn't understand why Larry didn't just leave the museum when all the creatures came to life.

Afterward, with everyone in their bedrooms, Marc sprawled out on the sofa with a beer, enjoying the peacefulness of the moment. He watched the flames flicker in the fireplace beneath the seven Christmas stockings that hung on the mantle—one for each member of the household, including Ralph the cat.

Completely relaxed, his thoughts drifted to how things had changed during the past ten months—how he had changed in so many respects.

He put his "I Hope You Dance" CD in the player for old time's sake, not because the song reminded him of Gabby so much, but because it had inspired him to figure out what he really wanted in life—what he had never had as a child, that "thing" for which he would be most grateful in the future—and they were all sound asleep upstairs.

Feeling sentimental, he picked up a photo album from the coffee table. It was his father's and had surfaced during the move. Hundreds of photographs, mostly taken in Germany in the late sixties and early seventies, had been carefully mounted with handwritten captions beneath each one. Marc flipped through them.

Since moving into their new home, his father had taken a few occasions to educate Josh and Riley about "the old country." He'd used the photos to guide him through stories about the German people, culture, and politics. Marc found it interesting that his father often couldn't remember his own name, but details of life in East Germany during the middle of the Cold War came easily. Marc knew more about his father's life from listening in on these story-telling moments than he had ever known before.

As he flipped through the book, one photo in particular attracted his attention. It was captioned EAST GERMAN WORKERS ADDING HEIGHT TO THE WALL BETWEEN EAST AND WEST BERLIN, 1961. His father was seventeen and working in a food processing plant when West Berlin decided to make the wall taller to keep the East Berliners from gaining entry. On his way home from work, he would walk along the wall and watch the tops of the workers' helmets bob up and down as they added concrete blocks atop of it. He had told the boys that one day he ran across a broken concrete block that the workers had apparently dropped over on his side and how he had lugged home a large piece of it to keep as a souvenir.

His father had been a good photographer, Marc thought, always capturing the complexity hidden within simple subjects and settings. There was one exceptional photo of three children playing ball on his side of the wall. He had told the boys he wished these children had had a nicer place to play. There was another poignant image of armed guards at a soccer game at the Olympiastadion in Berlin. Without the guards, it would have been just another soccer game.

His father's explanations beneath each image were also simple yet telling. GERMAN WOMEN PLANTING POTATOES IN A FIELD NEAR MESTLIN, 1975. The photograph showed four women sitting on a makeshift trailer behind a tractor and four other women standing behind them. Bundled up in heavy coats and scarves, all of them were smiling. He had told the boys the one on the far left was his next-door neighbor.

The more Marc studied the photographs, the more he realized how difficult it must have been for his father to adjust from socialism, where everything was provided to him by the government and people took care of each other, to a capitalist society in which he had to fend for himself. He had come to the U.S. looking for the American dream without any insight into how drastically different the culture was. No wonder he had struggled.

The doorbell rang. It was likely Jessica, who had called earlier wanting to drop off Christmas presents for the kids. On his way to the door, Marc quickly raked his fingers through his hair and picked at the dried remnants of strained carrots on his shirt from Emma's dinner.

He swung the door open, expecting to see Jessica with an armload of gifts.

"Hi," he said before even focusing on who it was standing before him. When he realized it wasn't Jessica, he took a step backward as he gazed at Gabby.

"Hi."

"Hi," he said again. She had changed her hairstyle, but the rest was just how he remembered her.

"I was hoping we could talk. Did I come at a bad time?"

"No. Not at all," he said sliding his hand up his shirt in an effort to hide the carrot stain.

"Maybe I could come in?"

"Of course. What's wrong with me?" He opened the door wider to let her in.

She took two steps into the living room, then stopped to listen to the end of the song.

And when you get the choice to sit it out or dance,
I hope you dance.

When it ended, she followed him to the sofa.

"How did you know to find me here?" he asked.

"Jessica has been keeping me up-to-date on what you've been up to."

"And you came by in spite of it all?" he asked laughing.

"No. I came by *because* of it all."

"I'm not following you."

She hesitated for a long moment before speaking. "These past several months, I've had a lot of time to think about that low period in my life when my brother was going through his drug addiction and what my parents did to save him. It shouldn't have been a low period at all—I was being immature and terribly selfish. My brother stole from my parents, Marc, was physically and verbally abusive toward them, pushed them into significant debt—yet they didn't give up on him. And look how he turned out—an Air Force master sergeant and a fine man." Her eyes fixated on his for a long moment. "I didn't realize it back then, but I know now that what my parents so unselfishly did to save my brother is indicative of the kind of person I want to be with. Someone like you."

He stood up and reached out for her hand.

"Would you care to dance, Miss Harding?" he asked.

"It would be my pleasure, Mr. Nussbaum."

I hope you enjoyed reading Living with Markus and will consider posting a short review on Amazon and/or Goodreads. Reviews and word-of-mouth referrals play an important role in helping authors promote their books, and your help in this regard is much appreciated.

Florence Osmund

Other books by Florence Osmund

Regarding Anna

For a fun, fascinating, and somewhat unpredictable mystery, look no further than Regarding Anna by Florence Osmund. Written in a friendly and straightforward style, readers will enjoy sleuthing alongside Grace as she seeks the truth about Anna. Don't be surprised if you have a hard time putting this novel down.
—San Francisco Book Review

After recovering from the shock of her parents' death, Grace Lindroth discovers clues in their attic that cause her to believe the people she called Mom and Dad her whole life may not have been her real parents. In her search for the truth, Grace encounters people whose actions cause her to be distrustful of everyone and believe that things that happen to you in the past can mold you into someone you're not.

Red Clover

Red Clover is a wonderfully written detailed story about a man overcoming his upbringing and becoming his own. The finished product, both the man and his story, are exemplary.
—Ray Paul, Windy City Reviews

The troubled son of a callous father and socialite mother determines his own meaning of success after learning shocking family secrets that cause him to rethink who he is and where he's going. Lee Winekoop's reinvention of himself is surprising; the roadblocks he confronts are unnerving; and the cast of characters he befriends along the way is both heartwarming and amusing.

The Coach House

This book is not only thought evoking but also a genuine pleasure to read.
—BestChickLit

1945 Chicago. Marie Marchetti flees from her devoted husband when she realizes he is immersed in local corruption, only to discover it's the identity of her real father that unexpectedly changes her life more than her husband ever could.

Daughters (sequel to The Coach House)

Civil rights, gender roles, and political postures are carefully, realistically, and sensitively present in this story.
—Pens and Needles

Discovering who her father is leads Marie Marchetti to discover who she really is and where she belongs, driving her to seek peace and truth in her life. But unexpectedly, the most life-altering consequence of her reunion grows out of an encounter with a twelve-year-old girl named Rachael.

Books are available on Amazon http://www.amazon.com/author/florenceosmund
Or the author's website http://florenceosmund.com/buy_the_authors_books
Or at book stores who order from distributors Ingram or Baker & Taylor

About the Author

After a long career working for large corporations, Florence Osmund retired to write novels. "I like to craft stories that challenge readers to survey their own beliefs and values," Osmund states. Striving to create stories that contain thought-provoking plots and characters with depth and complexity,

Florence lives in the heart of Chicago on the shore of Lake Michigan where she continues to write literary fiction.

If you are a new or aspiring novelist, visit Florence's website where she offers substantial advice on how to begin the project, writing techniques, building an author platform, book promotion, and much more.

Contact Information

E-mail	info@florenceosmund.com
Website	http://www.florenceosmund.com
Facebook	http://www.facebook.com/florenceosmundbooks
LinkedIn	http://www.linkedin.com/in/florenceosmund
Twitter	@FlorenceOsmund
Goodreads	http://www.goodreads.com/user/show/8800692-florence-osmund
Amazon	http://www.amazon.com/author/florenceosmund

www.ingramcontent.com/pod-product-compliance
Lightning Source LLC
Chambersburg PA
CBHW060955120726
47910CB00002B/640